PENGUIN  CLASSICS

THE VILLAGE OF STEPANCHIKOVO

AND ITS INHABITANTS

FYODOR MIKHAILOVICH DOSTOYEVSKY was born in Moscow in 1821, the second of a physician's seven children. When he left his private boarding school in Moscow he studied from 1838 to 1843 at the Military Engineering College in St Petersburg, graduating with officer's rank. His first story to be published, 'Poor Folk' (1846), was a great success. In 1849 he was arrested and sentenced to death for participating in the 'Petrashevsky circle'; he was reprieved at the last moment but sentenced to penal servitude, and until 1854 he lived in a convict prison at Omsk, Siberia. In the decade following his return from exile he wrote *The Village of Stepanchikovo* (1859) and *The House of the Dead* (1860). Whereas the latter draws heavily on his experiences in prison, the former inhabits a completely different world, shot through with comedy and satire. In 1861 he began the review *Vremya* (*Time*) with his brother; in 1862 and 1863 he went abroad, where he strengthened his anti-European outlook, met Mlle Suslova, who was the model for many of his heroines, and gave way to his passion for gambling. In the following years he fell deeply in debt, but in 1867 he married Anna Grigoryevna Snitkina (his second wife), who helped to rescue him from his financial morass. They lived abroad for four years, then in 1873 he was invited to edit *Grazhdanin* (*The Citizen*), to which he contributed his *Diary of a Writer*. From 1876 the latter was issued separately and had a large circulation. In 1880 he delivered his famous address at the unveiling of Pushkin's memorial in Moscow; he died six months later in 1881. Most of his important works were written after 1864: *Notes from Underground* (1864), *Crime and Punishment* (1865–6), *The Gambler* (1866), *The Idiot* (1869), *The Devils* (1871) and *The Karamazov Brothers* (1880).

IGNAT AVSEY was born in Ludza (Lucin), Latvia. He came to England in 1951, and was planning to enter upon a career in engineering, but subsequently changed to the humanities. He is currently a lecturer in Russian language and literature at the University of Westminster, London. His other major published translation is Dostoyevsky's *The Karamazov Brothers* and he is currently working on the first translation in ~~English of Dmitry Merezh~~kovsky's historical drama *Paul I*.

FYODOR DOSTOYEVSKY

THE VILLAGE OF STEPANCHIKOVO

AND ITS INHABITANTS

From the Notes of an Unknown

TRANSLATED WITH AN INTRODUCTION
BY IGNAT AVSEY

PENGUIN BOOKS

For Judie

PENGUIN BOOKS

Published by the Penguin Group
Penguin Books Ltd, 27 Wrights Lane, London w8 5tz, England
Penguin Putnam Inc., 375 Hudson Street, New York, New York 10014, USA
Penguin Books Australia Ltd, Ringwood, Victoria, Australia
Penguin Books Canada Ltd, 10 Alcorn Avenue, Toronto, Ontario, Canada m4v 3b2
Penguin Books (NZ) Ltd, 182–190 Wairau Road, Auckland 10, New Zealand

Penguin Books Ltd, Registered Offices: Harmondsworth, Middlesex, England

This translation first published in Great Britain 1983 by Angel Books
Revised edition published in Penguin Books 1995

17   19   20   18   16

Translation and introduction copyright © Ignat Avsey, 1983
All rights reserved
The moral right of the translator has been asserted

Filmset by Datix International Limited, Bungay, Suffolk
Printed in the United States of America
Set in 10/11.75 pt Monophoto Fournier

CONTENTS

The Village of Stepanchikovo and its Inhabitants is Dostoyevsky's fifth medium-length fictional work. It has remained in the shadow of his major novels since his lifetime, and in English it is less well known even than his second short novel *The Double*. Yet whereas *The Double* and the other 'novels' and stories of Dostoyevsky's pre-Siberian period are apprentice works, *The Village of Stepanchikovo* represents its author at a further stage of his development, poised to write the great fiction of his maturity.

Transitional work that it is, *The Village of Stepanchikovo* is a striking, accomplished and highly entertaining story, uniquely combining abundant humour with the seeds of Dostoyevsky's future concerns as a novelist. It contains in Foma Fomich Opiskin one of the most notorious characters in Russian literature, in D. S. Mirsky's words 'a weird figure of grotesque, gratuitous, irresponsible, petty, and ultimately joyless evil that together with Saltykov's Porfiry Golovlyov and Sologub's Peredonov forms a trinity to which probably no foreign literature has anything to compare'. (Mirsky's further somewhat shattered comment 'it must be confessed that though the element of humour is unmistakenly present, it is a kind of humour that requires a rather peculiar constitution to enjoy' catches the unusual nature of this work, though sixty years after his *History of Russian Literature* was written, readers' 'constitutions' are demonstrably tougher.)

The only previous English translations known to me are Frederick Whishaw's of 1887 in abridged form, under the title *The Friend of the Family*; Constance Garnett's of 1920 using the same title; and Olga Shartse's of 1961, included in a composite volume of short works by Dostoyevsky entitled *A Funny Man's Dream*, published in Moscow. It is with the strong feeling that this work should be altogether better known in English that the present translation is offered, in which I have aimed at as modern a rendering as seemed possible or appropriate, especially in dialogue.

The text I have used is the long-established one of 1866, which incorporates Dostoyevsky's slight revisions from the first serial printing. I am particularly indebted to Volume 3 of the 30-volume edition of

Dostoyevsky published in Leningrad in 1972, edited by G. M. Fridlender, A. Arkhipova and others, for my annotation.

I.A.

The Village of Stepanchikovo and its Inhabitants is unique among Dostoyevsky's works in that it is a sustained exercise in comedy. Successive generations of critics – nineteenth-century Russian, Soviet and English – have proved at variance with Dostoyevsky's approach in this work, so that a major component of its author's creativity, his humour – present in other works too, but nowhere in such concentrated measure as in *The Village of Stepanchikovo* – has been largely overlooked by the English-reading public.

The least discerning Russian critical approach has been to regard Dostoyevsky's fifth medium-length fictional work as a piece of frivolous 'revisionism' in which he sought to generate cheap humour out of human degradation at a time when the Russian conscience was at last moving towards socio-political reform. The work was neglected by critics and public on publication in 1859. Four eventful years later – which included, in 1861, the year of the 'emancipation' of the serfs, one of the most significant dates in Russian history – one critic compared *The Village of Stepanchikovo* unfavourably with the newly published *House of the Dead:*

> Whoever would see in literature the full benefit to be derived from a study of life and the positive influence of such a study, let him compare the two recent works *The Village of Stepanchikovo* and *The House of the Dead*; the forced melodrama of the former, with the genuine drama of the latter; the forced counterfeit humour of the one, designed merely to attract the reader's attention, with the real entertainment value of the second. As to the true worth of the two works one can only say that to the extent that one is socially edifying, the other is utterly useless.

A somewhat similar opinion was expressed by another critic in the year of emancipation itself. While conceding that *The Village of Stepanchikovo* was not devoid of 'remarkable qualities', he opined that Dostoyevsky was 'on the wrong tack', since humour 'is not Mr Dostoyevsky's *forte*'. Modern Soviet critics have continued to be muted about the work, L. Grossman, for example, finding Dostoyevsky's 'blessed village of Stepanchikovo' regrettably innocuous and socio-historically irrelevant.[1] (The novel actually contains a good deal more social relevance than most commentators seem to have noticed; it took some time for its underlying symbolism to work through – and indeed, for history to catch up with it, as we shall see. Early Soviet critics were more perceptive than those Russian commentators so far quoted.)

Even modern Western critics, with the notable exception of Ronald Hingley, who has given a penetrating analysis of *The Village of Stepanchikovo* in his *The Undiscovered Dostoyevsky*,[2] find it difficult to relate to Dostoyevsky as a humorist and either by-pass the subject altogether or, as in the case of E. H. Carr (writing in 1931 but more recently in print), ascribe it to an 'unwonted mood of light-heartedness, in which the world and its evils could for once be treated as a joke rather than as a problem'. Carr also comments that in this work Dostoyevsky 'no longer probes the psychological foundations of visible human relations; he is content to describe external phenomena in a spirit of exaggeration and caricature'.[3] Such views belittle not only Dostoyevsky's own artistic integrity, but more importantly, the intrinsic merits of a work which, besides being a delightful piece of comic entertainment, is also in a number of ways a fascinating small-scale prototype of 'the Dostoyevskian novel'.

The Village of Stepanchikovo is in form actually a *povest* – 'tale', the Russian term indicating a work on a larger scale than a short story or novella, and shorter than the fully developed form of the 'novel' (*roman*). It is not, therefore, a 'novel' in the sense that, say, *Crime and Punishment* is, or even the next fictional work that Dostoyevsky wrote, *The Insulted and Injured*, which is twice the length of *The Village*.

Dostoyevsky's writing career had been brought to an abrupt halt in April 1849 when he was arrested for being a member of the Petrashevsky Circle.[4] Nicholas I, fearful of the revolutionary movements which had been sweeping Europe, suspected danger and sedition in any form of outspoken protest, especially when it concerned legal reform and the emancipation of the serfs, and it was precisely these and related issues which a group of reform-minded journalists, writers and guards officers,

[1] L. Grossman, *Dostoyevsky*, Allen Lane, 1974.

[2] Hamish Hamilton, 1962.

[3] *Dostoyevsky 1821–1881*, 1931; reprinted Unwin Books, 1962, p. 65.

[4] Up to the time of his arrest he had written the short novels *Poor Folk* and *The Double*, the unfinished 'novel' *Netochka Nezvanova* (actually three linked stories), and some ten short stories. *Poor Folk*, his first work, published in January 1846, had been enthusiastically praised and established his reputation overnight; but *The Double* is considerably its superior.

Dostoyevsky amongst them, had been regularly gathering to discuss under the aegis of the eccentric intellectual M. V. Butashevich-Petrashevsky.

In 1847 the reform-minded critic Belinsky had written a blistering attack on Gogol for betraying his promise as an enlightened apologist for reform in his unexpectedly reactionary *Selected Passages from Correspondence with Friends*. In his *Open Letter to Gogol* Belinsky had accused the latter of adherence to despotism. Dostoyevsky read this letter out loud at one of the regular meetings of the Petrashevsky Circle and had thus, according to the Criminal Code of 1845, which strictly forbade any organized political discussion, committed a capital crime. His confinement in the Peter and Paul Fortress, his trial, his mock execution, enacted in every grim detail up to the last moment of 'reprieve' in order to teach the prisoners a lesson, his four years of penal servitude, and his subsequent six years of exile in Siberia, all inevitably left their mark upon his view of life.

Dostoyevsky started working on *The Village of Stepanchikovo* while serving his term of exile as a common soldier in the remote garrison town of Semipalatinsk in Western Siberia. He attached great importance to this work, and hoped that it would enable him to return to the literary scene after his enforced absence. There were two other projects on which he was engaged at the same time, one of which he completed, a mildly entertaining comic tale of manners *Uncle's Dream*, published in March 1859, and a long, unnamed novel to which, in a letter of 18 January 1858 to his brother Mikhail, he refers with gravity as his future *chef-d'œuvre*. In a letter of 9 October 1859, however, his brother is informed that this novel has been destroyed, but that the idea of writing a major serious work is still very much alive, and this time it may be concluded that Dostoyevsky referred to his plan for *Notes from the House of the Dead* which finally appeared in full in 1861/2. After his meteoric rise to fame with *Poor Folk* in 1846, this was his first truly successful publication, and it paved the way for his subsequent literary career, beginning with *Notes from Underground* published in 1864.

A far less ambitious work than the latter, and *Crime and Punishment* and the other monumental novels which succeeded it, *The Village of Stepanchikovo* is written in a spirit of fun, its primary aim being to amuse and entertain. Burdened as Dostoyevsky was at the time with unexpected ill-health, a capricious, irritable wife and lack of money, he may well have been motivated by a need for escapism, as can be surmised from a deceptively sanguine letter which he wrote to his friend Apollon Maykov in January 1856:

I began in fun to write a comedy and have managed to evoke so many comical scenes and characters and have grown to like my hero so much that I decided to drop the form of comedy, even though it was turning out quite well, for the sheer pleasure of prolonging the adventures of my new hero and enjoying a good laugh at him. This hero is not unlike myself. In short, I'm writing a comic novel.

Another friend, the young district procurator Baron Vrangel, whom Dostoyevsky met in Semipalatinsk, leaves us in his memoirs a vivid picture of Dostoyevsky's state of mind a short while earlier when he conceived the work. The exiled writer would regularly spend his evenings at Vrangel's house. 'Having undone his greatcoat,' Vrangel recalls,

with a Turkish pipe in his mouth, he would stride about the room, often conversing with himself . . . I see him now just as in one of such moments: at that time he set upon the idea of writing *Uncle's Dream* and *The Village of Stepanchikovo*. He was in a wonderfully cheerful mood, was laughing and telling me of uncle's adventures . . .[5]

The fact that *The Village of Stepanchikovo* was initially conceived as a play was revealed by Dostoyevsky's widow in conversation with Konstantin Stanislavsky when the latter was planning to adapt it for the stage in 1891. She declared, however, that the difficulties of mounting a production and obtaining the requisite public performance certificate from the censor at a time when her husband was in need of funds had persuaded him to revert to the genre of the novel. The work was in fact received with indifference by the first two publishers approached, and only at the third attempt, when his brother successfully negotiated with Krayevsky, the publisher of the journal *Otechestvennyye zapiski*, was it finally printed in serial form in the November and December issues of 1859.

It is difficult to say how far Dostoyevsky's approach to his subject-matter was governed by his undoubted maturing in exile, and how far by his equally undoubted need for circumspection before the censor. Certainly it took little enough provocation to excite the searching censorship of tsarist Russia, and Dostoyevsky's oblique and apparently detached rendering of provincial Russian society through the free play of humour and characterization was perhaps as much a protective device as an artistic achievement.

[5] Quoted in K. Mochulsky, *Dostoyevsky*, translated by M. A. Minihan, Princeton University Press, 1967, p. 156.

Dostoyevsky's disenchantment with Gogol's political stance had led to his ten years of penal servitude and exile, but he still had this enormously potent and influential writer very much in his blood when he wrote *Uncle's Dream* and *The Village of Stepanchikovo*. Indeed, as Richard Freeborn has commented, 'Once having seen a production of *The Inspector General* or having read *Dead Souls*, who could fail to regard the Russian provinces as comic?'[6] And the minute, closed society of Semipalatinsk, a town that boasted a single piano and a dozen subscribers to newspapers or periodicals, could not have been a very great distance from Stepanchikovo itself.

The 'spirit of exaggeration and caricature' that undoubtedly pervades *The Village of Stepanchikovo* is thoroughly Gogolian – and Gogol himself is the real-life model for its chief character, the despotic humbug Foma Fomich Opiskin. A. Arkhipova, in her commentary on the work in the 1972 Soviet edition of Dostoyevsky in 30 volumes, writes: 'Dostoyevsky saw in him [Gogol] a Russian typical of his time, with a characteristic duality in his soul, harbouring a deep spiritual "underground". It is this "underground" which, according to Dostoyevsky, had driven Gogol to write his *Selected Passages* in tones of exaggerated psychological exultation which at times acquired tragi-comic overtones.'[7] Into the figure of Foma Fomich Opiskin Dostoyevsky injected all his pent-up gall against the artist turned false prophet and erring philosopher, parodying Gogol's 'revisionist' view of Russian despotism as paternal benevolence through Opiskin's pompous, sanctimonious, self-aggrandizing, bombastic utterances, often drawing directly on Gogol's writings in the process, especially *Selected Passages* and his published letters. But creatively, Dostoyevsky still remained almost as much under the sway of his great predecessor as he had been at the time of writing *The Double* and his other early works, and in the very act of running down his former idol, he gave ample substance to one of his most candid and generous admissions – that 'we have all emerged from Gogol's *Greatcoat*'. The name of Foma Fomich Opiskin itself is in the tradition of Gogol, who liked repetitive patronymics such as Ivan Ivanovich, Pyotr Petrovich Petukh, and, the most famous of them all, Akaky Akakyevich.

Another literary presence stands behind Gogol in *The Village of Stepanchikovo* – Dickens. During penal servitude Dostoyevsky, starved of

---

[6] *The Rise of the Russian Novel*, Cambridge University Press, 1973, p. 168.
[7] F. M. Dostoyevsky: Collected Works in 30 volumes, vol. 3, edited by G. M. Fridlender and others, Leningrad, 1972, p. 503.

reading-matter, had eagerly devoured *David Copperfield* and *Pickwick Papers;* Dickens's works were available in Russia in translation not long after their original publication. Opiskin has been claimed as the 'spiritual progeny' of Uriah Heep and Mr Pecksniff, besides which it may be observed that Dostoyevsky's unbuttoned delight in caricature and the depiction of outrageous and eccentric characters is as much Dickensian as Gogolian.

Dostoyevsky has skilfully used the trappings of bucolic farce to weave a tight, dynamic story which seems to span a much longer period than the forty-eight hours into which all the main action is packed. *The Village of Stepanchikovo*, indeed, is a *tour de farce* of endless comic invention – of character, dialogue and plot – in which the principle of exaggeration is carried to glorious absurdity. The circumstance that brings the narrator to the remote country estate of his uncle, the retired Colonel Rostanev – he is summoned from his studies in St Petersburg by the urgent request to come to Stepanchikovo to marry a former ward of his uncle, the young and pretty Nastenka Yezhevikin (with whom the Colonel turns out to be in love himself), in order to save her from Opiskin's persecution – is patently far-fetched. As for the narrator himself, the wistfully romantic young Sergey Aleksandrovich (he is never given a surname, and Dostoyevsky's title-page bears the subtitle 'From the Notes of an Unknown'), he is not so much a narrator as an eye-witness addressing the reader from the midst of events, no more able to foretell or make sense of what happens than any of the inhabitants of Stepanchikovo. The latter are done in highly coloured caricature, and their obsessions and distorted viewpoints are given free and highly expressive rein in dialogue, which is the main vehicle of the novel. In a world of grotesque comedy, Opiskin, the most ridiculous figure of all, sounds darker notes of oppression and cruelty.

Before arriving at Stepanchikovo the narrator makes the acquaintance of the garrulous landowner Bakhcheyev, who warns him that all is not well in Stepanchikovo. Following the death of Rostanev's step-father, General Krakhotkin, Foma Fomich Opiskin, a vagrant of obscure origins first employed by the General as a reader when his sight fails, has installed himself in a position of power in the household and rules it with an iron rod, aided and abetted by the Colonel's mother, the General's widow. On arrival Sergey finds the worst reports he has heard fully confirmed, and he is soon brimming with indignation at the injustices which he sees being committed; but all his attempts to remedy the situation are ineffective. Moreover, his youthful pride suffers a severe blow through a painful awareness of his own inability to assert himself and to prevent himself from being turned into a figure of fun. The preoccupation of the narrator at this stage with his own image has much autobiographical content; Dostoyevsky himself in his young days is known to have been awkward, shy and highly strung.

The Colonel's household is a veritable haven for a variety of extraordinary individuals, and the scene in which most of them are introduced, Chapter 4, 'At Tea', is electric with their combined eccentricities. Prominent amongst them is old Yezhevikin, Nastenka's father – a truly original portrait of a proud man, crushed by circumstances and forced to play the jester, yet perversely revelling in his abject misery and always ready to throw down the gauntlet to society. Significantly, he has not taken up abode in the Colonel's house, and by maintaining his personal independence is not a *prizhivalshchik* or hanger-on in the sense that Opiskin is, or any of the minor characters such as the scheming poseur Mizinchikov, the rapacious Mme Obnoskin and son, the venomous spinster Miss Perepelitsyna, or the nameless, indigent gentlewomen, dependents and companions, who are all sheltering in the Colonel's house. The pathetic heiress Tatyana Ivanovna, also a *prizhivalshschitsa*, plays a rôle extraneous to the main plot, but for one moment she is allowed to occupy the centre of the stage when attention is focussed on her amorous misadventure in which Obnoskin junior and Mizinchikov are involved. The moment in question is her elopement – which as Ronald Hingley has observed,[8] can be traced to that of Jingle and the middle-aged heiress Miss Wardle in *Pickwick Papers*.

In the early part of the novel, narrative predominates. As the atmosphere builds up towards the first appearance of Opiskin, however, dialogue takes over from narrative, and the pace quickens under apparently effortless self-propulsion. D. S. Merezhkovsky has observed that everything of moment in Dostoyevsky's works is communicated by way of the spoken word: 'we see, because we hear'.[9] And the early Soviet critic V. F. Pereverzev agreed that each of Dostoyevsky's characters has his or her own verbal image. 'Take ... *The Village of Stepanchikovo*: Opiskin, Rostanev, Yezhevikin, and even the subsidiary characters, as for instance Bakhcheyev and the servants Grigory and Vidoplyasov, all speak their own, individually memorable language.'[10] In their discussion and argument, often in trivial terms, which heightens the absurdly comical effect,

[8] *The Undiscovered Dostoyevsky*, p. 35.

[9] Collected Works, vol. 7, M. O. Wolf, St Petersburg-Moscow, 1912, p. 234.

[10] *Gogol, Dostoyevsky, Issledovaniya*, Moscow, 1982, pp. 210–11.

the characters touch on the most sensitive aspects of Russian life from several sides at once, no one character clearly representing the author's view. It is thus that we hear Opiskin holding forth on the need of the house-boy Falaley to know the French language at a time when serfs were generally debarred from all forms of education; the petulant Bakhcheyev desperately clinging to his feudal privileges with emancipation of the serfs just around the corner; and the naive and totally ignorant Colonel Rostanev gasping in awe at the very mention of the words 'science' and 'learning' in a setting where no pursuit of knowledge has ever been undertaken. But debate is always motivated by deeply felt personal convictions, which enable the play that Dostoyevsky set out to write to sprout vigorously within the novel. This sense of life and spontaneity carries the work far beyond the stylized beginnings which critics have located in both plot and characterization of Molière's *Tartuffe*.

Schematically there is much in common between Molière's play and *The Village of Stepanchikovo*: the plot, the broad lines of the two chief characters and of a number of the minor ones. But it is in the psychology and motivation of Opiskin/Tartuffe that the vital difference is to be found. To quote A. Arkhipova once more: 'The situations of *Tartuffe* seem to be deliberately put forward by the author as likely motivations, but are then rejected.'[11] Whereas Molière's hero is a calculating crook pursuing a premeditated plan of action in order to take possession of his host's wife and money, Opiskin's moves are quite irrational and without any practical end-result in mind. He does not maintain improper relations with the General's Lady, however much she might worship him, he has no designs on Nastenka, and he rejects the offer of a substantial sum of money from Rostanev. Mizinchikov describes him as 'an artist'. He certainly acts intuitively. He persists in his grand act not for material gain but in response to irrepressible inner compulsions to dominate, to bluster and to oppress, deriving satisfaction from the very act of inflicting suffering. In the words of N. Mikhaylovsky, writing in 1882, Opiskin 'needs the unnecessary', and, paraphrasing Coleridge's words 'motiveless malignity' with reference to Iago, the critic typifies him as a case of 'unnecessary cruelty'.

Dostoyevsky wrote to Mikhail in May 1859 of *The Village of Stepanchikovo*: 'I have put my soul, my flesh, my blood into it ... It contains two colossal and typical characters that I've spent five years *conceiving* and *recording* ... characters wholly Russian, and poorly repre-

[11] F. M. Dostoyevsky: Collected Works, vol. 3, p. 502.

sented before in Russian literature.' To the figure of Opiskin Chekhov was to respond in *Uncle Vanya*, exploring and developing still further the curious combination of parasite, poseur, clown and domestic tyrant in the person of his Professor Serebryakov.

Opiskin is the irresistible, satanic force, dominating and moulding his domain in a totally unreasonable way. Long before we meet him, reports of his outrageous behaviour serve to whet our appetites and to build up his character to a degree only possible in the absence of contact, and above all to create suspense and a sense of deepening tension within the Rostanev household. Drawing complex and shifting reactions from the other characters, he is a threat to the established order of life in 'the blessed village of Stepanchikovo', a force of social upheaval rather than a mere villain. He continually sparks off fresh alliances and shifts of ground in the other characters as he develops and extends his own position.

Rostanev by contrast seems passive and even feeble. Pereverzev called him 'a palm in the snow',[12] because he is not a typical representative either of the landowning class or the military. His need for Sergey's presence and his absurd regard for the passing vagrant Korovkin, and even for Opiskin, can be explained in terms of his deep-seated feeling of inferiority and urge to hero-worship. Kindly, obliging and unwilling to see faults in others, he is at the same time the archetype of the reasonable man being pushed beyond all reasonable limits by the excessive demands both of Opiskin and members of his own family. But if Foma Fomich is not a simple villain, nor is Rostanev merely a weak hero. Whereas Opiskin lays claim to sensibilities and deep concern over the whole range of human activities down to the most absurd trivia, Rostanev's protective instincts operate over a relatively small area of life: protection of the weak and the innocent, and the ultimate requirements of honour. His defence of these is, however, absolute, and the oppressor's undoing is to push him to the point where that absolute is invoked.

Within this major struggle, which develops on Rostanev's side from a vague sense of unease to ruthless action, the minor characters play out their individual dilemmas between the force of tyranny on one side and the only potential power of resistance on the other. Rostanev's mother, the General's Lady, for example, finds a new and mystical sense of purpose in the shadow of Opiskin, who, like Tartuffe, is ready to don the mantle of a guru and play on the religious sensibilities of his admirers. Family conflict is set up and the mother brands her son as a base and

[12] Op. cit., p. 305.

egotistical detractor from a great man. Rostanev's nephew, a shadowy figure who provides the early narrative and later, after becoming dramatically redundant, serves to mark what may be supposed to be the author's general position, is Rostanev's main supporter. Bakhcheyev, an idle windbag whose kindliness is as rough and unconscious as his cruelty, starts out as an unreasoning devotee of the Colonel and manages, just as irrationally, to transfer his loyalties to Opiskin. Nastenka (one of Dostoyevsky's stock 'virtuous girls') preserves the emotional balance between herself and her intended by embracing her erstwhile tormentor. The accommodations made by these and by other members of the household are a kind of microcosm of the complex and diverse reactions seen in any society faced with major disruptive forces.

After the climactic clash in the major *skandal* scene of the novel, Dostoyevsky does not flinch from the logic of his own argument. When Rostanev casts out Opiskin and emerges as the most decisive and valiant of heroes, this could be the end of the story. Dostoyevsky's sense of reality and purpose will not allow this, however, and instead he accepts the implications of his own characterization by letting Opiskin's fate and his future relationship with Rostanev develop naturally out of the action. The oppressor overthrown and the Colonel triumphant, the sheer force of habit and the dull prospect of life without the tyrant persuade everyone to give up the fruits of freedom by urging the Colonel towards clemency and the reinstatement of Opiskin. The characters' knowledge even as they ask this that he is in no way likely to be reformed is a most telling image of Russian docility. The novel ends with the forgiving victor and the unrepentant vanquished living in bizarre equilibrium with Opiskin elevated almost to priestly status by a household which he continues to abuse. Interpreting Opiskin's reinstatement in terms of the philosophy of Ivan Karamazov's devil, it is the whole of humanity which would find his, the devil's, absence intolerable.

Suspense is the key factor in maintaining the pace of the novel, and each of the chapters concludes with a 'cliff-hanger' ending. Only once does Dostoyevsky presume rather too heavily on the reader's goodwill, and that is where, having announced Opiskin to be entering the room for our first encounter, the author then inserts an entire chapter in parenthesis. A more successful stratagem is the suspense and expectation built up regarding Korovkin's intended visit. As the Colonel's need for Korovkin's presence increases, so the prospects for his arrival seem to become more uncertain. Having been mentioned from time to time throughout the story, the mysterious guest begins to take on a significance which anticipates Godot. Unlike Godot, however, Korovkin does turn up, and with devastating effect.

Korovkin's arrival coincides with a display of Dostoyevsky's most effective and masterful structural device, the ensemble scene, which is often a *skandal* scene too. In *The Village of Stepanchikovo* there are plenty of opportunities here; some six of the eighteen chapters are devoted to gatherings of one sort or another (Chapters 4, 5 and 7 in Part I, and 3, 4 and 5 in Part II), with the participants revealing in spontaneous outbursts their inner preoccupations and the most startling and telling facets of their personalities. The early Soviet critic M. Bakhtin observed that on these occasions there is a pervading sensation of the Dostoyevskian unreality of life, a carnival atmosphere – 'life with all the stops out'.[13] Such scenes serve not only as firework displays for Dostoyevsky's brilliance as a writer of dialogue, but equally act as crucibles in which the next stage of the action is poured and compounded. It is here also that Dostoyevsky's comic gifts are most strikingly revealed. Pereverzev observed that in Dostoyevsky there are no funny people, only funny situations. 'Dostoyevsky does not concentrate on delineating portraits, but tries to depict movement and that spiritual state which is conveyed by the movement.'[14]

In these ensemble scenes, and the way in which the tensions and conflicts they contain move the action step by step towards the final climax, lies the structural dynamic of 'the Dostoyevskian novel', and it is in *The Village of Stepanchikovo* that Dostoyevsky first substantially employs the method. The final clash is preceded by significant minor clashes and their reverberations: in Chapter 5 of Part I, where Rostanev's daughter Sashenka bursts out against Opiskin before the assembled company; and in Chapter 7 of Part I, where the servant Gavrila also explodes, this time in Opiskin's face, and where shortly afterwards the narrator tells Opiskin that he is drunk. The last incident, for example, brings the brooding hostility that has hitherto existed between Opiskin and the narrator into the open, and 'fixes' their relationship for the rest of the novel.

Richard Freeborn has pointed out that this work's 'most important innovation' in Dostoyevsky's technique 'is its concern for exhibiting private contentions in a public form'. He continues:

> For Dostoyevsky this was the principle upon which he constructed the dramatic form of his greatest novels. The revelation of the private conflict

[13] Quoted in F. M. Dostoyevsky: Collected Works, vol. 3, p. 504.
[14] Op. cit., p. 215.

through subjecting it to group scrutiny and analysis involves the many in the single experience and in this most simple sense 'dramatizes' it. A drama demands spectators *who do not know* the truth about the private conflict, and the darker the object of revelation the more dramatic is the analysis. His *skandal* scenes enshrine this principle.[15]

Besides the dynamic principle of its action, *The Village of Stepanchikovo* contains further prototypes for future development in certain of its characters. Rostanev is the direct precursor of Prince Myshkin in *The Idiot*; unlike the latter, he has no intellectual view-point, however vaguely formulated, to support his stance of meekness and humility, and he clings to others for moral support. The lackey Vidoplyasov is an early version of the lackey Smerdyakov in *The Karamazov Brothers*, the tones of the sinister moralist already present in Vidoplyasov's utterance, with its constant emphasis on 'refinement'. The orphan Tatyana Ivanovna, lost in her dream-world, is an early version of the 'holy fool' Marya Timofeyevna in *Devils*.

Konstantin Stanislavsky, a founder-director of the Moscow Art Theatre, adapted *The Village of Stepanchikovo* for the stage in 1891; he also directed it as well as acted the part of Rostanev. Before the play could be staged, however, both the title and the names of the characters had to be altered for the benefit of the censor. Nor was the name of the author to be mentioned.[16] Ten years after his death Dostoyevsky was still a controversial figure in the eyes of the guardians of the Russian Empire. Much against his will Stanislavsky was thus obliged to pass off the play for official purposes as his own. However, not surprisingly, he refused to present himself to the public as its author, and consequently no author's name appeared on the programme notes.[17] Subsequently, the novel was again prepared for the stage to open the Moscow Art Theatre's 1917/18 season. Work began in January 1916 and went on for just under two years. The dramatization promised to be an important part of the repertoire. Stanislavsky saw Dostoyevsky not in the traditional reading of the 'cruel genius' morbidly probing the spiritual ulcers of humanity, but on the contrary, as the genial and witty author of a comedy with an enlightened perception of reality. In Stanislavsky's eyes the novel was

---

[15] *The Rise of the Russian Novel*, p. 169.
[16] See, K. Stanislavsky, Collected Works in Eight Volumes, Moscow, 1954: Vol. 1, p. 138 and ibid. Letter to Kisselevsky in vol. 7, p. 106.
[17] Ibid. Letter to A. G. Dostoyevskaya, vol. 7, p. 70.

uplifting in its assertion of the divine principle of love and humility against the satanic principle of egoism and false pride.

The part of Colonel Rostanev had a deep emotional appeal for Stanislavsky, and he claimed total spiritual identification with Dostoyevsky's character. '. . . this rôle enabled me to become Uncle, whereas in all previous rôles to a greater or lesser extent I merely aped, copied or mocked other people's images or my own'. But Stanislavsky's involvement with the play was to end on a deeply unhappy note, for in striving to interpret the nature of Rostanev's motivating force, he was unable to reconcile within himself the benign, submissive, pacifist element with the belligerent, aggressive strain needed to wage war on tyranny as epitomized by Opiskin. The numerous rehearsals in which Stanislavsky attempted to come to terms with the rôle dragged on, holding up other productions, and yet he did not appear to be anywhere near a satisfactory artistic solution. Finally, Nemirovich-Danchenko, who had by this time taken over the directorship, asked Stanislavsky to step down from the rôle of Rostanev – a devastating blow to his morale.[18]

The production itself in September 1917 was a critical sensation and a popular success. Critics saw in Opiskin the archetype of degenerate Russian tyranny, of which the most recent example had been that arch-*prizhivalshchik* Rasputin, who had been disposed of only the previous year. The gentle-hearted Rostanev, on the other hand, was taken to epitomize Mother Russia – inactive (except *in extremis*), gullible, and totally defenceless against its never-ending succession of Opiskins. The critic I. Zhilkin, writing in *Russkoye slovo*, pointed to the gravity of Dostoyevsky's message in the context of contemporary events. 'Is it not strange,' he asked, 'how Dostoyevsky seems to revive every time our way of life dissolves in a fiery ferment? Dostoyevsky appeared prophetically fresh in 1905–06, and now his voice resounds again.'

Stanislavsky's lifelong fascination with *The Village of Stepanchikovo*, and such reactions as these, argue strongly against contemporary and present-day suggestions that it is light-weight or trivial. It is for the reader to judge where this unusual tale will eventually stand in relation to Dostoyevsky's other works.

[18] See M. N. Stroyeva, *Rezhissyorskiye iskaniya Stanislavskogo* 1898–1917, Moscow, 1973, pp. 348–50.

PART I

I

Introductory

After his retirement from military service, my uncle, Colonel Yegor Ilyich Rostanev, moved to his inherited estate of Stepanchikovo and settled down there so readily that one would have supposed he had been born and bred on the estate and never left it. Some natures are completely satisfied with everything and are readily adaptive to all circumstances; such a nature was the retired Colonel's. It would be difficult to imagine a man more benign and compliant. If one had asked him for a ride on his back for a distance of say two versts, the Colonel would probably not have refused. His generosity was such that on occasion he would have been ready to part with everything on the spot, down to his last shirt, and hand it to any needy person he chanced to meet. He was very powerfully built: tall and well-proportioned, with a fresh complexion, ivory-white teeth, a full, reddish-brown moustache, and a rich sonorous voice which rang pleasantly when he laughed. His manner of speaking was hurried and uneven. At the time of his retirement, he was around forty; from about the age of sixteen he had spent all his life in the hussars. He had married very young and loved his wife dearly. When she died, he was left with a host of tender and grateful memories. Finally, after inheriting Stepanchikovo, which increased his estate to six hundred serfs, he decided to forsake military life and settle in the country with his children – eight-year-old Ilyusha (whose birth had cost his mother her life) and his elder daughter Sashenka, a girl of about fifteen who had been attending boarding-school in Moscow since her mother's death. But soon my uncle's house was to become a veritable Noah's Ark, and this is how it came about.

At the same time as he inherited his estate and retired from the army, his mother, the wife of General Krakhotkin, lost her husband. This had been her second marriage, contracted sixteen years earlier, when my uncle was only a second lieutenant and was himself thinking of taking a wife. For a long time his mother had refused to countenance such a union – she wept bitter tears, reproached him with selfishness, ingratitude, and disrespect; tried to prove that his estate – two hundred and fifty serfs in all – was barely sufficient to support his family as it was (that is, her own self with her establishment of hangers-on, pug and spitz dogs, Chinese cats, and so on); and then suddenly, quite unexpectedly, in the midst of all her reproaches, accusations and tantrums, even before her son, and notwithstanding her forty-two years, entered into matrimony herself. But even now she was able to find a pretext for directing further reproaches at my poor uncle, maintaining that the only reason she had taken a husband was to provide herself with a refuge in her old age – a refuge which her disrespectful, egotistical son had denied her by taking the outrageous step of setting up his own home.

It has always been a mystery to me why such an apparently level-headed person as the late General Krakhotkin should have chosen to marry a forty-two-year-old widow. It must be assumed that he suspected she had money. Some were of the opinion that he simply needed a nurse, as even at that time he probably foresaw the succession of maladies which were to plague him in old age. It is certain, however, that the old General had no respect for his wife during the entire period of their married life, and mocked her mercilessly at every available opportunity. He was a strange person. Semi-educated but by no means a fool, he hated all and sundry, submitted to no authority, took perverse pleasure in ridicule and mockery, and in old age, from ill-health that resulted from a none too regular or virtuous way of life, grew short-tempered, irritable and stony-hearted. His service career had been successful until, in consequence of some 'unpleasant incident', he had been obliged to resign his commission in undignified haste, narrowly escaping court martial and having to forego his pension. He became embittered. Almost completely without means, this owner of a hundred-odd impoverished serfs turned his back on the world, and for the rest of his life, twelve years or so, never bothered to inquire how or by whom he was being maintained; at the same time he insisted on enjoying all of life's comforts, refused to limit his expenses, and kept a carriage. Before long he lost the use of his legs and spent the remaining ten years of his life in a wheelchair, attended by two seven-feet-tall manservants upon whom he heaped every kind of abuse. Carriage, servants and wheelchairs were provided and maintained by the disrespectful son, who supplied his mother with cash borrowed on security several times over, denying himself necessities, incurred debts which he had practically no hope of settling from his meagre income, and who for all that remained in her eyes an ungrateful and hard-bitten egotist of a son. My uncle's character, however, was such that finally he too began to believe in his own egotism, and, in self-punishment and an attempt to prove he was otherwise, sent his mother more and more money.

The General's wife worshipped her husband. But her greatest pleasure was derived from the fact that he was a general, and that she could therefore rejoice in the title of 'General's Lady'. She had her own suite of rooms in the house where, during the whole period of her husband's semi-existence, she flourished in the company of numerous hangers-on, gossips and lap-dogs. In the little provincial town she was a person to be reckoned with. Invitations to weddings and christenings, kopeck-stake card games and universal adulation more than compensated for her domestic frustrations. Gossips called on her regularly with their latest reports; everywhere she went she was accorded a place of honour; in short, she exploited to the full all the privileges that her husband's title afforded. The General did not interfere in any of this, but he taunted her mercilessly in public. He would ask out loud, for instance, 'Whyever did I marry that sanctimonious old hag?' and no one dared to argue with him. One after another all his acquaintances turned their backs on him – a treatment ill-suited to his desperate dependence on society, for he loved to talk and argue, he simply loved to have a listener permanently seated before him. As a freethinker and old-style atheist, he had a need to discourse from time to time on lofty matters.

But the listeners of the town of N** had little time for lofty matters and came to see him less and less regularly. To humour him, an attempt was made to introduce members of the household to preference; but the game would normally end in disaster, with the General having such fits that his terror-stricken spouse and her retinue would be driven to lighting candles to the saints, offering prayers, divining their fortunes from tea-leaves and cards, even distributing alms at the prison gates, in trepidation at the thought of the afternoon session when they would yet again have to expose themselves, for every mistake, to shouts, howls, cursing and all but physical assault. The General, when displeased, overstepped all bounds of propriety: sometimes he would tear up and scatter the playing cards all over the floor, chase his partners out of the room, and even weep in anger and exasperation, for no other reason than that somebody had put down a jack instead of a nine. Finally his eyesight began to fail, and he needed someone who would read to him. It is at this juncture that Foma Fomich Opiskin first appears on the scene.

I must confess, it is with more than a little awe that I introduce this new personage. He is undoubtedly one of the principal characters of my tale. But what sort of claim he has on the reader's attention I shall not presume to judge: the reader will be better able to make up his own mind.

Foma Fomich joined General Krakhotkin's household as a pickthank in dire need – no more, no less. Where exactly he came from is shrouded in mystery. However, I did make a few enquiries about the former circum-stances of this remarkable person. First, it was said that he had been in government service but had suffered for a cause – needless to say, a just one. It was also rumoured that he had tried his hand at literature in Moscow. That in itself is not surprising, for however abysmal his ignorance, it could hardly have constituted an obstacle to his literary career. Only one thing was beyond dispute – he was finally obliged to enter martyrdom in the General's service as a reader. There was no humiliation that he was not obliged to suffer for his keep. Of course, after the General's death, when Foma quite unexpectedly began to play an important and unique rôle, he was at pains to assure us all that in agreeing to play the clown, he had made a selfless sacrifice in the name of friendship; that the General, his benefactor, had in fact been an outstanding person, sadly misunderstood by all, and that only to him, Foma, had he confided the innermost secrets of his soul; and furthermore that if he, Foma, had portrayed various animals and *tableaux vivants* at the General's behest, it was solely to comfort and amuse a wretched bedridden invalid and a dear friend. However, the protestations of Foma Fomich in this matter are open to grave doubt. Meanwhile, at the same time as serving the General as fool, he came to play a vastly different rôle in the women's wing of the house. How he managed to achieve this no one but an expert in such matters could attempt to explain. The General's Lady held him in a kind of mystical reverence. Why? We do not know. Gradually he gained an astonishing ascendancy over the ladies, reminiscent of that exercised by such prophets and men of vision as Ivan Yakovlevich Koreysha,[1] whom certain ladies are so fond of visiting in lunatic asylums. Foma Fomich would give readings from devotional books and hold forth with eloquent tears on Christian virtues; recount his life story and achievements, attend midday and even morning service, and even foretell the future; he was particularly adept at analysing dreams, and a past-master at running down his fellow-men. The General had a vague idea of what was going on in the female quarters at the rear of the house, and tyrannized his victim all the more. But the martyrdom of Foma Fomich only gained him greater respect in the eyes of the General's Lady and her companions.

At last everything changed. The General died. The manner of his death, it must be owned, was original. The erstwhile freethinker and confirmed atheist turned out to be a thorough coward. He wept, repented, kissed icons, summoned priests. Liturgies were sung, he was anointed. The poor wretch cried that he had no wish to die, and with tears streaming down his face even begged Foma Fomich for forgiveness. This latter act subsequently gave an enormous boost to Foma Fomich's prestige. However, before the final separation of the General's soul and body the following incident occurred. The daughter of the General's Lady by her first marriage, my aunt Praskovya Ilyinichna, who had long before resigned herself to spinsterhood and settled in the General's house only to become his favourite victim throughout his ten wheelchair-bound years, proving herself an indispensable nurse who alone, in her meek and simple-hearted way, was able to attend to all his whims and caprices, approached his bedside with a tear-sodden face and was about to straighten his pillow when the invalid managed to catch hold of her hair and tug it three times all but foaming at the mouth with venom. Ten minutes later he was dead. The Colonel was duly informed, although the General's Lady announced that she had no intention of seeing him, and that only over her dead body would he be allowed anywhere near her at such a time. The funeral was a splendid one, needless to say arranged at the expense of the disrespectful son, who himself was forbidden to appear.

In the bankrupt estate of Knyazyovka, owned jointly by a number of landowners, the General's share having been about one hundred serfs, stands a white marble mausoleum emblazoned with laudatory inscriptions on the wisdom, talent, probity and military prowess of the departed. Foma Fomich was in large part responsible for these inscriptions.

For a long time after her husband's death, the General's Lady stubbornly resisted any suggestion of relenting towards her disobedient son. Surrounded by her coterie of cronies and lap-dogs, she insisted, weeping and wailing, that she would sooner live on dry crusts – and of course 'wash them down with her tears' – she would sooner go out and beg for charity than accept the *disobedient one's* invitation to come and settle in Stepanchikovo; that never, never, never would she so much as set *foot* in his house. The word *foot* when enunciated in this sense by some ladies has a particularly meaningful quality, and the General's Lady was a supreme artist in enunciating it . . . In short, she displayed no end of eloquent indignation on the subject. It ought to be mentioned, however, that amid all the ranting and raving, preparations were steadily under way for her eventual move to Stepanchikovo. The Colonel nearly flogged his horses to death racing the forty-odd versts from Stepanchikovo to town every day, and yet it was a fortnight after the General's funeral before he received permission to appear before his outraged parent. Foma Fomich acted as an intermediary in the negotiations. Throughout the two weeks he reproached and scolded the disobedient son for his 'inhuman' behaviour and reduced him to tears of shame and abject despair. Thus began Foma

Fomich's extraordinary and inhuman domination of my poor uncle. Foma saw the kind of man he had to deal with, and immediately realized that his days as clown and scapegoat were over, that in the land of the weak he himself could be tsar. And he certainly missed no opportunity to make up for the past.

'What would be your feelings,' Foma would say to him, 'if your own mother, the prime source of your existence, as it were, had to stumble about clutching a pauper's staff with hands trembling and weak from hunger — actually begging? Would it not be monstrous in view of her august title and many personal virtues? Could you describe your feelings if she were suddenly to turn up here — accidentally, of course, but it could happen — on your doorstep, in rags, starving, while you, her own son, were wallowing in the lap of luxury! Dreadful, dreadful! And the worst part of it is — let me tell you frankly, Colonel — that even now you stand before me like a wooden post, with mouth hanging open and eyes popping — it's positively indecent ... whereas the very thought of such an appalling spectacle ought to be making you tear out your hair by the roots and weep floods ... What am I saying! Rivers, lakes, seas, oceans of tears! ...'

In short, Foma Fomich would get carried away in the heat of the moment. But that was always the way with his outbursts of eloquence. The upshot of it all was that the General's Lady, accompanied by her hangers-on, her lap-dogs, Foma Fomich, and her principal confidante, Miss Perepelitsyna, finally graced Stepanchikovo with her arrival. Her sojourn, she announced, would only be long enough to *test* her son's devotion. It may be imagined what the Colonel had to go through while his devotion was being put to the test. To begin with, as a result of her recent bereavement, the General's Lady felt it incumbent upon herself to indulge at least two or three times a week in bitter despair at the slightest mention of her departed spouse; and invariably it was the Colonel who, for some reason or other, had to bear the brunt of her displeasure. Often, especially in the presence of visitors, having summoned her little grandson Ilyusha and fifteen-year-old granddaughter Sashenka and seated them beside her, the General's Lady would fix on them her sad tormented eyes as on children brought to ruin by *such a father*, and then, sighing deeply, release a silent and mysterious flood of tears lasting for at least an hour. Woe betide the Colonel if he failed to *understand* those tears! But the poor man never could, and in his naivety would turn up in her presence at just such tearful moments, and invariably find himself put to the test. His own devotion, however, showed no signs of diminishing, and eventually

reached untold proportions. Both the General's Lady and Foma Fomich now realized that the thundercloud which had loomed over them for so many years in the shape of General Krakhotkin had finally and irrevocably been dispersed. There were occasions when the General's Lady, for no apparent reason, would go into a swoon on the sofa, and the whole house would be in turmoil. The Colonel would stand confounded, shaking like an aspen leaf.

'Heartless son!' the General's Lady would cry, regaining consciousness, 'you have rent my entrails . . . *mes entrailles, mes entrailles!*'

'Mamma, how could I have done such a thing?' the Colonel would protest meekly.

'You have! You have! No more of your excuses! The insolence of the man! You cruel creature! I'm dying!'

The Colonel, of course, would feel utterly crushed.

Miraculously, however, the General's Lady would always recover. And half an hour later the Colonel, having buttonholed someone, would be heard explaining away his mother's antics.

'You must understand how it is with her, my dear fellow: *une grande dame*, wife of a General, you know! She's the kindest old lady; but you see, she's used to every refinement in life . . . it's different for a ruffian like me. She's furious with me now. Don't even know what I'm supposed to have done, my dear fellow, but, of course, it's clear I'm to blame . . .'

Occasionally the old spinster Perepelitsyna, a dried-up creature embittered with the whole world, with tiny rapacious eyes devoid of eyebrows, paper-thin lips, hands washed in pickled gherkin juice, and wearing a chignon, would feel duty bound to treat uncle to a lecture:

'It's all because you've no consideration, sir. Because you're selfish! Shame on you for treating your dear mother so: she's used to better, sir. You're still only a Colonel, sir, you ought to have some respect for her title.'

'Miss Perepelitsyna, my friend,' the Colonel would observe to his listener, 'is a remarkably fine lady – so protective towards Mamma! A rare lady! No mere hanger-on, God forbid. As a matter of fact, she's a Lieutenant-Colonel's daughter herself. Yes, really!'

Of course, all this was just the beginning. The same General's Lady who was capable of such antics as these was in her turn like a mouse before her former dependant. Opiskin had bewitched her completely. She doted on him, she heard with his ears, and she saw with his eyes. A distant cousin of mine, also retired from the hussars though still in his prime, but a reckless profligate who had come to the end of his tether and

at one time sought shelter in my uncle's house, declared without ado that the General's Lady maintained improper relations with Foma Fomich. Naturally, I immediately rejected such a supposition with indignation as altogether too insulting and facile. No, I believed there was another explanation, and this I can only begin to explain to the reader by giving some preliminary account of the character of Foma Fomich Opiskin as I eventually came to understand it.

Imagine the most craven and insignificant of social outcasts, utterly useless to man or beast, utterly vile, but inordinately vain, and without a single personal virtue to justify his cankered vanity. Let me state at the outset: Foma Fomich Opiskin was the embodiment of the most boundless vanity, but vanity of a peculiar sort, to be found only in complete nonentities; vanity nurtured by crushing, long-festering past insults, and from then on oozing envy and poison at every human contact, every encounter with another's good fortune. Needless to say, all this was seasoned with the most exaggerated sense of offence, the most insanely developed mistrust of the world. Suppose one were to ask where such vanity is born, how it is conceived in such nonentities, such miserable creatures who by virtue of their social status alone ought to know their place – what would the answer be? Maybe there are exceptions, among which my hero did in truth belong. He was indeed an exception to the rule, as the subsequent course of events will prove. Be that as it may, one may well ask the following question: how can one ever be sure that even those who have come to consider it their honour and happiness to be at your beck and call and to play the fool for your exclusive pleasure, how can one be sure that such people have completely renounced all vanity? And what of the jealousies, the intrigues, the malice, the backbiting, the surreptitious hissing in distant corners of one's own house, somewhere in the same room, at one's elbow, at one's very table? . . . Who knows but that some of these ill-fated outcasts, your clowns and God-forsaken wretches, instead of being cowed by humility, have had their vanity augmented still further by this very humiliation, by the sycophancy, wretchedness and obligation to play the fool enforced upon them, by the extirpation of all individual personality? Who knows but that such warped vanity might perhaps merely be a deceptive manifestation of initially corrupted personal dignity, dignity which might have sustained its first reverses perhaps in childhood, in circumstances of oppression, poverty, filth – perhaps been degraded in the persons of the parents themselves of the future outcast, before his very eyes? But I stated that Foma Fomich was an exception to the general rule. And so he was. He had once tried his

hand at literature, and had suffered disappointment and rejection; but, of course, literature has ruined mightier men than Foma Fomich – especially rejected literature. It is also likely, though I don't know for sure, that attempts to establish himself prior to his literary period had been none too successful either, and that wherever he turned, a smart kick in the pants had been his due rather than a decent wage. I have no definite facts to hand, but according to some inquiries I made, it seemed that Foma Fomich had actually produced a 'novel' rather resembling such works as *The Liberation of Moscow, Ataman Storm, Filial Love* – or *Russians in 1104*,[2] etc., etc., which in the thirties used to appear every year by the score and afforded such delectable food for the wit of Baron Brambeus.[3] All this, of course, is past history, but the serpent of literary self-love bites deep and the wound never heals, especially when its chosen victims are the insignificant and the feeble-minded. Humiliated at his first literary attempt, Foma Fomich there and then joined the countless ranks of the embittered whence all hapless spiritual vagrants and God-forsaken simpletons emerge. I presume that his monstrous vainglory, his need to be universally acclaimed, admired and applauded, also dated from that particular moment. Even as the General's fool, he managed to surround himself with a troupe of loyal and devoted idiots. His was an insatiable need to dominate, to play the oracle, to show off whatever the circumstances. If he failed to receive praise from others, then he would set about praising himself. I can clearly recollect his words when he spoke to us in my uncle's house at Stepanchikovo after becoming virtual lord and master: 'I'm no lodger in this house,' he announced mysteriously, 'I'm no lodger here! Just give me a little time to arrange everything, to show you the way of things, and then adieu: to Moscow, to publish a journal! Thirty thousand people will throng every month to attend my lectures.[4] My fame will spread far and wide, and then – woe betide my enemies!' But his genius, even before it had established itself, insisted upon immediate reward. The prospect of being paid in advance is always alluring, and in his case especially so. I know he seriously tried to convince my uncle that he, Foma, was destined one day to perform a great feat,[5] a feat for which he had been expressly brought into this world, and that in hours of solitude and darkness a winged creature or something of that kind was providing him with the necessary strength and inspiration. Namely, he was to compose a profoundly searching *magnum opus* of a spiritually edifying nature that would shake the world and stun all Russia.[6] And then, after all Russia had been stunned, he, Foma, scorning glory, would withdraw to a monastery, spend the rest of his days and nights praying in the caverns of Kiev for the salvation of his motherland?[7] My uncle, of course, was deeply impressed by all this.

Now imagine Foma Fomich, the lifelong martyr, downtrodden and beaten into submission, perhaps actually beaten, Foma the secretly carnal and self-loving, Foma the embittered man of letters, Foma the indigent buffoon and despot at heart however humble and pathetic his origins, Foma the arch-bluffer with a penchant for insolence whenever things were on the mend – imagine this Foma risen to honour and respect, cheered and applauded on all sides thanks to his semi-demented benefactress and his besotted, totally compliant benefactor, in whose house he ended up after so many arduous years of wandering. My uncle's character, of course, requires a more detailed explanation, for without it the meteoric rise of Foma Fomich is impossible to grasp. For the time being, however, suffice it to say that Foma proved the truth of the old proverb: seat a pig at a table and it will put its feet on it. He more than made up for his past! A base nature subjected to tyranny will always tyrannize others as soon as it has secured its own release. Foma Fomich had been tyrannized, and he too experienced an immediate compulsion to tyrannize others; he had been abused, and he too set about abusing others. He had had to play the clown, and he too immediately surrounded himself with a company of clowns. He turned into a shameless braggart; he gave himself the most ludicrous airs, he demanded the impossible, he bullied mercilessly, and the outcome was that sensible and decent people, even before they had personally witnessed his antics and had only heard reports, considered him to be possessed of the devil, made the sign of the cross and spat with disgust at the sound of his name.

I mentioned my uncle. Without, I repeat, my shedding some light on this remarkable personage, the impudent ascendancy of Foma Fomich in the household, his metamorphosis from a base clown into a man of stature, can never be properly understood. Apart from being unusually kind-hearted, my uncle, in spite of his somewhat rugged looks, was the most delicate and sensitive person imaginable; he was a man of the utmost nobility of soul and of courage tried and tested. I say 'courage' without reservation, because no matter what the obstacles, he never neglected or shirked his obligations or hesitated in the performance of his duties. In spirit he was as innocent as a child. Indeed, he was a child at the age of forty: totally uninhibited and full of good cheer, he considered all men to be saints, blamed only himself for other people's shortcomings and exaggerated their virtues out of all proportion, even ascribing them where there were none. He was one of those uncontaminated souls who are ashamed to see bad in others, who hasten, on the contrary, to endow their fellow-men with all the virtues, and to take delight in their success, living perpetually in an ideal world in which they accuse no one but themselves whenever disappointments occur. Sacrifice of their own interests for the good of others is the vocation of such souls. One might have suspected my uncle of being timid, spineless and weak. Of course, he was weak and altogether too soft-hearted, but not for any want of backbone, simply because he had a terror of giving offence, of performing a cruel act, which sprang from an excessive respect for his fellow-men and for humankind in general. Besides, he was irresolute and faint-hearted only where his own personal interests were concerned, which he neglected to an extraordinary degree, and as a result of which he was subjected, all his life, to taunts and ridicule, even from those on whose behalf he sacrificed such interests. He never believed that he could have enemies, and if he happened to come across any, he somehow failed to notice them. He had an unholy dread of domestic squabbles, and would always give in at once rather than lift a finger in his own defence. His compliance was born of a shy generosity of spirit, a bashful considerateness towards others: 'I only want', he would readily pronounce, dismissing any suggestion of leniency and weakness, 'I only want to see everybody happy and contented.' Needless to say, he could never resist championing all manner of noble causes, and conse-quently fell easily under the spell of any charlatan who took the trouble to disguise his motives. My uncle was credulous to an unbelievable degree, and in this respect was often the victim of grievous deception. And when at last, after much torment, he would be forced to admit that the person deceiving him was a scoundrel, he would place the blame upon himself above all, and at times, himself alone. Now picture a capricious idiot of a woman having just installed herself in his peaceful household together with another idiot, her idol; a woman who all her life had feared only her husband the General, but now had no one to fear, who moreover imagined that recompense was due to her for past sufferings — an idiotic woman whom my uncle felt bound to revere out of sheer filial duty. She and Foma Fomich immediately began by impressing upon my uncle that he was rude, impatient, inconsiderate, and, above all, egoistic in the extreme. The amazing thing was that the stupid old woman sincerely believed what she preached. But I think Foma Fomich did too, to a certain extent at least. They also convinced my uncle that it was the Almighty Himself who had sent him Foma to save his immortal soul and subdue his unbridled passions; they convinced him that he was arrogant, vainglorious of his wealth, and capable of the sin of begrudging Foma

Fomich every morsel of his keep. Very soon my poor uncle ceased to have any doubts about his moral degradation, and was ready to tear out his hair and grovel for pardon.

'It's all my fault, you know,' he would say to whoever was listening. 'I'm to blame for everything! You've got to be doubly considerate to someone in your debt[8] ... That is to say ... My word! ... what am I saying! In *my* debt? I'm lying again! Just the opposite, he puts me in *his* debt by staying with me! And I begrudged him his keep! ... Though I did nothing of the sort really, a mere slip of the tongue, happens with me all the time ... And if you must know, my dear sir, the fellow's had a frightfully difficult life but has managed to do an enormous amount of good — ten solid years he tended a sick friend and received nothing but insults in return — all this calls for a reward! And don't forget, he's a man of learning ... A writer! A highly educated man! A most noble spirit, in short.'

The picture of Foma, erudite and miserable, acting the part of a clown to a capricious and cruel master, filled my uncle's heart with pity and indignation. He was quick to attribute all that was outlandish and mean in the character of Foma Fomich to the suffering, humiliation and bitterness of former days. In his gentle and lofty-minded way he immediately concluded that the poor devil could not be held responsible for his behaviour and that he must not only pardon him but soothe and heal his wounds with tenderness and compassion, so as to reconcile him to humanity. Having made up his mind on this point, he was carried away completely and proved utterly incapable of realizing that his newly found friend was nothing but a lascivious, capricious, selfish, indolent brute. In the genius and erudition of Foma Fomich he had supreme belief. I should mention that the very words 'science' and 'literature' inspired in my uncle the most naive and artless awe, although he had never studied anything himself in his life. This was one of his principal, if quite harmless, foibles.

'He's writing an essay!' he would say, on tiptoe, though Foma's study was two rooms away. 'Haven't a clue what it's all about,' he would add with a proud and mysterious air, 'probably just a lot of drivel, my friend ... that is to say, drivel in the best sense, you understand. Crystal-clear to some, no doubt, but for the likes of us, just plain gibberish ... something about forces of production, so he said. Something to do with politics, very likely. Yes, he'll be famous yet! And we may get a chance to bask in his glory. That's what he told me, my friend ...'

I have positive proof that on Foma's express orders my uncle was compelled to shave off his splendid reddish-brown side whiskers.[9] It seemed to Foma Fomich that they made him look too much like a Frenchman, which was, of course, unpatriotic. Little by little Foma began to interfere in the running of the estate and to put forward clever suggestions. These clever suggestions had a disastrous effect. The peasants soon realized what was going on and who was the real master and scratched their heads in puzzlement. One day I overheard one conversation that Foma Fomich had with the peasants; I confess I was eavesdropping. He had previously declared how fond he was of talking to the 'shrewd Russian peasant'. And now he had called in at the threshing barn; first he spoke to the peasants about farm management, although he could not tell oats from wheat, then in suave tones explained the sacred duties of the peasant to his master, touching in passing upon the subject of electricity and the division of labour, of which, of course, he understood not a jot, went on to explain the revolution of the earth around the sun, and finally, in a state of euphoria at his own eloquence, turned to discussing the ministers of the crown. I understood this. Was it not Pushkin who wrote about a certain father who tried to impress on his four-year-old son that he, his papa, 'was so terribly brave that the Tsar loved him'? How desperately that papa needed his four-year-old listener. The peasants, as always, listened submissively to Foma Fomich.

'And what kind of wages did the holy Tsar pay you, master?' one grey-headed old man by the name of Arkhip Korotky suddenly asked him, in an obvious attempt to ingratiate himself. But the question struck Foma Fomich as being unduly familiar, and familiarity he detested above all else.

'And what's that to you, you clod?' he replied, looking contemptuously at the poor peasant. 'Take your ugly face away before I spit on it!' Foma Fomich invariably adopted this tone when conversing with the 'shrewd Russian peasant'.[10]

'Father,' another peasant intervened, 'we're ignorant folk. You may be a major, or a colonel, or His Eminence himself for all we know – we don't know how to address you.'

'Listen, you clod,' replied Foma Fomich, but in a gentler voice this time, 'there are wages and wages, blockhead! Somebody may well be a general, but be paid nothing, because the Tsar has no use for him. If you must know, my salary at the Ministry came to twenty thousand rubles, but I never took a kopeck because I served for the honour of it, and besides, I had my own means. All my salary went towards state education and aid for the destitute victims of the fire in Kazan.'

'My word! Then it was you who rebuilt the town?' replied the peasant, astonished.

The peasant folk were always full of astonishment at Foma Fomich.

'I had a hand in it,' Foma replied reluctantly, as though *such* a subject was much too lofty for *such* an audience.

With my uncle he would adopt a completely different tone.

'Who exactly were you to begin with?' he once inquired suddenly, lolling back in his easy chair after a sumptuous meal, while a servant armed with a freshly plucked lime branch fanned him from behind to keep the flies away. 'What sort of person were you before I arrived? But I have kindled a spark of the divine fire in you, and it will glow in your soul forever. Have I kindled a divine spark in you or not? Answer me: have I, or have I not, kindled a spark in you?'

If the truth be known, Foma Fomich did not know himself why it was that he had asked such a question. But my uncle's silence and confusion suddenly infuriated him. Formerly meek and long-suffering, he was now apt to flare up like a tinder-box at the least provocation. Uncle's silence offended him and he had to insist upon an immediate answer.

Uncle hesitated, hummed and hawed, and did not know what to say.

'May I remind you that I'm still waiting for a reply,' continued Foma Fomich in offended tones.

'*Mais répondez donc, Yegorushka!*' the General's Lady chimed in, with an impatient shrug of the shoulders.

'I'm asking you: have you got this spark in you or not?' repeated Foma in a patronizing tone, helping himself to a bonbon from a box which, on the express orders of the General's Lady, was always placed at his side.

'Good heavens, I don't know, Foma,' my uncle replied at last in despair, 'perhaps there may be something of the kind . . . you really oughtn't to ask me such questions, I'm afraid I might tell a lie . . .'

'Very well! It follows then that I'm not even worthy of a reply – is that what you wanted to say? All right then, so I am a nobody!'

'Not at all, Foma, bless your soul! I didn't mean that at all!'

'No, I know exactly what you meant.'

'But I swear I never did!'

'Oh, very well! Then I'm a liar too! Have it your way: I'm out to pick a quarrel, is that it? What's one insult more or less! I can bear them all . . .'

'*Mais mon fils . . .*', the General's Lady cried out in terror.

'Foma Fomich! Mamma!' my uncle exclaimed in despair. 'Honestly, I am not to blame! A slip of the tongue maybe, no more! . . . You mustn't look at me like that, Foma. Of course I'm stupid – I can feel myself how stupid I am – I can hear myself uttering the most infernal nonsense sometimes ... Say no more, Foma! I know it all!' he continued with a wave of his hand. 'Would you believe it, I've lived forty years, and up till now, up to the time you came along, I always thought I was a normal person ... It never occurred to me that I was as sinful as a goat and an egoist of the first order – I've piled up such a heap of evil, it's a wonder the earth can bear the weight of it all!'

'Yes, you're an egoist all right!' remarked Foma Fomich, well satisfied with himself.

'Yes, now I know that I am! But no more! From now on I'll mend my ways!'

'May God assist you in the task,' concluded Foma Fomich with a pious sigh, rising from the table to take his after-dinner nap. Foma Fomich always took a nap after dinner.

Allow me to say something, as a conclusion to this chapter, about my own relationship with my uncle, and how it came about that I was so unexpectedly brought face to face with Foma Fomich and thrown headlong into the midst of the most momentous events that had ever disturbed the peaceful routine of the blessed village of Stepanchikovo. My introduction will then be at an end and I shall proceed to the story proper.

At an early age I found myself an orphan, alone in the world, and my uncle took the place of my father and brought me up at his own expense; in short, he did for me more than my own father would have done. From the day he took me into his home I became immensely attached to him and loved him with all my heart. I was about ten at the time, and I remember we very quickly became great friends and understood each other perfectly. Together we spun peg-tops, and once we stole a bonnet from a cantankerous old lady, a relative of ours; I promptly tied it to the tail of my kite and sailed it up into the sky. We met again briefly many years later in St Petersburg where I was completing my university studies for which he was paying. On this occasion I again responded to him with the full ardour of youth, completely won over by his extraordinarily noble, meek, honest, genial and simple-hearted disposition – which cast everyone who met him under its spell. After completing my studies I spent some time in St Petersburg, without employment, flushed by the youthful conviction that soon, very soon, I was destined to perform great and remarkable things. I had no wish to leave St Petersburg, from where I maintained an infrequent correspondence with my uncle, and then only when I needed money, which he never refused me. One day word reached me through one of my uncle's house-staff who happened to arrive in St Petersburg on business that strange things were afoot in Stepanchikovo.

These initial rumours astonished and intrigued me. I began to be more regular in my correspondence. My uncle's replies were always very guarded and evasive, full of references to the sciences and the high and proud hopes he held for my future success in the field of learning. Suddenly, after a long spell of silence, I received a most amazing letter, which was quite unlike any of the previous ones. It was so full of strange hints and such a maze of contradictions, that at first I could not make head nor tail of it. The writer had evidently been in a state of unusual agitation. On closer perusal, however, one thing emerged clearly; my uncle earnestly entreated me to marry without delay his former ward, the daughter of an impoverished provincial clerk named Yezhevikin. The girl had received an excellent education in a Moscow boarding-school at my uncle's expense, and was now engaged as his children's governess. He went on to say that she was very unhappy and that I could bring her happiness by performing this noble act; he appealed to the generosity of my heart, and promised to give her a dowry. It must be said that he spoke of the dowry in veiled and apprehensive terms and concluded by enjoining me to treat everything in the strictest confidence. This letter bowled me over, and when I had finished reading it my head was spinning. It was hardly surprising that such a romantic proposition should have had the effect it did on a newly fledged youngster like me. Besides, I had heard it said that the young governess was an uncommonly pretty thing. Although I didn't know what to do for the best, I immediately informed my uncle that I was setting off at once for Stepanchikovo. With his letter he had enclosed money to cover the expenses of the journey. However, as a result of my doubts and even fears it was three more weeks before I finally left St Petersburg. Quite by accident I came across a former colleague of my uncle's who had stopped at Stepanchikovo on his way back to St Petersburg from the Caucasus. He was an elderly, level-headed man and a confirmed bachelor. He spoke of Foma Fomich with indignation, and suddenly informed me of something which was quite new to me, namely that Foma and the General's Lady were plotting to marry off my uncle to a strange spinster well past her prime and semi-demented, with an extraordinary life-story and close on half a million rubles for dowry; that the General's Lady had succeeded in convincing the bride-to-be that they were already as good as relatives and on these grounds had enticed her into the household; that uncle was in despair and would probably end up marrying the half million rubles; and, finally, that the two plotters were waging a fearful persecution of the poor defenceless governess in a desperate bid to turn her out of the house, probably fearing that my uncle might fall in love with her, or perhaps, indeed, because he had already done so. I was astonished by these last words. To all my inquiries as to whether my uncle was really in love, my informant either could not or would not give a straight answer, and on the whole spoke tersely and with a marked avoidance of detailed explanation. All this news gave me considerable food for thought; it was in such stark contrast to my uncle's letter and the proposal it contained! ... But time was short. I decided to go to Stepanchikovo to comfort him and try to make him see reason, to rescue him – to get rid of Foma Fomich and put an end to the hateful marriage with the aged spinster – and ultimately, convinced as I was that Uncle's romance was merely a destructive fabrication by Foma Fomich, I hoped to bring happiness to the unfortunate but highly desirable young girl by my offer of marriage, and so on and so forth. Little by little I became so carried away that, young and idle pup that I was, I went to the opposite extreme: instead of doubting and hesitating, I was now consumed by a desire to perform great and prodigious deeds. It even struck me that I was acting with rare magnanimity in my self-sacrifice to bring happiness to an innocent and lovely creature – in short, I was well pleased with myself the whole length of the journey. It was July; the sun was shining brightly; around me spread the immense expanse of fields of ripening corn ... I had spent so much time cooped up in St Petersburg that it seemed to me I was only now looking upon God's earth for the first time.

2

Mr Bakhcheyev

I was nearing the end of my journey. On my way through the little town of B** from where it was only ten versts to Stepanchikovo, the rim of the front wheel of my tarantass broke and I was obliged to stop at a blacksmith's near the town gate. The repair was not going to take long, as all I needed was something temporary to cover the last ten versts, and so I decided to wait on the spot while the men got on with their work. As I stepped down from the tarantass, I noticed a stout gentleman who had also pulled in to have his vehicle attended to. It turned out that he had already been waiting a solid hour in the sweltering heat, all the while scolding and shouting with peevish impatience at the workmen who were bustling round his splendid calash. From the very first glance this angry gentleman struck me as being an extraordinarily petulant individual. He was about forty-five years old, of medium height, enormously fat and with a mottled complexion. His corpulence, double chin and puffed-out cheeks spoke of the blissful life of a landowner. There was something old-womanish in his whole bearing which immediately caught my eye. He was neatly dressed in loose-fitting, comfortable clothes that made no claim to fashion.

For some reason he was angry with me too, all the more baffling since he had never spoken to me or even seen me before in his life. The moment I stepped out of the tarantass, I noted the particularly unfriendly manner in which he eyed me. For my own part, however, I was very eager to make his acquaintance. To judge by the chatter of his servants he was on his way from my uncle's and here, therefore, was an opportunity to ask a few questions. I was about to raise my cap and had just started to comment, in tones of the utmost civility, on how irritating delays can be on a journey, when the fat man measured me from head to toe with a particularly pained and querulous look, mumbled something under his breath, and deliberately turned his ample back on me. This part of his anatomy, though of considerable visual interest, offered no prospect of amicable dialogue.

'Grishka! Stop growling under your breath or you'll be flogged!' he suddenly shouted at his manservant as though he had not even heard my remarks about delays on the road.

'Grishka' happened to be an old silver-haired servant dressed in a long frock-coat and sporting enormous grey sideburns. At a glance it was evident that he too was in a state of anger as he kept up a low mutter of protest. An argument immediately ensued between master and servant.

'Flog me then, loudmouth!' Grishka muttered as if to himself, but loudly enough for all to hear, and turned away in disgust to attend to the calash.

'What? What did you say? "Loudmouth"? . . . I'll teach you to be insolent!' the fat man shouted, going red in the face.

'Why on earth do you keep snapping at me, sir? Can't even say a single word!'

'What do you mean, snapping? Did you hear that? He can grumble at me but I'm not allowed to snap at him!'

'What would I have to grumble about?'

'What indeed . . . Of course you grumbled! And I know why – it's because I left and didn't stay for dinner, that's why!'

'As if I cared. It wouldn't worry me if you stopped dining altogether. It's the smiths I'm grumbling at, not you.'

'The smiths? . . . What are you grumbling at the smiths for?'

'Well, if it's not them, it's your carriage I'm grumbling at.'

'And why should you grumble at the carriage?'

'Because it's broken down. It won't do to break down on the road. See you don't do it again.'

'The carriage, is it? . . . No, you're on at me, not the carriage. It's his own fault, and I get the blame!'

'But, sir, why do you keep on at me? Leave off, I beg you!'

'And why did you scowl the whole journey and not say a single word to me, eh? You're not so dumb at other times!'

'A fly was trying to crawl into my mouth, so I kept it shut: that's why I sat scowling. Did you want me to tell you fairy tales, is that it? You'd better get yourself a nanny if you're fond of fairy tales.'

The fat man opened his mouth and was about to retort but stopped short, apparently unable to think of a suitable reply. His servant, meanwhile, well pleased with his rhetoric and influence over his master, displayed in front of witnesses, turned to the workmen with redoubled smugness and resumed giving instructions.

All my efforts to scrape an acquaintance with the fat gentleman proved futile, especially in view of my awkwardness and shyness; however, an unforeseen incident saved the day. A dirty, hairy, sleepy-eyed face suddenly appeared at a window of a coach which, locked up and its wheels removed, looked as if it had been standing there since time immemorial, vainly awaiting its turn to be repaired. The appearance of the face drew a general burst of laughter from the workmen. The joke was that the man who had peered out of the carriage had been confined there drunk, and, having slept it off, was now clamouring to be released. Finally he called out to somebody to fetch him his tools. All this provoked the crowd to unbounded merriment.

There are some people who take enormous delight in the most unexpected things. A drunken peasant pulling a face, a man tripping and falling on the road, a couple of washerwomen squabbling, and so on and so forth, for some unknown reason puts them in a mood of the most innocent rapture. The fat landowner was just such a person. Little by little his stern and sullen features began to light up and mellow until finally he was positively beaming.

'Well, if it isn't Vasilyev!' he exclaimed with concern. 'But how did he get stuck in there?'

'Vasilyev, sir, it's Vasilyev!' everybody shouted in chorus.

'He's been on a spree, sir,' one workman added, a tall, lean, elderly man with a stern and affected expression, who appeared to claim precedence among his fellows. 'Been on a spree, sir, three days now he's been on the run from his master, hiding here with us, a proper nuisance he is! Wants his chisel now. You don't need any chisels, you blockhead! He'd pawn his last tool!'

'Oh, Arkhip! Money comes and money goes. God in heaven, let me out,' Vasilyev implored in a pitifully thin warble, poking his head out of the coach.

'Now you're trapped, you rogue, you can stay there!' Arkhip replied sternly. 'Two days he's been on the bottle now; they dragged him off the street at dawn this morning; thank the Lord we hid you and told Matvey Ilyich you'd gone down with unexpected stabbing pains.'

There was another burst of laughter.

'And where's my chisel?'

'Our Zuy's got it! There he goes again! He's as tipsy as they come, Stepan Alekseyevich, sir.'

'Ha-ha-ha! Oh, you scoundrel! So this is what you get up to in town: pawning your tools!' The fat man wheezed and choked with laughter in a sudden access of geniality.

'And what a craftsman! There isn't another like him outside Moscow. But the rogue is always up to tricks like this,' he added, turning to me quite unexpectedly. 'Let him out, Arkhip, perhaps he does need something after all.'

The gentleman's request was carried out. The nail that had been knocked into the door of the coach in order to make fun of Vasilyev when he woke up was pulled out, and a dirty, clumsy, ragged creature emerged into the daylight. The sunlight stung his eyes; he sneezed and swayed on his feet; then, shielding his eyes with the flat of his hand, he looked about him slowly.

'What a crowd, what a crowd!' he said, shaking his head, 'and everybody sober, I b-bet.' There was a note of personal reproach in his drawling, pensive voice. 'Well, good morning, my friends, how d'you do all, what a lovely day!'

Again laughter all round.

'A lovely day indeed! Can't you see there's precious little left of your day, you dimwit!'

'You're a good one, you are.'

'An hour's as good as a day when I get going.'

'Ha-ha-ha! Just listen to him!' the fat man cried, shaking with laughter, and again looked at me amiably. 'Aren't you ashamed of yourself, Vasilyev?'

'It's misfortune drove me to it, sir, misfortune,' Vasilyev replied gloomily, with a wave of his hand, evidently glad of an opportunity to talk about his troubles.

'What misfortune, you idiot?'

'Misfortune such as you've never heard of before: Foma Fomich is to be our new owner.'

'Who? When?' the fat man yelled out, unable to contain himself.

I took a step forward myself: I was suddenly and unexpectedly involved in the situation.

'Why, all of us at Kapitonovka. The Colonel, our master, God bless him, is about to hand over the whole of the Kapitonovka estate to Foma Fomich, all the family lands and us seventy souls with it. "There, Foma," he says, "you've been a pauper till now, hardly a landowner; all you've got is a couple of smelts in Lake Ladoga, so to speak – that's all the workforce your father left you. Now this father of yours,"' Vasilyev continued with a kind of malicious relish, garnishing his story with choice references in all that related to Foma Fomich, '"this father of yours, assuredly of noble stock, though no one knows where he came from, like you, used to scrape a living at the kitchen doors of gentlefolk. But wait till I transfer Kapitonovka to you and make you a landowner with a noble title thrown in, as well as serfs of your own and leisure enough for you to lie back at your ease . . ."' '

But Stepan Alekseyevich was no longer listening. The story which the half-drunk Vasilyev had told produced a shattering effect upon him. The fat man was so incensed that he turned almost purple; his double chin began to throb, his small eyes grew bloodshot. I feared he would have a fit on the spot.

'That's all we needed!' he said, half choking himself, 'that scoundrel, Foma, that toady, a landowner! Bah! Go to hell, the lot of you! You there, get a move on! We're going home!'

'Excuse me, please,' I said, hesitantly stepping forward, 'I just heard you mention somebody called Foma Fomich: if I'm not mistaken, his surname is Opiskin. You see . . . I'd like to . . . that is, I have reason to be interested in this gentleman and for my own part I'd very much like to know whether it really is true, as this good man has just stated, that his master, Yegor Ilyich Rostanev, is willing to pass one of his estates to this Foma Fomich. I should very much like to know, and I . . .'

'Begging your pardon, kind sir,' the fat man interrupted, 'why should you be interested in this gentleman, as you call him — a godless scoundrel is what he really is! And that's what he should be called! You think that toad's got a face? It's a disgrace, not a face.'

I hastened to explain that I could not comment on his appearance as I had never seen him in my life, but as for Yegor Ilyich Rostanev, he happened to be my uncle, my own name being Sergey Aleksandrovich So-and-So.

'Ah, the man of learning? Well, well, they're all eagerly waiting for you, I can tell you!' the fat man exclaimed, genuinely overjoyed. 'I've just come from there, from Stepanchikovo — walked out before I had my pudding: couldn't stand the sight of Foma any longer! I quarrelled with the whole household over that confounded Foma . . . Well, I never! I do beg your pardon, sir. I am Stepan Alekseyevich Bakhcheyev and I can remember you when you stood so high . . . Who would have thought . . .? Allow me . . .'

And the fat man reached out to embrace me warmly.

The initial moment of excitement over, I immediately resumed plying him with questions: the opportunity was not to be missed.

'But who on earth is this Foma?' I asked. 'How is it he has come to lord it over the whole household — why doesn't someone chase him away with a broom? I must confess . . .'

'Chase Foma Fomich away? Are you out of your mind, sir? Why, the

Colonel himself is always the first to bow before him. You know, Foma once decreed that a Thursday was going to be Wednesday and nobody in the house dared object. "I don't want Thursday, I want it to be Wednesday." And they ended up with two Wednesdays that week! You think I'm making it up? Not a bit of it. Even Captain Cook couldn't have managed that.'

'Yes, I did hear about that, but I must admit . . .'

'Must admit, must admit! The way he keeps on! What's the use of admitting! You'd do better to ask me what forests I've trekked through. Take the Colonel's mother, a worthy lady if ever there was one, and besides, the wife of a general – but completely crack-brained, if you ask me: she's besotted with Foma Fomich and it's thanks to her first and foremost that he's been able to install himself in the household. He's so bewitched her with his learning that she's no longer able to speak for herself, even though she still has the title of "Your Excellency" – imagine marrying General Krakhotkin at fifty! As for Praskovya Ilyinichna, the Colonel's sister, forty and still an old maid – she's not even worth talking about. It's oohs and ahs, clucking like an old hen all day long – I'm fed up with her – to hell with her! The fair sex, they tell me, and I'm expected to respect her just because of her sex! Oh, but I shouldn't gossip; she'll be your aunt. There's only one sane person there and that's the Colonel's fifteen-year-old daughter, Aleksandra Yegorovna, a mere child but wiser than everybody else put together, if you ask me; hasn't got a scrap of respect for Foma – a joy to behold. What a darling creature! And who is he to be respected? Foma used to play the buffoon for the old General, he used to imitate different animals to amuse His Excellency! But Ivan the clown now wears a crown. Your uncle has put the scoundrel on a pedestal, treats him like his own father, grovels at his feet – when he's a hanger-on in the Colonel's household! Blast him!'

'Being poor is hardly a crime . . . and . . . I must admit . . . allow me to ask, is he clever or handsome?'

'Foma? Handsome?' Bakhcheyev replied with an extraordinary tremor of malice in his voice. (My questions for some reason seemed to irritate him and he was beginning to eye me with some misgiving.) 'Handsome! Listen to him: he thinks he's found a beauty! He's a monster, if you really want the truth, sir. All right if he had some wit, if only the rascal had a scrap of wit – well, perhaps then I'd grin and bear it for the sake of his wit, but not a bit of it! He's given them a potion and drugged the lot, the charlatan! Damnation! I've lost my voice! There, I'll say no more. You've quite put me out of sorts with all your talk, kind sir! Hey, you! Is it ready or not?'

'Blackie still needs re-shoeing,' Grigory replied morosely.

'Blackie indeed! I'll show you Blackie! ... Yes, my good friend, I could tell you things that would make your mouth hang open, and you'd stay with your mouth hanging open till the Second Coming. You see, there was a time when I respected him. What do you think? I confess, I openly confess: I was a fool – there's no getting away from it! I was taken in by the scoundrel. A know-all! A universal expert who's mastered all the sciences! He gave me drops: you see, I'm sick, I've got humours, my friend. You mightn't believe it, but I have. So he started feeding me these drops – they nearly knocked me out cold. No, don't say a word, just listen to me. You'll be there soon enough to see it all for yourself. He'll have the Colonel shed tears of blood yet; yes, the Colonel will shed tears of blood, but it'll be too late. All the neighbours are already avoiding them because of Foma – curse him. Anybody who comes to the house gets abused. Who am I to complain, though – even rank isn't spared! Whoever comes gets treated to a sermon; he's sold on morals now, the scoundrel. "I'm the wisest of the wise," he says, "everybody listen to me. I'm a learned man!" So what if you have learning, damn it! Must you persecute everyone who hasn't, just because you have learning? ... And you should hear that learned tongue of his at work, bla-bla-bla! bla-bla-bla! Such a wagging tongue, I tell you, that if you cut it out and threw it on a dunghill, it'd still go on wagging till a crow pecked it all up. The conceit of the man! He's as puffed-up as a mouse in a granary! Just too big for his boots. What's the use? He's now taken it into his head to teach the servants French! Don't believe me, if you don't want to! It's going to do him good, he reckons, that uncouth lout of a servant! Bah! It's a scandal – it really is! What does a yokel want to know French for, I ask you? What do the likes of us want to know French for, come to that? To mince mazurkas with the ladies, prance about with other people's wives? Debauchery, that's all it is. To my mind, drink a carafe of vodka and you'll be talking all the languages under the sun. That's what I think of your French! You're a French-speaker, too, I wouldn't be surprised: "La-la-la! la-la-la, Tom the cat has got it pat!"' Bakhcheyev surveyed me disdainfully. 'You're a learned one too, my friend, eh? Been delving in the sciences, haven't you?'

'Well, yes, up to a point ...'

'Master of all manner of studies, I bet?'

'Yes, I mean, no ... I'm more of an observer at the moment. I've been in St Petersburg all the while and I'm now off to my uncle's ...'

'And what's the attraction at your uncle's? You ought to have stayed at home, wherever that may be! No, my good friend, you can take it from me, none of your learning will help you there, nor your uncle himself; you're as good as trapped! Why, I lost weight overnight there. You don't believe I did? Yes, I can see you don't believe me. Well, please yourself.'

'No, sir, really, I do believe you. But I still can't understand . . .' I replied, growing more and more confused.

'There we go again: I do believe you, I don't believe you. You're all glad to strut about spouting science. Any excuse is good enough to cut a dash! Can't stand all that learned stuff myself; it sticks here in my gullet! I've met your Petersburg types before – a useless crowd! Godless freemasons, all of them: shying away from a glass of vodka as if it would bite. Bah! You've made me angry, my friend, and I don't want to talk to you. I'm not obliged to entertain you with stories, you know, and anyway, my tongue's worn out. You can't go on ranting at the whole world, my good man, and besides, it's a sin . . . But let me just tell you that your uncle's valet, Vidoplyasov, has been turned into a proper idiot by your man of science. He's crazy now, is Vidoplyasov, thanks to Foma Fomich . . .'

'If I had my way, I'd take that Vidoplyasov,' broke in Grigory, who had been listening to the conversation in respectful silence, 'if ever he came my way, I'd give that Vidoplyasov such a hiding, I'd soon knock all that German nonsense out of him. I'd give him such a walloping he wouldn't know if he was coming or going.'

'Silence!' his master shouted. 'Hold your tongue; speak when you're spoken to!'

'Vidoplyasov,' I said, utterly confused and hardly able to think of what to say next. 'Vidoplyasov . . . Don't you think it's a strange name?'

'What's so strange about it? You're at it too, you man of learning!'

My patience snapped.

'I beg your pardon,' I said. 'Why are you angry with me? What have I done? I don't mind telling you, I've been standing here listening to you for the last half-hour and I don't begin to know what you're talking about . . .'

'No need to take offence, my friend,' the fat man replied, 'no need at all! I said it for your own good. You shouldn't take it to heart that I'm such a loudmouth and shouted at Grigory just now. He's a confounded wretch, is my Grishka, but I love him just the same, the scoundrel. I'm altogether too soft, that's my trouble, but it's all Foma's fault, you know. He'll be the end of me, I swear he will. Two solid hours I've had to swelter here on his account. I thought of dropping in on the archdeacon while these fools get on with the job. He's an excellent man, our archdeacon. But Foma Fomich has got me into such a state, I don't want to face the archdeacon! I've had enough! There isn't even a place to have a drink around here. Everybody's a scoundrel I say, one and all! . . . Now if he had some sort of unusual rank,' Bakhcheyev continued, again referring to Foma Fomich, whom he obviously could not get off his mind, 'well, I'd grin and bear it; but he hasn't got any sort of rank, I know he hasn't. Years back, in forty something or other, he was supposed to have suffered for a cause, and just for that we're now supposed to grovel at his feet! Hell! The slightest excuse and he's on his feet yelling: "I'm being insulted and taken advantage of because I'm poor and helpless and no one respects me!" Don't anyone dare sit down to a meal without Foma Fomich, even if he deliberately refuses to appear: "I've been insulted – I'm a poor defenceless castaway, a crust of bread is all I need." The moment everybody's settled down, in he comes and starts scraping away at the same old tune: "Why didn't you wait for me? Is this all you think of me?" What a performance! I put up with it for a long time, my friend. He thought I'd get up on my hind legs before him like an obedient pooch! He had another think coming! You might have your hand on the bridle, my friend, but I'm already in the cart. Look, Yegor Ilyich and I served in the same regiment. I resigned as a cadet, but he stayed on until he retired to his estate last year with the rank of Colonel. I said to him: "You'll come to no good giving in to Foma! You'll rue the day!" "No," he says to me, "he's an excellent fellow" – (Foma – I ask you!) – "he's my friend, he's teaching me correct behaviour." Well, how can you go against that! If he's teaching correct behaviour, that's the end. And do you know what all the fuss was about today? Tomorrow is St Ilya's Day' (Mr Bakhcheyev made the sign of the cross) 'and it's your little cousin's name-day. So I thought I'd spend the day with them and stay for dinner. Had a toy specially ordered from town: a clockwork German kissing his lady's hand and she wiping a tear with a handkerchief – a lovely little thing! (But all that's ruined *morgen-früh!* Look, it's lying with a broken nose in the back of my carriage. I'm taking it back.) Yegor Ilyich himself wasn't against having a bit of a celebration on a day like that, but Foma stopped it: "Why are you fussing with Ilyusha? Am I to be forgotten now?" Now what do you make of that? Grudging even an eight-year-old his name-day celebration. "I won't have it," he said. "It's my name-day too today!" And St Ilya's Day will become St Foma's, you can be sure of it. "No," he says, "it's my name-day as well." I was as patient as I could be. So what happens? They're walking about on tiptoe whispering what to do next, wondering whether to congratulate Foma on St Ilya's Day or not. If they don't, he might be offended; if they do, he might think they're trying to be funny. Hell and Damnation! We sat down to dinner ... Look here, my friend, are you listening to me or not?'

'Yes, yes, I am; I'm really fascinated, because I've learned from you ... and I must admit ...'

'"Fascinated!" I know all about your "fascinated" ... You're not by any chance trying to be funny, are you?'

'Funny, not at all! On the contrary. Besides ... you have such a way of putting things that I wish I could write down everything you say.'

'What d'you mean, "write down"?' Mr Bakhcheyev asked in some alarm, eyeing me suspiciously.

'Well, I didn't exactly mean "write down" ... just in a manner of speaking.'

'You're not trying to flatter me?'

'What do you mean, "flatter"?' I asked, taken aback.

'Simple. You flatter me; I tell you everything like a fool and then you go and write about me in some paper.'

I hastened to reassure Mr Bakhcheyev that I wasn't that sort, but he still continued to eye me with suspicion.

'Well, that's your story! But I don't know you! You might go one better. Foma threatened to write to the press about me too.'

'May I ask,' I interrupted him, to change the subject, 'is it true that my uncle wants to get married?'

'So what if he does? There's nothing wrong in that. Marry, if you've nothing better to do. That's only half the trouble, though ...' Mr Bakhcheyev looked thoughtful. 'Hm! It's very difficult for me to explain. All sorts of womenfolk have assembled there like bees round a honeypot and you can't tell which one is the marrying type. Now let me be frank with you, my good friend: I don't like women! They're said to be human, but in fact there's nothing but shame in them, they can bring damnation upon your soul. But that your uncle is in love like a Siberian cat, I don't doubt. Still, I'll say no more about it: you'll see it all for yourself. He shouldn't keep putting things off, though. If you want to get married, go ahead I say; but he's afraid to tell Foma; afraid to tell the old lady, who'll create merry hell, seeing as she is all for Forma: "What! A wife in the house! Foma will be mortified!" Mortified, indeed! He'd be picked up by the scruff of his neck and slung out of the house! He wouldn't last five minutes with her! If she wasn't a fool, she'd manage it in some other way, she'd give him such a to-do that he wouldn't find anywhere to put himself. That's why he's now plotting with Mamma to palm some crackpot off on your uncle . . . Now don't interrupt me, my friend! I was just coming to the main part of my story and you interrupted me! I'm older than you; it won't do to interrupt your elders . . .'

I apologized.

'No need for apologies. As you're a man of learning, I was going to let you be the judge of how he insulted me today. Now just think about it, if you're a fair-minded man. We sat down to dinner, and I could see he'd have gladly eaten me alive! Right from the start he sat there absolutely fuming. He'd have drowned me in a spoonful of water! The viper! The man is so stuffed full of vanity it's bursting out of him! He decided to pick on me and teach me morals and manners too, if you please. Why am I so fat, he asks? Why fat and not thin, the fellow wants to know. Now, I ask you, what sort of question is that? Is there anything clever in it? I gave him a sensible answer: "That's the way God has arranged it, dear Foma: one man is fat, another thin; and it's not for us mortals to question Divine Providence." Reasonable — don't you agree? "Oh, no!" he says. "You own five hundred serfs, they wait on you hand and foot and what good are you to your country? You ought to work; instead, all you do is sit at home and tootle on your harmonium?" As it happens, that is something I do like to indulge myself in a little, to cheer myself up occasionally. Again I gave him a sensible answer: "And what kind of work do you think would suit me, Foma? Can you think of a uniform that would accommodate this fat body of mine? Say I did squeeze myself into one, and then sneezed — all the buttons would go pop, maybe in front of important officials; good God, they might think I was being deliberately offensive — what then?" Now tell me, my friend, is there anything funny in what I said? You should have seen him giggling and tittering, rolling about with laughter no end at my expense . . . I say there's not a scrap of decency in him; why, he even used French on me: "*Cochon*," he says. Well, that's one word I do understand. So I thought: you damned scholar — you think I'm your booby? I could take so much and no more. I rose from the table and addressed him, in front of all the good people there: "I confess I have thoroughly mistaken you, gracious Foma: I almost thought you were a man of breeding; but it turns out you're a swine like the rest of us," and I left the room just as the pudding was being served. "To hell with your pudding!"'

'Excuse me,' I said, after Mr Bakhcheyev had come to the end of his story. 'Of course, I thoroughly agree with all you say. However, I'm still not at all clear about the facts . . . You see, I now have certain ideas of my own about all this.'

'What ideas, may I ask?' Mr Bakhcheyev inquired suspiciously.

'You see,' I began, a little confused, 'it may not be altogether relevant, but you might as well know. The way I look at it, it's possible we are both wrong about Foma Fomich; maybe beneath it all lies an exceptional nature, perhaps even a highly gifted one – who knows? He may be bitter and broken by his sufferings, as it were, wreaking his vengeance on humanity. I hear he used to be something of a jester; perhaps he was humiliated, demoralized, completely undone by that? You see, a man of quality ... perception ... forced to play the jester! Hence his distrust of mankind and ... and, perhaps, if he were to be reconciled with humanity ... that is to say, with people, maybe he would turn out to have a remarkable nature ... a unique one in fact and ... and surely there must be something in this man? After all, there must be a reason why everyone bows down before him!'

In short, I realized I had said the wrong thing entirely. I could have been excused on account of my youth, but Mr Bakhcheyev was implacable. He looked long and hard into my eyes and suddenly went as red as a turkey-cock.

'What, Foma, a remarkable person?' he asked abruptly.

'Please, I scarcely believe a word of what I just said myself. I was only surmising ...'

'My dear sir, allow me to ask you one thing out of curiosity: have you ever studied philosophy?'

'In what sense?' I asked, nonplussed.

'Forget about sense; you just give me a straight answer and leave sense out of it: have you studied philosophy or not?'

'I must admit, I do intend to, but ...'

'I thought as much!' Mr Bakhcheyev exclaimed, giving full vent to his indignation. 'Even before you opened your mouth I knew you were a philosopher! *Morgen-früh!* You can't fool me! I can smell a philosopher a mile off! Go and kiss your precious Foma Fomich! A remarkable person indeed! Bah! To hell with the lot of you! I almost took you for a reasonable person, but it turns out ... Come on!' he called out to his coachman, who was already mounting the newly repaired calash. 'Home!'

Somehow I managed to placate him. He relented at last; but it was a good while before anger gave way to good spirits. Meanwhile, he had clambered into the calash assisted by Grigory and Arkhip, that same elderly workman who had previously admonished Vasily.

'I beg your pardon,' I said, walking up to the calash, 'I don't suppose you'll ever visit my uncle again?'

'Not visit Yegor Ilyich ever again, you say? That's a lie! You think I'm a man of my word – you think I'd be able to stay away? I'm weak and lacking in manly resolve, that's my undoing. Before the week's out I'll be making my way back, that's for sure. Don't ask me why! I've absolutely no idea, but I shall go, to do battle with Foma again. It's my undoing, good sir! The Lord has sent him to punish me for my sins. It's my womanish character, spineless creature that I am. I'm a coward, sir, a coward of the first order ...'

In spite of all, we parted friends, and Mr Bakhcheyev even invited me to his home for dinner.

'Come, my friend, do come for dinner. I've got vodka that's come walking all the way from Kiev and my cook's been to Paris. The scoundrel will lay on such a beast of a feast you'll be begging on your knees for more. A learned man! He's not been flogged lately, though; he's taken to the bottle again ... good of you to remind me ... Do come! I'd have invited you to dine with me today, but I'm quite out of sorts, at sixes and sevens – sick inside. I'm a sick man, you know ... It's my corpulence. You probably don't believe me ... Well, look after yourself, my friend! It's time I was on my way. There, your transport has been put right too. And tell that Foma to keep away from me, or I'll give him such a reception that he ...'

But his last words were no longer audible. The calash, eagerly drawn by four powerful horses, vanished in a cloud of dust. My own carriage was brought up; I climbed in, and soon the little town was left behind. 'Of course that gentleman was exaggerating,' I thought, 'he was too carried away by anger, he can't possibly be impartial. On the other hand, it's fascinating what he had to say about my uncle. That's two people now who agree he's in love with this girl ... Hm! I'm beginning to wonder if our marriage will take place after all.' For the first time I was assailed by strong doubts.

3

Uncle

I must admit my spirits had flagged a little. As soon as I drove into Stepanchikovo all my romantic notions suddenly struck me as extremely out of place and even foolish. It was about five in the afternoon. The road led past the garden of the manor. Once again, after long years of absence, I saw the huge garden which I remembered from the happy but all too brief days of my early childhood, days of which I was to dream fondly later in the dormitories of the various boarding-schools charged with my education. I alighted briskly and went straight through the garden towards the house. I was most anxious to arrive unannounced, to buttonhole somebody to find out what was going on and above all, to have a good heart-to-heart talk with my uncle. I was not disappointed. At the end of the avenue of ancient lime-trees I came to the terrace, where a French window led into the house. The terrace was surrounded with flower beds and pots of exotic plants. Here I ran into one of the servants, old Gavrila, who had looked after me when I was a child and was now my uncle's valet. The old man was wearing spectacles and clutched an exercise book, to which he kept referring with unusual attention. Two years previously my uncle had brought him to St Petersburg where we had seen each other, and he therefore recognized me immediately. With tears of joy he rushed to kiss my hands, and his spectacles flew off his nose to the ground. I was deeply touched by such devotion. However, I was so disturbed by what Mr Bakhcheyev had said that I had eyes only for the suspicious exercise book which Gavrila was holding.

'What's that, Gavrila? Surely you too aren't being made to study French?' I asked the old man.

'I am, sir, like a parrot in my old age,' he replied sadly.

'Is it Foma himself who teaches you?'

'Yes, sir. And a clever man he must be.'

'Yes, indeed. Does he teach you by the spoken word?'

'No, by exercise book, sir.'

'Is that what you have there? Ah! French words in the Russian alphabet – very clever! And you're not ashamed, Gavrila, to be taken in by this blockhead, this blithering idiot?' I exclaimed, in a flash forgetting all my noble surmises for which Mr Bakhcheyev had only just taken me to task.

'How can he be a fool, sir,' the old man replied, 'and lord it over all the household?'

'Hm! You may be right, Gavrila,' I mumbled, stopped short by this remark. 'Take me to my uncle!'

'Oh my good sir! I wouldn't show my face there, I daren't. I'm even scared of him now. That's why I sit here moping and nip behind the flower beds every time he comes by.'

'What are you afraid of exactly?'

'I didn't know my lesson the other day. Foma Fomich tried to make me get down on my knees as a punishment, but I wouldn't do it. I'm too old, my good Sergey Aleksandrovich, to have that kind of joke played on me! My master was annoyed with me for being so contrary. "Can't you understand, you old fool, it's your education he's concerned about, he wants to improve your elocution." So here I am, swotting up vocabulary. Foma Fomich said he'd give me another test tonight.'

Something did not seem to make sense. I felt there was more to this business with the French language than Gavrila was able to explain.

'One more question, Gavrila: what is he like? Is he good-looking, tall or what?'

'Foma? Foma Fomich? No, sir, he's a shabby-looking creature if ever there was one.'

'Hm! Wait, Gavrila; everything will probably turn out all right; in fact, I promise it will. But . . . where's Uncle?'

'Behind the stables talking to the peasants. The old men of Kapitonovka have come with a petition. They've heard that they're to be signed over to Foma Fomich. They've come to plead for mercy.'

'But why behind the stables?'

'He's scared, sir . . .'

And indeed, I found my uncle behind the stables. He was standing in a yard facing a group of peasants who were bowing and earnestly pleading with him. Uncle was explaining something to them with fervour. I called out and approached him. He turned and we rushed to embrace each other.

He was overjoyed to see me; his happiness knew no bounds. He kept embracing me, shaking my hands . . . as if his own son had been restored to him from some mortal danger; indeed, as if he too had found himself delivered from mortal danger and as a result of my arrival his fears had been dispelled and eternal luck and happiness lavished on him and all his loved ones. My uncle could never be happy in isolation. After the initial moments of excitement he suddenly grew agitated, and then became totally flustered and confused. He kept showering me with questions and offered to take me immediately to meet the family. We were just on the point of going, when instead he turned back and decided to introduce me to the Kapitonovka peasants first. Then, I remember, without rhyme or reason, he began to talk about a certain Mr Korovkin, an unusual person whom he had met on the high road three days before and whom he was now anxiously expecting to arrive on a visit. The next moment he was off on another topic quite unconnected with Korovkin. I watched him with admiration. In reply to his hurried questions I explained that I intended to continue my studies of the sciences rather than to take up a post. As soon as the conversation touched upon science, my uncle wrinkled his brow and assumed an unusually grave countenance. On learning that I had lately become interested in mineralogy, he raised his head and looked about him proudly, as if it was he, without any outside assistance, who had discovered mineralogy and written all there was to write about it. The word 'science', as I have already mentioned, commanded his utmost respect, the more so since he himself understood nothing of it.

'It's marvellous! There are people who know everything there is to know,' he had once said to me, his eyes sparkling with delight. 'You sit amongst them listening to all their talk, and you know you can't make any sense of any of it, yet what a treat it is to listen! And why? Because it's good, it's wise, it will lead to universal happiness! That much I do understand. Take me now, steaming along by train – one day this little Ilyushka of mine will probably fly through the air . . . Then there is trade, industry – various branches, as it were . . . what I mean is, no matter how you look at it, the benefit is indisputable . . . it is, isn't it?'

But let us return to our meeting.

'You just wait, you wait and see,' he rattled on, rubbing his hands gleefully. 'You'll see a man! A rare man indeed, I tell you, a man of learning, a man of science; he'll go down in history. Not bad, is it: "go down in history"? Foma explained it to me . . . Just wait, I'll introduce you.'

'Are you talking about Foma Fomich, Uncle?'

'No, no, my boy! I'm talking about Korovkin now. Foma as well, of course, he too . . . But this time I was thinking of Korovkin.' For some reason he blushed and looked embarrassed as soon as Foma was brought into the conversation.

'What is his field of study, Uncle?'

'Oh, he just studies, my boy, just studies, studies in general. I'm not really quite sure what, but he studies all right. The things he had to say about the railways! – And you know what?' Uncle added in a whisper, conspiratorially screwing up his right eye: 'A touch of the free-thinker in him too, I noticed; especially when he started talking about family happiness . . . A pity, though, I followed so little of what he had to say – there wasn't the time – or I'd have given it all to you in detail. And what's more, he's a thorough gentleman! I invited him to stay with us for a while. He'll be here at any moment.'

All this while the peasants had been staring at me with round eyes and mouths agape, as at some freak.

'Listen, Uncle,' I interrupted, 'don't let me stop these good people talking to you. They've come on business. What is it? I must admit, I suspect what it might be, and I'll gladly listen to what they have to say . . .'

Uncle became restless and flustered again.

'Oh yes! I nearly forgot! Well, you see . . . what's to be done with them? They've got it into their heads – I'd like to know whose bright idea it was in the first place – that all of them on the Kapitonovka estate – do you remember Kapitonovka? Those long walks we used to go on there in the evenings, with Katya, bless her soul . . . that the whole lot of them, sixty-eight souls in all, are to be signed over to Foma! "We don't want to leave you," they tell me, "and that's that."'

'So it's not true, Uncle? You're not giving him Kapitonovka?' I cried in something akin to exultation.

'Not at all! I wouldn't dream of it! Who told you that? It was a slip of the tongue on my part long ago, and now everyone's repeating it. But why should everybody dislike Foma so? Just wait, Sergey, I'll introduce you to him.' He glanced timidly at me as if already sensing my opposition to Foma. 'What a man . . .'

'We want nobody else but you! Nobody else!' the peasants suddenly wailed in chorus. 'You're our lord and we're your children!'

'Listen, Uncle,' I replied, 'I've not met Foma Fomich yet, but . . . you see . . . I have heard a little about him. You may as well know, I happened to meet Mr Bakhcheyev today. And anyway, I've got my own ideas. Now, Uncle, please don't keep these people waiting any longer. Let's go and talk, just the two of us. That's what I came for . . .'

'That's right, that's right!' Uncle agreed, 'that's right! We'll deal with the peasants and then have a friendly, thorough, heart-to-heart talk! Well,' he continued to talk rapidly, turning to the peasants, 'you may go now, my good lads. And in future come to me, always come to me whenever you need to: just come straight to me, any time you like.'

'Bless you, kind sir! You're our lord and we're your children!' the peasants cried out again. 'Don't let Foma Fomich take advantage of us! We beg you, poor folk that we are!'

'Listen to the fools! Nobody's getting rid of you, I tell you!'

'Them studies will be the end of us, sir! He's already taught the living daylights out of people round here.'

'Do you mean to say he's trying to teach you French too?' I exclaimed, almost terrified by the thought.

'No, sir, the Lord has spared us so far!' one peasant replied, evidently a great talker, a ginger-haired man with a huge bald patch on the back of his head and sporting a long, wispy, wedge-shaped beard which seemed to acquire a life of its own whenever he opened his mouth. 'No, master, the Lord has spared us so far.'

'What in heaven's name does he teach you?'

'Well, sir, if you ask me, it's like buying a golden casket to store copper coins.'

'What do you mean, copper coins?'

'Seryozha! You've got it all wrong; it's all lies!' my uncle exclaimed, turning red in acute embarrassment. 'These fools misunderstood what he said to them! He merely ... what's it got to do with copper coins? And there's no need for you to act so clever and talk so much' – Uncle turned to the ginger-haired peasant reproachfully – 'it was all for your own good, you idiot, so why don't you keep your mouth shut if you don't understand!'

'I beg your pardon, Uncle, what about the French lessons?'

'For elocution, Seryozha, just to improve their elocution,' my uncle retorted in a plaintive tone. 'He said himself it was for their elocution ... Besides, something most unusual has happened here – you know nothing about it, so you can't judge. Make sure of the facts before you criticize ... It's easy enough to criticize!'

'And what have you got to say for yourselves!' I cried out, turning to the peasants in a temper. 'Couldn't you have come straight out with it and told him plainly what ought and what ought not to be done? Have you lost your tongues?'

'It's not for the mice to bell the cat, sir! "I'm teaching you manners and clean habits, you clod-hopper," he says. "Why's your shirt filthy?" 'Cos it lives in sweat, that's why! Can't change it every day. Not just the clean I say'll go to heaven, nor all the dirty down to hell.'

'He turns up at the threshing shed the other day,' another peasant chimed in, a tall, lean man in patched clothes and wearing the thinnest

bast sandals imaginable, and evidently one of those people for whom
grumbling is second nature and who seem to lie in wait for every
opportunity to release some poisonous comment. He had been hiding
behind the backs of the other peasants listening in gloomy silence with an
ironic, bitterly cunning smile playing about his lips. 'He turns up at the
threshing shed and says: "Do you know how many versts it is to the
sun?" Now who would know a thing like that? Such learning is for the
gentlefolk, not for the likes of us. "You're an idiot, a yokel," he says,
"you don't know what's good for you! But I," he says, "I'm an
astrolomer! There isn't a planid in God's heaven I can't put a name to."'

'Well, and did he tell you how many versts it is to the sun?' Uncle
butted in, cheering suddenly and winking joyfully at me as if to say: 'Just
wait and see now!'

'Yes, he said it was a lot,' the peasant replied reluctantly, obviously
unprepared for such a question.

'Well, how many did he say, how many exactly?'

'Your honour will know better; we're ignorant folk.'

'No, my friend, I know how far it is, but do you remember?'

'A few hundred, or thousand, he said. Quite a lot. More than three
cart-loads.'

'And what did you think? You probably expected it to be no more than
a verst, within arm's reach? No, my good man, the earth, see, is like a
round ball – do you follow? . . .' my uncle continued, describing a
spherical shape in the air with his hands.

The peasant smiled bitterly.

'Yes, just like a ball! It's up in the air all by itself, spinning round and
round the sun. But the sun itself is motionless. It only looks as though it's
moving. Wonderful, isn't it? Captain Cook, the navigator, discovered all
this . . . Or was it someone else, dammit?' he added in a lowered voice,
turning to me. 'I'm dreadfully ignorant really, my boy . . . Do you know
how far it is to the sun?'

'I do, Uncle,' I said, observing the whole scene in astonishment, 'only
the way I look at it, though ignorance is tantamount to slovenliness . . .
on the other hand . . . to teach astronomy to the peasants . . .'

'Precisely, precisely, precisely – slovenliness!' Uncle echoed, delighted
with my words which struck him as being particularly apt. 'It's a splendid
thought. Of course, slovenliness! I always said so . . . all right, I never
said so, but I felt it. Do you hear me!' he cried to the peasants. 'Ignorance
is slovenliness, it's filth. That's precisely why Foma was so keen to teach
you. He meant it all for your own good. Science, like military service, can

lead to every rank and honour. There, that's science for you now! All right, all right, my good lads! God be with you and I'm glad, very glad . . . rest assured, I shan't abandon you.'

'Protect us, dear father!'

'Don't let us come to grief!'

And the peasants fell at his feet.

'Now, now, what nonsense. You kneel only for the Tsar or the Almighty, not for me . . . Well, off you go now, behave yourselves and you'll be kindly treated . . . and all that . . . You know,' he said, suddenly turning to me and beaming with joy after the peasants had departed, 'there's nothing like a kind word to the poor devils, and a little present won't do any harm either – eh? What d'you think? To celebrate your arrival . . . shall I give them something or not?'

'Uncle, you really are a Frol Silin, a charitable man,[11] it seems to me.'

'There's no other way, no other way, my boy: don't worry. I've been wanting to make them a gift for some time now,' he added, as if apologizing. 'Did it strike you as ridiculous, Seryozha, to see me doling out science to the peasants? It was nothing but the sheer joy of seeing you, Seryozha, my boy. All I wanted was to let the peasants find out how far it is to the sun and see them gape in wonder. It's a rare sight, my boy, to see them gape in wonder . . . I pity the poor devils, really. One thing, though, not a word to anybody in the drawing-room that I've spoken to the peasants. I deliberately took them behind the stables to be out of sight. It couldn't be done out in front, my boy: a very tricky business; and they came along peacefully enough. I did it for their own good . . .'

'And so here I am, Uncle!' I began, changing the subject in order to get to the main point as soon as possible. 'I must admit your letter was such a surprise to me that . . .'

'My boy, not a word about this!' Uncle interrupted in a low voice, as if in fear. 'Later, later, everything will be clear. I may have done you an injustice, a very serious injustice come to that, but . . .'

'An injustice, Uncle – to me?'

'Later, later, my boy, later! Everything will sort itself out. My, what a fellow you have grown! Dear boy! And how I waited for you! I wanted to pour out my heart to you, so to speak . . . You're a learned man, the only one I know . . . you and Korovkin. By the way, you might as well know that everybody's taken against you here. So be careful you don't do the wrong thing!'

'Taken against me?' I asked, staring at my uncle in disbelief and wondering how I could have incurred the displeasure of people who were complete strangers to me. 'Against me?'

'Taken against you, my boy. Can't be helped. It's Foma really . . . and therefore Mother too. Anyway, be careful, be respectful, don't argue, but above all, be respectful . . .'

'To Foma Fomich, Uncle?'

'There's no other way, my boy! I'm not defending him or anything. It's true he may have faults as a person, and perhaps this very minute . . . Oh, Seryozha, my boy, I'm so worried about it all! And yet there should be no need for any of this trouble, everybody could so easily be happy and contented! . . . Still, who hasn't got his faults? We're not perfect ourselves, are we?'

'Uncle, please! Just consider what he's doing . . .'

'My dear boy! It's all such petty bickering, nothing else! For instance, let me tell you something: I'm in his bad books at the moment, and do you know why? . . . Still, perhaps I'm to blame myself, after all. I'll tell you about it later . . .'

'Uncle, I've a special theory of my own on this subject,' I interrupted him, anxious to voice my views. We both seemed to be rather impatient. 'To begin with he was a clown: this embittered and wounded him, degraded his ideals; consequently he has developed a warped and poisoned outlook, with thoughts of wreaking revenge on the whole of mankind . . . But if mankind were to befriend him and his peace of mind were restored . . .'

'Exactly, exactly!' Uncle exclaimed joyfully, 'that's just it! A splendid thought! It's uncharitable, disgraceful of us to criticize him! You're absolutely right! . . . Oh, you really do understand me, my boy; you've brought me comfort! If only things could be put right at the house. You know, I'm even afraid to show my face there. Your arrival is bound to get me into trouble!'

'Uncle, if that's so . . .' I began, nonplussed by such an admission.

'No, no, no! Not on your life!' he exclaimed, grabbing my hands. 'You're my guest, and that's how I want it!'

I found all this most perplexing.

'Uncle, tell me at once,' I began firmly, 'why did you want me to come, what do you expect me to do, and above all, what injustice could you possibly have done me?'

'My dear boy, don't ask! Later, later! Everything will be clear later! I may have done you a very grave injustice, but I only wished to be fair and . . . and . . . and you will marry her! If there's a grain of decency in you, you will marry her!' He blushed deeply in a sudden surge of emotion and went on, clasping my hand firmly and fervently. 'But enough, not another word! You'll soon find out everything for yourself. It'll all depend on you ... You must try to please them now, that's the main thing; make a good impression. Above all, don't lose your nerve.'

'But listen, Uncle, who are they? I see so few people that to tell the truth —'

'A little scared?' Uncle interrupted with a smile. 'It's all right! You're among friends, cheer up! Cheer up and don't be afraid. I'm a little concerned about you though. You want to know who's there, do you? Well, let's see ... First of all there's Mother,' he began hurriedly. 'Do you remember her or not? She's the kindest, sweetest old lady; no pretence about her — that's a fact; a little old-fashioned, but no harm in that. Well, she does occasionally go over the top, she says outlandish things; I'm in her bad books at the moment, but I can't blame her for that ... it's my own fault, I know! After all, she's the *grande dame*, the General's Lady ... What an outstanding man her husband was: first, a general, a highly educated man; true, he didn't leave a fortune, but he was battle-worn and scarred; he strove for glory! Then there's Miss Perepelitsyna. Well, I don't know about her ... lately she's been a bit odd ... it's her character. Still, I can't go on criticizing everybody ... Good luck to her ... Don't go thinking she's just a hanger-on. She's a Lieutenant-Colonel's daughter no less; Mother's confidante, bosom friend! Next, Praskovya Ilyinichna, my sister. Well, no need to say very much about her: simple and good-natured, a bit of a fusspot, but what a heart of gold! — the heart's the thing, I tell you — no longer in her prime, but, you know, Bakhcheyev, funny man, has designs on her, I suspect, wants to woo her. But mum's the word! Keep it secret! Well, who else is there? No need to mention the children: you'll see them for yourself. It's Ilyusha's name-day tomorrow ... Oh, and I nearly forgot: Ivan Ivanych Mizinchikov has been staying with us for over a month now. He's second cousin to you if I'm not mistaken; yes, that's right, second. He gave up his commission in the hussars not so long ago; quite young still. A very worthy soul! But what a spendthrift! I simply can't imagine how he could have turned into such a spendthrift. He hardly ever had a kopeck to his name, but he still managed to run up debts! ... He's a guest of the house now. I didn't even know him until he arrived and introduced himself. Very pleasant, kind, good-natured, respectful. I doubt if anybody's ever heard him speak! Very untalkative. Foma has nicknamed him "the silent stranger" — but he doesn't mind. Foma is pleased with him; he reckons Ivan is a little slow-witted. To be sure, Ivan never contradicts him, in fact he says yes to everything. Hm! a sad case ... Anyway, God help him!

You'll see for yourself. Then there are some people from the town. Pavel Semyonych Obnoskin with his mother; young, but exceptionally clever; something mature, you know, and steadfast about him . . . Pity I can't put it any better. And he's of impeccable morals! And finally we've a certain Tatyana Ivanovna staying, may well be a distant relative of ours – you don't know her – a lady no longer in her prime, no use denying that, but . . . with certain other attributes; she's so rich she could buy Stepanchikovo twice over; she's recently come into money, you understand, she was quite destitute before. So Seryozha, please be considerate: she's highly strung and excitable . . . there's something phantasmagoric in her character. But I know you're a gentleman, you'll understand, she's had her share of bad luck. Discretion, above all discretion with people who've tasted misfortune! Still, don't get the wrong idea. Of course she has her weaknesses: she won't stop to think sometimes, she will say the wrong word too hastily sometimes, not to deceive, you understand . . . but out of, as it were, pure innocence of heart, that is, even if she does tell the occasional lie, it's her good nature speaking pure and simple – if you follow me?'

It appeared to me that Uncle was terribly embarrassed.

'Listen, Uncle,' I said, 'I'm so fond of you . . . pardon my frankness: but are you going to marry somebody here or not?'

'Who told you?' he replied, blushing like a child. 'Now look here, my boy, I'll tell you everything: first, I'm not getting married. Mother, and to some extent my sister, and above all Foma, whom Mother adores – and rightly so, rightly so, he's done a lot for her – they all want me to marry Tatyana Ivanovna; to do the sensible thing and benefit the whole household. Of course, it's my welfare they're concerned with – that much I do understand; but nothing will ever induce me to marry – my mind's made up! However, I've not been able to bring myself to say yea or nay. It's the same old story with me, my boy. And they think I've agreed, and insist I should propose tomorrow, on the day of the family celebrations . . . there's going to be such a commotion tomorrow, I wish I knew what to do! Besides, for some unknown reason Foma has been very short-tempered with me recently; Mother too. My boy, I do admit, I have been so wanting to see you, you and Korovkin . . . to unburden myself, as it were . . .'

'Come, come, Uncle, what good can Korovkin do?'

'He can, my boy, he can help – my, what a man; just think of it: a man of science! I rely on him as on a solid rock: a providential personality! You should hear him talk of family happiness. Of course, I've been relying on you too. I was hoping you'd make them see reason. Judge for yourself: well, so I am guilty, really guilty – I accept that, I'm not so insensitive. But surely I could be forgiven once in a while! What a life we would all have then. How my Sasha has grown, almost ready to wed! And you should see Ilyusha! Tomorrow's his name-day. I'm a bit worried about Sasha though! . . .'

'Uncle! Where's my suitcase! Let me get changed and I'll be back directly, and then . . .'

'It's in the mezzanine, my boy, in the mezzanine. I made sure that you would be taken straight to the mezzanine when you arrived, so that nobody would spot you. Yes of course, of course, get changed! That's good, very good, wonderful! In the meantime I'll go and prepare them all as well as I can. God bless! One is driven to cunning, you know. I'm worse than Talleyrand sometimes. Never mind though! They're all having tea now. That's the way here, very early. Foma likes to have his tea as soon as he wakes up; frankly, it's better that way . . . I'll leave you now, but don't keep me waiting; I hate to be on my own with them . . . Oh! I say! There's just one other thing: don't shout at me, like you did just then! Later if you must, when we're alone, you can point things out to me; but in the meantime try to control yourself and just wait! You see, I've stirred things up there already. They're frightfully cross . . .'

'Listen, Uncle, from what I see and hear, it seems you're –'

'A real dummy? Go on – say it!' he interrupted me quite unexpectedly. 'What's to be done, my boy! I'm aware of it myself. Well, you will come and meet them, won't you? Don't be too long, please.'

I hurried upstairs and opened the suitcase, with Uncle's words not to delay fresh in my ears. As I was changing, it struck me that although I had spent nearly an hour talking to him, I still knew next to nothing about what I had come to find out. This astonished me. One thing was clear: my uncle still wished me to marry; consequently all rumours to the contrary, namely that he was in love with the same person, were unfounded. I remember I felt most alarmed. It occurred to me, further-more, that arriving as I had and saying very little to Uncle, I had tacitly expressed my agreement, given my word, and bound myself for life. It was the easiest thing in the world, I thought, to let yourself be bound hand and foot through an inadvertent word. And I hadn't even seen my bride yet! And then again, why was the whole family up in arms against me? Why should my arrival, as Uncle claimed, have antagonized them? And what strange rôle was Uncle himself playing in his own household? Why this secretiveness? Why so much fear and anxiety? I must admit, everything suddenly seemed to me quite meaningless; all my romantic and heroic notions vanished clean out of my head at the first contact with reality. Only now, after my conversation with Uncle, did I suddenly realize the incongruousness, the utter ridiculousness of his suggestion, and it became clear to me that such a proposal, and in such circumstances, could only have come from my uncle. I realized too that in making the journey as I had post-haste, delighted at his proposal, at the first summons, I had come dangerously close to acting like a fool. I dressed hurriedly and was so engrossed in my troubled thoughts that it took me some time to notice the manservant in attendance.

'What colour necktie would you prefer – Adelaide blue, or this fine check one?' the manservant inquired, suddenly addressing me with absurdly cloying deference.

I glanced at him, and it turned out he too was a sight worth seeing. He was a young man remarkably well dressed for a lackey, quite the equal of any provincial dandy. His brown tailcoat, white trousers, pale yellow waistcoat, patent leather boots, and pink necktie were evidently matched with exquisite care so as to draw attention to the young fop's refined taste. His fob-chain, prominently displayed, served the same purpose. His complexion was deathly pale, almost green; his long, aquiline nose was unnaturally white, as if moulded in china clay. The smile playing about his thin lips suggested melancholy, but refined melancholy. His large, goggling, glassy eyes had an air of extraordinary dullness that at the same time also managed to share something of the same refinement. His soft thin ears were stopped – for the sake of his refined hearing – with cotton wool. The long thin strands of his fair hair were curled and moist with pomade. His hands were white and spotless, no doubt washed in scented rose water, and his delicate fingers displayed long pink manicured nails. Everything suggested a spoilt, idle fop. He talked with a lisp and, according to the latest fashion, would not pronounce the letter 'r', all the while raising and lowering his eyes in undisguised affectation. He reeked of perfume. He was short of stature, flabby and feeble, and kept bobbing up and down as he walked, apparently regarding this as the peak of refinement – in a word, he was steeped in affected mannerisms, feigned delicacy and an inordinate sense of his own dignity. For some reason this last characteristic annoyed me intensely.

'So this necktie is Adelaide blue, is it?' I asked, looking hard at the young lackey.

'Adelaide blue – correct,' he replied, his 'refinement' unruffled.

'You're sure it's not Molly pink?'

'No sir. No such colour is possible.'

'Why is that?'

'The name Molly is vulgar.'

'What do you mean, vulgar? Why?'

'It stands to reason, sir: Adelaide's a foreign name, and therefore civilized; whereas any washerwoman could be called Molly.'

'You're mad!'

'Not at all, sir, I'm quite sane. But if it pleases you to abuse me, that's your affair. I'd have you know though that my conversation has been found pleasing by many a general and even certain counts from the capital.'

'Tell me, what's your name?'

'Vidoplyasov.'

'Ah! So you're Vidoplyasov?'

'I am, sir.'

'Well, we'll meet again, my dear fellow, I can assure you.'

'This is real Bedlam,' I thought as I descended the stairs.

4

At Tea

Tea was being served in the room which opened out onto the terrace where earlier on I had met Gavrila. Uncle's mysterious forebodings about the reception which awaited me made me very uneasy. Youth is sometimes given to excessive pride, and youthful pride is almost always cowardly. Hence my extreme anguish when, coming through the door and suddenly finding myself face to face with the whole party assembled at the tea-table, I tripped on the carpet, and, trying to regain my balance, unexpectedly stumbled into the middle of the room. I stood there staring at the assembled company in dumb embarrassment, red-faced and motionless, believing my career, honour and good name to have been ruined at a stroke. I mention this incident, which in itself was quite insignificant, only because it had a profound effect upon my state of mind all that day and consequently upon my attitude to some of the personages of my story. I started to make a bow, hesitated, blushed more deeply still, then rushed towards my uncle and seized him by the hand.

'Hello, Uncle,' I brought out, gasping for breath and wishing to say something quite different and much more witty, but, quite unexpectedly, managing only 'Hello'.

'How do you do, my boy, how do you do?' Uncle replied, sharing my suffering. 'We've already greeted each other, though. Please don't feel embarrassed,' he added in a whisper, 'it can happen to anybody, and worse! I know you wish the earth would open up and swallow you! Well, and now, Mother dear, allow me to introduce — here is our young man; he's a trifle embarrassed, but I'm sure you'll grow to like him. My nephew, Sergey Aleksandrovich,' he announced, addressing everybody in general.

But before I continue my story, allow me, dear reader, to introduce individually the assembled company in whose midst I suddenly found myself. For this is essential to the proper sequence of my tale.

The company consisted of several ladies and only two men, apart from my uncle and myself. Foma Fomich, whom I was so eager to meet and whom I perceived immediately to be the undisputed master of the house, was not present: but he was conspicuous by his absence, which appeared to have deprived the room of its only source of light. Everybody looked preoccupied and despondent. It was impossible not to notice this from the outset; in spite of my own confused and distraught state I could see that Uncle, for instance, was as upset as I was, however hard he tried to conceal his agitation under a mask of unconcern. Something was weighing heavily on his mind. One of the two men present was still quite young – about twenty-five, the same Obnoskin whom Uncle had previously extolled for his intelligence and morals. I took an intense dislike to this gentleman. Everything about him had an air of modishness and poor taste; his suit, in spite of its elegant cut, looked shabby and tattered; there was something shabby about his face too. Pale, struggling, cockroach whiskers and a miserable tufted beard were apparently intended to mark a man of an independent attitude, perhaps even inclined to free thought. He kept striking poses in his chair, screwing up his eyes and contorting his features into a malicious grin as he eyed me through his lorgnette which he would timidly drop as soon as I turned to face him. The other gentleman, also fairly young, about twenty-eight years of age, was my second cousin Mizinchikov. He was indeed a man of extraordinarily few words. Through the whole of tea he said absolutely nothing, did not laugh when others laughed, but not, as Uncle seemed to think, through any feelings of inferiority; quite the contrary, his light-brown eyes radiated confidence and a certain incisiveness of character. Mizinchikov looked rather handsome with his dark hair and swarthy complexion; he was dressed very presentably – at Uncle's expense, as I found out later. Of the ladies, my attention was first attracted by Miss Perepelitsyna because of her bloodless and singularly vicious features. She was sitting close to the General's Lady – whom I shall describe separately later – not next to her, but at a respectful distance behind her, from where she constantly leant across her benefactress's shoulder and whispered in her ear. Another two or three elderly ladies, indigent members of the household, sat mutely in a row by the window respectfully awaiting their turn to be served tea and staring wide-eyed at the General's Lady. My interest was also aroused by a gaudily clad, fat and flabby woman of about fifty, with rouged cheeks and such teeth as she had black and broken, which did not deter her from tittering, smiling and showing off to the point of flirtation. Her dress was festooned with tiny chains, and she kept staring at me through her lorgnette in the manner of Monsieur Obnoskin. She turned out to be his mother. My aunt, the dutiful Praskovya Ilyinichna, was serving tea. After our long separation it was evident she wanted to embrace me and, naturally, burst into tears, but she did not dare. Everything seemed to be under some kind of prohibition. Next to her sat a lovely dark-eyed girl of fifteen who kept looking at me with intense childish curiosity – this was my cousin Sasha. The last and perhaps most striking of all was a very strange lady dressed with a magnificent and youthful abandon which belied her age. She was at least thirty-five years old, with drained, haggard but extremely animated features. Her pale cheeks would flush deep crimson with her every movement, every surge of emotion. She seemed to be in a perpetual state of excitement, fidgeting on her chair, incapable of keeping still even for a minute. She scrutinized me with frantic curiosity and all the while kept leaning towards Sasha or anybody else close by to whisper a remark before bursting into the most innocent and childishly merry laughter. Yet all her eccentricities, to my surprise, passed completely unnoticed as though everybody had conspired in advance to ignore them. I guessed that this must be Tatyana Ivanovna, whom Uncle had earlier referred to as being 'phantasmagorical', and who was being foisted upon him in marriage and generally much fêted on account of her wealth. Oddly enough, I found her gentle blue eyes strangely attractive; although there were lines under them they shone with a sincerity, cheerfulness and kindness that made it a pleasure to encounter them. But of Tatyana Ivanovna, who is one of the principal 'heroines' of my tale, I shall speak more fully later; her life story is quite remarkable. About five minutes after my arrival in the drawing-room my cousin Ilyusha, a sweet boy, whose name-day was to be celebrated the following day, burst into the room from the garden with both his pockets full of knuckle-bones and a spinning-top in his hand. He was followed by a graceful young girl, a little pale in the cheek and tired-looking, but all the same very attractive. She swept the room with an inquisitive yet apprehensive, not to say timid glance, gave me a stare, and took a seat next to Tatyana Ivanovna. I remember feeling my heart jump involuntarily. I realized this must be the governess . . . I recall too that when she appeared, Uncle shot a glance at me, blushed, then hurriedly lifted up Ilyusha and brought him to me to kiss. I also could not help noticing that Madame Obnoskin first stared at my uncle, then, with a sarcastic smile, turned her lorgnette on the governess. Uncle, who appeared very uneasy and at a loss what to do, called on Sasha to come and introduce herself to me, but she merely rose, bobbed with serious dignity, and quickly sat down again without uttering a syllable. This in fact became her, and I liked her for it. At the same instant the kindly Praskovya Ilyinichna, who could no longer restrain herself, stopped pouring tea and rushed over to shower me with kisses;

but I had not managed to say two words to her before Perepelitsyna's penetrating voice echoed through the room with the complaint that it seemed Mamma (the General's Lady) had been forgotten, Mamma had asked for some tea and nothing was being done about it and she was being kept waiting; whereupon Praskovya Ilyinichna left me and rushed to resume her duties.

The General's Lady, quite the most important member of the present gathering, before whom everybody walked in trepidation, was a withered and bilious old woman dressed in black – her bile obviously stemming from old age and the loss of the last of her faculties, which indeed had been feeble enough at the best of times. Even in her early years she had been demanding and petulant; marriage to the General had made her still more stupid and overbearing. During her fits of anger all hell would break loose in the house. Her tantrums would take two forms. The first was characterized by total speechlessness, when for days on end not a word would pass her lips and she would push away or throw onto the floor anything that was placed before her. The other form was the exact opposite – garrulity. It would begin with Grandmother – she was after all my grandmother – sinking into a slough of despond, when she would foresee the end of the world and her estate, and anticipate poverty and every calamity; then she would become intoxicated with her own presentiments to the point of gleefully enumerating on her fingers all her future disasters and finally whipping herself into a state of jubilant hysteria. It would transpire, of course, that she had foreseen everything long ago and had kept quiet only because 'in this house' she was forced to do so. But if only she had been shown respect, if only she had been listened to, then ... etc., etc. All this would immediately be seconded by her ranks of hangers-on led by Perepelitsyna, and then solemnly affirmed by Foma Fomich. At the particular moment when I was introduced to her she was in the grip of terrible anger apparently of the first type, the silent and more terrifying variety. Everybody was looking at her in trepidation. Only Tatyana Ivanovna, who was allowed to do just as she pleased, remained in excellent spirits. With deliberate solemnity, Uncle led me to my grandmother; but the old lady, making a sour grimace, angrily pushed away her cup.

'Is that the *vol-ti-geur*?' she exclaimed in a sing-song tone through clenched teeth, addressing Perepelitsyna.

This inane question completely disconcerted me. I had no idea why she referred to me as the *voltigeur*, but such questions were not unusual for her. Perepelitsyna leaned over and whispered something in her ear at which the old woman irritably waved her hand. I stood agape, looking inquiringly at my uncle. Everybody exchanged glances, and Obnoskin even bared his teeth, which I found particularly repugnant.

'She doesn't always talk sense,' Uncle whispered to me, also slightly shaken, 'but it's nothing, it's all because she's so kind-hearted, it's her heart that counts.'

'Ah yes, the heart! the heart!' the clarion voice of Tatyana Ivanovna suddenly resounded, her eyes never leaving my face as she shifted restlessly on her chair. The whispered word 'heart' had evidently reached her ears.

However, she did not finish her remark, even though she was clearly anxious to say something. Either from embarrassment or for some other reason, she stopped abruptly, blushed, bent over to whisper something to the governess, and then suddenly covering her face with her handkerchief, threw herself back against her chair and burst into an almost hysterical fit of laughter. I looked round the room in utter consternation; to my surprise, however, everybody remained quite composed and carried on as though nothing remarkable had occurred. Of course, I understood who Tatyana Ivanovna was. At last I was offered tea, and I began to feel more at ease. I cannot explain why, but it suddenly occurred to me that I should enter into polite conversation with the ladies.

'You were quite right, Uncle,' I began, 'to warn me that it's difficult to keep one's nerve here. I'll not conceal,' I turned with an ingratiating smile to Madame Obnoskin, 'I've hardly known female company until recently, and when I made such a clumsy entry just now I must have cut a very funny figure standing in the middle of the room – the simpleton all over, don't you think? ... Have you read *The Misfit*?'[12] I concluded with mounting embarrassment and, blushing with shame at my tone of obsequious frankness, I stared hard at Monsieur Obnoskin, who had bared his teeth and was scrutinizing me from head to toe.

'Exactly, exactly, exactly!' Uncle suddenly exclaimed in an unusually animated voice, genuinely grateful that conversation of sorts was finally under way and that I appeared to be more at ease. 'My boy, what you just said about being unnerved is nothing. All right, so you were unnerved, and that's the end of the matter! But when I made my first entry into society, I went so far as to tell a lie – don't believe me if you don't want to. Now I tell you, Anfisa Petrovna, this is worth listening to. I had just become a cadet in the army and had arrived in Moscow with a letter of introduction to a very eminent lady – an imperious woman, if ever there was one, but in fact extremely kind-hearted, whatever people might have been saying about her. I arrived, and she was receiving guests. The drawing-room was packed with people, real bigwigs. I made my bow and took a seat. At the second word she says to me: "Have you, my good fellow, any estates?" Of course, I hadn't a chicken to my name, but what was I to say? I was embarrassed out of my life. Everybody was staring at me as if to say: Well now, young cadet! Now, why couldn't I have just said: "I've nothing"? I should have acquitted myself with honour, because I'd have told the truth. But that was too much to ask. "Yes," I replied, "one hundred and seventeen serfs." Why the odd seventeen, I'll never know. After all, if you're going to tell a lie, do it in round figures, don't you agree? Anyway, the letter immediately revealed that I was as poor as a church mouse, and a liar to boot. Impossible situation! I took to my heels and never went back there again. And I was penniless at the time, you know. All I possess now has been inherited since then: three hundred serfs from Uncle Afanasy Matveyich, and before that two hundred that came with Kapitonovka from grandmother Akulina Fanfilovna – that's a total of five hundred odd. So from then on I promised never to tell a lie again – and I haven't!'

'Well, wasn't it a rash promise to make? God only knows what may happen,' Obnoskin remarked with a derisory leer.

'Yes, of course, that's true! God only knows what may happen,' Uncle agreed simply.

Obnoskin threw himself back in his chair and burst out laughing; his mother smiled; there was something decidedly vile in the way Miss Perepelitsyna sniggered too; and for some reason Tatyana Ivanovna began to laugh, even clap her hands – in short, I clearly saw that nobody respected Uncle even in his own house. Sasha's eyes flashed angrily as she fixed her gaze on Obnoskin. The governess blushed and hung her head. Uncle seemed surprised.

'What! What's the matter?' he repeated, looking round, quite lost.

All this time my cousin Mizinchikov was sitting in silence a little apart from everybody, and didn't so much as venture a smile when everybody else was laughing. He busily sipped his tea, philosophically studying the company, and several times, as if to relieve the excruciating boredom, would begin to whistle, an old habit no doubt, but always checked himself just in time. I noticed that Obnoskin, who delighted in mocking Uncle and making sallies at me, hardly dared glance at Mizinchikov. I also noticed that my taciturn cousin would occasionally cast curious glances in my direction as though anxious to establish just who the devil I might be.

'I am certain,' Madame Obnoskin suddenly chirped, 'I am certain, *Monsieur Serge* – that is your name, is it not? – that in that St Petersburg of yours you showed no great love for women. I know there are now many, a great many young people who completely reject female company. To my mind they're all free-thinkers: I can only regard it as unpardonable free-thinking. And I must admit to you, it astonishes me, young man, simply astonishes me!'

'I've not been in society at all,' I hastened to reply with unusual animation. 'But . . . I don't think there's any harm in that . . . I lived, that is, I had rooms . . . still, be that as it may . . . I shall get to know people, whereas before I stayed at home most of the time . . .'

'At his studies,' Uncle remarked solemnly.

'Oh, Uncle, you do go on about studying! . . . Imagine,' I continued in an unnaturally casual tone, turning again to Madame Obnoskin and smiling ingratiatingly, 'my dear uncle is so devoted to science that he has unearthed, God knows where from, some miracle-performing practical philosopher, a certain Mr Korovkin, and the first word I hear from him today, after all these years, is that he's expecting this marvel in feverish excitement . . . all for the love of science, it would appear . . .'

And I began to giggle, hoping to draw some general laughter in recognition of my wit.

'What was that? Who's he talking about?' croaked the General's Lady in a harsh voice, turning towards Perepelitsyna.

'Yegor Ilyich has been tramping up and down the highways inviting scientists to the house,' the spinster squeaked with relish.

Uncle looked completely lost.

'Oh yes! I'd quite forgotten!' he exclaimed, casting a look of reproach at me. 'I'm expecting Korovkin. A learned man this Korovkin, a man who'll go down in history . . .'

He hesitated and stopped. The General's Lady threw up her arms, this time with such deadly accuracy that her cup of tea flew across the room and smashed to smithereens on the floor. General confusion ensued.

'She always throws something on the floor when she loses her temper,' Uncle whispered in acute embarrassment. 'But only when she loses her temper . . . Try not to notice, don't look, my boy, pretend you haven't seen . . . you *would* have to mention Korovkin! . . .'

But I was not looking in any case. Just at that moment I met the governess's eyes, and could read in them reproach bordering on contempt; a flush of indignation suddenly coloured her pale cheeks. I understood the meaning of this, and realized how little I must have gained in the girl's estimation through my cowardly and despicable attempt to ridicule Uncle in order to appear less ridiculous myself. I felt too ashamed for words.

'We were talking about St Petersburg, weren't we?' Anfisa Petrovna trilled again after the excitement occasioned by the broken cup had subsided somewhat. 'I have such, as it were, exquisite memories of our life in that most enchanting of capitals ... At that time we were on very close terms with a famous family – remember, *Paul, mon cher?* General Polovitsyn ... Ah, what a delightful, what a *de-light-ful* creature was Madame Polovitsyna! Well, you know, the aristocracy, the *beau monde*! ... I dare say you have met them ... I must admit, I was so anxious to see you: I expected to hear such a lot from you about our St Petersburg friends ...'

'I'm terribly sorry, I can't ... you must excuse me ... I did mention that I've moved very little in society, and I've no idea who General Polovitsyn is, haven't even heard of him,' I replied brusquely, suddenly switching from politeness to extreme exasperation and annoyance.

'He spent all his time studying mineralogy!' my incorrigible uncle remarked proudly. 'Study of pebbles and such like, that's mineralogy, isn't it?'

'Yes, Uncle, pebbles ...'

'Hm ... so many different sciences, and each one of them so useful. But you know, my boy, I really didn't know what mineralogy was – all Greek to me. In other things I'm so-so, but when it comes to science, I'm nowhere – I admit frankly!'

'At least he admits it,' Obnoskin hastened to remark with a sneer.

'Papa!' Sasha exclaimed, looking reproachfully at her father.

'Yes, darling? Oh, I beg your pardon, I keep on interrupting you, Anfisa Petrovna,' Uncle exclaimed with a start, having completely missed the point of Sasha's exclamation. 'Forgive me, for God's sake!'

'Oh, don't mention it!' Anfisa Petrovna replied, puckering her lips in a sour smile. 'Anyway, I've said all I have to say to your nephew, though in conclusion, *Monsieur Serge* – that is your name, is it not? – I will add that it is absolutely essential for you to mend your ways. I do believe that science, art ... sculpture, for example ... in short, all these, so to speak, intellectual pursuits, are *att-rac-tive* in themselves – but they cannot replace ladies! ... Women, women, young man, mould you, and life without them is impossible, impossible, young man, *im-po-ssible*.'

'Impossible, impossible!' echoed Tatyana Ivanovna in her strident voice. 'Listen,' she began again in a sort of childish patter, and, of course, blushing deeply, 'listen, I want to ask you ...'

'At your service!' I replied, turning to her attentively.

'I meant to ask you: have you come to stay here for long, or not?'

'I really don't know, as soon as my business ...'

'Business! He says he's here on business! . . . You madman! . . .'

And Tatyana Ivanovna, blushing crimson, hid behind her fan and leaned over towards the governess to whisper something in her ear. Then she suddenly burst out laughing and began to clap her hands.

'Wait, wait!' she cried, tearing herself away from her confidante and addressing me hastily as if afraid that I would leave her. 'Listen, you know what I am going to tell you? You remind me most awfully of a young man, of a most charming young man! . . . Sashenka, Nastenka, remember? Doesn't he look just like that madman – remember, Sashenka? We met him while we were out driving . . . he came by on horseback, in a white waistcoat . . . The way he turned his eye-glass on me, the shameless rascal! Remember, I hid my face behind my veil, but I simply couldn't restrain myself, I put my head out of the window and cried: "You shameless rascal!" and then I threw my bunch of flowers out on the road . . . Do you remember all that, Nastenka?'

And the love-crazed spinster, trembling with excitement, buried her face in her hands; then, suddenly jumping from her seat, darted towards the window, plucked a rose from a flower-pot, threw it at my feet and ran out of the room. This produced some confusion, though the General's Lady, as before, managed to preserve her equanimity. Anfisa Petrovna, for instance, seemed not so much surprised as suddenly concerned, and she cast an anxious glance at her son; the young ladies blushed, while Paul Obnoskin got up with a show of annoyance, which I could not account for at the time, and stalked over to the window. Uncle began to make signals to me, but at that moment, another person entered the room, drawing everybody's attention.

'Ah, welcome, Yevgraf Larionych! We were just talking about you!' Uncle exclaimed, genuinely delighted. 'Straight from town, are you?'

'It's as if all the freaks of the neighbourhood have conspired to meet here,' I thought to myself, still without any clear understanding of what was going on before me, and not suspecting that by appearing among them myself, I only added to their number.

5

Yezhevikin

There entered, or rather squeezed into the room (though the door opened widely), a little figure of a man, who bobbed and bowed and bared his teeth as soon as he appeared in the doorway, surveying all the guests with the utmost curiosity. He was an old man, slightly built, and balding, with a mottled face, quick roguish eyes and a subtle, indeterminate smile playing about his rather thick lids. He was dressed in a threadbare, probably second-hand frock-coat. One of the buttons was barely hanging on and two or three were missing altogether. His worn-out boots and grubby cap matched his pitiable attire. He was clutching a filthy cotton handkerchief with which he kept dabbing his perspiring brow and temples. I noticed that the governess blushed slightly and darted a glance at me. I fancied there was something proud and defiant in her eyes.

'Straight from town, my dear benefactor! Straight from town, kind sir! I'll tell you everything, only give me time to pay my respects,' the old man said and made straight for the General's Lady but stopped half-way and again addressed my uncle.

'For your gracious information, my dear benefactor, I'm a charlatan, a downright charlatan! You see, as soon as I arrive, I make a beeline for the most important person in the house to seek favours and protection. A rogue, sir, a rogue, dear benefactor! Allow me, dear kind lady, to kiss the hem of your dress lest my lips sully Your Excellency's precious hand.'

The General's widow extended her hand to him, rather graciously to my surprise.

'And greetings to you too, beauteous maiden,' he continued, turning to Perepelitsyna. 'Can't be helped, gracious Madam: a villain! Back in 1841 I was pronounced a villain when they dismissed me from public service, when Valentin Ignatyich Tikhontsov was promoted to assessor; an assessor-ship for him, a villainship for me. It's my open nature all over, I won't hide anything. Can't be helped! I did try to lead an honest life, indeed I did, now it's time for a change ... Aleksandra Yegorovna, succulent apple that you are,' he continued, working his way round the table towards Sasha. 'Let me kiss your frock; there is, sweet lady, the smell of apples and all nice things about you. Our respects to the hero of the day: a bow and arrow for you, sir, which my boys spent the morning helping me to make; we shall have such fun. Soon you'll grow up to be an officer and chop the Turk's head off. Tatyana Ivanovna . . . oh, she isn't here – my benefactress! Or I'd have kissed the hem of her dress too. My dear, kind Praskovya Ilyinichna, what a pity I can't reach you, or I'd have smothered your dainty foot with kisses, let alone that hand of yours – that's right! Anfisa Petrovna, I profess my every respect for you. This very morning I was down on my knees praying with tears for you and your son, my benefactress, that the Almighty might bless you both with rank and talent: especially talent! And while I'm about it, Ivan Ivanovich Mizinchikov, your humble servant too, sir. God grant you all that you yourself desire. Not that it's ever easy to tell what exactly you do desire: ever so sparing with your words, sir, you are . . . Hello Nastenka, all my small fry send you their greetings; they remember you every day. And now my deepest bow to the master of the house. Yes, I come straight from town, your honour, straightaways from town. And this must surely be your learned nephew, fresh from the faculty of sciences? Our esteemed respects to you, sir; your hand, please.'

Somebody tittered. It was clear the old man was playing the self-appointed rôle of jester. His arrival cheered the gathering enormously. Most people missed his sarcasm, although he addressed almost every person individually. Only the governess, whom to my surprise he had simply called Nastenka, stood blushing and frowning. I made an attempt to withdraw my hand, but apparently that was just what the old man was waiting for.

'With your permission, sir, I only wanted to shake it, not kiss it. You thought I was going to kiss your hand? No, sir, for the moment I shall just shake it. You, my benefactor, surely mistook me for the jester of the house!' he concluded, looking at me mockingly.

'N-no, really, I . . .'

'Well, well, sir! Even if I am a fool, I'm not the only one here. And you ought to respect me. I'm not the villain you take me for, though of course I am a clown. A slave too, and so is my wife – besides, a little flattery, a little flattery will never come amiss – might win an extra morsel for the little ones. Sugar, sugar, don't spare the sugar for your health. There's a tip for you – in confidence, mind: who knows, it might come in useful one day. Fortune has played me false, kind sir, or why should I play the clown?'

'Ha-ha-ha! How funny that little old man is! He always makes me laugh!' piped Anfisa Petrovna.

'My dear lady benefactress, had I but known it's easier to go through life being a fool, I'd have become one straightaway in my early youth. Who knows, I might have been a wise man now. But untimely wisdom is the stuff that fools are made of – and I've ended up a proper one.'

'Tell me, please,' Obnoskin chipped in (obviously not happy with the remark about 'talent'), ostentatiously stretching full-length in his chair and viewing the old man through his monocle as though he required magnification, 'tell me your name, please. I keep forgetting your name ... What the deuce was it again?'

'Ah, sir, I'm afraid it's Yezhevikin, and much good it has done me. Why, to tell you the truth, I've been out of employment these nine years, and I've survived only by the Grace of God. And my children – I've more children to support than the Kholmsky family.[13] You know how the saying goes: "The rich rear cattle, the poor breed kids" ...'

'Hm ... cattle ... let that pass. I've been meaning to ask you for a long time: why is it you always look behind you whenever you enter a room? It's so funny!'

'Why do I look behind me? Because I'm afraid somebody's going to creep up and swat me like a fly, that's why I look behind me. I've turned into a monomaniac, sir.'

Again there was laughter. The governess jumped to her feet and made as if to leave the room but then sat down again. In spite of the colour in her cheeks, she looked pained and distressed.

'You know who that is, my boy?' Uncle whispered. 'It's *her father!*'

I stared at my uncle wide-eyed. The name Yezhevikin had completely flown out of my head. I had spent the journey to Stepanchikovo daydreaming and building heroic plans for my intended, but had completely forgotten her surname, or, to be more precise, had not paid any attention to it at the outset.

'Father?' I replied, also in a whisper. 'I thought she was an orphan.'

'Father, my boy, father. And do you know he's a thoroughly honest, upright fellow; and he doesn't even drink, just likes to act the fool sometimes. Frightfully poor, you know – eight children! Nastenka's wages are all they have to live on. Lost his job for being too sharptongued. Comes here every week. But proud as Lucifer – won't accept a thing. Many's the time I've tried to help him, indeed I have – but no. An embittered soul!'

'Well, my dear Yevgraf Larionych, what other news have you brought us?' Uncle inquired, dealing him a hearty slap on the shoulder as he noticed that the suspicious old man was already beginning to eavesdrop on us.

'News, my dear benefactor? Yesterday Valentin Ignatych was giving evidence in the Trishin case. Some flour turned out to be short weight in his stores. Trishin, by the way, lady, is the one who looks at you as though he's blowing on charcoal to light a samovar, if it be your pleasure to recall. Anyway, this is what Valentin Ignatych says about Trishin: "If the oft-mentioned Trishin proved himself incapable of guarding his own niece's honour," – she ran off with an army officer last year – "how then can he be expected to look after government property?" That's word for word what he put down in his statement – I'm not lying.'

'For shame! The stories you tell!' cried out Anfisa Petrovna.

'Exactly so, exactly so! You're going too far, dear Yevgraf,' Uncle assented. 'One of these days your tongue will be the death of you! You're a righteous, honourable, upstanding man – that I declare, but your tongue is sheer venom! And I'm amazed you don't get on with them! After all, they're good simple folk, I believe . . .'

'My dear sir and benefactor! The simple man is the one I'm afraid of most of all!'[14] the old man exclaimed with great fervour.

I liked his reply. I quickly strode over to Yezhevikin and shook his hand heartily. To be honest, I wanted to protest against the general opinion by openly declaring my sympathy for the old man. But who knows! Maybe I wanted to gain favour in Nastasya Yevgrafovna's eyes. Anyway, my move completely misfired.

'Could you tell me please,' I asked hurriedly, and blushing as usual, 'Have you heard of the Jesuits?'

'No, kind sir, I haven't; or perhaps something once. But who am I to hear of such matters? Why do you ask?'

'Well, it just occurred to me . . . But we'll let it pass, remind me some other time. As for now, rest assured that I completely understand and . . . do appreciate . . .'

Utterly confused, I once more clasped his hand.

'I will remind you, sir, I will definitely remind you! I'll have it inscribed on my memory in gold lettering. With your permission, I'll even tie a knot to remind myself.'

And having selected a dry corner of his filthy, tobacco-stained handkerchief, he proceeded to tie a knot in it.

'Yevgraf Larionych, your tea,' said Praskovya Ilyinichna.

'Thank you, most kind lady, or should I say princess, not just lady! My compliments for the tea. On my way here, kind lady, I met Stepan Alekseyevich Bakhcheyev! Full of excellent high spirits! Not getting married is he, I thought? Gently does it! Gently does it!' he whispered, winking and pulling a face as he passed me with his tea. 'And wheresoever would our principal benefactor be, I wonder – Foma Fomich? Is he not joining us for tea?'

Uncle started as if he had been stung and cast a timid glance at the General's Lady.

'Well, actually, I don't know,' he replied uneasily in some strange embarrassment. 'He has been told, but ... I don't rightly know, perhaps he's indisposed. I did send Vidoplyasov and ... maybe I ought to go myself?'

'I did go in to see him just now,' Yezhevikin remarked, intoning his words mysteriously.

'You did?' Uncle exclaimed in alarm. 'Well?'

'I called on him first of all to convey my respects. He said he'd have his tea in private and later added that a crust of dry bread would be enough for him, he did, sir.'

These words seemed to strike real terror into my uncle.

'You should have explained to him, Yevgraf Larionych, you should have reasoned with him,' Uncle exclaimed, looking at the old man with reproach and anguish.

'I did, I did.'

'Well?'

'He didn't deign to answer me for a long time, seeing as he was engrossed in figures, calculating some mathematical problem, and a deuce of a hard one, if you ask me. He sketched the Pythagoras theorem – saw it with my own eyes. Three times I spoke to him, and only after that did he raise his head as though he'd seen me for the first time. "I shan't go down, they say there's a *learned man* there now, so who am I next to such a luminary?" That's exactly how he put it, "next to a luminary".'

And the old man measured me with a sidelong glance full of mockery.

'Just as I expected!' Uncle exclaimed, throwing up his arms. 'Just as I thought! Do you realize it was you, Sergey, he was referring to as the "learned man"? What's to be done now?'

'To tell you the truth, Uncle,' I replied, proudly shrugging my shoulders, 'his refusal to join us for tea is ridiculous, surely he can't be serious – I am amazed you take it so much to heart ...'

'Oh, my dear boy, you don't know a thing!' exclaimed my uncle, with a wild gesture of his arm.

'Too late for regrets now,' Miss Perepelitsyna suddenly chipped in, 'seeing as all the evil stems from you originally, Yegor Ilyich. No good crying over curls when the head's chopped off! If only you'd listened to your mother in the first place, there'd be no cause for tears now.'

'Now what have I done wrong, Anna Nilovna? for heaven's sake!' Uncle exclaimed in a pleading voice, as though beseeching her for an explanation.

'I'm a God-fearing person, Yegor Ilyich; but the whole trouble is you're an egoist, and have no love for your mother,' Miss Perepelitsyna replied with dignity. 'Why did you ignore her wishes in the first place? She is your mother, isn't she? And I'm not one to tell you lies, sir. I'm a Lieutenant-Colonel's daughter myself, sir, not just anybody.'

The sole reason for Perepelitsyna's interjection, it seemed, was to impress her audience, and me as a newcomer in particular, with her illustrious parentage.

'He will even insult his own mother,' the General's Lady exclaimed menacingly.

'Mother, be merciful! How have I insulted you?'

'By being an infernal egoist, Yegorushka,' the old lady continued with mounting ire.

'Mother, Mother! What do you mean, an infernal egoist?' Uncle exclaimed almost in despair. 'It's five days now, five days you've been in a rage with me and refused to speak to me. What have I done? What? Let everybody be my judge! At last my side of the story is going to be heard too. I've kept quiet for too long, Mother; you've refused to listen to me: so let everyone hear me now. Anfisa Petrovna! Pavel Semyonych, dear Pavel Semyonych! Sergey, my boy! You're a newcomer, a bystander, so to speak, your verdict will be impartial . . .'

'Calm down, Yegor Ilyich, calm down,' cried Anfisa Petrovna. 'You'll be the death of your mother!'

'She'll come to no harm, Anfisa Petrovna; but here is my chest – go on, hit me!' Uncle continued, pushed to the limits of his endurance, as often happens with weak-willed people when they are sorely tried, although their passion is as short-lived as the flame of a burning straw. 'I want it to be known, Anfisa Petrovna, that I'd insult no one, and I'll begin by saying that Foma is the most honest and honourable of gentlemen, and in addition blessed with the highest of qualities, but . . . but for all that, he has been unfair to me on this occasion.'

'Hm!' Obnoskin muttered, as if to needle Uncle still more.

'Pavel Semyonych, my dear, kind Pavel Semyonych! Do you really believe I have such a heart of stone? Of course I see, of course I appreciate, with heart-felt tears, as it were, I appreciate that these misunderstandings result from *his* burning love for me. But say what you will, he has . . . by God he has done me an injustice this time. I'll tell everything.

I want to tell the whole of this story now, Anfisa Petrovna, down to the last detail so that everyone can hear how it all began, and then judge for himself if Mother is justified in blaming me for being unfair to Foma. Sergey, you hear me out too,' he added, turning to me, and he continued to address me throughout the rest of his story, as though afraid of the other listeners, and doubtful of their goodwill, 'you listen too and decide whether I'm right or not. You see, it all began like this: about a week ago – yes, definitely not more than a week – my former commanding officer, General Rusapetov, happened to be passing through the town with his wife and sister-in-law, and stopped off for a while. I was overwhelmed. I was determined not to miss the opportunity, and rushed round to pay my respects and invite them to dinner. He promised he'd try to come. A true gentleman, overflowing with virtues, and a man of authority as well! Showered a fortune upon his sister-in-law, arranged a brilliant match for an orphan girl (the young man is a notary in Malinov now, a brilliant fellow with an all-round education!)[15] – in short, a general in a million. Naturally there was an almighty panic in the house, hustle and bustle, cooks everywhere, *fricassées* and so on. I even hired an orchestra specially for the occasion. I was pleased as Punch, of course, and looked it! But Foma couldn't bear to see me so pleased. We were at table, I remember; his favourite dish, fruit jelly and cream, was being served – he just sat there without saying a word: suddenly up he jumps: "I'm being insulted!" – "How so, Foma? Who's insulting you?" – "You've set your mind on ignoring me," he says, "you only have time for generals now; generals are of more concern to you than I am!" Well, of course, I'm cutting a long story short, as it were, it's only the gist of what he said; but you should have heard the rest . . . he really cut me to the quick! What was I to do? I was utterly demoralized; shocked and shattered, and felt like a drowned cat. Well, came the eventful day. A message arrived from the General saying he couldn't come; he was very sorry, but he just couldn't come. I dashed to Foma: "Well, Foma, relax! He's not coming!" You'd think he'd have forgiven me – not a bit of it. "You've insulted me, yes you have!" I tried reasoning. "No," he says, "you go off to your generals, they have more to offer you than I have. You have ruptured," he says, "the bonds of friendship." Of course, my boy, I knew why he was furious with me. I'm not a numskull, I'm not an ass, I'm not a nincompoop! Why, it was all because of his devotion to me he was jealous, I suppose – he said as much himself – jealous of the General, afraid of losing my sympathy, so he was putting me to the test, to see what sacrifices I'd be capable of for his sake. "No," he says, "to you I am the equal of a general, to you I am 'Your Excellency'! I'll be reconciled with you when you prove your respect for me." "How can I prove my respect for you, Foma?" "By addressing me," he says, "all day long as 'Your Excellency': that's how you'll prove your respect." You could have knocked me down with a feather! "It'll serve you right to get carried away with your generals when there are other people around who are worth more than all your generals." Well, this is where I could stand it no longer, I admit! I openly admit! "Dear Foma," I said, "this is quite impossible. How can I take such a thing upon myself? How can I, where is my authority for promoting you to a general? Just think who it is that bestows the rank of general. How could I call you 'Your Excellency'? To do so would surely be an encroachment upon the highest decrees of Providence! A general is the pride and joy of his country: a general has fought the enemy, he has shed his blood on the field of glory! So how can I possibly call you 'Your Excellency'?" Would he listen to me? Not at all! "You may ask me to do anything you like, I'll do it all, Foma," I said. "You told me to shave off my sideboards, because they're not patriotic, and I've shaved them off – reluctantly, true, but they're off. And I'll do anything else you want, only please don't ask for a general's rank!" "No," he says, "there'll be no reconciliation until I'm addressed as 'Your Excellency'! It'll be an edifying exercise in humbling your spirit," he says. That was a week ago and he's not spoken to me since; and he'll let fly at anybody who comes to the house. "So I'm not good enough to be a scholar, then?" I shudder to think what he'll do when he finds out about Korovkin! I ask you, be my judge, what have I done wrong? Should I really have called him "Your Excellency"? How could one live with such a thing? And why did he have to chase poor Bakhcheyev from the table today? Admittedly, he didn't found astronomy; but neither did I, and nor did you, for that matter . . . So why, why?'

'Why? Because you're jealous, my dear Yegorushka,' the General's Lady muttered.

'Mother!' Uncle exclaimed in complete despair, 'you'll drive me crazy! These are not your words, you're just repeating what others say, Mother. I'm gradually turning into a lump of wood, a stump, a lamp-post – I'm not your son!'

'I heard, Uncle,' I interrupted, utterly astounded by his story, 'I heard from Bakhcheyev, I don't know whether it's true, that Foma Fomich is jealous of Ilyusha's name-day and insists that it ought to be his own tomorrow. I confess, this side of his character surprises me so much that I . . .'

'It's his birthday, my boy, birthday, not name-day, birthday,' Uncle interrupted me hastily. 'He just made a slip, but he's perfectly right: it *is* his birthday tomorrow. He's right, my boy, first because . . .'

'No, it isn't!' cried Sashenka.

'What do you mean, it isn't?' Uncle exclaimed, dumbfounded.

'It's not his birthday at all, Papa! You're simply not telling the truth, you're just deceiving yourself to please Foma Fomich. His birthday was in March – remember, we went just before to hear the service at the monastery, and he wouldn't let anybody sit still in the carriage, he kept shouting that the cushion was hurting his ribs, and then he started pinching everybody and he pinched Auntie twice in a temper! And later when we wished him many happy returns, he flew into a temper because there were no camellias in the flowers we gave him: "I'm fond of camellias," he said, "because I have a refined taste – and you begrudge me a few sprays from the greenhouse!" All day long he fretted and sulked and wouldn't speak a word to any of us . . .'

I believe a bomb bursting in the middle of the room would have occasioned less shock and pandemonium than this rebellious outburst – and to think that it could have come from a girl who was not even allowed to speak above a whisper in her grandmother's presence! The General's Lady, struck dumb with rage and consternation, rose majestically to her feet and glared at her insolent granddaughter with utter incredulity. Uncle was terror-stricken.

'Such a liberty! This will kill Grandmamma!' Perepelitsyna exclaimed.

'Sashenka, Sashenka, take a hold on yourself! What's the matter with you, Sashenka?' Uncle cried, darting backwards and forwards between his mother and Sashenka in an attempt to restrain the girl.

'No, I won't keep quiet, Papa!' shouted. Sashenka, and suddenly jumped to her feet and stamped on the floor, her eyes flashing furiously. 'I refuse to keep quiet! We've been putting up with this vile, horrible Foma Fomich of yours for too long! He'll be the end of us all – nobody ever stops telling us how clever, noble, gentlemanly and scholarly he is; a paragon of all the virtues – and Foma Fomich, like the idiot that he is, takes it all in! He's been served so many good things, it would put a decent person to shame, but not Foma Fomich; he gobbles up everything put before him and keeps coming back for more. Just you wait, he'll eat us all up and Papa will be the one to blame! Horrible, horrible Foma Fomich! I'll say it straight out! I'm scared of no one! He's nasty, stupid, capricious, ungrateful, cruel, slanderous, deceitful and a bully . . . I wish I could kick him out of the house this very minute, but Papa adores him, Papa worships him!'

'Ah!' cried the General's Lady and swooned on the sofa.

'Darling, Agafya Timofeyevna, my angel!' Madame Obnoskin cried, 'take some of this! Water, quick, water!'

'Water, water!' cried Uncle. 'Mother, Mother, please calm down! I beg you on my knees, calm down!'

'You should be shut up in a dark closet and kept on bread and water, you murderess!' Perepelitsyna hissed at Sashenka, shaking with venom.

'Shut me up on bread and water, it won't worry me!' screamed Sashenka, also in a peak of excitement. 'I'm defending Papa because he can't defend himself. Who is he, who is this Foma Fomich of yours compared with Papa? He eats Papa's bread and then goes and humiliates him — what ingratitude! I'll tear him to pieces, your Foma Fomich! I'll challenge him to a duel and shoot him dead on the spot with a pair of pistols –'

'Sashenka, Sashenka!' Uncle cried in despair, 'one more word – and I'm doomed, doomed forever!'

'Papa!' cried Sashenka, in tears, suddenly rushing up to her father and clasping her arms around his neck. 'Papa! You're so good, happy, clever and wonderful, why must you punish yourself so? Why must you submit to this wicked, ungrateful man, why must you let yourself be a plaything in his hands and a laughing-stock to everyone? Dear, precious Papa . . .'

She broke into sobs, buried her face in her hands, and rushed from the room.

A terrible commotion ensued. The General's Lady lay unconscious. Uncle knelt beside her, kissing her hands. Miss Perepelitsyna hovered around them, casting angry but triumphant glances at us. Madame Obnoskin kept dabbing the General's Lady's brow and fiddling with her vial of smelling salts. Praskovya Ilyinichna trembled and wept uncontrollably; Yezhevikin looked for somewhere to make himself inconspicuous and the governess stood pale and petrified with fear. Mizinchikov alone was completely unruffled. He got up, strode over to the window and stood there, absorbed in what he saw outside, without paying the slightest attention to the scene in the room.

Suddenly the General's Lady sat bolt upright on the sofa and fixed her terrible eyes upon me.

'Out!' she cried, stamping her foot.

I must admit this came as a complete surprise to me.

'Out! Out of this house – out! Why is he here? Out of my sight! Out!'

'Mother! Mother, stop it! This is Seryozha,' Uncle mumbled, trembling all over with fear, 'he's come to visit us, Mother.'

'What Seryozha? Rubbish! I don't want to hear – out! It's Korovkin! I'm sure it's Korovkin! My eyes don't deceive me! He's come to turn Foma Fomich out – he's been specially invited. My heart tells me . . . Out, you scoundrel!'

'Uncle, if it's come to this,' I said, gasping with righteous indignation, 'if it's come to this, then I . . . excuse me . . .' and I grabbed my hat.

'Sergey, Sergey, what are you doing?' Uncle cried. 'Now Mother! This is Seryozha . . . Sergey, upon my soul!' He chased me and tried to snatch my hat. 'You're my guest, you must stay – I insist! . . . It's only one of her moods,' he added in a whisper, 'she's only like this when she's angry . . . Just go and find somewhere to hide . . . anywhere – till it all blows over. She'll forgive you – I assure you! She's good at heart, only never to be taken at her word . . . You see, she's mistaken you for Korovkin, and in the end she'll forgive you, really . . . What do you want?' he yelled at Gavrila, who had entered the room and was standing quaking with terror.

Gavrila was not alone; he was accompanied by a charming peasant lad of about sixteen, who, as I later discovered, had been admitted to the house because of his good looks. His name was Falaley. He was got-up in a remarkable costume: a red silk shirt with ruche trimming round the collar, gold galloon belt, black velveteen breeches and kid boots with red turn-overs. This costume was of the General's Lady's own creation. The boy was sobbing bitterly, and tears rolled one after the other from his large blue eyes.

'What's all this?' Uncle exclaimed. 'What's happened? Speak up, you rogue!'

'Foma Fomich told us to come here; he'll be here shortly himself,' replied Gavrila in a pained voice. 'I'm to have my examinatation, and he . . .'

'What about him?'

'He's been dancing, sir,' Gavrila replied in tears.

'Dancing!' gasped Uncle, horrified.

'Yes, dancing!' wailed Falaley.

'The kamarinsky?'

'The ka-mar-in-sky.'

'And Foma Fomich caught you?'

'He did!'

'That's it!' exclaimed Uncle. 'I'm done for!' and he clasped both his hands around his head.

'Foma Fomich!' announced Vidoplyasov, entering the room.

The door swung open and Foma Fomich in person appeared before the bewildered gathering.

6

Concerning the White Bull and a Peasant Named Kamarinsky

But before I have the honour of personally presenting Foma Fomich to the reader, I consider it absolutely necessary to say a few words about Falaley, and to explain why it should have been so scandalous for him to have danced the kamarinsky and for Foma Fomich to have caught him at this merriest of pastimes. Falaley was a house-boy, an orphan from the cradle and godchild of my uncle's deceased wife. My uncle loved him dearly. This alone would have given Foma Fomich, after he had settled in Stepanchikovo and assumed dominance over my uncle, sufficient reason to take a violent dislike to the boy: but, since the General's Lady took a particular liking to Falaley, he remained, to Foma's extreme annoyance, upstairs in attendance on the family. The General's Lady was adamant on this point, and Foma Fomich was obliged to submit, but he retained a deep-seated grudge — it was his wont to regard everything as a personal offence and took it out on my blameless uncle at every convenient opportunity. Falaley was unusually handsome. He had a girl's features — the features of a village beauty. The General's Lady indulged, pampered and treasured him as some rare and precious pet; and it was far from certain which she loved more: her small curly-haired bitch Ami, or Falaley. We have already remarked upon his dress, which was entirely of her own creation. The young ladies of the house would supply him with pomade, and for feast days the barber Kuzma had the duty of curling his hair. This boy was a very strange creature indeed. It would have been unfair to have called him an outright freak or idiot, but he was so naive, so guileless and simple-hearted, that one could easily have taken him for a simpleton. If he had a dream, he would relate it to his masters first thing in the morning; and he would think nothing of interrupting their conversation, not in the least concerned that he was making a nuisance of himself. He would ply them with stories such as ought never to be told to masters. He would burst into bitter tears at the sight of the General's Lady swooning or his master receiving an unusually severe dressing-down. He responded with compassion in any calamity. Often he would come up to the General's Lady, kiss her hands and beg her not to be angry — and the General's Lady would magnanimously overlook such liberties. He was extraordinarily sensitive, as innocent and gentle as a lamb, happy and carefree as a child. People rewarded him with titbits from the table. He was always to be found behind his mistress's chair. He was enormously fond of sugar, and as soon as he was given a lump, he would immediately crunch it between his strong, pearl-white teeth, his jovial blue eyes and handsome features beaming with sheer delight.

Foma Fomich fretted for a long time; but having finally concluded that anger was to no avail, he decided to become Falaley's benefactor. Upbraiding my uncle for neglecting the education of the house servants, he immediately took upon himself the task of instructing the poor boy in morals, good manners and the French language.

'Why,' he would exclaim in defence of his misbegotten idea (an idea which the author of these lines can vouch has occurred to others besides Foma), 'Why! Is he not constantly upstairs in his mistress's presence! Suppose she suddenly forgets his ignorance of the French tongue and says to him, for example, "*Donnez-moi mon mouchoir*" – how could he rise to the occasion and perform his duty?' But it transpired that not only was it impossible to teach Falaley French, but that the cook Andron, his uncle, who in the goodness of his heart had diligently tried to initiate him in the rudiments of Russian, had long ago abandoned the attempt and allowed the text-book to gather dust on a shelf. Falaley was so hopeless in the matter of learning that he simply could not grasp a thing. As it happened, this led to a minor incident. The peasants nicknamed Falaley 'Frenchie', and old Gavrila, Uncle's faithful valet, had the temerity openly to dispute the advantage of knowing the language anyway. This reached Foma's ears, and in a temper he ordered the fractious Gavrila himself to take up the study of French as a punishment. Thus began the whole affair with the French language that had incensed Mr Bakhcheyev so deeply. In the matter of manners, it was even worse: Foma was quite incapable of reforming Falaley, and in spite of all injunctions the lad persisted each morning in recounting a catalogue of his dreams, which Foma regarded as intolerable familiarity and the height of bad manners. But Falaley stubbornly refused to reform. Once again my uncle was the first to suffer for this. 'Do you know – do you know – what he did today?' Foma had shouted on one occasion, selecting for maximum effect a moment when everybody was present. 'Do you realize, Colonel, what your systematic indulgence has led to? Today he gobbled a piece of pie you gave him from the table, and do you know what he said? Come here, come here, you son of perdition, you imbecile, you red-faced monkey!'

Falaley went up to Foma, crying and wiping his eyes with both hands.

'What did you say after you gobbled up your pie? Repeat it so that everybody can hear!'

Falaley, tears streaming down his cheeks, could not bring himself to say a word.

'Well then, I'll answer for you. You said, slapping your tight, revolting belly: "I've stuffed myself with pie like Martin full of soap!"[16] Colonel, I ask you, such expressions in educated society – indeed, in *refined* society. Isn't that what you said? Speak up!'

'I – did,' Falaley agreed, sobbing.

'Well, can you tell me now, does Martin eat soap? Where have you seen anybody called Martin eating soap? Speak up! Tell me about this legendary Martin!'

Silence.

'I'm asking you,' Foma insisted, 'who exactly is this Martin? I want to see him, I want to get to know him. Well, who is he? A clerk, an astronomer, a peasant, a poet, a captain-at-arms, a household serf – he must be somebody? I'm listening!'

'A – serf,' Falaley finally replied, amid continued sobs.

'Whose serf? Who would his masters be?'

But Falaley had no idea who his masters were. Naturally the result was that Foma Fomich flew out of the room in a passion, shouting that he had been insulted; the General's Lady immediately resumed her fits, while Uncle, quietly cursing the hour of his birth, implored everybody for forgiveness and spent the rest of the day tiptoeing round his own rooms.

Now to make matters worse, the very next day Falaley, after bringing Foma his tea and contriving to forget all about Martin and the woes of the previous day, informed him that he had dreamt about a white bull. That was the last straw. Foma Fomich's rage knew no bounds. He at once summoned my uncle into his presence and proceeded to berate him for the vulgarity of *his* Falaley's dream. On this occasion tough measures were resorted to. Falaley was punished; he was made to kneel in a corner and forbidden to have any more such uncouth peasant's dreams. 'It makes me livid!' cried Foma Fomich, 'Quite apart from his effrontery in coming to me with his dreams at all – but a white bull! You must agree, Colonel, what is a white bull but proof of the boorishness, ignorance and lowly birth of your precious Falaley? His dreams are every bit as bad as his daytime thoughts. Didn't I warn you from the start that he's a bad lot, that he ought never to have been allowed upstairs to wait on his masters? Never, never will you be able to lead this dim rustic clodhopper to elevated, poetic notions. Could you not,' he continued, turning towards

Falaley, 'could you not dream of something refined, delicate, edifying, some scene from polite society – say, gentlemen playing cards or ladies promenading in a fine park?' Falaley solemnly promised that next time he would dream of gentlemen or ladies promenading in a fine park.

Before retiring to bed Falaley, in tears, beseeched God for help and thought for a long time how he could possibly avoid dreaming of the accursed white bull. But human hopes are frail. Next morning he recalled with horror that again, all through the night, he had been dreaming of the hated white bull, and he had not had a glimpse of a single lady promenading in a fine park. This time the consequences were particularly grave. Foma Fomich categorically refused to believe in the possibility of such a repetition of dreams, and declared that Falaley must deliberately have been worked upon by a member of the household, possibly Uncle himself, expressly to annoy him, Foma. There ensued tears, reproaches and wailing in abundance. By evening the General's Lady had fallen ill, and everybody in the house put on a long face. Only one slender hope remained, that on the following, that is the third night, Falaley might still save the day with a vision of refined society. What was the general indignation then, when every night for a whole week running, Falaley dreamt of the white bull and the white bull alone, with not a single glimpse of refined society!

But the most curious thing of all was that it never occurred to Falaley to tell a lie, simply to say for instance that, instead of the white bull, he had seen a carriageful of ladies with Foma in their midst; and all the more so since under the circumstances a lie would have constituted no grave transgression. But Falaley was incapable of deceit, even had he desired it. Nobody even tried to put the idea in his head. Everyone knew that he would betray himself the moment he opened his mouth, and Foma would immediately catch him out. What was to be done? Uncle's predicament grew unbearable and Falaley remained incorrigible. The poor boy even grew thin with worry. Malanya, the house-keeper, declared that he had fallen under the evil eye, and she sprinkled him with charcoal dipped in holy water. The tender-hearted Praskovya Ilyinichna assisted her in this salutary operation. But even that failed to bring results. Nothing seemed to be of any use!

'The devil take that creature!' Falaley kept repeating. 'Every night I see it! Every night I say my prayers: "Don't dream about the white bull, don't dream about the white bull!" And then there he is, the dreadful thing, standing in front of me with his horns, fat-lipped and huge. Ugh!'

Uncle was desperate. Fortunately, however, Foma Fomich suddenly seemed to forget about the white bull. Of course, nobody thought it likely for a moment that he could totally neglect such an important matter. Rather it was assumed with trepidation that he was merely amassing evidence to make the better use of it at the first opportune moment. In due course it turned out that the white bull was in fact of secondary importance to him, and that he had other tasks, other projects growing and ripening in his resourceful and prolific mind. This is why Falaley was granted respite. Everybody breathed a sigh of relief. The lad grew merry and even began to forget what had happened; even the white bull began to appear less frequently in his dreams, although now and again it still reared its phantom head. In short, everything would have been perfectly all right had it not been for the kamarinsky.

It must be observed that Falaley was an excellent dancer; it was his principal skill, something approaching a vocation; he danced with inexhaustible energy and abandon, and he was especially fond of the 'kamarinsky muzhik'. Not that he liked the frivolous and inexplicable behaviour of the ne'er-do-well peasant – no, he liked to dance the kamarinsky simply because to listen to the kamarinsky and not to dance to it was totally impossible for him. Sometimes, in the evening, two or three house servants, the coachmen, the gardener, who played the fiddle, and even a few of the ladies' maids, would gather in some remote spot on the estate to escape Foma's attention, music and dancing would begin, and then finally and triumphantly the whole event would be crowned by the kamarinsky. The band consisted of two balalaikas, a guitar, a fiddle and a tambourine[17] which the coachboy Mitushka handled with consummate skill. What Falaley then got up to had to be seen to be believed: egged on by the cries and laughter of the audience, he danced himself into a state of frenzy and total exhaustion; he whooped, shouted, laughed and clapped his hands; he danced as if impelled from within by an intangible force over which he had no control as he stamped his heels and strained to catch up with the ever-increasing tempo of the infectious tune. These were moments of pure delight for him, and everything would have turned out happily had not rumour of the kamarinsky finally reached Foma Fomich.

Foma was shocked and immediately sent for the Colonel.

'Pray tell me one thing, Colonel,' he began. 'Is it, or is it not, your ultimate intention to ruin this poor idiot? If it is, then I shall not interfere; if not, then I . . .'

'What is it? What's happened?' Uncle exclaimed, panic-stricken.

'What's happened? Do you realize he was dancing the kamarinsky?'

'Well . . . what about it?'

'What do you mean, "What about it?"' roared Foma. 'How can you say such a thing? You who are their master and, in a sense, their father! Have you any idea what the kamarinsky stands for? Do you know that this song depicts a vile peasant in a state of drunkenness, who is about to commit a highly immoral act? Do you realize what this debauched yokel did? He violated the most sacred ties, and as it were trampled upon them with his huge peasant boots that are accustomed to nothing but stomping the floors of drinking dens! Do you realize that your reply has insulted my noblest feelings? Do you realize that your reply has insulted me personally? Do you realize all this, or not?'

'But Foma . . . it's only a song, Foma . . .'

'What do you mean, only a song! And you are not ashamed to admit you know this song – you, a member of decent society, a father of fine and innocent children and a Colonel to boot! Only a song! I'm sure this song is based on a real occurrence! Only a song! How can a person with a grain of propriety admit that he knows this song without dying of shame, that he has even heard of it? How, how?'

'Well, you have, Foma, seeing as you are asking,' Uncle replied in all simplicity and confusion.

'What was that? *I* know? Me . . . Me, you really mean me! The insolence!' Foma Fomich suddenly yelled, jumping to his feet and choking with anger. He never expected such a stunning reply.

I shall not attempt to describe Foma Fomich's rage. The custodian of morality banished the Colonel from his sight for the indecency and *ineptitude* of his reply. Foma Fomich now swore to apprehend Falaley at the scene of the crime, as he danced the kamarinsky. In the evenings, when everybody thought that he was occupied with some task in hand, he would steal out into the garden and, skirting the vegetable beds, conceal himself in the long grass, from where there was a good view of the patch of ground on which the dancing was supposed to take place. He lay in wait for poor Falaley like a hunter stalking his prey, and gleefully looked forward to the distress he would bring upon the whole household, and especially upon Uncle, if ever he were successful. At last his unrelenting vigilance was rewarded: he caught Falaley at the kamarinsky!

No wonder, then, that Uncle was beside himself when he saw the boy in tears and heard Vidoplyasov solemnly announcing Foma Fomich, who was about to make his unexpected personal appearance at a very awkward moment for us all.

7
Foma Fomich

I studied this gentleman with intense curiosity. Gavrila was quite right in referring to him as a shabby sort of man. Foma Fomich was short of stature, with greying fair hair, a hooked nose and face densely lined with tiny wrinkles. A large wart sat prominently on his chin. He entered the room with an even gait, his eyes lowered to the ground. None the less his features and pedantic bearing exuded an air of arrogant self-assurance. To my surprise he appeared in a dressing-gown – of foreign cut, true, but in a dressing-gown all the same – and in bedroom slippers. The collar of his open-necked shirt was neatly folded back à *l'enfant*, and this made him look exceedingly ridiculous. He went up to a vacant chair, moved it to the table and sat down without uttering a word. In an instant all the excitement and commotion had ceased. The silence became so intense that one could have heard a pin drop. The General's Lady went as quiet as a lamb. The reverence in which this poor idiot held Foma Fomich now became clear to see. She could not stop admiring her treasure, and feasted her eyes upon him. Miss Perepelitsyna bared her teeth and rubbed her hands, while poor Praskovya Ilyinichna shivered visibly from fright. Uncle immediately began to fuss.

'Tea, tea, sister darling! Plenty of sugar, dearest! Foma likes his tea sweet after his sleep. You do, don't you, Foma?'

'I've no time for tea now,' Foma Fomich pronounced with slow deliberation, waving his hand with an abstracted air. 'All you care about is making things sweet.'

These words, and the ludicrously affected dignity of his entry, greatly aroused my interest. I was curious to know what extremes of indecency this insolent little humbug of a man was capable of reaching.

'Foma!' Uncle exclaimed, 'may I introduce my nephew, Sergey Aleksandrovich! He has just arrived.'

Foma Fomich surveyed Uncle from head to toe.

'I'm surprised you so deliberately insist on interrupting me, Colonel,' he said after a pregnant pause, paying me not the slightest attention. 'I'm speaking to you about important matters, and you go off . . . at a *tangent* . . . Have you seen Falaley?'

'I have, Foma . . .'

'Oh, you have, have you! Well, you shall see him again. Take a good look at your masterpiece . . . in the moral sense, that is. Come here, you idiot! Come here, you Dutch-faced moron! Come on, move yourself! Don't be afraid!'

Falaley approached open-mouthed, gulping down his tears in a convulsion of sobs. Foma Fomich viewed him with sinister delight.

'I called him a Dutch-faced moron deliberately, Pavel Semyonych,' he remarked, making himself comfortable in his chair and half-turning to Obnoskin who was sitting next to him. 'I find it quite unnecessary ever to mince words. Truth must out. No matter how you cover up filth, filth it will remain. So why go to the trouble of deceiving oneself and others? Only a stupid society dimwit could conceive of such senseless niceties.[18] Judge for yourself – can you detect anything beautiful in that face? I mean refined, beautiful, noble, and not just an ugly red mug?'

Foma Fomich spoke with haughty indifference in a soft, measured drawl.

'Him, beautiful?' Obnoskin replied with a dismissive sneer. 'All he reminds me of is a good joint of roast beef, that's all.'

'Happened to stand in front of the mirror today and had a close look,' continued Foma Fomich, solemnly omitting the pronoun 'I'. 'Far be it from me to regard myself as handsome, but I was nevertheless obliged to conclude that there is something in this grey eye of mine to distinguish me from the Falaleys of this world. There is thought, there is life, there is wit in this eye. I'm not just praising myself. I'm speaking of our class in general. Now tell me, do you think that this lump of raw beef could have the least trace, the least particle of a soul in it? No, really, Pavel Semyonych, observe the revoltingly coarse freshness, the stupid freshness in the complexion of these *people* who feed on nothing but beef and lack all power and thought and imagination. Would you care to find out the range of his intellect? Here, you *ob*ject! Come closer, let's have a good look at you! And shut your mouth! You're not trying to swallow a whale! Are you beautiful? Answer: are you beautiful?'

'I am beau-ti-ful,' Falaley replied, amid stifled sobs.

Obnoskin rolled about with laughter. I felt myself beginning to shake with anger.

'Did you hear that?' Foma Fomich went on, turning triumphantly to Obnoskin. 'And that's not all! I've come to give him a test. You see, Pavel Semyonych, there are people who have an interest in corrupting and undoing this pathetic idiot. I may judge too harshly, maybe I'm wrong, but I speak out of love for mankind. Just now he danced the most indecent of dances. Yet no one here seems to care. But now you can hear for yourselves. Answer: what did you do? Answer, answer at once, do you hear?'

'I – danced . . .' Falaley gasped with redoubled sobs.

'What did you dance? What is the name of the dance? Speak up!'

'The kamarinsky . . .'

'The kamarinsky? And who is this "Kamarinsky"? What does "kamarinsky" mean? Do you expect me to make sense of such a reply? Well then, give us some idea: who is this Kamarinsky of yours?'

'A pea-sant . . .'

'A peasant! Just a peasant? I'm surprised! Then it follows he must be a wonderful peasant! It follows he is some famous peasant, if there are poems and dances composed in his honour? Well, answer!'

It was in Foma Fomich's nature to indulge in slow, deliberate inquisition. He played cat and mouse with his victim; but Falaley sobbed wordlessly, utterly confounded by the question.

'Answer me!' Foma Fomich insisted. 'I'm asking you – What kind of peasant was he supposed to be? Speak! Was he a manorial peasant, a crown peasant, a free peasant, an obligated or economical peasant?[19] There are all kinds of peasants.'

'E-co-no-mi-cal . . .'

'Ah, economical! Did you hear that, Pavel Semyonych? A new historical fact: Kamarinsky was an economical peasant. Hm! . . . Well, what did this economical peasant do? What were his achievements, now that he is being celebrated in song . . . and dance?'

The question was awkward and fraught with danger in as much as it was directed at Falaley.

'Now . . . now . . .' Obnoskin said, after glancing at his mother, who was beginning to shift uneasily on the sofa. But there was nothing to be done. Foma Fomich's caprices were a law unto the household.

'Please, Uncle, if you don't restrain this fool, he'll . . . Do you see what he's getting at? Falaley will talk himself into trouble, I assure you . . .' I whispered to Uncle, who seemed lost and totally irresolute.

'Listen now, Foma . . .' he began, 'may I introduce my nephew to you, a young man who has studied mineralogy . . .'

'I beg you, Colonel, not to interrupt me with your mineralogy, of which, as far as I am aware, you know nothing, and that goes for the *others* too probably. I'm not a child. He will reply to me that this peasant, instead of toiling for the good of his family, got blind drunk, drank away his sheepskin in a tavern and ran sozzled into the street. Such, as we all know, is the content of a poem extolling drunkenness. Have no fear, *now* he knows what to reply – well, speak up: what did this peasant do? I've helped you all the way, I've put the words into your mouth. Now I want to hear you speak: what did he do to distinguish himself, whence his fame, whence his claim to immortality, that even troubadours sing of him? Well!'

The unfortunate Falaley kept looking around in utter bewilderment and distress, not knowing what to say, opening and shutting his mouth like a gasping carp left to lie out on the sand.

'I'm too ashamed – to say!' he brought out at last, in utter despair.

'Ah – too ashamed!' echoed Foma Fomich triumphantly. 'That's just the reply I was after, Colonel! Ashamed to speak, but not ashamed to misbehave? That's the morality which you have sown, which has sprouted and which you are now ... watering. But let us not bandy words! Off with you to the kitchen, Falaley. I shan't say anything more to you in deference to the present company; but today without fail you will be punished, severely and painfully punished. If not, if I am to be thwarted yet again for your sake, then stay here and entertain your gentlefolk with your kamarinsky, I shall not remain a moment longer in this house! Enough! I have spoken. Go!'

'Well now, it seems to me that is rather severe ...' murmured Obnoskin.

'Indeed, indeed, indeed!' Uncle was about to say something, but stopped abruptly as Foma Fomich fixed his menacing gaze upon him.

'I'm astounded, Pavel Semyonych,' he continued. 'What do our modern men of letters do – our poets, scholars and thinkers? Why do they pay no attention to what songs the people of Russia sing, what songs the Russian people dance to? What have all these Pushkins, Lermontovs, Borozdnas been doing up to now?[20] I am astonished! People are dancing the kamarsinky, this apotheosis of drunkenness,[21] and all we get from them are the praises they sing to forget-me-nots! Why don't they compose more edifying songs for the use of the people, and give up their forget-me-nots? Here we have a social problem! Let them portray a peasant, but an ennobled peasant, a settled and responsible villager and not simply a peasant. Let them portray a rural sage in all his simplicity, wearing bast shoes if need be – I'll accept even that – but enhanced by virtues, which – I say this without fear – may even be the envy of some greatly overrated Alexander the Great. I know Russia and Mother Russia knows me:[22] that's precisely why I'm saying this. Let them portray this peasant, if they

like, burdened by family responsibilities, advancing old age, cooped up in
a stuffy hut and maybe starving too, yet perfectly content and uncomplain-
ing, glorifying his poverty and indifferent to the gold of the wealthy.[23]
Now let the rich man, his heart moved to tenderness, bring his gold to
him; let there even be a merging of the peasant's virtues and the virtues of
his lord and maybe master. The rustic and the lord, placed so far apart on
the ladder of society, are finally united in their virtues – there's an
elevated thought! But what do we see? On the one hand, forget-me-nots –
on the other, a disorderly wretch running through the streets after
boozing in a tavern! Well, what is poetic about such a sight? What is
there to admire in it? Where is the wit, the grace, the morality? It defeats
me!'

'A hundred rubles I owe you, Foma Fomich, for such words!' breathed
Yezhevikin, his eyes filled with rapture.

'The devil he'll get it,' he whispered to me softly. 'Flattery, flattery!'

'Yes, yes . . . what a beautiful picture you painted,' Obnoskin said.

'Indeed, indeed, indeed!' exclaimed Uncle who had been listening with
profound attention and eyeing me triumphantly all the while.

'What a topic!' he whispered, rubbing his hands. 'A many-sided
conversation indeed, damn it! Foma, this is my nephew,' he added,
overcome by emotion. 'He has studied literature too – may I introduce
him?'

Foma Fomich, as before, paid not the slightest attention to Uncle's
introduction.

'For God's sake, stop introducing me! I really mean it,' I whispered
sternly.

'Ivan Ivanych!' Foma Fomich suddenly began again, turning to Mizinchikov and fixing him with a steadfast gaze, 'what would your opinion
be regarding what we have been talking about?'

'Me? You're asking me?' said Mizinchikov in surprise, as though he had
just been woken up.

'Yes, you sir. I'm asking you because I value the views of truly clever
people, as opposed to those of doubtful sages whose only claim to wit is that
they are *constantly being proclaimed as wits and scholars*, and are sometimes
specially summoned to be paraded, as in some fairground booth.'

This thrust was clearly aimed at me. And there was not the slightest
doubt that Foma Fomich, while doing his best to ignore me, had initiated
this conversation about literature solely in order to blind, destroy and put
down at one blow the would-be wit and scholar from St Petersburg. I at
any rate had no doubt that this was the case.

'If you wish to know my opinion, then I . . . I completely agree with all you say,' was Mizinchikov's apathetic and reluctant reply.

'You all agree with me! This is beginning to get rather sickening,' Foma Fomich observed. 'Let me tell you frankly, Pavel Semyonych,' he continued after a brief silence, turning to Obnoskin again, 'if there is one thing for which I respect the immortal Karamzin, it is not his History, not *Marfa Posadnitsa* or *Russia Old and New*, but because he wrote *Frol Silin*:[24] a grand epos – true people's art, destined to live to the end of time! Epos in the grand manner indeed!'

'Indeed, indeed, indeed! Grand *epoch*! Frol Silin, a charitable man! I remember reading it: he bought the freedom of two *more* wenches and then cast his eyes to heaven and wept. Nobility indeed,' Uncle concurred, beaming with delight.

Poor Uncle! He was utterly unable to resist joining in a *learned* conversation. Foma Fomich contorted his face into a malicious grin, but said nothing.

'There are entertaining writers today too,' Anfisa Petrovna cautiously put in. 'Take *The Mysteries of Brussels*,[25] for example.'

'I wouldn't have said so,' replied Foma Fomich in a tone of regret. 'I read one poem recently. Nothing very much – another forget-me-not! But if you will, of the modernists I admire "The Scribe"[26] best of all – such lightness of touch!'

'"The Scribe"!' Anfisa Petrovna exclaimed, 'the one who writes letters for the magazine? Oh, how enchanting he is! What witty play with words!'

'Precisely, his play with words. He plays with the pen, so to speak. Incredible felicity of style!'

'Yes, but he is a pedant,' Obnoskin remarked nonchalantly.

'A pedant, a pedant he may well be – I don't dispute it; but a charming pedant, a gracious pedant! True, not one of his ideas will stand up to serious criticism; but the ease of his style is disarming. He is a windbag – I agree; but what a charming, what a stylish one! For instance, you remember in one literary essay he speaks of owning some estates?'

'Estates?' Uncle echoed, 'That's good! Which province?'

Foma Fomich paused, measured Uncle with a piercing look, and continued in the same tone as before: 'Can somebody please tell me in plain language: why should I, the reader, need to know that he is a man of property? If he is – good luck to him! But how charmingly, how amusingly he refers to it! He sparkles with wit, he bubbles over with it, he's on fire with it! He's a fountain of wit! That's the way to write! I believe that's how I would have written, if, that is, I had consented to write for publication . . .'

'Maybe even better,' Yezhevikin remarked respectfully.

'There is something melodious in his imagery!' Uncle added.

Foma Fomich's patience was at an end.

'Colonel,' he said, 'may I ask you — with all due respect, of course — to let us finish our discussion in peace and not interrupt. You have nothing to contribute to our discussion, nothing! So please do not disturb our agreeable literary discussion. Go about your own business, drink tea, but . . . leave literature alone. It'll be to its advantage entirely, I can assure you!'

This overstepped all bounds of propriety. I was speechless.

'But you said yourself, Foma, there was something melodious . . .' Uncle exclaimed, sadly perplexed.

'Agreed, sir. But when I spoke, I knew what I was talking about, which is more than can be said for you!'

'Yes, we certainly know what's what,' Yezhevikin chimed in, twisting and turning at Foma Fomich's side. 'Not that our brains amount to a great deal — we have to work hard with what we've got, there's just enough to manage two ministries, but we're willing to take on a third — that's how we are.'

'Well, I've done it again!' Uncle concluded with his usual good-natured smile.

'At least he admits it,' remarked Foma Fomich.

'It's all right, Foma, I'm not angry. I know you pulled me up just then for my own good, as a friend, a brother. It was I who told you to do it, I actually asked you to do it. It was only right and proper, for my own good in the end! I thank you kindly, and I'll take heed!'

My patience was beginning to wear thin. All I had previously heard about Foma Fomich had seemed somewhat exaggerated. Now that I was able to see it all for myself, my astonishment knew no bounds. I could not believe my own eyes; I could not reconcile the insolence, the unabashed arrogance on the one hand, with the self-imposed submissiveness, the credulous good nature on the other. Furthermore, it was clear that even Uncle was shocked by such a display of impudence. I was aching for a confrontation with Foma Fomich, aching for a clash so as to insult him to the quick — whatever the consequences! The thought of it lent me strength. An opportunity was all I needed, and in my eager expectation I completely crumpled up the brim of my hat. But the opportunity never presented itself. Foma Fomich steadfastly refused to acknowledge my presence.

'You're right, Foma, every inch of the way,' Uncle continued, doing his best to recover himself and to make up for the acrimony of what had just been said. 'You hit the nail on the head, Foma, and I thank you. Never speak unless you know what you're talking about. I confess, though, it's not the first time I've been in such a predicament. Imagine, Sergey, I once even sat on an examination panel . . . You're laughing! Well, there you are! I really did – funny, isn't it? Somebody invited me to an educational establishment to attend an examination, and placed me amongst the examiners as a mark of distinction because there was a vacant place to fill. I'm afraid my heart sank within me, I was positively scared; I didn't know a single subject! What was I to do? Supposing I myself had been called upon to explain something at the blackboard? Everything turned out all right in the end; I even managed to put in a question or two myself, such as: who was Noah? I got excellent answers on the whole; we had lunch afterwards and drank champagne to the flourishing of learning. An excellent establishment.'

Foma Fomich and Obnoskin were helpless with laughter.

'I couldn't stop laughing at the time, either,' Uncle exclaimed, sharing in the mirth in the most good-natured way, pleased that things had taken such a jovial turn. 'Now, Foma, here goes. Just to amuse you all I'll tell you how I once really did come a cropper . . . Imagine us, Sergey, stationed at the time in Krasnogorsk . . .'

'Permit me to ask you, Colonel: how long is this story of yours going to take?' Foma Fomich interrupted.

'Oh, Foma! It's a marvellous story; you'll die laughing. Just listen: it's good, I swear it really is good. I'll tell you how I came a cropper.'

'It's always such a pleasure to listen to that sort of story from you,' Obnoskin drawled with a yawn.

'We can't help it, we'll have to listen,' decided Foma Fomich.

'Yes, really, my God, it will be good, Foma. It'll show you how I really came a cropper once, Anfisa Petrovna. You listen too, Sergey: it'll be a lesson to you. We were stationed at Krasnogorsk.' (Uncle began speaking rapidly with countless parentheses and beaming with excitement, as he always did when setting out to tell a story for his listeners' amusement.) 'On the evening that we arrived, we all went to the theatre. There was a marvellous actress, Kuropatkina; later she ran off with the Cavalry Captain Zverkov in the middle of a performance; the curtain had to be brought down . . . Zverkov was a real devil for drinking and gambling – not that he was a drunkard, but there was never a dull moment with him. When he really hit the bottle, my word, he'd forget

everything: his address, the country he was living in, his own name –
everything; deep down a likeable fellow all the same . . . Anyway, there I am
in the theatre. In the interval I happened to meet my old friend Kornoukhov
. . . splendid fellow. Hadn't seen him for about six years. Well, he'd been in
action, his chest was covered in medals . . . heard the other day he's joined
the civil service, and going up and up . . . We were glad to see each other.
We talked of this and that. In the box next to ours sat three ladies. The one
on the left was as ugly as sin . . . Later it turned out she was a most excellent
lady, mother of a family, happily married . . . So like a fool, I blurted out to
Kornoukhov: "Tell me, friend, who is that scarecrow?" "Which one?"
"That one." "That's my cousin." You can imagine how the devil I felt! So
to make up for it: "No, not that one. Can't you see! That one sitting
opposite: who's she?" "That's my sister." Damnation! And what's more,
she was as pretty as a rosebud, a real peach; decked out like an angel – gloves,
brooches, bracelets; later she got married to a splendid fellow called Pykhtin;
she eloped and married him without getting her parents' consent: but that's
all over now and they're living in the lap of luxury; the in-laws are as happy
as can be . . . So anyway: "No, no!" I cried, wishing the ground would
swallow me up. "Not that one! The one in the middle!" "The one in the
middle? Well, my friend, that's my wife . . ." Between you and me there was
never a more handsome woman! You could swallow her whole and smack
your lips . . . "Well now," I said, "have you ever seen a real fool? If not,
there s one before you now. Here's his head: you can chop it right off!" He
just laughed. After the performance he introduced us and the scoundrel
probably told them all that had happened. I could tell it by the way they
laughed! Must admit, I had the time of my life with them. So you see, Foma,
my friend, one can really come a cropper sometimes! Ha-ha-ha!'

But poor Uncle laughed in vain; his kind and merry glances, which he
pleadingly cast around the room, were to no avail: a stony silence greeted
his merry story. Foma Fomich sat glum and mute and so did everybody
else; only Obnoskin smiled faintly in anticipation of the dressing-down
which was now to follow. Uncle was overcome with confusion and
embarrassment. That was just what Foma Fomich was waiting for.

'Have you quite finished?' he asked, turning haughtily towards the
embarrassed story-teller.

'Yes, Foma.'

'And are you happy?'

'What do you mean, happy, Foma?' poor Uncle replied, pained.

'Do you feel better now? Are you pleased you've disrupted a pleasant
literary discussion amongst friends to satisfy your own petty vanity?'

'Oh Foma! I only wanted to amuse you all, but you —'

'Amuse us?' Foma cried, flaring up with indignation. 'All you can do is bore people, not amuse them. You think you're amusing! Do you realize your story bordered on the immoral — quite apart from being indecent? It's plain to anyone. Just now you announced, betraying an astonishing lack of sensibility, that you ridiculed an innocent and noble lady simply because she did not have the honour of being attractive to you. What's more, you wanted us to laugh and thereby condone your rude and shocking behaviour, and all because you are the master of this house! It's up to you, Colonel; you may seek toadies, flatterers, partners, you may even summon them from far-off lands to increase the strength of your entourage in violation of all decent humane principles; but never will Foma Opiskin become a yes-man, a boot-licker, a hanger-on of yours! Anything else — but not that, I assure you! . . .'

'Oh, Foma! you really have misunderstood me, Foma!'

'No, Colonel, I know your type; I saw through you long ago! You are consumed by insatiable self-love; you have pretensions to be a master of wit, forgetting that pretension is the very death of wit. You . . .'

'Foma, for goodness sake! Have you no shame before all these people!'

'Colonel, how do you expect me to see all this and keep silent; it saddens me, and I can't keep silent. I'm poor, I'm *surviving* on the bounty of your mother. My silence may be misconstrued as flattery; and I don't want some *milksop* to regard me as your toady! Perhaps when I entered this room a short while ago I purposely exaggerated my blunt frankness; I may have been forced to the point of rudeness, solely because you left me no alternative. You are too high-handed with me, Colonel. I may be looked upon as your slave, your lackey. It may be your pleasure to demean me in front of *strangers*, whereas in point of fact I am your equal, do you hear me, sir? Equal in every respect! It may even be *I* who am doing *you* a favour by residing with you. I am being insulted; hence it is my duty to exalt myself — that's natural! I cannot keep silent, I have to speak out, I must protest immediately, and I therefore flatly and openly declare that you are a monstrously jealous man. For instance, you observed how, in the course of a simple, friendly discussion, somebody spontaneously revealed his erudition, his knowledge of literature, his taste; and you're immediately consumed with jealousy and you say to yourself: "I must show off my taste and erudition too!" And may I ask what taste you have to speak of! You, if I may say so, Colonel, have about as much appreciation of beauty and refinemen as a bull has of the Holy Scriptures! That was rude and cruel, I admit; but at least it was honest and just. None of your toadies will ever tell you anything like that, Colonel.'

'Oh, Foma! . . .'

'"Oh, Foma", indeed. It hurts to know the truth. Well – we'll talk about this some other time, but now allow me my turn to entertain the company a little. The right isn't exclusively yours, you know. Pavel Semyonych, have you seen this sea monster in human form? I've been watching him for a long time now. Look at him closely: he wants to devour me, gobble me up alive in one gulp!'

The reference was to Gavrila. The old servant was standing by the door, looking on with considerable distress at the treatment meted out to his master.

'I too want to entertain you with an amusing spectacle, Pavel Semyonych. Listen, you scarecrow, come here! Closer, closer, if it be your pleasure, Gavrila Ignatych! – You see, Pavel Semyonych, this is Gavrila; as a punishment for his insolence he is studying the French tongue. I, like Orpheus, wish to mellow the morals of the masses, but with the French tongue instead of songs. Well, Frenchman, *Monsieur Chematon*[27] – he can't stand being called *Monsieur Chematon* – do you know your lesson?'

'Yes, I've learnt it,' replied Gavrila, his head hung low.

'And *parlez-vous français*?'

'Oui, monsieur, *je-le-parle-on-purr* . . .'

I don't know if it was Gavrila's doleful expression when he spoke the French sentence or if it was in anticipation of Foma Fomich's desire that everybody should laugh, but as soon as Gavrila opened his mouth everybody simply doubled up with laughter. Even the General's Lady could not forbear to join in. Anfisa Petrovna threw herself back in the settee and shrieked a high-pitched falsetto, hiding her face behind her fan. The general mirth reached its peak when Gavrila, seeing what the examination had turned into, could not contain himself any longer, spat, and pronounced with indignation:

'To think I'd live to suffer such shame in my old age!'

Foma Fomich started.

'What? What did you say? Are you being insolent?'

'No, Foma Fomich,' replied Gavrila with dignity, 'what I have to say is no impudence, and it's not for me, your underling, to insult a born gentleman such as you be. But each and every man bears the image and likeness of God. I've passed the ripe old age of sixty-two. My father could remember the monster Pugachov, and my grandfather, together with his master, Matvey Nikitich – may their souls rest in everlasting peace – were both hanged by Pugachov on the same tree: for this my father was honoured above all others by our late master Afanasy Matveyich who made him his valet, and he ended his days as the master's steward. And I, sir, even though I am just a common serf, I've never witnessed such shame as this in all my born days!'

With these words Gavrila spread out his hands and bowed his head. Uncle regarded him with an anxious eye.

'Now, now, Gavrila!' he exclaimed. 'No need to go on like that; that'll do!'

'Leave him, leave him,' said Foma Fomich, growing pale and forcing himself to smile. 'Let him have his say; this is all your doing . . .'

'Yes, I'll say everything,' Gavrila continued, in a peak of excitement, 'I'll hold back nothing! You can tie my hands but not my tongue! I stand a poor wretch before you, Foma Fomich, in a word a slave, but I can feel insult. I'm forever bound to you in service and submission, because I was born a slave and I must carry out every duty to my master, in fear and trembling. If you sit down to write a book, I must stop anyone annoying you – that's the nature of my duty. If you desire any service – I'll always do it with the greatest of pleasure. But having me yap in some outlandish tongue in my old age and be laughed at by others! I can't go into the servants' quarters now without someone saying: "A Frenchman, a Frenchman!" No, sir, it's not just a fool like me, other good people too have been saying with one voice that you've turned into a cruel and vicious person, that our master is just like a little child before you; you may well have been born a general's son, and probably weren't far off a general's rank yourself – but now I must say, you've turned into a thorough fiend.'

Gavrila stopped. I was beside myself with exultation. In the confusion which ensued Foma Fomich sat pale with rage, unable to recover himself after Gavrila's sudden onslaught; he seemed to be debating how far to give vent to his anger. At last he exploded.

'What! he dared to abuse me – me! Open rebellion!' he yelled, jumping up from his chair.

Even the General's Lady sprang to her feet, and clasped her hands. Total commotion followed. Uncle rushed forward and jostled the delinquent Gavrila out of the room.

'Chain him, chain him!' shouted the General's Lady. 'Take him to the town, Yegorushka, sign him on for the army – or I'll refuse you my blessing! Put him in the stocks immediately and sign him on for the army!'

'What!' shouted Foma Fomich, 'A slave – a yokel – a peasant dared to abuse me! That – that rag I wipe my boots with! He dared to call me a fiend!'

I stepped forward with extraordinary resolve.

'I admit that in this case I am in full agreement with Gavrila,' I said, looking Foma Fomich straight in the eye and quivering with excitement.

He was so surprised by this sally of mine that it took him some time to realize his ears were not deceiving him.

'What was that?' he yelled out at last in a frenzy, fixing me with his small bloodshot eyes. 'And just who are you?'

'Foma . . .' Uncle began in acute embarrassment, 'this is Sergey, my nephew . . .'

'The scholar!' bellowed Foma Fomich, 'so this is the man of learning, is it? *Liberté, égalité, fraternité! Journal de Débats!* Lies, I say, all lies! This isn't Petersburg for you, you won't make fools of us! Worse than Saxon lies! To hell with your *débats!* What you call *débats*, we call fiddlesticks! A man of learning, indeed! What you've just learned, I've already forgotten seven times over! That's what your learning means to me!'

If somebody had not held him back he would have attacked me with his fists.

'He's drunk,' I said, looking around in confusion.

'Who? Me?' yelled Foma Fomich in a voice that was not his own.

'Yes, you!'

'Drunk?'

'Drunk.'

This was more than Foma Fomich could bear. He shrieked as if somebody had stuck a knife into him, and charged out of the room. The General's Lady seemed about to faint but decided to follow him instead: everybody else did likewise, Uncle last of all. When I had recovered and looked round, the only person I saw left in the room was Yezhevikin. He was smiling and rubbing his hands.

'That Jesuit you promised to tell us about,' he said slyly.

'What?' I asked, not knowing what he was talking about.

'You promised to tell us about a Jesuit . . . a funny story . . .'

I dashed out onto the terrace, and then into the garden. My head was spinning.

8

Declaration of Love

I must have been pacing about the garden for a quarter of an hour, in acute irritation and highly displeased with myself, wondering what to do next. The sun was setting. Suddenly, at the corner of a shady walk, I came face to face with Nastenka. There were tears in her eyes which she wiped away with a handkerchief.

'I was looking for you,' she said.

'And I was looking for you,' I replied. 'Tell me: am I in a madhouse or not?'

'Not at all,' she answered reproachfully, giving me a sharp look.

'In that case, tell me what's going on. For the love of God, give me some advice! Where has Uncle got to? Can I see him? I'm very glad to have met you: perhaps you can suggest something.'

'No, don't go in. I've just left them.'

'Well, where are they now?'

'Who knows? They might have gone back to the orchard,' she said, irritated.

'What orchard?'

'Last week Foma Fomich shouted that he didn't want to stay in the house and rushed out into the garden, took a large spade from the shed and started digging the ground. Everybody was so surprised we thought he had gone mad. "That's to stop people accusing me of being a parasite, I'll dig the earth and earn my keep here, and then I'll leave. See what you've made me do!" People were crying and ready to go on their knees in front of him, trying to wrench the spade out of his hands, but he wouldn't stop and dug up all the turnips. They let him do it that time — he's probably at it again. I wouldn't put it past him.'

'And you ... and you can stand here calmly telling me about it!' I shouted, filled with indignation.

Her eyes flashed.

'Please forgive me; I don't know what I'm saying! Listen, do you know why I'm here?'

'N-no,' she replied, blushing, and a shadow of vexation flitted across her sweet face.

'You must excuse me,' I continued. 'I'm rather upset. I feel this is no way to begin talking about it . . . to you of all people . . . But never mind! Honesty is the best policy in such cases. I admit . . . that is, I meant to say . . . do you know Uncle's plans? He instructed me to ask for your hand –'

'Oh, what nonsense!' she interrupted, suddenly flaring up. 'Don't start on that!'

I was perplexed.

'What do you mean, nonsense? But he wrote to me.'

'So he did, did he?' she asked with animation. 'And he promised not to! What nonsense! God, what utter nonsense!'

'Forgive me,' I muttered, lost for words, 'maybe I was inconsiderate and rude . . . but at a time like this! You see: we're surrounded by God knows what . . .'

'Oh, for God's sake, don't apologize. Believe me, it's embarrassing enough for me to have to listen to it all: but I did mean to talk to you myself . . . to see what I could find out . . . Oh, what shame! So he wrote to you, did he? That's just what I was afraid of most of all! My God, he's such a strange man! And you believed him and rushed here like a madman? Whatever next?'

She did not seek to hide her irritation. I was in a most unenviable position.

'I must admit, I didn't expect,' I said in the most acute embarrassment, 'such a turn . . . on the contrary, I thought . . .'

'Ah, did you?' she said with a trace of irony and lightly bit her lip. 'Now, let me see that letter of his.'

'Very well.'

'And please don't be angry or offended with me; we've got enough trouble as it is!' she said pleadingly, and yet a faint smile of derision flitted across her sweet lips.

'Oh, please don't take me for an idiot!' I exclaimed passionately. 'Perhaps you're prejudiced against me? Perhaps somebody has been spreading tales about me? Perhaps it's because I disgraced myself in there just now? But that's as may be – I assure you. I appreciate what a fool I am in your eyes now. Please don't laugh at me! I don't know what I'm saying . . . And it's all because I'm only twenty-two, damn it!'

'Good God! What does that matter?'

'What do you mean, what does it matter? Any twenty-two-year-old has got it plainly stamped on his face; for example, take the way I bounced into the middle of the room just now, or at this moment, in front of you . . . It's a terrible age!'

'No, no, no!' replied Nastenka, trying hard not to laugh. 'You're good, sweet and wise, I'm certain, I honestly mean it! But . . . you're too proud. You could improve, though.'

'I'm no more proud than I should be.'

'Yes you are. You got embarrassed in there — and why? Because you tripped when you entered . . . What right did you have to mock your good, noble uncle, who's done so much for you? Why did you have to make a laughing-stock of him when you were so ridiculous yourself? It was bad of you, and you ought to be ashamed! It does you no credit, and let me tell you, I really hated you then — so there you are!'

'It's true! I was an idiot — and worse: I behaved despicably! You noticed it, and that's my punishment! You can scold me, you can laugh at me, but you must listen: maybe you will change your mind in the end,' I added, urged on by some strange emotion. 'As you know me so little, perhaps later, when you get to know me better, then . . . maybe . . .'

'For goodness' sake, let's drop this subject!' Nastenka exclaimed, with evident exasperation.

'All right, all right, let's drop it! But . . . when can I see you?'

'What do you mean — see me?'

'It can't be that we've said all there is to say to each other, Nastasya Yevgrafovna! For goodness' sake, tell me when I can see you again — today? No, it's getting dark. Well then, if it's at all possible, early tomorrow morning; I'll make sure I'm woken up in good time. There's a summer-house by the pond. I remember it; I know where it is. I lived here when I was a child.'

'But what on earth do you want to see me for? We're talking to each other now, aren't we?'

'But I still don't know anything, Nastasya Yevgrafovna. Let me find out everything from Uncle first. He'll have to tell me everything, and then I may be in a position to say something important to you . . .'

'No, no! No need! No need!' exclaimed Nastenka. 'Have done with it now, and don't ever bring up the subject again. You'll be wasting your time going to that summer-house: I assure you, I shan't come, so please get all this nonsense out of your head — I'm asking you seriously . . .'

'So it turns out Uncle treated me as though I were mad!' I cried in a fit of unutterable anguish. 'Then why did he ask me to come? . . . But listen! What's that noise?'

We were quite close to the house. Through the open windows we could hear an extraordinary commotion.

'Good heavens!' she said, going pale. 'Not again! I knew it was going to happen!'

'You knew? One more question, Nastasya Yevgrafovna. Of course, I've no right whatsoever, but for the good of all concerned I'll be so bold as to put it to you. Tell me – and to my dying day you'll hear no more from me – tell me honestly: is Uncle in love with you or not?'

'Get this nonsense out of your head once and for all!' she cried in a sudden fit of anger. 'Honestly! If he'd been in love with me, would he have wanted to marry me off to you?' She smiled bitterly. 'Where did you get the idea? Don't you understand what's behind all this? Just listen to the shouting!'

'But . . . that's Foma Fomich . . .'

'Exactly, Foma Fomich. They're talking about me, repeating the same rubbish you were saying; they too suspect that he's in love with me. And as I'm poor and insignificant and my honour means nothing to them, they want to marry him off to somebody else, they are insisting he should turn me out of the house and have me stay with Father to be out of the way. And if anybody speaks to him about it, he loses his temper – even with Foma. That's what they're all shouting about now, I can tell.'

'So it's true! He really will marry this Tatyana?'

'What Tatyana?'

'You know, the half-wit.'

'She's no half-wit. She's a kind woman. You've no right to say such things! She's got a good heart, which is more than can be said for others. The poor thing can't help her misfortune.'

'I'm sorry. Let's assume you are right; but aren't you wrong about the most important thing? Tell me, how is it they're so kind to your father? If they had been as angry with you as you say they are and had been trying to get rid of you, surely they would have been angry with him and treated him badly?'

'But can't you see what my father is doing for me! He's acting the fool! He's being tolerated precisely because he's managed to win Foma Fomich's favour. And as Foma himself was once a clown, it flatters him to have a clown of his own. What do you think: who does my father do it for? He does it for me, for me alone. He has nothing to gain himself; he wouldn't bow to anybody for his own sake. He may seem ridiculous to some people, but he is noble, he is the noblest of men! He imagines, God knows why – and not at all because I'm getting good wages here, I assure you – he imagines it's better for me to stay in this house. But now I've managed to change his mind completely. I've written to him firmly. He has come to take me away, if the worst comes to the worst tomorrow, because things have got so bad: they want to tear me limb from limb, I'm positive it's me they're shouting about now. Because of me they'll tear him apart, they'll destroy *him*. And he is like a father to me – do you hear, even more than a father! I don't want to wait any longer. I know more than anyone else. I'm leaving tomorrow, tomorrow! Who knows: perhaps because of this they'll postpone *his* marriage to Tatyana Ivanovna if only for a short time . . . Now I've told you everything. You pass it all on to him, because I mustn't even be seen speaking to him now: we're being watched, especially by this Perepelitsyna. Tell *him* not to worry about me, that I'd rather eat black bread and live in father's hut than be the cause of his suffering here. I'm poor, and I have to live accordingly. But, Good Lord, the noise! the shouting! What's going on there? I'm going to see, no matter what happens! I'll tell them all this straight to their faces, come what may! I must. Goodbye!'

She ran away. I stood stock-still, fully aware of the comical rôle which I had been made to play and not at all sure what the outcome would be. I was sorry for the poor girl, and afraid for my uncle. Suddenly Gavrila appeared beside me. He was still holding his exercise book.

'Your uncle wants to see you,' he said in a downcast voice.

I started.

'Uncle? Where is he? What's the matter with him?'

'In the drawing-room, where you were having tea, sir.'

'Who's with him?'

'No one. He's waiting.'

'Who for? Me?'

'He's sent for Foma Fomich. Our golden days are over!' Gavrila sighed deeply.

'Foma Fomich? Hm! And where are the others? Where is the General's Lady?'

'In her rooms. She fainted, and now she's lying there out of her mind – and weeping.'

Still in conversation, we reached the terrace. It was now almost completely dark. Uncle was indeed alone, pacing up and down the room where my confrontation with Foma Fomich had taken place. Lighted candles were standing on the tables. When I entered the room he rushed towards me and shook my hands warmly. He was pale and his chest was heaving with agitation; his hands were shaking, and a nervous shudder would from time to time convulse his whole body.

9

Your Excellency

'My boy! it's all over, everything has been decided!' he uttered in an almost tragic whisper.

'Uncle,' I said, 'I heard shouting.'

'Shouting, my boy, shouting; yes, there was shouting. Dear Mother has fainted and everything's in a turmoil. But I've made up my mind and nothing will make me budge. Now I'm no longer afraid of anybody, Seryozha. I want to show them that I have a mind of my own too – and I will. I sent for you so that you can help me show them ... It breaks my heart, Seryozha ... but I must, I must act with the utmost rigour. Justice is implacable!'

'But do tell me what happened, Uncle!'

'Foma and I are parting,' Uncle announced resolutely.

'Uncle!' I shouted with joy, 'that really is the best thing that could have happened! And if I can help you in any way to carry out your plan ... I'm at your service for evermore.'

'Thank you, my dear boy, thank you! The final decision has been taken. I'm expecting Foma. I've already sent for him. It's either him or me! We must part. Either Foma leaves this house tomorrow, or, I swear, I'll throw it all up and join the hussars again! They'll take me on all right and give me a division. To hell with this way of life! A new life will begin. What's that French exercise book for?' Uncle turned towards Gavrila in a rage. 'Get rid of it! Burn it, tear it up, destroy it! *I'm* your master, and *I* command you not to study French. You cannot, you dare not disobey me, because *I'm* your master, not Foma Fomich!'

'Thank God!' Gavrila muttered to himself. Things had obviously taken a serious turn.

'My dear boy!' Uncle continued in great agitation, 'they're asking me for the impossible! You'll be my judge. You will stand between us as an impartial arbiter. You've no idea, no idea what they've been demanding of me and have actually requested formally; now they've come out with it! What an affront to human dignity, decency, honour ... I'll tell you everything, but first ...'

'I already know everything, Uncle!' I exclaimed, interrupting him. 'I can guess ... I've just been talking to Nastasya Yevgrafovna.'

'My boy, say no more about this, not a word!' Uncle interrupted me in great haste as though afraid of something. 'I'll tell you everything afterwards myself, but in the meantime ... Well?' he called out to Vidoplyasov who had just come in, 'where is Foma Fomich?'

Vidoplyasov returned bearing a message that Foma Fomich did not wish to come in view of the excessive impertinence of the demand and because he now considered himself to have been grossly insulted.

'Bring him here! Drag him here! Drag him here by the head and ears!' Uncle shouted, stamping his foot.

Vidoplyasov, who had never seen my uncle in such a frenzy, retired in a state of shock. I was amazed.

'Something really must have happened,' I thought, 'to have driven a person of his gentle character to such anger and desperation.'

For a few seconds Uncle paced up and down the room in silence, evidently in deep conflict with himself.

'On second thoughts, don't tear up that exercise book,' he said at last to Gavrila. 'Wait, don't go away: you may be needed. My boy!' he said, turning to me, 'I've a feeling that I got carried away a bit. Things ought to be done with dignity, courage, but without shouting, without abuse. That's right. You know, Seryozha, wouldn't it be better if you left the room? Surely it's all the same to you. Afterwards I'll tell you everything myself – eh? What do you think? There's a good boy.'

'You're afraid, Uncle! you're regretting your decision now!' I said, looking hard at him.

'No, no, my boy, I'm not regretting it!' he exclaimed with redoubled fervour. 'I'm not afraid of anything now. I've taken drastic, very drastic measures! You've no idea, you can't imagine what they were demanding of me! Was I really supposed to agree? I'll show them! I have rebelled; I'll show them! I had to prove it some time or other! But you know, my boy, I do regret I called you: perhaps it wouldn't be fair on Foma if you too, as it were, were to witness his downfall. You see, I want to turn him out of the house in a civil manner, without loss of face. However, that's easier said than done – without loss of face. Things have got to the point where no amount of honeyed words can smooth over the indignity. And I'm rough and unmannerly, I daresay I shall come out with something – fool that I am – that I shan't ever forgive myself for later. The fact is, he's done such a lot for me ... Off you go now, my boy ... Here they come, here they come! Seryozha, go, I beg of you! I'll tell you everything afterwards. Do leave us, for God's sake!'

And Uncle ushered me out onto the terrace just as Foma was entering the room. But I confess that I did not go away. I decided to stay on the terrace, where it was dark and consequently difficult to see me from inside the room. I decided to eavesdrop.

I am not trying to exonerate myself, but I will say without hesitation that the half hour I spent on the terrace, struggling to restrain my temper, was an act of high martyrdom. From where I stood I could not only hear, I could see everything through the French window. Now picture Foma Fomich *summoned* to appear under threat of physical force if he refused.

'Have my ears deceived me, Colonel?' he whined as he entered the room. 'Have I been informed correctly?'

'You have, you have, Foma, calm down,' Uncle replied bravely. 'Sit down. Let's talk it over seriously, in a friendly, brotherly fashion. Sit down, Foma.'

Foma Fomich gravely settled into an armchair. Uncle continued to pace up and down the room in quick, uneven steps, evidently uncertain where to begin.

'Yes, in a brotherly fashion,' he repeated. 'You'll understand me, Foma, you're no child; neither am I – in short, we're both advanced in years . . . Hm! Look here, Foma, we haven't been seeing eye to eye on certain points . . . Yes, that's right, on certain points, and so, Foma, old fellow, wouldn't it be better for us to part? I'm sure you're a gentleman and would wish me only the best, and so . . . But what's the use of talking! Foma, I'm your friend till the end of time – I swear to it by all the Christian saints! Here is fifteen thousand rubles in silver: that's all I've got, my friend; all I've been able to scrape together at my family's expense. Take it, don't be afraid! I must, it's my duty to provide for you! Most of it is in securities and a little bit of cash. Go on, take it! You owe me nothing because I'll never be in a position to repay all you've done for me. Yes, yes, indeed, this is what I feel, even though our views don't coincide on the main issue at the moment. Tomorrow or the day after . . . or whenever it suits . . . we must part. Why don't you move into town, Foma? It's only about ten versts from here. Behind the church, the first turning you come to, there's a beautiful little house with green shutters belonging to the priest's widow; it could have been built specially for you. She'll sell it. I'll buy it for you on top of what I'm giving you now. You'll be practically next door to us. You can study literature, science: your fame will spread . . . All the civil servants there are gentlemanly, friendly, unselfish people; the parish priest is a scholar. At holiday time you'll come to visit us – what a life it'll be, a real paradise! Do you agree, or not?'

'So these are the conditions on which Foma is being dispatched!' I thought. 'Uncle didn't say anything to me about money.'

For a long time there was total silence. Foma was sitting in the armchair thunderstruck, staring hard at my uncle, who was evidently becoming disconcerted by the silence and such a gaze.

'Money!' Foma uttered at last in an affectedly feeble tone, 'where is it, where is this money? Give it to me, hand it to me quickly.'

'Here it is, Foma: my last scrapings, fifteen thousand exactly, that's all I have. There are some credit notes and securities – you'll see for yourself . . . here!'

'Gavrila! you take this money,' Foma said gently, 'it may come in handy to you, old man. – No!' he suddenly yelled in an unusually high voice, leaping to his feet. 'No! Give it to me first, this money, Gavrila! Give it to me! Give it to me! Give me these millions to trample underfoot, give them to me to tear up, spit on, scatter about, vilify and desecrate! . . . I, I am being offered money! I'm being bribed to leave this house! Do my ears deceive me? Have I lived to witness this final degradation? Here, here they are, your millions! Look: there, there, there and there! This is how Foma Opiskin conducts himself, in case you didn't know, Colonel!'

And Foma scattered the bundle of money all over the room. Strangely enough, he neither tore nor spat on a single note as he had boasted, but only crumpled them, and even then, none too severely. Gavrila rushed to pick them up and later, after Foma had departed, carefully handed them back to his master.

Foma's response produced a shattering impression upon my uncle. It was his turn now to stand stock-still, dumbfounded and open-mouthed. Meanwhile Foma settled back in his chair, panting as though in extreme agitation.

'You're a peerless fellow, Foma!' Uncle exclaimed, having finally recovered his composure. 'You're the noblest of men!'

'That I know,' Foma replied in a weak voice, but with enormous dignity.

'Foma, forgive me! I'm a scoundrel compared with you, Foma!'

'Yes, compared with me,' Foma agreed.

'Foma! It's not your nobility that astounds me!' Uncle continued rapturously, 'but rather that I could have been so uncouth, blind and mean as to offer you money under such circumstances! But Foma, you were mistaken in one respect: I never intended to bribe you, I wasn't paying you off to leave the house; I merely wanted you to have some money so that you wouldn't be destitute when you left me. I swear it! On my knees, on my bended knees I'm ready to ask your forgiveness, Foma, and if you wish, I'll kneel down before you now . . . you only have to say the word . . .'

'I don't need your bended knees, Colonel!'

'My God! Just think, Foma: I was worked up, all in a tizz, I was beside myself . . . But speak, tell me, how can I make up for this offence? Instruct me, guide me . . .'

'No need, no need, Colonel! And rest assured that tomorrow I shall be shaking the dust off my feet outside this house.'

And Foma began to rise from his chair. Much alarmed, Uncle rushed forward in an attempt to make him sit down again.

'No, Foma, you're not going anywhere, I assure you!' Uncle shouted. 'No need to talk of dust or feet, Foma! You're not to stir from here, or I shall follow you to the ends of the earth, I won't leave you until you forgive me . . . I swear, Foma, that's what I'll do!'

'Forgive you? You are guilty?' Foma said. 'But I wonder if you have any idea at all of the extent of your guilt? Do you realize that you are guilty before me now by the very fact of offering me a crust of bread in your house? Do you realize that in a matter of seconds you have poisoned all previous crusts of which I have partaken in your house? You made me feel beholden for every morsel, for every mouthful of bread that I had already eaten here; you have demonstrated to me that I was a slave in your house, a lackey, a duster for your patent leather boots! When in the purity of my heart I fondly imagined that I was a friend and brother under your roof! Didn't you yourself, with your serpent's tongue, assure me thousands of times of this friendship and brotherhood? Why then did you secretly weave the noose in which I have now been caught like a damned fool? Why under cover of darkness did you dig a pit and push me into it? Why didn't you strike me down at a blow, with this club? Why didn't you wring my neck like a farmyard cockerel's in the very beginning, because . . . well, because, for instance, it couldn't lay eggs. Yes, that's right! I stand by this comparison, Colonel, even though it has a provincial flavour about it and is reminiscent of the trivial tone of our contemporary literature. I stand by this comparison because it illustrates the absurdity of your charges; for I am no more guilty before you than this hypothetical cockerel might have been, offending his scatter-brained master by his inability to lay eggs! Now Colonel! Whoever pays his friend or brother money – what for? What for, that's the point? Saying: "Here, take it, my beloved brother, I owe it to you: you saved my life: so take these pieces of silver – Judas did – and clear out of my sight!" How naive! How brutally you have treated me! You thought I coveted your gold, when I cherished nothing but the purest thoughts for your well-being. Oh, how you have wounded my heart! You've played with my noblest feelings like a boy with his jacks! I've been anticipating this from the very beginning, Colonel — that's why your hospitality has been sticking in my throat and throttling me all along! That's why your eiderdowns have been crushing me — crushing me instead of giving me comfort! That's why your sugar and sweets have turned to cayenne pepper in my mouth! No, Colonel! You live and thrive on your own, and let Foma plod his own weary way with a bag over his shoulder. So be it, Colonel!'

'No, Foma, no! It won't be so, it can't be so!' Uncle whined, feeling he had been utterly annihilated.

'Yes, Colonel, yes! it has to be so and there is no other way. Tomorrow I shall leave you. You can scatter your millions, carpet my whole way with banknotes, every inch of the highway as far as Moscow itself — and I will proudly and disdainfully walk on your banknotes; this same foot, Colonel, will trample, crush and defile those banknotes, and Foma Opiskin shall live by the rectitude of his soul alone! I have spoken, and I have revealed my mind! Farewell, Colonel. Fare-well, Colonel! . . .'

And Foma Fomich made another attempt to rise from his chair.

'Forgive me, forgive me, Foma! and try to forget! . . .' Uncle entreated.

'"Forgive!" you say? But what use is my forgiveness to you? Well, supposing I do forgive you: I am a Christian; I can't help forgiving; I've nearly done so already. Now tell me: would it not be a violation of good sense and spiritual dignity for me to remain a minute longer in this house? And anyway — you have shown me the door!'

'It wouldn't be a violation of anything, it wouldn't, Foma! I assure you, it woudn't!'

'Really? But how can we be equals from now on? Can you understand that I have, as it were, crushed you with my nobility of spirit, that you have indeed crushed yourself by your despicable behaviour? You have been crushed, and I have been exalted. So how can there be talk of equality? And how can there be friendship without equality? I say this with a bleeding heart and not, as you may perhaps suspect, to exult and elevate myself above you in triumph.'

'My heart bleeds too, Foma, I assure you.'

'And this is he,' continued Foma Fomich, changing his tone from severe to sanctimonious, 'this is he on whose account I spent so many sleepless nights! How many times I used to get up during my sleepless nights, light the candle and say to myself: "Now he sleeps peacefully, he puts his trust in you. So you must not sleep, Foma, keep vigil for him; you may devise something for his well-being." Such were the thoughts that went through Foma's head during his sleepless nights, Colonel! And this is how this same Colonel has rewarded him! But enough! enough! . . .'

'But Foma, I will redeem your friendship, I will, I swear to it!'

'"Redeem"? Where is your guarantee? As a Christian I forgive and even love you; but as a man, a man of honour, I've no alternative but to despise you. I'm obliged to despise you, I must in the name of decency, because you have − I repeat − you have disgraced yourself, whereas I have acted in the noblest way possible. Which *of all of you* could do anything to equal what I have done? Who would find it in him to turn down a colossal sum of money such as the penniless and universally despised Foma Fomich has spurned in the name of glory? No, Colonel, if we are to be quits, you've a long list of good deeds to perform. And what good deeds are you capable of, I ask you, if you can't even address me properly and keep calling me "Foma" as if I were a common servant?'

'But, Foma, I did it to be friendly!' Uncle cried. 'I had no idea you didn't like it . . . Good God! If only I had known . . .'

'You were incapable,' Foma continued, 'you were incapable of granting, or rather unwilling to grant, the most trivial, the most insignificant request − to address me as "Your Excellency", as one addresses a general . . .'

'But surely that would have been, should I say, supreme arrogation, Foma?'

'Supreme arrogation! You've read too many high-flown phrases, you keep repeating them like a parrot! Do you realize you have debased and dishonoured me by your refusal to refer to me as "Your Excellency" − you dishonoured me because in failing to understand my motives, you made me appear a capricious fool who ought to be put away in an asylum! Do you really suppose I couldn't see how ridiculous I'd look if I were to choose to assume the title of "Your Excellency", I who despise all titles and earthly honours, which are pure humbug in themselves unless they be illumined by virtue? Not a million rubles would persuade me to accept the rank of general without the light of virtue! And you thought I was out of my mind! For your benefit alone I sacrificed my pride and let you, yes *you*, think I was insane, you and your *band of scholars*! The only reason I asked you to address me as a general was to enlighten your mind, to improve your morals and to bathe you in the light of new ideas. Above all else I wanted to see to it that you stop revering generals as though they were the highest luminaries on this earth; I wanted to prove to you that rank is worth nought without true nobility, and that you needn't gloat over the arrival of your general, when at your side, perhaps, there are people who shine with virtue! But you've flaunted your colonel's rank in my face for so long that you just couldn't bring yourself to say "Your Excellency" to *me*. There lies the cause of it all, that is where it is to be found – not in "supreme arrogation"! It all revolves around the fact that you're a Colonel and I'm simply Foma . . .'

'No, Foma, no! I assure you, that's not so at all. You're a learned man, and not simply Foma . . . I respect –'

'You do! Good. Pray tell me then, seeing that you do respect me: am I worthy of general's rank or not? I want a straight answer! Am I worthy of it or not? I want to see how developed your mind is.'

'As regards your honesty, your generosity, your wit, your supreme spiritual nobility – of course, you're worthy!' Uncle replied sincerely.

'And if I am worthy, why won't you say "Your Excellency"?'

'Foma, perhaps . . . I will . . .'

'I insist! I insist, Colonel, that you should do so now, I insist and demand! I can see how difficult it is for you to agree, and that's why I insist. Let this sacrifice be the first of many spiritual acts which – don't forget – you will have to perform to raise yourself up to my level; you will have to learn to master yourself, for only then will my faith in your sincerity be restored . . .'

'I'll call you "Your Excellency" tomorrow, Foma!'

'No, not tomorrow, Colonel, tomorrow will look after itself. I insist you address me as "Your Excellency" now, immediately.'

'Well then, Foma, I'm ready . . . Only why now, Foma . . .?'

'And why not now? Are you ashamed? If it shames you, I'll feel offended.'

'Well, all right then, Foma, I suppose I'm ready . . . even proud to . . . Only, Foma, what's the point, without rhyme or reason – simply: "Hello, Your Excellency?" It doesn't make sense . . .'

'No, not "Hello, Your Excellency", that's an offensive tone; you mustn't turn it into a joke or farce. I will not allow such jokes from you. Come, come, Colonel! I demand you mend your tone immediately!'

'You're not joking, Foma, are you?'

'In the first place, I am not "Foma", Yegor Ilyich, but "Foma Fomich". Don't forget: I'm not "Foma", but "Foma Fomich".'

'Of course, Foma Fomich, I'll make every effort . . . Only what am I to say?'

'You're not sure what to add after "Your Excellency" – that I can well understand. You should have said so at the beginning! It is quite pardonable, especially in one who is not *creative*, to put it politely. I'll help you, since you are not creative. Repeat after me: "Your Excellency".'

'Very well, "Your Excellency".'

'No, not "Very well, Your Excellency", but simply "Your Excellency"! I told you to watch your tone, Colonel! I also trust you will not be offended if I suggest you make a slight bow and at the same time incline your body forward a little. When conversing with a general keep the body inclined forward, so as to indicate respect and also, as it were, readiness to dash off on an errand for him. I've been in the company of generals myself, so I know what I'm talking about ... So "Your Excellency".'

'Your Excellency ...'

'I'm overjoyed and delighted that at last I have the opportunity to apologize for failing to appreciate from the start Your Excellency's true nature. Let me assure you that in future I shall not spare any of my feeble efforts for the common good ... Well, that'll do!'

Poor Uncle! He was obliged to repeat all this nonsense phrase by phrase, word by word! I stood blushing with shame, as though it had been my own fault. Anger was seething within me.

'Well, don't you feel,' the tormentor continued, 'that you've now been spiritually uplifted as though an angel had been sent to calm your heart? ... Do you feel the presence of this angel? Answer me!'

'Yes, Foma, I suppose I do feel a bit more at ease,' Uncle replied.

'As though your heart had been dipped in some kind of balm the moment you learnt to master yourself?'

'Yes, exactly that, Foma – as if rubbed with some unguent.'

'Unguent, you say? Hm ... I wouldn't know about unguents ... Well, no matter! The point is that you know now how it feels to have performed one's duty! Learn to master yourself! You are proud, inordinately proud, Colonel!'

'Yes, proud, Foma, I agree,' Uncle replied with a sigh.

'You are an egoist, and a sordid egoist at that ...'

'An egoist, yes, that's right, Foma, I can see that. I realized that as soon as I got to know you, Foma.'

'I'm speaking to you as your father, as your gentle, loving mother ... you're alienating everyone from yourself and forgetting that it is the gentle calf that has two mothers to suckle it.'

'That's true too, Foma!'

'You're a bore, you're a trespasser upon the hearts of men of goodwill, you're so selfishly eager to draw attention to yourself that any decent person would run to the ends of the earth to escape from you!'

Uncle again heaved a deep sigh.

'Why not be more gentle, loving and understanding towards your fellow-men? Forget yourself, remember others and you too perhaps will not be forgotten. Live and let live, that is my motto! Patience, toil, prayer and hope are the precepts I should like to instil into every human heart! If you lived up to them, I should be the first to open my heart to you, weep bitter tears on your shoulder . . . if necessary . . . Instead you're so full of yourself, you, yourself and your Reverence! In the end your Reverence can be altogether too much, Colonel, if I may put it that way!'

'What sweet words!' Gavrila said humbly.

'That's true, Foma, I appreciate it all,' Uncle agreed, overcome by emotion. 'But I'm not to blame for everything, Foma; it's my upbringing; I've lived amongst soldiers. And I swear to you, Foma, I haven't been insensitive. When I left my regiment, all the hussars, the whole battalion was simply in tears. They swore they'd not find anyone else like me . . .! I thought then that perhaps there was hope for me.'

'There's the egoist in you again! There's your vanity again! First you glorify yourself, and then in passing I get your hussars' tears rammed down my throat. Oh well, I shan't brag of anybody's tears. Though indeed I could, though indeed I could.'

'That was just a slip of the tongue, Foma, I couldn't resist recalling the good old times.'

'They're not to be snatched out of the blue, the good old times — we make them ourselves, they're locked in our hearts, Yegor Ilyich. Why is it I am always happy, always content, in spite of all my anguish; calm in spirit and a burden to no one except fools, upstarts, *men of learning*, for whom I neither have nor wish to have any pity at all.[28] I can't abide fools! And what of these learned men, what of this "man of science"! His science is pure bluff, nothing else! What was it *he* said? Get him here! Bring all the scientists here! I can explode everything; I'll explode every theory they can put up! And as for the nobility of the soul . . .'

'Of course, Foma, of course. Nobody doubts it!'

'For instance, a while ago I revealed wit, talent and extraordinarily wide reading. I proved my knowledge of humanity, of contemporary literature, I gave a brilliant exhibition of how a talented person may turn even the kamarinsky into a topic for lofty debate. And may I ask, did any one of the company appreciate me according to my deserts? No, everybody averted their gaze! I'm sure *he's* already told you that I know nothing. For all he knew, it might have been Machiavelli or Mercadante sitting before him[29] — my only fault is that I happen to be poor and obscure . . . No, they shan't get away with it! . . . And then there's this Korovkin. What sort of goose is he?'

'Foma, he's a clever man, a man of learning . . . I'm expecting him. He'll turn out a good man, Foma!'

'Hm! I doubt it. Some modern ass laden with books. They've no soul, these people, Colonel, no heart! And what good is learning without virtue?'

'No, Foma, no! You should have heard him speak of family happiness! It was straight from the heart, Foma!'

'Hm! We'll see. We'll examine Korovkin too . . . But enough,' Foma concluded, rising from his chair. 'I still can't forgive you completely, Colonel; the offence was too deep, you know, but I shall say a prayer and perhaps God will vouchsafe peace to an injured heart. We'll speak again about this tomorrow, but now allow me to leave. I feel tired and weak . . .'

'Oh, Foma!' Uncle began to fuss. 'You really are tired! Why not have a little something? I'll have it brought up in a moment.'

'A little something! A little something!' Foma replied with derision. 'First they give you poison to drink, and then they ask if you want a little something! They expect to heal wounds of the heart with stewed mushrooms and preserved apples! What a pitiable materialist you are, Colonel!'

'Oh, Foma, I really meant no harm . . .'

'Well, all right. Enough. I will go now. However, you must go at once to your mother: go down on your knees, cry, sob, but you've got to obtain her forgiveness — that's your duty now, your obligation!'

'Oh, Foma, that's what I think about all the time; even now, talking to you. I would be ready to kneel before her till dawn. But think, Foma, what it is I'm being expected to do. It's unfair, it's cruel, Foma! Be generous to the last, think of my happiness, reconsider, make your decision, and then . . . then . . . I swear . . .'

'No, Yegor Ilyich, no, that's none of my business,' replied Foma Fomich. 'You know I don't want to interfere at all; that is to say, you may be convinced I'm to blame for everything, but I assure you, I've had nothing to do with this affair from the very start. Your dear mamma alone has willed it so, and, of course, she has nothing but your interests at heart . . . Go then, hurry, fly to her and try to mend matters by pledging your obedience! Let not the sun go down upon your wrath! I . . . I shall be praying for you all through the night. I have quite forgotten what sleep is, Yegor Ilyich. Farewell! ... I pardon you too, old man,' he added, turning to Gavrila. 'I know that the blame rests with others for what you did. So forgive me any offence I may have caused you ... Farewell, farewell, farewell all, and may the Good Lord bless you . . !'

Foma Fomich departed. I immediately rushed into the room.

'You were eavesdropping!' Uncle exclaimed.

'Yes, Uncle, eavesdropping! How could you bring yourself to call him "Your Excellency"!'

'What could I do, my boy? I'm proud of it ... that was nothing when so much is at stake; but what a noble, selfless, remarkable man! Sergey – you heard him, didn't you? ... And how I dared offer him that money is simply beyond me! My boy! I got carried away! I was in a rage; I didn't understand him; I suspected him, accused him ... but no! he could never have been my enemy – I can see it now ... You remember how dignified he looked when he refused the money?'

'Very well, Uncle, be as proud as you wish, but I'm leaving: I've had enough! For the last time: what is it you want of me? Why have you called me here and what is it you're after? If everything is over and I'm no longer of any use, I'm leaving. I'm sick of these charades! I'm leaving today.'

'My dear boy ...' Uncle began to fuss as usual, 'stay for two more minutes: I'm going to see Mamma ... I've got to settle something vitally important, an affair of great moment! ... Why don't you go to your room? Gavrila will take you to the summer wing. You know the summer wing? It's actually in the garden. I've had your bags taken there already. As for me, I'll go back to her and implore her forgiveness – I know exactly how to go about it – and then I'll be back immediately and tell you everything, everything, everything, in the minutest detail, I'll bare my soul to you ... And ... and ... there'll be better times for us too! Two minutes, just two more minutes, Sergey!'

He shook my hand and hurried out. There was nothing for it but to follow Gavrila again.

Miʒinchikov[30]

The part of the house where Gavrila conducted me was called 'the new wing' merely as a matter of usage; in fact, it had been built by the previous owner a long time before. It was a pretty timber building standing close to the old house and within the bounds of the garden itself; it was surrounded on three sides by tall lime-trees whose branches touched the roof. Its four rather well furnished rooms were kept ready for guests. On entering the room which had been prepared for me and where my suit-case had already been brought, I noticed on a little bedside table a sheet of notepaper covered in beautiful writing in different styles, full of flourishes and curlicues. Ornate capitals and borders were worked over in various colours. The whole formed a most pretty exercise in calligraphy. From the first words I read I recognized the document as a pleading letter addressed to me, in which I was referred to as 'the enlightened benefactor'. It was headed: *Vidoplyasov's Laments.* I continued to read it, but despite all my efforts I could not make head or tail of the contents; it seemed to be the most inflated nonsense, couched in the high-flown phraseology peculiar to flunkeys. All I could surmise was that Vidoplyasov, finding himself in a dire predicament, entertained high hopes of my ability to help him in view of my education, and was anxious to secure my cooperation in interceding for him with Uncle, who was to be prevailed upon with the aid of 'my machine', as he literally put it at the end of this missive. I was still absorbed in reading when the door opened and Mizinchikov entered.

'I hope you'll permit me to make your acquaintance,' he said, extending his hand in a relaxed but most cordial manner. 'I didn't have an opportunity to say a word to you before, but I felt from the start I'd like to get to know you better.'

I immediately replied that I was delighted and so on and so forth, although in fact I had seldom been in such an unsociable mood. We both sat down.

'What's that?' he said, looking at the sheet of paper which I was still holding in my hand. 'It's not Vidoplyasov's Laments? Just as I thought! I was sure he wouldn't leave you in peace. He gave me a sheet just like that, with just the same laments; he knew you were coming and he must have got one ready in advance. Don't be surprised: there's no end of weird things going on here, there's always something to laugh at.'

'To laugh at – is that all?'

'Well, you don't expect me to cry, do you? If you like, I can tell you Vidoplyasov's life-story, you'll be thoroughly amused, I'm sure.'

'I'm sorry, I can't be bothered with Vidoplyasov now,' I replied with vexation.

It was clear that Mr Mizinchikov's pleasant chatter and interest in me were pursued with an ulterior motive and that he was after something from me. In the drawing-room he had been sullen and pensive, whereas now he was cheerful, smiling and ready to tell lengthy stories. He was clearly a cool, self-possessed person with an insight into human nature.

'Confounded Foma!' I said, angrily bringing down my fist upon the table. 'I'm sure he's the cause of all the mischief here and mixed up in everything! The brute!'

'Aren't you being rather hard on him?' Mizinchikov ventured.

'Rather hard!' I shouted, my temper suddenly rising. 'Certainly I got carried away and anyone is entitled to criticize me. I know I went and thoroughly disgraced myself on all counts, but I don't think there's any need to remind me of it! ... Of course, that's not the way to behave in polite society; but just think, how could I have kept cool? This is a real madhouse, if you want my opinion ... and ... and I'll simply pack up and leave – I will!'

'You smoke?' Mizinchikov asked calmly.

'Yes.'

'Then you won't mind if I do. They won't let me smoke over there and frankly it's a bore. I agree,' he continued, lighting up a cigarette, 'it is a bit like a madhouse, but far be it from me to criticize you because in your shoes I'd probably have lost my temper far sooner.'

'And why didn't you, if you really were so upset? On the contrary, I recall you were completely unconcerned, and I must say it's a shame you didn't speak up for poor Uncle who's always ready to do good to others ... to everyone without exception!'

'You're right: he's helped a lot of people; but I still think it would have been quite useless to have stood up for him: first, it wouldn't have done him the least bit of good, it might even have hurt his dignity; and secondly, I would have been kicked out of the house the very next day. I'll be frank with you: my personal circumstances are such that I daren't take risks with the hospitality of this house.'

'I've no wish to be drawn into your confidence on the subject of your circumstances ... But, seeing that you've been living in this house for over a month, I'd be interested to ask ...'

'Why of course, I'm at your service,' Mizinchikov replied eagerly, drawing his chair closer.

'For instance, how do you explain the fact that Foma had his hands on fifteen thousand rubles in silver and turned it down? I saw it with my own eyes.'

'Is that so? Well, I never!' Mizinchikov exclaimed. 'Do tell me what happened!'

I told him without revealing the 'Your Excellency' episode. Mizinchikov listened with rapt interest, his countenance undergoing a change when I reached the fifteen thousand rubles.

'Brilliant!' he said when I had finished. 'I never thought Foma would be capable of that.'

'All the same, to turn down a sum of money like that! How do you explain it? Could it really be nobility of soul?'

'He turned down fifteen so as to go for thirty later. On second thoughts,' he added after short deliberation, 'I very much doubt if Foma had any definite plan. He is a most impractical person, an artist you could say, in his way. Fifteen thousand ... hm! You see: he'd have gladly accepted the money, but he couldn't resist the temptation to impress, to strike a pose. I tell you, the fellow's such a lily-livered, snivelling old woman – and so puffed up with pride as well!'

Mizinchikov could not conceal his vexation. It was clear he was thoroughly annoyed, perhaps even jealous. I studied him with great curiosity.

'Hm! There are great changes in the air,' he added thoughtfully. 'Yegor Ilyich now worships Foma. Out of the goodness of his heart he may even consent to marry.' Mizinchikov clenched his teeth.

'So you think that idiotic, abnormal marriage with that demented half-wit of a woman will take place after all?'

Mizinchikov looked hard at me.

'The scoundrels!' I burst out.

'As a matter of fact their reasoning is quite sound: they insist it's about time he did something for the family.'

'As if he hadn't done enough!' I cried indignantly. 'How *can* you, how *can* you call marriage to a vulgar fool "sound reasoning"!'

'Of course, I do agree, she is a fool ... Hm! I'm glad you're so fond of your uncle; I have every sympathy for him myself ... her money wouldn't come amiss on the estate, though. Still, they've other reasons too; they're afraid Yegor Ilyich might marry that governess ... you know that rather interesting girl?'

'Surely not ... surely that's impossible!' I exclaimed in extreme agitation. 'I expect it's just idle rumour. Tell me more, for goodness' sake, I'm dying to know ...'

'Oh, he's head over heels in love! But of course, he's trying to keep it secret.'

'Trying to keep it secret! You're sure of that? And what about her? Is she in love with him?'

'It's quite possible that she is. After all, she's got everything to gain by marrying him: she's very poor.'

'But what evidence have you for assuming that they're in love?'

'You can't help noticing it. They're seeing each other on the quiet, I believe. Some people say they're having improper relations. But please – not a word to anyone. This is strictly between ourselves.'

'This is preposterous!' I exclaimed. 'And you, you even admit that you believe it?'

'Of course I don't believe all of it. I wasn't present. On the other hand, it may well be true.'

'*May well be true?* Don't you consider Uncle's dignity, his honour!'

'Naturally; but people do get carried away, and then end up in wedlock. This is not uncommon. However, I repeat, I'm not insisting upon the absolute truth of these stories, especially as the girl herself has been much maligned in this house: they've even said that she had an affair with Vidoplyasov.'

'There you are!' I exclaimed. 'With Vidoplyasov! How can that be true? Isn't the very thought enough to make you squirm? Don't tell me you believe that too?'

'As I said, I've no strong reasons for believing,' Mizinchikov replied coolly. 'On the other hand, it could well have happened. Lots of things happen in this world. I wasn't there, and besides, I don't think it's any of my business. However, seeing as you're so concerned, I feel bound to admit that the suggestion of an affair with Vidoplyasov does seem rather far-fetched. Anna Nilovna's behind it all, you know, Perepelitsyna; it was she who spread the rumour, from sheer jealousy, because she once had designs on Yegor Ilyich herself – honestly! – she reckoned she had a claim on him just because her father was a lieutenant-colonel. Now she's been disappointed, and she's absolutely furious. Well, I think I've told you everything – and let me tell you, I hate gossip, it's such a waste of precious time. You see, I've come to ask you a small favour.'

'A favour? I'd be pleased! Any way in which I can be of service to you . . .'

'I understand, and indeed perhaps I might even be able to persuade you to take an interest in this affair, because I see you are fond of your uncle and seem very concerned about his fate as regards this marriage. But before I go any further I have another preliminary favour to ask.'

'What is it?'

'Well, it's like this: you may or you may not agree to my main request, but whatever happens, before I ask you, I'd humbly beg you to give me your word as an honourable gentleman and a man of principle that what you are about to hear will remain the most closely guarded secret between us, and that under no circumstances whatsoever will you reveal it to anyone, nor will you seek to make personal use of the idea which I must now disclose to you. Do you agree or not?'

It was a very solemn preamble. I gave my consent.

'Well, sir?' I said.

'It's a very simple matter indeed,' Mizinchikov began. 'You see, I want to abduct Tatyana Ivanovna and marry her; you know, like Gretna Green.'

I looked Mizinchikov straight in the eyes and for a while remained totally speechless.

'I must admit, I just don't understand you,' I confessed at long last; 'and what's more,' I continued, 'I thought I was dealing with a person of sense, and for my part I hardly expected –'

'Assumed, expected . . .' Mizinchikov interrupted: 'translated into plain language, you don't think much of me or my idea, am I right?'

'No, not at all . . . but . . .'

'Oh, please don't be afraid to speak your mind! You'll do me a great pleasure: we'll get to the point. I'll agree that this whole business must strike you as rather out of the ordinary. But let me assure you – there's nothing stupid about my plan, on the contrary, it's an extremely sensible proposition; if only you would be so good as to listen to the circumstances as a whole . . .'

'Please go on! I'm waiting to hear.'

'Well, there's nothing much to tell. You see, I've run into debt and I haven't a kopeck to my name. On top of that, I've a sister of about nineteen, an orphan living with a family, practically destitute, you know. I'm partly to blame. We inherited an estate of forty serfs which, as bad luck would have it, coincided with my commission in the cavalry. Well, at first I borrowed on security but then came wine and women. I lived like a fool, I set the fashion, like Burtsov,[31] I gambled, drank — in short, I couldn't have behaved more stupidly . . . I'm ashamed to talk about it. Now I've come to my senses, I'm going to turn over a new leaf. But I've got to get a hundred thousand in cash. As I've no hope of earning anything, I have no practical skill and hardly any education, there are only two ways open to me: either to steal or marry into money. I came here on foot, yes, I walked all but barefoot. My sister gave me her last three rubles when I started out from Moscow. Here I came across Tatyana Ivanovna, and that's when I got the idea: I decided to sacrifice myself and get married. You must agree, this makes perfect sense. Besides, I'm doing it more for my sister . . . of course, for myself as well . . .'

'Just a moment — are you going to propose to Tatyana Ivanovna?'

'God forbid! That would be asking to be kicked out of the house, anyway she'd refuse; but she'll jump at the idea of running away, eloping. As long as I make it romantic and exciting for her. Of course we'd get married legally immediately afterwards. But I must lure her away from here first!'

'What makes you so sure she will definitely elope with you?'

'Oh, don't worry! I'm positive about that. Everything depends on Tatyana Ivanovna's readiness to start an affair with literally anyone she meets, anyone who cares to respond to her. That's why I've asked you to give me your word beforehand not to try and take advantage of me. You will appreciate, I am sure, that it would have been foolish of me not to make use of the opportunity, especially considering my circumstances.'

'She must be totally mad . . . oh! I beg your pardon,' I said, stopping short, 'now that you have designs on her . . .'

'Please don't be embarrassed, I've asked you already. You ask if she really is mad? Well, how shall I put it? Of course she isn't, otherwise she would have been put away; and what's more, I don't see anything specially disturbing in this craze for love affairs. She's an unusually honest girl, in spite of all. You see, she was dreadfully poor until last year, and since the day she was born she'd been under the heel of benefactresses. She's fearfully sensitive, and conscious of never having had a proposal. So you must understand — what with her hopes, desires, aspirations, passions, which have always been bottled up, and the endless taunts from her benefactresses, it's hardly surprising that she's been reduced to such a state. And then suddenly she comes into money; you must agree, that would have unsettled anybody. Now of course they're all after her, she is the centre of attention and all her hopes have been raised. You heard her story about the dandy in the white waistcoat: it's true, it all happened just as she said. This should give you an idea about the rest: secret *billets-doux*, suppressed sighs, love poems, and she's as good as yours; but if in addition you mention silken ladders, Spanish serenades, and all that nonsense – you can do anything you like with her. I've propositioned her already, and got a secret rendezvous. But for the moment I've decided to leave things as they are till a better moment. But in about three or four days' time I've definitely got to get her away from here. First I'll woo her with sweet words and sighs; I can strum on the guitar and sing. A rendezvous at night in the arbour, and by dawn my carriage will be waiting: I'll lure her into it and we'll be away, away! You see, there's no risk: she's of age, and besides, she'll have done it of her own free will. And of course, once she's eloped with me, she'll be under an obligation to me . . . I'll put her in the care of a poor but respectable family – there's one about forty versts from here – where she'll be looked after and cared for till the wedding day, so that nobody else gets their hands on her. In the meantime I'll be making the wedding preparations – shouldn't take me more than three days. Of course I'll need money, but I've worked it out, the whole thing won't cost more than five hundred in silver, and I'm counting on Yegor Ilyich to help me out: he'll give me the money without knowing what's going on. Now do you understand me?'

'Yes,' I said, having grasped the situation fully. 'But tell me, where do I come into all this?'

'Oh, quite a lot, I assure you. Otherwise I'd never have approached you. As I said, I've got a respectable but impoverished family in mind. I'll need your help in various ways – and of course as a witness. Frankly, I'd be lost without your help.'

'Let me ask you: to what do I owe the honour of your confidence in me? I've only been here a few hours and I am a total stranger to you.'

'I'm glad you asked me,' Mizinchikov replied with a friendly smile; 'frankly, your question makes me very happy because it gives me an opportunity to express my profound respect for you.'

'Oh, you do me too much honour!'

'Not at all, you see I've already studied you a little. You may be a trifle emotional and . . . and . . . well, young too; but there's one thing I'm certain about: if you've promised to keep a secret, you'll never break your word. First, you're not like Obnoskin. Secondly, you're honest and would never think of stealing my idea from me, unless of course you decided to enter into a friendly deal with me. In that case I might perhaps be willing to concede you my idea, that is, Tatyana Ivanovna, and I'd do my level best to help you with the elopement – on one condition though, that one month after the wedding you pay me fifty thousand in cash; naturally I'd appreciate some security in advance – say an I O U without interest.'

'What?' I cried, 'you're offering her to me?'

'Naturally I'm quite willing to let you have her, if you should feel so inclined. I shall be the loser, of course ... but the idea is mine and it's worth hard cash. Thirdly, I turned to you because there really isn't anybody else to choose from and, bearing in mind the present circumstances, delay would be disastrous. And what's more, the Fast of the Assumption will soon be upon us and there are no weddings then. You understand me now, I hope.'

'Indeed I do, and let me assure you once again that your secret will remain inviolate with me; but I cannot be your accomplice in this affair, I feel duty bound to make it clear to you here and now.'

'Why?'

'What do you mean, "why"?' I cried, at last giving full vent to my indignation. 'Don't you see that it's a mean trick to play on anybody? Of course your calculations are faultless, based as they are on the frustrations and unhappiness of this pathetic spinster – but that alone should have been enough to deter you as a gentleman! You said yourself she deserves respect even though she is ridiculous. And now you're ready to take advantage of her misfortune so as to squeeze a hundred thousand out of her! You've no intention of being a dutiful husband who will stand by her and accept his responsibilities: you're bound to leave her ... The whole plan is so outrageous that I'm amazed you dared ask me to be your accomplice!'

'My God, what a romantic you are!' Mizinchikov exclaimed, looking at me with unfeigned surprise. 'Come to think of it, it might not be that you're romantic – just that you don't understand what's at stake. You're accusing me of being dishonourable, and yet she and she alone stands to gain in this, not me ... just consider!'

'I'm sure as far as you're concerned, marriage to Tatyana Ivanovna would be the most magnanimous arrangement possible,' I replied with a sarcastic smile.

'How else? Of course it would be the most magnanimous arrangement possible!' shouted Mizinchikov, his temper rising too. 'Just consider: first, I'm sacrificing myself by agreeing to be her husband – isn't that worth something? Secondly, even though she's got at least a cool hundred thousand in silver, I'm only ever going to take one hundred thousand in notes, I have solemnly promised myself not to touch any more in all my life, though I could easily do so — that's worth something too! Finally — try to understand: can she ever have a moment's peace in life? If she's to lead a life of peace, she's got to be relieved of her wealth and committed to a lunatic asylum. Otherwise, she'll be prey to some waiting, fortune-hunting, guitar-strumming, serenading confidence-trickster like Obnoskin, complete with moustachio and goatee beard, who'll seduce her, marry her, pocket all her money and then leave her stranded by the roadside. Take this household, highly respectable you'd think: but she's tolerated here only because everybody is speculating with her money. She must be protected from all these risks! Now, as soon as she's married to me, you understand, there will be no more dangers of that sort. I'll see to it that she comes to no harm whatsoever. First, I shall immediately settle her in Moscow with a respectable, destitute family — not the one I mentioned earlier, another one; my sister will be at her side all the time and she'll be under strict surveillance. She'll be left with at least two hundred and fifty thousand — perhaps three hundred thousand — in cash: imagine how you could live on that! All the pleasures of life will be hers, balls, masquerades, concerts. I shan't even object if she indulges in a little flirtation, but I'll have to safeguard my interests — it will have to be strictly in the realm of fancy, not beyond. At present, anybody can insult her, but all that will stop once she's my wife, Mrs Mizinchikov, for I'll not allow my good name to be sullied, sir! Isn't that worth something? Naturally we shan't be living together. She'll live in Moscow, I'll be somewhere in Petersburg. You might as well know this because I'm not hiding anything from you. Well, what if we do live apart? You've seen her and observed her character: I ask you, is she capable of being a wife who maintains a conjugal relationship with her husband? Could one ever expect her to be constant? She's the most irresponsible creature under the sun! She must have continual variety; she could get married one day and forget all about it the next. And I should make her very miserable indeed if I were to stay with her and expect strict observance of her marital obligations. Naturally, I'll be coming to see her from time to time, once a year or even more, and not just for the sake of her money, I assure you. I said I shan't take more than a hundred thousand, and that's the end of it! I'll be perfectly honourable with her in money matters. By coming to see her for a day or two I shall give her a lot of happiness, and prevent her turning into a bore; I shall laugh with her, tell her jokes, take her to balls, make love to her, give her souvenirs, serenade her, buy her a pekinese; we'll have romantic partings and I'll go on writing love-letters to her. She'll be positively delighted to have such a romantic, amorous and happy husband!

To my mind this is all quite reasonable: if only all husbands behaved like that. Wives never appreciate their husbands more than when they're away: I'll follow my theory and capture Tatyana Ivanovna's affections, I'll hold her in sweet bliss for life. What more could she want, I'd like to know? Life will be sheer heaven for her!'

I listened, too astonished to speak. I could see it would be futile to contradict Mr Mizinchikov. He was obsessed with the righteousness, the grandeur of his plan, and spoke of it with the passion of an inventor. However, there still remained one tricky matter which had to be resolved.

'Have you considered,' I said, 'that she's already virtually Uncle's fiancée? If you elope with her, you'll hurt him badly; you'll be abducting her on the eve of her wedding-day, and on top of that, you'll be borrowing the money to finance your project from him!'

'Ah, that's where you're wrong!' Mizinchikov cried out in excitement. 'Don't worry, I was expecting you to raise that objection. First and most important: as yet your uncle has not actually proposed; so I could have been unaware of any plans afoot for her betrothal. And don't forget, I conceived my plan three weeks ago, when I still knew nothing at all about what was going on here, and therefore as far as he's concerned I'm morally perfectly within my rights; strictly speaking, I'm not taking his bride away from him at all, it's more like the reverse, and – remember – I've already had a secret midnight meeting with her in the summer-house. And lastly, if I may say so, just now you were fuming with indignation that your uncle was being made to marry Tatyana Ivanovna, and now you're suddenly defending this marriage and talking of honour and insults to the family! No – it's me who's doing your uncle an enormous favour – I'm rescuing him – surely you understand that! He's dead set against this marriage, and what's more he's in love with somebody else! What sort of a wife would Tatyana Ivanovna make him? And on top of everything, she's bound to be unhappy with him because sooner or later someone will have to stop her throwing roses at strange young men. But once I've abducted her in the night, neither Foma nor the General's Lady will be able to do anything about it. It'll be too scandalous to bring back a bride who has fled from the altar. Now isn't that doing your uncle a service, a really good turn?'

I must admit this last remark really made me stop and think.

'But what if he proposes tomorrow?' I said. 'Surely it'll be too late then? They'll be officially engaged.'

'Of course it'll be too late! That's exactly why we have to work fast to prevent it. Why do you think I'm asking for your cooperation? I couldn't possibly handle it on my own, but the two of us could make sure that Yegor Ilyich doesn't propose to her. We've got to stop him! We may even have to give Foma a beating to divert everybody's attention – they'll not think of weddings then. Of course, this would only be a last resort; I'm only making a suggestion. You're my only hope.'

'One final question: have you told anybody else besides me about this scheme?'

Mizinchikov scratched his head and made a very wry face.

'I must admit,' he replied, 'your question is worse than the most bitter pill for me. I have, that's the whole trouble ... what a fool I've been! I mentioned it to Obnoskin, of all people! I can hardly believe it myself now! I've no idea how I came to do it! He was always snooping about; I hardly knew him at the time, and when the idea first occurred to me I was in a daze; the one thing I was clear about was that I needed an accomplice, so I turned to Obnoskin ... Unforgivable, unforgivable!'

'Well, what did he have to say?'

'He jumped at the idea, and early the very next day he vanished. A couple of days later he came back with his mother. Kept avoiding me and wouldn't say a word, as though he was afraid. I immediately guessed what was going on. His mother's a sly one – she's been up to every trick you can imagine. I know her of old. Of course, he told her everything. I'm waiting now and keeping quiet, while they snoop around. The situation is rather tense ... That's why I'm in a hurry.'

'What exactly are you afraid of?'

'There's not much they can do – but they're bound to make some sort of mischief. For a start they'll want money to keep quiet and not interfere: that I can expect ... Only I'm not in a position to give them much – my mind's made up; they won't get more than three thousand in notes. Judge for yourself: three thousand here, five hundred in silver for the wedding which I'll have to pay back to your uncle; then some old debts of my own – well, something for my sister, just a little. A hundred thousand won't go very far! I'll be ruined again! ... By the way, the Obnoskins have left.'

'Left?' I asked with interest.

'Yes, straight after tea; anyway, to hell with them! They'll be back again tomorrow, you'll see. Well then, can I rely on you?'

'To be honest,' I replied, wincing inwardly, 'I don't know what to say. It's a tricky proposition ... Of course, your secret is quite safe with me, don't mistake me for an Obnoskin ... but I'd rather you didn't rely on me.'

'I can see,' said Mizinchikov, getting up, 'you're still prepared to put up with Foma and the old lady, and fond though you are of your kind, noble uncle, you don't fully appreciate what he's being subjected to. You're new here . . . But patience! If you stay here tomorrow, you'll see for yourself, and by the end of the day you'll agree. Otherwise your uncle is doomed — you understand? They're certain to marry him off. Don't forget, he may even propose tomorrow. It'll be too late then; tonight is the time for a decision!'

'I do wish you every success, but as for helping . . . I honestly don't know.'

'Very well! Let's wait till tomorrow,' Mizinchikov decided with a derisive smile. '*La nuit porte conseil. Au revoir.* I'll see you first thing in the morning. Think it over . . .'

He turned and left, whistling a tune.

I went out after him for a breath of fresh air. The moon was not up yet; the night was dark, warm and close. The foliage in the trees was motionless. Though I was extremely tired, I decided to take a short stroll to refresh myself and collect my thoughts in peace, but I had not walked ten paces when I suddenly heard Uncle's voice. He was mounting the flight of steps to the house and talking excitedly to someone. I immediately turned back and called to him. He was with Vidoplyasov.

'Uncle!' I said, 'there you are at last!'

'My boy, I've been dying to see you myself. Just let me finish with Vidoplyasov — and then we'll talk our hearts out. I've got a lot of things to tell you.'

'What! Not Vidoplyasov again! Leave him be, Uncle!'

'Give me five or ten minutes more, Sergey, and then I'll be at your disposal. I really am busy.'

'He's probably just fooling about,' I said, disappointed . . .

'Well, what do you want me to say to you, my friend? Some people just will not learn! Really, my good Grigory, you couldn't have picked a worse time for your complaints! So what can I do for you? Have pity on me, you of all people. You've all done for me — eaten me alive and whole! I'm at the end of my tether, Sergey!'

And Uncle waved both his arms in the utmost distress.

'Well, what's so important that it can't wait? I have an important matter myself, Uncle . . .'

'My dear boy, I'm forever being blamed for neglecting my servants' morals! What if he complains tomorrow that I've not even bothered to hear him out? . . .'

And Uncle waved his arm again.

'All right, try and get it over quickly! And let me help you. Why don't we go inside? . . . What's the matter with him? What's he up to?' I asked as we went indoors.

'Well, you see, my boy, he's taken a dislike to his own surname and he wants to change it. What do you make of that?'

'Surname? How so . . .? Uncle,' I said, my arms spread in consternation, 'before I listen to him — let me tell you that your house must be the only one where such goings-on are possible.'

'That's all very well, my boy,' Uncle remarked sadly, 'I can wave my arms too, but what's the use! You just try and talk to him yourself. He's been at me for the last two months . . .'

'It's an unbecoming surname!' declared Vidoplyasov.

'Why unbecoming?' I inquired with surprise.

'Well, it is. It's vulgar and base.'

'Why base? Anyway, how do you propose to change it? Whoever heard of such a thing?'

'And whoever heard of such a surname?'

'I do agree that your surname is a trifle unusual,' I continued, still unable to overcome my astonishment, 'but what can you do now? After all, your father rejoiced in the same name.'

'That's the scandal of it all,' Vidoplyasov replied, 'that I should suffer eternally because of my father, and have to endure insults and gibes on account of my name.'

'I'll wager a bet that Foma is behind all this, Uncle!' I exclaimed bitterly.

'No, no, my boy; you're mistaken. True, Foma does favour him. He's made him his secretary and absolved him from all other obligations. Well, naturally this has had an edifying effect upon him, it has spiritually renewed him and, in a sense, opened his eyes ... You see, there's so much to tell you ...'

'Just so!' Vidoplyasov interrupted. 'Foma Fomich is my true benefactor, and being my true benefactor he has inculcated in me the knowledge of my own insignificance, puny worm that I am, and a vision of my own destiny has for the first time been revealed to me through him.'

'There you are, Sergey, there – you see how it is?' Uncle continued, his words falling over each other as usual. 'First he lived in Moscow, from childhood more or less, working for a teacher of calligraphy. You should see how he learned to write there: coloured and gold letters with cupids all round – a real artist, I tell you! Now he's teaching Ilyusha – he's charging me one-and-a-half rubles. He visits three other neighbouring landowners and they pay up too. See how he dresses! And he writes poetry too.'

'Poetry! That's all we need.'

'Poetry, my boy, poetry, and I'm not joking either, true poetry, real versification on any subject you like – you name it, he'll rhyme it. A deuce of a talent! Take the huge poem he delivered on Mother's name-day. Left us all speechless: full of mythology and Muses on the wing, so lifelike you could almost see their ... dash it, what was it again? – rotundity of form ... and all in strict and regular metre. With Foma's help, you understand. Well, of course, I had no objection. On the contrary, I'm glad, as long as it keeps him out of mischief. I'm now speaking to you as your father, my dear Grigory. Anyway, Foma has been giving him every encouragement and has engaged him as his reader and copyist – in short, educated him. He's every reason to be grateful. Hence his refined romantic notions and feeling of independence – Foma explained it all to me. Yes, I quite forgot, I was planning to grant him his freedom anyway. After all, one can't help feeling it's wrong somehow ... But Foma talked me out of it as he needs Grigory's services and he's very fond of him; and besides, he said to me: "It's a matter of pride that a landowner like me should keep a versifier among his serfs" – some baron he knows keeps one too. "That really is living *en grand*," he said. Well, if he wants to live *en grand*, let him! I've developed a respect for him myself, do you see? ... Only, my God, the way he behaves now. The worst of it is that he's turned into a perfect snob because of his poetry – he won't even speak to the rest of them. No offence, Grigory, I'm only speaking to you as your father. Last winter he promised he would get married: there's an excellent girl here, Matryona, one of the serfs, you know, very sweet, industrious, honest and lively. Now he just won't have her: he refuses point blank. I wonder if it's all gone to his head, or perhaps he wants to see himself famous first and then look around for a better match ...'

'It's more on advice from Foma Fomich,' Vidoplyasov interposed, 'he, as my true benefactor ...'

'Yes indeed, is anything ever possible without Foma Fomich!' I couldn't help myself exclaiming.

'No, my boy, that's not the point!' Uncle interrupted hastily. 'You see, he's in a bad way now. The girl is a high-spirited and mischievous thing, she has set everybody against him: wherever he turns he gets laughed and jeered at, even the village children make a fool of him ...'

'And it's Matryona that's to blame,' Vidoplyasov remarked. 'She really is a stupid, silly girl, that Matryona – she's a woman of unruly temperament – it's because of her I have to endure a life of insults.'

'My dear Grigory, when will you learn?' Uncle said, glancing reproachfully at Vidoplyasov. 'You see, Sergey, they made up a couple of disgusting lines to rhyme with his surname and now he's complaining and begging me to have it changed; he says he's never been really happy with the way it sounds.'

'Yes, it is a graceless name,' Vidoplyasov put in.

'Keep quiet, Grigory! Foma has given his approval ... well, he hasn't exactly approved, but you see, there is this to remember: if the verses get printed, as Foma plans, then a name like his might turn out a handicap – don't you think?'

'So, Uncle, he wants to publish his poems, does he?'

'Yes, quite, my boy. It's all been settled – I'm paying for it. On the title-page it will say: "The bonded serf of ** " and there will be an introduction with the author's acknowledgement to Foma for providing his education. The book will be dedicated to Foma, and Foma himself will write the introduction. Now just imagine if, after all this, the work is called *Vidoplyasov's Compositions* . . .'

'*Vidoplyasov's Laments*, sir,' Vidoplyasov corrected.

'Well, there you are, it's *Laments* now! Anyway, how can the author be called Vidoplyasov? It's an offence to the finer feelings; that's what Foma says too. Then again, you've got to consider the critics – what a merciless lot they can be: Brambeus, for instance . . . They'll stop at nothing! Any excuse for tearing an author to pieces, even his name! They'll give you such a going-over, you'll be smarting for evermore – that's true, isn't it? So I said: look here, as far as I'm concerned, you can put any name you like to the verses – a pseudonym, that's what they call it, isn't it? Some *nym* anyway. Oh no, he says, I want you to see that everybody in the house calls me by my new name, and it should be refined, as befits my talent . . .'

'And I bet you agreed, Uncle?'

'My dear Seryozha, anything for a quiet life; let him! I had my hands full with Foma at the time. And then it started: every week he used to come up with a new version; very genteel, some of them: Oleandrov, Tulpanov . . . Just think, Grigory, first you wanted to be called simply "The Faithful" – "Grigory the Faithful"; then you wanted it changed, because some damned fool turned it into "Disgraceful".[32] You complained – the culprit was punished. You spent the next two weeks looking for a new surname – think how many you tried! – finally you settled upon "Uhlanov". Now tell me, my friend, what could be more ridiculous than Uhlanov?[33] But I didn't object: I put in a second order for your surname to be changed – to "Uhlanov". I assure you, my boy,' Uncle added, turning to me, 'just to get him off my back. For three days you walked around as "Uhlanov". You made a mess of every wall and window-sill in the summer-house with pencil scrawls of your new signature. "Uhlanov". Do you know, the summer-house was in such a state it had to be repainted. You ruined reams of best parchment paper with "Uhlanov, *sample signature*", "Uhlanov, *sample signature*". Finally, disaster again – somebody added: "Silly old Bolvanov".[34] You didn't like it – another change of surname! What did you choose next, I forget now?'

'Tantsev,' Vidoplyasov replied. 'If I am to present myself as a dancer through my name, let it have a refined, foreign-sounding flavour, Tantsev.'

'That's right, Tantsev. I gave in yet again, my dear Sergey. Only this time they rhymed it with something I daren't repeat. So he's back today with something new again. I bet you anything, he's got another surname ready. Have you or have you not? I want the truth, Grigory!'

'Yes – I've been wanting to submit my refined name to you for a long time.'

'What is it?'

'Essbouquetov.'

'Shame on you, shame on you, Grigory! Straight off a powder box! And you call yourself a sensible fellow! Why couldn't you have given it a bit of thought! It's a name you see on a bottle of perfume.'

'Uncle, please,' I said in a half-whisper, 'he's just a fool, a half-wit!'

'Can't be helped, my boy!' Uncle replied, also in a whisper. 'Everybody thinks he's clever and that it's his noble qualities at work . . .'

'Get rid of him, for heaven's sake!'

'Listen, Grigory! – you see I'm busy, have a heart, my friend!' Uncle began plaintively, as if Vidoplyasov too was somebody to be afraid of. 'You've got to understand, I can't deal with your troubles now! You say you've been insulted again? Very well: I give you my word – I'll go into it all tomorrow, but be off with you now . . . Wait! How is Foma Fomich?'

'He's retired to rest. If anyone inquires, I'm to say he'll be at prayer long into the night.'

'Hm! Well, off you go now, off you go, my friend! You see, Seryozha, he and Foma are inseparable now, so I'm wary of him. The servants aren't fond of him either because he reports everything back to Foma. He's gone now, but who knows what he'll come up with tomorrow! You see, my boy, I've just managed to get everything settled, so it's a weight off my chest . . . I was in such a hurry to see you. At last we're together again!' He shook my hand with feeling. 'You know, I thought you'd be mad with anger and give me the slip. I even had someone keep an eye on you. Everything's fine now, thank God! What did you think of Gavrila's little act though, eh? And then Falaley, then you – one thing after another! Anyway, thank God, thank God! Now I can talk to you to my heart's content. Sergey, you mustn't leave me: you're all I've got now, you and Korovkin . . .'

'Just a minute, Uncle, what is it that you've managed to settle? And by the way – what's the point of my staying here after what's happened? My head's reeling!'

'And you suppose mine isn't? It's been whirling in a waltz for the last six months if you want to know! But, thank God, everything has been settled now. First, I've been granted a pardon, a full pardon, with some conditions attached, of course; but at least I'm not afraid of anything any more. Sasha has also been pardoned. Sashenka, Sashenka, bless her heart! ... She got carried away a little this afternoon, but her heart's in the right place! I'm proud of this girl of mine, Seryozha! May the Good Lord bless and protect her always! You've been pardoned too – and you know how generously? You are free to do anything you wish, you may enter any of the rooms and go into the garden, even when there are guests – in short, you are free to do whatever you please; but on one condition only, that tomorrow you don't say a word in front of Foma and Mamma – this is an essential condition, not a syllable, understand? I've promised already that you will – just listen to what your elders and betters ... I mean what the others have to say! They say you're very young still. Don't be cross, Sergey; you really are young, you know ... Anna Nilovna said so too ...'

Of course I was very young, and immediately gave proof of it by flying into a rage at such humiliating conditions.

'Listen, Uncle,' I shouted, fairly choking with anger, 'just tell me one thing to put my mind at rest: have I wandered into a madhouse or have I not?'

'Now, now, my boy, what an impulsive fellow you are! Pull yourself together, my boy,' Uncle replied, visibly distressed. 'Who said anything about a madhouse? You lost your temper as much as he did. You must admit you went rather too far. My, how you tore into him – a man of his years commands respect.'

'A man like him commands no respect, whatever his age, Uncle!'

'Well, that's really too much, my boy! That's free-thinking! I'm all for rational free-thinking, but not if it goes to such lengths, I mean, you really do surprise me, Sergey.'

'Don't be angry, Uncle. I'm in the wrong, but only as far as you're concerned. As for your Foma ...'

'There you go again, why *your*? My dear Sergey, don't judge him too harshly: he's a misanthrope, that's all, sick at heart! You can't ask too much of him. He's a noble man, the noblest alive, there's no getting away from it! You've just seen him yourself – wasn't he magnificent? As for his little tantrums, they're not worth talking about. It happens to all of us!'

'But Uncle, on the contrary, who does it happen to?'

'There you go again! You haven't any compassion, Seryozha; you don't know what it is to forgive! ...'

'All right, Uncle, all right! Let's not talk about it any more. Tell me, have you seen Nastasya Yevgrafovna?'

'My boy, she's the cause of it all. Look here, Seryozha, first things first: we've all decided to wish him many happy returns tomorrow on his birthday, Foma I mean, because it really is his birthday tomorrow. Sashenka's a fine girl, but she's wrong. Anyway, we're all going together in a congregation, nice and early, before the service. Ilyusha's going to read him some poems, which will please him no end – flattery's the best policy. Seryozha, if only you too would join us in congratulating him! He would probably forgive you altogether! Wouldn't it be marvellous if you made it up with him! Stop feeling sorry for yourself! You know you wronged him too . . . He's the worthiest of men!'

'Uncle! Uncle!' I exclaimed, my patience exhausted. 'I want to discuss something serious, while you . . . Do you know – I repeat, do you *know* what Nastasya Yevgrafovna is having to endure?'

'Hush, my boy, hush! Don't shout! Why do you think it all blew up just now? I mean, it really started long ago, but I kept it from you so as not to upset you too much. They were planning to turn her out of the house and insisted that I should be the one to do it. Can you imagine my position . . . Well, thank God, everything's been settled now. You see, they thought – I might as well be perfectly frank with you – that I was in love with her and wanted to marry her myself; in short, that I was set to bring about my own downfall – because it really would have been my downfall; they explained it all to me . . . so in order to save me, they decided to turn her out. It's all Mamma's idea, but Anna Nilovna's most of all. Foma hasn't said anything yet. But I've managed to put their minds at rest, and you might as well know, I've announced that you're already engaged to Nastenka, and that's why I asked you to come. Well, this eased their minds somewhat, and she can stay on now, not permanently but for a trial period, anyway, she's staying. You rose in their estimation too when I announced your engagement. Mamma at all events seemed to calm down. The only one who keeps grumbling is Anna Nilovna! I wish I could think of some way of humouring her. What on earth can she want, this Anna Nilovna of ours!'

'Uncle, how you deceive yourself! Don't you realize that Nastasya Yevgrafovna is leaving tomorrow, if she hasn't left already? Don't you realize her father has come today for the express purpose of taking her away, that everything has been decided and that she personally told him all about it today and asked me to say goodbye to you for her? Do you or don't you realize this?'

Uncle stared at me open-mouthed. It seemed to me he shuddered and let out an involuntary groan.

I wasted no time in recounting to him the whole of my conversation with Nastenka: my proposal, her outright rejection, her indignation that he should have sent for me by letter; I explained that by departing now she was hoping to save him from marriage to Tatyana Ivanovna – in short, I concealed nothing and even took extra care to exaggerate the unpleasant aspects of events. My aim was to shock Uncle so as to compel him to take a firm stand – and I certainly succeeded in shocking him. He uttered a cry and buried his head in his hands.

'Where is she, do you know? Where is she now?' he said at last, pale with fright. 'What a fool I am,' he added in despair, 'relaxing and imagining everything had been settled.'

'I don't know where she is now,' I replied, 'except that she was on her way to see you after the shouting started, to discuss the matter openly, in everybody's presence. I expect somebody stopped her.'

'Of course they stopped her. Heaven knows what she might have done! Oh, the proud, reckless thing! Where can she go? Where? Where? And you, you're a nice one! Why should she have turned you down? What foolishness! You ought to have won her over. Why didn't you? Answer me, for God's sake, don't just stand there!'

'That's a fine question to ask! I give up, Uncle!'

'That's no way out! You must marry her, you must. Why do you think I made you come all the way from Petersburg? You've got to make her happy! They won't let her stay as she is – but as your wife and my niece, nobody would be able to lay a hand on her. But where can she go now? What will become of her? Will she be a governess again? How idiotic – a governess! And how will she survive while she's looking for a place? Her old father has nine mouths to feed; they're starving as it is. And if this vile gossip means she'll have to go, she'll not accept a penny of my money, nor will her father. Anyway, how can she just pack up and leave? It's all dreadful! There's bound to be a scandal – I know it. All her salary's been paid in advance to cover the family needs: she's the one who feeds them. Well, suppose I do recommend her as a governess, and manage to find her an honest, decent family ... Damnation! Where do you start looking for these honest, decent people? Of course, don't misunderstand me, God forbid, they're there, plenty of them! But, my boy, it's still a risk: how can you trust people? Besides, poverty breeds suspicion; the poor are never sure they're not expected to demean themselves in return for the charity they receive! What if she's insulted?

She's quick to take offence. Then what? . . . What then? And if on top of it all some rogue were to seduce her? . . . She'd spit in his face – I know she would – but all the same, the rascal would still have abused her, her good name would still have been tarnished, there'd be suspicion, and then . . . My head's spinning like mad! Dear God!'

'Uncle! I do beg your pardon, but I must ask you one question,' I said solemnly. 'Don't be angry with me – your answer may solve a lot of problems: in a way I have the right to insist on an answer, Uncle!'

'What, what? What question?'

'Tell me before God, truthfully and plainly: do you not feel a little in love with Nastasya Yevgrafovna, and wouldn't you like to marry her yourself? After all, remember that's precisely why they're trying to turn her out.'

Uncle made a convulsive gesture indicating that he had reached the limit of his patience.

'Me – in love? With her? Everybody's gone stark raving mad – or is it a conspiracy against me? Why do you think I sent for you if it wasn't to prove that they've all gone off their heads? Why am I asking you to propose to her? Me – in love? With her? You're as crazy as the rest of them!'

'If that's the case, then you'd better listen to me, Uncle. I can tell you, in all sincerity, that I see absolutely nothing wrong in the idea. On the contrary, you could make her very happy if you love her so much, and – God grant it may be so! May the good Lord send you love and good counsel!'

'The things you say!' Uncle exclaimed, visibly shocked. 'I really am surprised you can talk about all this so coolly . . . and . . . anyway my boy, you always seem to be in such a hurry – I notice this about you. Well, isn't what you are saying preposterous? Tell me, how could I marry her if I regard her as my daughter pure and simple? It would be downright disgraceful to look upon her in any other way, it would be sinful. Here I am, an old man – and she a sweet little rosebud! Even Foma explained it to me in these very words. My heart is full of paternal concern for her – and you talk of marriage! Out of sheer gratitude, she might be prepared to give in to me – but wouldn't she despise me later for taking advantage of her! I'd be the ruin of her, and lose her affection. Why, of course, I'd sacrifice my soul for her, my darling girl! I love her just as much as Sashenka, even more, you might as well know. Sashenka is my rightful, lawful daughter; but the other is my daughter by choice of love alone. I rescued her from poverty, I brought her up. My angel Katya, may her soul rest in peace, loved her too, and left her in my care as a daughter. I educated her: she can speak French, and play the piano, and read books, and everything . . . What a smile she has! Have you noticed, Seryozha? You'd almost think she's mocking you, and yet nothing of the kind, she's full of love . . . So I thought you'd come and propose to her to satisfy them I've no designs on her, and stop them spreading all those nasty rumours. She'd then stay with us here in peace and quiet, and how happy we'd all be together! You're both my children, as good as orphans, I brought you both up . . . How I'd love you both, how I'd love you! I'd give my life for you, we'd always be together; always as one! Oh, how happy we could all be! Why is it people are angry, bitter, full of hatred for one another! If only – if only I could explain everything to them! If only I could lay the whole simple truth before them! Oh, my God!'

'This is all very well, Uncle, but she still turned me down.'

'Turned you down, did she? Hm! . . . You know, I had a feeling she would,' Uncle said thoughtfully. 'No, no!' he exclaimed, 'I don't believe it! It's impossible! Well, in that case, everything's off! You must have been careless in your approach, you may have offended her in some way, or started overdoing the compliments . . . Tell me again what happened, Sergey!'

Again I repeated everything in the minutest detail. When I reached the point where Nastenka had expressed the hope that her departure would save Uncle from marriage to Tatyana Ivanovna, he smiled wryly.

'Save me indeed!' he said. 'Save me till tomorrow morning!'

'You don't mean to tell me, Uncle, that you're going to marry Tatyana Ivanovna?' I exclaimed in alarm.

'Well, that's the price I have to pay for letting Nastenka stay on! Tomorrow I propose; I've promised.'

'And your mind's made up, Uncle?'

'What's to be done, my boy, what's to be done! It breaks my heart, but my mind's made up. Tomorrow I propose; we've agreed the wedding will be a quiet one, just the family; it'll be better if it's just the family. You'll probably be best man. I've already dropped the hint to them, so they won't try to get rid of you just yet. Couldn't be helped, my boy! They've been saying, "The children will be wealthy!" And, of course, what wouldn't one do for one's own children? I'd stand on my head if it were any use; it's only fair, I suppose. I've got to do something for the family, you know. Can't be a sponger all my life!'

'But, Uncle, she's mad!' I cried, beside myself, and my heart tightened in pain.

'What do you mean — mad! She's not mad at all, she's had a raw deal from life ... What can I do, my boy? I suppose I'd have preferred somebody brainier ... but the brainy ones can be a handful too! She has such a kind heart, if only you knew!'

'Good God! He's already reconciled to the thought!' I said to myself in desperation.

'What else could I have done? They're trying to help me, you know, and besides, I could see it was bound to happen sooner or later — I'd never have got out of it: they'd have married me off. So why not have it over and done with and not go on quarrelling. I'll be frank with you, Seryozha, I'm downright glad in a way. No point in shilly-shallying once your mind's made up — might as well be done with it and have some peace. When I came here, I really imagined I'd nothing to worry about. Such is my luck! The main thing was that Nastenka was going to stay on. That was my condition ... And now she wants to run away! It's out of the question!' He stamped his foot. 'Listen, Sergey,' he added in a firm tone, 'wait here, don't go away! I'll be back directly.'

'Where are you off to, Uncle?'

'Perhaps I might be able to see her, Sergey. Everything will be cleared up, believe me, everything will be cleared up and ... and ... and you will marry her — I give you my word of honour!'

Uncle quickly left the room and turned away from the house into the garden. I watched him through the window.

Catastrophe

I was alone. My position was intolerable: my suit had been rejected and here was Uncle set on marrying me off by default, it would seem. I was confused and lost in a tangle of thoughts. Mizinchikov and his proposition haunted and obsessed me. Uncle had to be rescued at all costs.

It even occurred to me to go and look for Mizinchikov and tell him everything. But where could Uncle have gone to? He had said he would look for Nastenka, but why had he gone into the garden? Thoughts of secret meetings flashed through my mind, and my heart was gripped by a most unpleasant feeling. Mizinchikov's words about a clandestine relationship were still fresh in my memory ... After a moment's thought I indignantly thrust aside all my suspicions. Uncle was above deception: that much was clear. My disquiet was mounting rapidly. I stepped out on the porch and wandered off aimlessly into the garden, following the same path that Uncle had taken. The moon was beginning to rise. I knew the garden well and was in no fear of getting lost. Reaching the ramshackle summer-house which stood isolated on the bank of the old overgrown pond, I suddenly stopped dead: voices were coming from inside. I can hardly describe the feeling of vexation that suddenly overcame me. I was convinced it was Uncle and Nastenka, but walked on, salving my conscience with the thought that, as I had not changed my pace, I was not trying to steal up on them. Suddenly there was the unmistakable sound of a kiss, then an animated exchange of words, followed immediately by a woman's piercing scream. The next moment a female form in white rushed out of the summer-house and flashed past me like a swallow. I even had the impression she was shielding her face with her hands to avoid being recognized; in all probability I had been spotted from within. But what amazed me even more was that hard on the heels of the affrighted lady came Obnoskin, the self-same Obnoskin who, according to Mizinchikov, had departed long ago! On seeing me, he became terribly embarrassed; gone was all his former arrogance.

'I beg your pardon, but ... I never expected to meet you,' he said, smiling and stuttering.

'Nor I you,' I replied with derision. 'Especially as I heard you had left.'

'No ... that is ... I just saw Mamma off to a place not far from here. But may I appeal to you as to the most honourable man in the world?'

'What about?'

'There are occasions – and I trust you will agree with me – when an honourable man is obliged to appeal to all that is honourable in another honourable man ... I hope you understand me ...'

'Don't build up your hopes – I haven't the least idea.'

'Did you see the lady who was with me in the summer-house?'

'I did, but I didn't recognize her.'

'Ah, so you didn't recognize her! ... This lady I shall soon call my wife.'

'Congratulations. But how can I be of service?'

'In just one thing: by keeping it absolutely secret that you saw me with this lady.'

I wondered who it could have been – surely not ...

'Really, I don't know,' I replied. 'I hope you'll excuse me, but I cannot make any such promises ...'

'For the love of God, please,' Obnoskin implored. 'Try to understand the position I'm in: it's a secret! You may get married one day, then I, in my turn ...'

'Shh! Someone's coming!'

'Where?'

And sure enough, a faint, shadowy figure appeared for a moment not thirty paces from where we were standing.

'It's ... it's probably Foma Fomich,' Obnoskin whispered, trembling in every limb. 'I recognize the way he walks. Oh my God! Someone else is coming from the other direction! Do you hear? ... Goodbye! Thank you, and ... I do beg you ...'

Obnoskin vanished. A few seconds later Uncle appeared before me, it seemed from nowhere.

'Is that you?' he called out. 'All is lost, Seryozha! All is lost!'

I noticed that he too was trembling in every limb.

'What is lost, Uncle?'

'Come!' he said breathlessly as he grabbed me firmly by the arm and dragged me after him. He said not a word all the way back to my room, nor would he let me speak. I was expecting something quite out of the ordinary, and was hardly disappointed. When we entered, he fainted; he was as pale as a corpse. I immediately threw some water over him. 'Something really terrible must have happened,' I thought, 'to make a man like him faint.'

'Uncle, what's the matter with you?' I asked at last.

'Everything's ruined, Seryozhya. Foma caught me and Nastenka in the garden just as I was kissing her.'

'Kissing? In the garden!' I exclaimed, looking at him in astonishment.

'Yes, in the garden, my boy. Don't know what came over me. I simply had to go out and see her; I wanted to tell her everything and make her see reason — about you, that is. And it turned out she had been waiting for me one whole hour on that broken bench on the far side of the pond . . . She often goes there when we have something to discuss.'

'Often, Uncle?'

'Yes, my boy! Lately we've been meeting there nearly every night. So they must have spied on us — in fact I know they have, and it's Anna Nilovna's doing. We had stopped seeing each other for a while — four days we held back; but tonight we just had to meet again. You know yourself how necessary it was — how could I have spoken to her otherwise? I went there hoping to find her, and she'd been waiting a whole hour for me: she had something important to tell me too . . .'

'My God, how careless of you! You must have known you were being watched!'

'It was an emergency, Seryozha; there was such a lot to be discussed. I never dare so much as look at her during the day. We both look in different directions as though the other didn't exist. But at night we meet and talk our hearts out . . .'

'Well, what next, Uncle?'

'I had hardly spoken two words, d'you see, my heart had begun to pound and I was on the point of tears. As soon as I began to try to persuade her to marry you, she said: "You obviously don't love me — you obviously don't see what's going on," and then she flung her arms round my neck and began to cry and sob! "You're the only one I love," she said, "and I shan't marry anybody else. I've been in love with you a long time now, but I shan't marry you either because I'm off to a nunnery tomorrow . . ."'

'Well I never! Did she really say that? Then what, Uncle, then what?'

'I looked up and there was Foma! No idea where he came from, he may have been hiding behind a bush waiting for his chance for all I know!'

'The wretch!'

'I was struck dumb. Nastenka began running, while he walked past us without saying a word and shook his finger at me. Do you realize, Sergey, what a to-do there'll be tomorrow?'

'Yes, I can imagine!'

'Do you understand,' he cried in despair, jumping to his feet, 'do you understand they want to ruin her, disgrace her, dishonour her, they want to cast a slur upon her and then turn her out of the house? And now they've got an excuse! After all, they did say I was having an improper relationship with her! And the villains did say she had an affair with Vidoplyasov! It's Anna Nilovna who started it all! What's going to happen now? What will happen tomorrow? Will Foma really tell everyone?'

'You can be sure of that, Uncle.'

'He wouldn't dare, he wouldn't dare . . .' Uncle said, biting his lips and clenching his fists. 'No, I don't believe it! He won't tell anybody, he'll understand . . . he's a thorough gentleman! He will spare her!'

'Whether he will or whether he won't,' I replied resolutely, 'in any case it is your duty to propose to Nastasya Yevgrafovna tomorrow.'

Uncle stared at me.

'Do you understand, Uncle, that if word spreads, her reputation will be ruined? Do you understand that to prevent disaster you must act as soon as possible; that you must look everybody proudly in the eye, announce your engagement, and to hell with all their objections? As for Foma, you must grind him into the dust if he says anything against her!'

'My dear boy!' Uncle exclaimed, 'that's just what I was thinking on my way here!'

'And have you decided?'

'Absolutely! My mind was made up even before I spoke to you!'

'Bravo, Uncle!' And I embraced him warmly.

Our conversation continued for a long time. I put before him all the arguments, all the pressing reasons for his marrying Nastenka, which I must say he appreciated even better than I did. I got carried away by my own eloquence. I was overwhelmed with joy for Uncle. I did my best to spur him on, convinced that otherwise he would never dare to stand up for himself. Duty and obligation were sacred to him. Nevertheless, I still had no idea how things would actually turn out. I knew without a shadow of doubt that Uncle would never go back on anything he considered to be his duty; but I was still not convinced he would have the strength to go against his household. And so I did my best to inspire him and urge him on with all the youthful fervour at my command.

'That's the whole point, that's the whole point,' I said. 'Everything has been settled and all your doubts resolved! Something you never expected has become clear – although everybody else has been aware of it for some time: Nastasya Yevgrafovna loves you! Surely,' I cried, 'you would never let this pure and innocent love bring shame and dishonour upon her?'

'Never! But, my dear boy, is it really true I am going to be so happy?' exclaimed Uncle, embracing me heartily. 'How is it she has fallen in love with me? What does she see in me? What? I'm an old man beside her! I'm staggered! My angel, my angel! ... Listen, Seryozha, you asked me a while ago if I was in love with her; did you have anything in mind when you asked me that?'

'I meant, Uncle, that you were as much in love as anybody could be and you didn't even know it. Just think! You brought me here to marry her simply so that she could stay on with you as your niece ...'

'And ... and do you forgive me, Sergey?'

'Oh, Uncle!'

And he embraced me again.

'But be careful, Uncle! Everybody's against you. You've got to stand up and fight – and tomorrow, mind.'

'Yes ... yes, tomorrow!' he repeated thoughtfully, 'and yes, we'll go about it with courage, strength of character, and true nobility of spirit ... yes, that's right, with nobility of spirit!'

'Don't give in, Uncle!'

'Never, Seryozha! Just one thing: how do I go about it, how do I start?'

'Don't think about it, Uncle. Everything will be settled tomorrow. Just rest today. The more you think about it, the worse it will be. And if Foma so much as opens his mouth – kick him out immediately, grind him into the dust.'

'But maybe there's no need to kick him out? This is what I've decided, my boy. I'm going straight to him tomorrow morning, at daybreak, to have a good long chat with him, like I've had with you. Surely he'll understand; he's a thorough gentleman! But it worries me that Mamma may have mentioned something to Tatyana Ivanovna about my proposal tomorrow. That may spell trouble!'

'Don't worry about Tatyana Ivanovna, Uncle!'

And I told him about the incident with Obnoskin in the summer-house. Uncle was most surprised. I made no mention of Mizinchikov.

'She's a phantasmagorical woman! Quite phantasmagorical!' he exclaimed. 'Poor soul! They're all after something, trying to take advantage of her weakness! I'm surprised about Obnoskin ... Wasn't he supposed to have gone away? ... Strange, very strange indeed! I don't quite know what to say, Seryozha ... We've got to look into this tomorrow at the latest and do something about it . . . But are you quite sure it was Tatyana Ivanovna?'

I replied that although I hadn't seen her face, I had reason to believe it could have been none other than Tatyana Ivanovna.

'Hm! Perhaps he's just carrying on with one of the servant girls whom you mistook for Tatyana Ivanovna? Dasha, the gardener's girl for instance? She's a crafty, saucy thing, you know – and been caught at it before by Anna Nilovna, that's how I know! . . . But no! He did say he wanted to get married. Strange! Very strange!'

Finally we parted. I embraced Uncle and blessed him.

'Tomorrow, tomorrow,' he repeated, 'everything will be settled – before you wake up. I'll go straight to Foma and have everything out honourably with him, I'll not conceal a thing from him, I'll treat him like a brother – he's to know everything down to the innermost workings of my heart. Goodnight, Seryozha. Go to sleep, you're tired. I doubt if I'll have a wink of sleep tonight.'

He departed. I went to bed immediately, utterly exhausted. It had been a hard day. My nerves were on edge, and before I managed to fall finally asleep, I started and woke up several times. But, strange as were the impressions with which I went to sleep, they were as nothing compared with the strangeness of my awakening next morning.

PART II

I

Pursuit

I had a sound, dreamless sleep. Suddenly I felt as though a ten-ton weight had descended upon my feet. I let out a cry and woke up. It was already daylight; the sun was streaming in at the window. And there on my bed, or rather on my feet, sat Mr Bakhcheyev.

There was no doubt about it: it was he. Having somehow extricated my feet, I sat up and stared at the man in the dumb bewilderment of one not yet fully awake.

'Look at him staring!' the fat man exclaimed. 'What are you gaping at? Get up, young man, get up! I've been trying to wake you for the last half hour, rub your eyes now!'

'What's happened? What time is it?'

'It's early still, my friend, but our Aphrodite has given us the slip before dawn! Get up, we're going after them!'

'Aphrodite?'

'Our very own, bless her! She's up and away! Gone before sunrise! I only dropped in for a minute to wake you up and I've wasted two hours already! Come on, young man, your Uncle's waiting too.' And he added with a malicious tremor in his voice: 'A fine way to see in the festive day!'

'What on earth are you talking about?' I said impatiently, although to tell the truth, I was beginning to get a shrewd idea. 'You don't mean Tatyana Ivanovna, do you?'

'And who else? The very same! Didn't I say it, didn't I warn you — nobody would listen! So there, that's her way of marking the festive occasion! Lovesick, dotty woman with Cupid on the brain! Bah! And he's a good one too — that streaky-bearded pipsqueak!'

'Surely not Mizinchikov?'

'Bah! Why don't you rub your eyes and sober up, young fellow, for this great day at least! You must have had one too many at supper last night, if you're still feeling it! Mizinchikov? It's Obnoskin, not Mizinchikov. Ivan Ivanych Mizinchikov is an honourable man and he's coming with us to chase them.'

'Well, I never!' I exclaimed, sitting up in bed with a start. 'Obnoskin — are you sure?'

'You're impossible!' the fat man replied, jumping to his feet. 'I came to pass a piece of news to a man of education and I'm taken for a liar! Well, young man, up you get, if you want to come with us, on with those trousers of yours – this is not time for tongue-wagging: I've wasted too much precious time on you already!'

And he left the room in high dudgeon.

Utterly amazed, I jumped out of bed, dressed hurriedly and ran downstairs. I wanted to find Uncle. It seemed everybody in the house was still asleep and quite unaware of what had occurred. I quietly mounted the steps of the main porch and in the hall ran into Nastenka. She had evidently dressed in a hurry, slinging a morning peignoir or some kind of dressing-gown over her shoulders. Her hair was dishevelled – it was obvious she had just got out of bed and was probably waiting to meet someone in the hall.

'Tell me, is it really true Tatyana Ivanovna has eloped with Obnoskin?' she asked quickly in a cracking voice, pale and frightened.

'So they say. I'm looking for Uncle; we want to go after them.'

'Oh! Do, do bring her back quickly! It'll be the end of her if you don't.'

'But where's Uncle?'

'He's probably at the stables – they're getting the carriage ready. I was waiting for him here. Listen, tell him I've made up my mind to leave today; that's final. Father has come to fetch me. I'm going immediately if I can. This is the end! There's no more hope!'

She looked distraught with grief as she spoke and suddenly burst into tears. I feared she was on the verge of hysterics.

'Now, now!' I implored. 'It's all for the best – you'll see ... Nastasya Yevgrafovna, what's the matter?'

'I ... I don't know ... what it is,' she said, gasping for breath and squeezing my hands feverishly. 'Tell him ...'

At this moment we heard a noise coming from the next door on the right.

She let go of my hand and, without finishing her sentence, rushed upstairs.

I found the company, that is Uncle, Bakhcheyev and Mizinchikov, assembled in full strength in the back yard by the stables. Fresh horses were being harnessed to Bakhcheyev's calash. Everything stood ready for departure; they were waiting only for me.

'Here he is!' Uncle exclaimed as soon as I appeared. 'Heard what's happened, my boy?' he added with a strange expression on his face.

Fear, panic and a kind of expectation were evident in his looks, voice and movements. He was conscious that a turning-point in his life had been reached.

I was immediately apprised of the circumstances in detail. Mr Bakhcheyev, having spent a most uncomfortable night, had left home in the early hours to attend morning service at the monastery which was situated about five versts from his village. As he drew up at the turning leading off the highway, he suddenly saw a tarantas rushing by at full speed. In it crouched Obnoskin and a seemingly terrified Tatyana Ivanovna, her face red and puffed with crying. She cried out and stretched her hands towards Bakhcheyev as if imploring his protection, or so it appeared from his narrative. 'And that bearded little scoundrel,' he continued, 'struck with mortal terror, tried to hide his face; but not so fast, my fellow!' Mr Bakhcheyev immediately turned round and raced back to Stepanchikovo, where he woke up Uncle, Mizinchikov, and last of all me too. It was decided to organize immediate pursuit.

'Obnoskin, Obnoskin . . .' Uncle said, looking hard at me as if there was something else that he wanted to communicate to me at the same time, 'who would have thought it!'

'Any dirty trick was to be expected from that despicable creature!' Mizinchikov spat vehemently, and immediately turned his head to avoid looking me in the eyes.

'Well, are we going or not? Unless you want to hang about till nightfall spinning fairy tales?' Mr Bakhcheyev interrupted, taking his seat in the calash.

'We're going, we're going!' Uncle cried.

'Everything's for the best, Uncle,' I whispered to him. 'You see, it has all turned out just right in the end.'

'Enough, say no more, my boy . . . Oh dear me! Now they'll kick *her* out from sheer spite because their plans have been ruined, do you see? How dreadful it's all going to be!'

'Now look here, Yegor Ilyich, do you want to stay behind and jabber away or shall we get a move on?' Mr Bakhcheyev exclaimed for the second time. 'Perhaps we ought to call the whole thing off and bring out the food – what do you think? You don't feel like a glass of vodka, do you?'

These words were spoken with such biting sarcasm that it was quite impossible not to oblige Mr Bakhcheyev immediately. We all hastily took our seats and the horses galloped off at speed.

For a while we sat in silence. From time to time Uncle would cast meaningful glances at me, although he did not want to start up a conversation with me in front of the others. He was often lost in deep thought, but would then come to with a start and look about him in alarm. Mizinchikov appeared calm as he sat smoking a cigar with the dignified air of a wronged man. Bakhcheyev, on the other hand, fretted for us all. He grumbled under his breath, he eyed us all with undisguised indignation, he flushed red, he wheezed, he constantly spat on the road, and was quite unable to settle himself.

'Stepan Alekseyevich, are you sure they've gone to Mishino?' Uncle asked suddenly. 'It's twenty versts from here,' he added to put me in the picture, 'a tiny village with hardly more than thirty souls in it; a former district clerk recently acquired it from the previous owners. The fellow's incorrigibly litigious! Or so they say, maybe he's nothing of the sort. Stepan Alekseyevich is sure that's where Obnoskin has gone, and the clerk is helping him.'

'Where else could he have gone?' Bakhcheyev exclaimed with a start. 'Of course he's gone to Mishino. Only he may have put a good few versts between himself and Mishino by now! We wasted three solid hours in idle chatter in the yard!'

'Don't worry,' Mizinchikov remarked. 'We'll catch them.'

'Yes, we'll catch them! You'll be lucky. You expect him to be sitting there waiting for you? Now he's laid his hands on the jewels, you'll not see him for dust!'

'Calm down, Stepan Alekseyevich, calm down, they won't get away,' Uncle said. 'They've not had time to do anything yet – you'll see who's right!'

'Not had time to do anything?' sneered Mr Bakhcheyev. 'Who knows what she's not had time to do, all meek and mild though she is! "She's so meek and mild," ' he added in a shrill voice as though mocking somebody, ' "she's so meek and mild. She's suffered." She's taken to her heels, the poor thing! And here we are chasing her up and down the highways at the crack of dawn with our tongues dangling in the wind! A man can't even be left in peace to say his prayers on a holy day any more! Bah!'

'Look here, she's of age,' I remarked. 'She's nobody's ward. No one can make her come back against her will. So what are we to do?'

'True enough,' Uncle replied, 'but she'll want to come back – I assure you. It's only now she's . . . The moment she sees us, she'll want to come back – I guarantee. So we mustn't leave her in the lurch, at the mercy of fate – it's our duty . . .'

'Nobody's ward!' cried Bakhcheyev, immediately launching into an attack against me. 'She's a fool, my friend, a certifiable idiot – never mind a ward. I didn't want to say anything to you about her yesterday, but I happened to walk into her room by mistake the other day and there she was with her arms akimbo doing an *écossaise* in front of the looking-glass! And you should have seen her get-up: something out of this world! I just spat and left her to it. I could have told you there and then it was going to end up like this!'

'You're too hard on her,' I remarked a little uncertainly. 'We all know Tatyana Ivanovna . . . is not in good health . . . or rather, she has got a certain mania . . . It seems to me Obnoskin is to blame, not her.'

'Not in good health, you say! Well now, what are we to do with him!' the fat man responded immediately, turning crimson with anger. 'The man has sworn to drive me out of my wits! He's been at it since yesterday! She's a crackpot, I repeat to you, my friend, a complete crackpot – not in good health indeed! She's had Cupid on the brain since childhood! Now she's at the end of her tether for Cupid. And as for that streaky-beard, don't even mention him! He's not sparing the horses now with all that money in his pocket! What a laugh he'll be having!'

'Do you really think he'll just abandon her?'

'What else? He's not going to lug a treasure like her with him everywhere he goes! She's of no use to him! After he's fleeced her she'll find herself sitting on the roadside under a bush smelling daisies!'

'Come, come, Stepan, don't get carried away! It won't be as bad as that!' Uncle exclaimed. 'Why are you taking it to heart so much? I'm surprised you should worry so, Stepan!'

'Am I human or not? It makes me angry – angry on principle. Perhaps you think I've a soft spot for her? . . . The whole world be damned! Why did I have to come along now? Why didn't I just carry on where I was going – minding my own business? Yes, minding my own business!'

Thus Mr Bakhcheyev fretted; but I was no longer listening to him – all I could think of was Tatyana Ivanovna, whom we were presently pursuing. Here is a short account of her which I subsequently compiled from highly reliable sources and which forms an essential commentary on her adventures. Brought up a poor and neglected orphan in a family that had no love for her, poor as a young girl, poor as a spinster, and then poor as a woman of a certain age, Tatyana Ivanovna, in all her poverty-stricken years, had been made to drain a full cup of sorrow, loneliness, humiliation and censure, and to suffer the gall of eating other people's bread. Cheerful by nature, impressionable and frivolous to a degree, she somehow managed at first to put up with her bitter lot and could even bring herself to laugh in her own charmingly carefree way; but with the years, the ravages of fate began to tell on her. Little by little Tatyana Ivanovna grew sallow and thin, turned irritable and morbid, and fell into the most impenetrable and boundless reverie, frequently interrupted by hysterical tears and convulsive sobbing. The fewer of life's blessings that were left to her, the more she entertained and comforted herself in her fanciful imagination. The more irrevocably her last substantive hopes waned and finally perished altogether, the more her extravagant and insubstantial dreams took hold of her. Unimaginable wealth, unfading beauty, elegant suitors, rich, renowned, of princely and distinguished stock, chaste and spotless of heart, expiring at her feet with infinite love, and, finally, *the one* − *the one*, the paragon of beauty, the seat of all the virtues, passionate and loving; an artist, a poet, a general's son in turn or all at once − all this made up not only the substance of her dreams, but even of her waking hours. Her mind was already beginning to exhibit symptoms of deterioration as a result of indulging in this uninterrupted succession of opiate fantasies, when suddenly fate decided to play her a final trick. In the last stages of her degradation, demoralized by hopeless, totally oppressive circumstances while serving as a paid companion to a senile, toothless, and the world's most ill-tempered mistress, blamed for everything, begrudged every meal, every cast-off scrap of clothing, insulted with impunity by everyone, protected by no one, exhausted by her miserable existence and yet revelling in her febrile and delirious fantasies, Tatyana Ivanovna was suddenly informed of the demise of a distant relative, whose remaining next of kin had long since passed away (a circumstance which in her frivolity she had never bothered to enquire about), a man unusual in every respect, who had led a sequestered life somewhere at the back of beyond − lonely, grim, unobtrusive, amassing wealth unobtrusively through usury and the practice of phrenology. At a stroke, enormous riches, a full hundred thousand rubles in silver, fell as if by magic at her feet as the last remaining legal heiress of the deceased relative. This quirk of providence was the final blow. For how could this already clouded understanding not now believe with full confidence in dreams, when they were actually beginning to come true? Thus the poor thing parted for ever with her last vestiges of common sense. Transported with delight, she totally immersed herself in her world of impossible fantasies and enchanting visions. Away with all counsel and restraint, away with all the barriers of reality, with its crystal-clear, inexorable laws of two-times-two. Thirty-five years of age and thoughts of stunning beauty, the sad chill of autumn and the luxury of love's infinite bliss, these thrived together in complete harmony in her inner being. On one occasion in her life her hopes had already materialized: why indeed should they not continue to do so? Why indeed should *he* not appear too? Tatyana Ivanovna did not reason, she simply believed. But in anticipation of *him*, her idol, suitors and admirers of every rank and position, military and civilian, army and cavalry, magnates and plain poets, those who had been to Paris and those who had only been to Moscow, moustachioed and clean-shaven, Spanish and non-Spanish (but mainly Spanish), began to haunt her day and night in such a staggering multitude as to give all onlookers cause for very serious concern – it was but a step to the lunatic asylum. Dazzling, beguiling visions crowded her imagination in an endless, intoxicating succession. Each moment of her everyday life was filled with fantasies: a mere glance, and somebody was hopelessly in love; a passer-by, and he was bound to be a Spaniard; a funeral, and somebody had surely expired of love for her. And sure enough, all this was beginning to be substantiated in her eyes by the appearance of the likes of Obnoskin, Mizinchikov and dozens of others, all with the same intentions. Suddenly people began to indulge, pamper and flatter her. Poor Tatyana Ivanovna refused to suspect that this was simply because of her money. She was perfectly convinced that, as a result of the will of some mysterious agency, all men had suddenly improved their moral natures, turned good-humoured, sweet-tempered, kind-hearted and virtuous. *He* had not yet appeared in person; but, although there was not a shadow of doubt that *he* would eventually come, her present mode of life was so entertaining, so alluring, so full of pleasant surprises and delights, that she could well afford to wait a little longer. Tatyana Ivanovna ate sweets, read novels, and gathered the blossoms of delight. The novels inflamed her imagination even more, and she usually abandoned them on the second page. She could not sustain the strain of reading further – the first few lines would be enough to carry her into dreams, the merest suggestion of love, sometimes simply the description of a place or of a room or somebody's dress. She indulged herself in an endless supply of new fashions, lace, hats, hair decorations, ribbons, dress patterns, designs, guipure, sweets, flowers and lap-dogs. Three girls in the women's quarters spent days on end stitching, while the lady herself from morn till dusk, and even in the dead of night, tried on her finery and corsets and gyrated in front of full-length mirrors. It must be owned that, on acquiring her inheritance, her appearance had somehow improved and she even seemed to grow younger. To this day I have no idea how she was related to the late General Krakhotkin. I was always convinced that the kinship was a lie perpetrated by the General's Lady in order to gain a hold over Tatyana Ivanovna and, come what may, ensure that Uncle married her money. Mr Bakhcheyev was quite right in maintaining that Cupid had turned her head completely; and Uncle's suggestion, when her elopement with Obnoskin was discovered, to bring her back by force if necessary, was the most sensible yet. The poor thing was incapable of surviving without protection and would surely come to grief if she were to fall into bad hands.

It was after nine o'clock when we arrived in Mishino. The village was small and poor and lay in a kind of hollow about three versts off the main road. Six or seven smoke-blackened huts, leaning crazily and barely covered with grimy thatching, greeted all arrivals with sullen enmity. For a quarter of a verst around not a green bush nor patch of garden was to be seen. A solitary willow drooped sleepily over a greenish puddle which passed for a pond. Such a new home was hardly likely to put Tatyana Ivanovna in a cheerful mood.

The master's abode was a newly erected long, narrow, hastily thatched log hut with six windows in a row. The former clerk turned landowner was just beginning to set himself up in the running of his estate. The courtyard had not yet been fenced off, although work had been started at one end of the house on a wattle fence to which shrivelled walnut leaves still clung. Close by stood Obnoskin's tarantas. Our arrival came like a bolt out of the blue for the runaways. Cries and the sound of weeping issued from an open window.

In the hallway we encountered a barefooted boy who turned on his heels and darted away from us like a shot. In the very first room we entered we saw Tatyana Ivanovna seated on a long chintz-upholstered divan, her eyes stained with tears. On seeing us she cried out and buried her face in her hands. Next to her stood Obnoskin, pitifully frightened, and so embarrassed that he rushed forward to shake our hands as if overjoyed at our arrival. A corner of a woman's dress was visible through the crack of a slightly open door; someone was standing on the other side eavesdropping and spying on us through a peephole. There was no sign of the owners of the house, but they were probably just hiding.

'There she is, our bird of passage! Won't help to hide your face now!' Mr Bakhcheyev exclaimed, waddling into the room after us.

'Contain yourself, Stepan Alekseyevich! This is most unbecoming. The only person who has the right to speak is Yegor Ilyich, the rest of us have no say here,' Mizinchikov remarked brusquely.

Uncle measured Bakhcheyev with a stern glance and, pretending not to notice Obnoskin, who had rushed forward to shake his hand, approached Tatyana Ivanovna as she sat, still hiding her face, and addressed her in soft tones full of sincere and courteous concern.

'Tatyana Ivanovna, we all love and respect you so much that we decided to come ourselves to inquire about your intentions. Would you be so good as to come back with us to Stepanchikovo? It's Ilyusha's name-day. Mother is impatiently awaiting you and I'm sure Sashenka and Nastenka have not stopped crying for you all morning . . .'

Tatyana Ivanovna meekly raised her head, looked at him through her fingers and, weeping bitterly, flung her arms around his neck.

'Oh do, do take me away from here this minute!' she said, sobbing, 'as quickly as possible!'

'Look at her turning tail after all that!' Bakhcheyev hissed, nudging me in the ribs.

'So the game is up,' Uncle said curtly to Obnoskin, hardly looking at him. 'Tatyana Ivanovna, your hand. We're going!'

There was a rustling noise behind the door as it creaked and opened a little wider.

'Now suppose we look at it from another angle,' Obnoskin remarked, anxiously eyeing the widening gap in the doorway, 'then you must admit, Yegor Ilyich . . . your behaviour in my house . . . and you wouldn't even acknowledge my greeting, Yegor Ilyich . . .'

'Your behaviour in *my* house, sir, was contemptible!' Uncle replied, looking sternly at Obnoskin, 'and this is not your house anyway. You heard: Tatyana Ivanovna does not wish to stay here a minute longer. What more do you want? Don't say a word – you hear me, not another word, please! I want to avoid all unnecessary explanations – which would be to your advantage too.'

But at this point Obnoskin broke down completely, uttering the most unexpected nonsense.

'Don't despise me, Yegor Ilyich,' he began in a half-whisper, on the brink of tears of shame and still casting anxious glances at the door, evidently afraid that he might be overheard, 'it wasn't my idea at all, it was Mother's. I wasn't doing it for any personal gain, Yegor Ilyich; it just happened that way. Of course, I did expect some gain, Yegor Ilyich . . . but my intentions were honourable, Yegor Ilyich; I would have used the capital for the good of mankind . . . I would have helped the poor. I also wanted to contribute towards the modern educational movement, I was even hoping to establish a university scholarship . . . that's how I was planning to use my wealth, Yegor Ilyich; there's nothing more to it than that, Yegor Ilyich . . .'

We all suddenly felt highly embarrassed. Even Mizinchikov blushed and averted his face; as for Uncle, his confusion became so intense that he was completely lost for words.

'Now, come, come!' he said at last. 'Calm down, Pavel Semyonych. Can't be helped! It could happen to anyone . . . Look here, come and have dinner with us, my friend . . . I'm really glad, glad . . .'

But Mr Bakhcheyev reacted otherwise.

'Endow a scholarship!' he spluttered in rage, 'a likely story! You'd sell your grandmother given half a chance, I bet! . . . Get yourself a decent pair of trousers before you talk of scholarships, you miserable little rag-and-tatter man! Fancy yourself a lover, do you! Where is she now, I wonder, your mother, hiding, is she? I'll be damned if she's not sitting there behind those curtains or she's crept under the bed in holy terror!'

'Stepan, Stepan!' Uncle yelled.

Obnoskin blushed deeply and was about to protest; but before he had time to open his mouth, the door flew open and the enraged Anfisa Petrovna, red in the face and eyes flashing, burst into the room.

'What's all this?' she exploded. 'What's going on? Yegor Ilyich, how dare you intrude into this peaceful house with your band of ruffians, and terrorize ladies, and order everybody about! . . . This is intolerable! I've not yet taken leave of my senses, thank God, Yegor Ilyich! And you, you dim-wit!' she continued to rail, turning on her son. 'Why don't you stop snivelling and stand up for yourself! Your mother is being insulted in her own house and all you can do is gape and gawk! Call yourself a proper young man after this! You're just a chicken-hearted cissy!'

Gone were yesterday's airs and graces and even the lorgnette had been dispensed with. Anfisa Petrovna now appeared in her true colours. She was a veritable fury, a fury unmasked.

The moment Uncle saw her, he grabbed Tatyana Ivanovna under her arm and made for the door; but Anfisa Petrovna immediately barred the way.

'No, you shan't get away that easily, Yegor Ilyich!' she ranted on. 'What right have you to take Tatyana Ivanovna away by force? It makes you mad to know she's escaped the vicious snares you've been setting for her with the help of your Mamma and that idiotic Foma Fomich of yours! You'd love to be married to her yourself, out of sheer greed! We in this house haven't sunk that low, thank you very much! Tatyana Ivanovna realized you were all plotting to ruin her and she put all her trust in Pavlusha. She herself begged him, yes she did, to rescue her from your snares; she was forced to flee your house in the dead of night – yes, that's what you drove her to! Isn't that correct, Tatyana Ivanovna? Of course it is, so how dare you and your cronies disturb the peace of noble gentlefolk in their own house and use force to abduct a virtuous lady, in spite of her tears and screams? I shan't allow it! I shan't allow it! I'm not mad! ... Tatyana Ivanovna will stay here because that's what she wants! Come along, Tatyana Ivanovna, they're not worth listening to: they're your enemies, not your friends! Don't be afraid, come along! I'll see them out immediately!'

'No, no!' Tatyana Ivanovna cried, overcome with fear. 'I don't want to, I don't want to! Him – a husband! I don't want to marry your son! I don't want him for my husband!'

'You "don't want to"!' Anfisa Petrovna shrieked, choking with anger. 'You "don't want to"? You agreed to come and now you don't want to! Pray tell me then, what right had you to deceive us? Pray tell me, how dare you make promises, foist yourself upon him, run away with him in the dead of night, embarrass us and put us to all sorts of expense? My son may have lost a splendid match because of you! He may have lost tens of thousands in dowry because of you! ... No, you'll pay for this, you'll have to pay up now! We've evidence against you: you ran away at night ...'

But we did not stop to listen to the end of this tirade. With Uncle in the middle, we all moved in a tight phalanx straight at Anfisa Petrovna and out onto the porch. The calash was drawn up immediately.

'Only blackguards and scoundrels would do such a thing!' yelled Anfisa Petrovna from the porch, completely beside herself. 'I'll sue you! You'll pay for this! ... You're going to a house of ill repute, Tatyana Ivanovna! You can't possibly marry Yegor Ilyich; he keeps a mistress under your very nose, yes, the governess! ...'

Uncle shuddered and went pale. He bit his lip and hurriedly helped Tatyana Ivanovna to her seat. I approached from the other side of the calash and was waiting for my turn to get in when Obnoskin suddenly appeared alongside, clutching at my hand.

'At least permit me to seek your friendship!' he said and squeezed my hand hard with a look of desperation on his face.

'What do you mean, friendship?' I said, one foot already resting on the treadboard of the calash.

'Just so. I recognized a most educated man in you yesterday. Don't judge me too hard ... My mother led me on. I've nothing to do with all this. I'm more inclined towards literature – I assure you; all this is Mother's doing ...'

'I believe you, I believe you,' I said. 'Goodbye!'

We took our seats and the horses moved off sharply, Anfisa Petrovna still ranting and raving after us. Strange faces suddenly appeared at all the windows and stared at us with wild curiosity.

There were now five of us in the calash; but later Mizinchikov climbed onto the box, vacating his seat for Mr Bakhcheyev, who found himself sitting directly opposite Tatyana Ivanovna. Tatyana Ivanovna was very pleased that we had taken her away but she still continued to cry. Uncle tried to comfort her as best he could. He himself was sad and pensive; Anfisa Petrovna's vitriolic remarks regarding Nastenka had clearly cut him to the quick. But our return journey would have passed quite peacefully had it not been for Mr Bakhcheyev.

Having taken his seat opposite Tatyana Ivanovna, he seemed to lose control of himself; he fretted and fumed, he fidgeted about, he flushed crimson and rolled his eyes ominously; in particular, when Uncle attempted to comfort Tatyana Ivanovna, the fat man would lose all restraint and begin to growl like an incensed bulldog. At last Tatyana Ivanovna became aware of the extraordinary state of mind of her fellow-passenger and she began to scrutinize him closely; with a glance and a smile at us she suddenly picked up her parasol and daintily tapped Mr Bakhcheyev on the shoulder.

'Madman!' she said with exquisite playfulness, and immediately hid her face behind her fan.

This prank was the last straw.

'Wha-a-t?' the fat man yelled. 'What was that, madam? So you're going to pick on me too now, are you?'

'Madman! madman!' Tatyana Ivanovna repeated and suddenly burst out laughing and clapped her hands with glee.

'Stop!' Bakhcheyev called out to the coachman. 'Stop!'

We stopped. Bakhcheyev opened the door and hurriedly began to clamber out of the calash.

'What's come over you, Stepan Alekseyevich? Where are you off to?' Uncle exclaimed in astonishment.

'I've had enough!' the fat man replied, quivering with indignation. 'To hell with everything! I'm too old, madam, to play at lovey-dovey. I'd much rather die a slow death on the roadside! Goodbye, *madame, comment vous portez-vous!*'

And he stalked off. The calash crawled behind him.

'Stepan Alekseyevich!' Uncle called out, finally losing his patience. 'Stop fooling around, that's enough, get in! We've got to get home!'

'Get away from me!' Stepan Alekseyevich retorted, breathless from walking, for which his stoutness had rendered him totally unfit.

'Drive on, as fast as you can!' Mizinchikov called out to the coachman.

'What's this, hey, stop!' Uncle exclaimed, but the calash had already shot full speed ahead. Mizinchikov was not mistaken: the desired effect followed immediately.

'Stop! Stop!' a voice full of desperation resounded in our rear. 'Stop, you bandit! Wait, you cut-throat, you! . . .'

At last the fat man was allowed to catch up with us, exhausted and completely out of breath, his face dripping with perspiration; he had loosened his necktie and taken off his cap. Sullenly and without uttering a word, he got back into the calash. This time I offered him my seat so that at least he would not be obliged to sit opposite Tatyana Ivanovna, who for the remainder of the journey continued to roll with laughter and clap her hands heartily, quite unable to keep a straight face every time she looked at Stepan Alekseyevich. The latter, for his part, said not a word and all the way to the house kept stolidly staring at the rear wheel as it performed its revolutions.

It was midday when we pulled into Stepanchikovo. I went straight to my room and Gavrila immediately brought me tea. I anxiously began to ply the old man with questions, but he was closely followed by Uncle who at once sent him out of the room.

'I only popped in for a minute, my boy,' he rattled on in haste, 'to tell you the news . . . I've found out everything. None of them has even been to church today, except Ilyusha, Sasha and Nastenka. They say Mamma has had her convulsions again. They rubbed and massaged her and only just managed to revive her. Everyone's now been called to assemble before Foma, and I'm supposed to be there too. I wish I knew whether Foma wants me to congratulate him on his name-day or not – it's most important! And how will they react to all that business this morning? It's dreadful, Seryozha, I fear the worst . . .'

'On the contrary, Uncle,' I replied just as hastily, 'everything is turning out all right. There's no question of your having to marry Tatyana Ivanovna now – that alone is worth something! I wanted to tell you that when we were on our way back here.'

'That's all very well, my boy. But there's more to it than meets the eye; the hand of the Almighty is in all this, of course, as you rightly say, but that's not what I meant . . . Poor Tatyana Ivanovna! The things that happen to her! . . . But Obnoskin, what a villain! Still, who am I to say "villain"? If I married her, wouldn't I be just as bad? . . . But that's not what I came to talk about . . . Did you hear what that harpy Anfisa was shouting about Nastenka!'

'I did, Uncle. Do you see now there's no time to waste?'

'Absolutely – come what may!' Uncle replied. 'The moment of truth is upon us. There's only one thing we didn't think of yesterday, and afterwards it kept me awake all night: will she accept me or not – that's the question!'

'For heaven's sake, Uncle! She told you herself she was in love with you!'

'But my boy, she immediately added: "I'll never marry you."'

'Oh, Uncle! She wasn't serious about that; besides, the situation is different today.'

'You think so? No, my dear Sergey, this is a delicate matter, a frightfully delicate matter! Hm! . . . You know, even though I was sad, I couldn't help feeling really thrilled all night! . . . Well, goodbye, I must

fly. They're waiting; I'm late as it is. I only dropped in for a little natter.
Oh, my God!' he exclaimed, turning back. 'I've forgotten the main thing
– I've written Foma a letter!'

'When?'

'Last night. Vidoplyasov delivered it to him at crack of dawn. I set
everything out before him on two pages, I told the whole story frankly
and truthfully. In short, I made it clear that I must, I simply must – you
understand? – propose to Nastenka. I begged him not to say anything
about our meeting in the garden and appealed to all that is holy in him to
intercede for me with Mother. I didn't make a good job of it, I know, but
I wrote straight from the heart and wept tears over it, so to speak . . .'

'And what's happened? Any reply?'

'Not so far; only as we were setting out on our chase this morning, I met
him in the hall. He had just got out of bed and was still in his slippers and
nightcap – he wears one in bed. He didn't say a word, didn't even look
up. I peered into his face like this, from below – not a word!'

'Uncle, don't trust him; he'll play some dirty trick on you.'

'No, no, my boy, don't say that!' Uncle exclaimed, wringing his hands.
'I'm sure he won't. Anyway, it's my only hope. He'll understand: he'll
appreciate . . . He can be difficult and capricious – I wouldn't deny that;
but the moment he's called upon to show his nobility, he'll shine like a
pearl . . . yes, just like a pearl. The trouble is, Sergey, you haven't seen
him at his noble best . . . But, my God! If he were to reveal yesterday's
secret, then . . . I really don't know what would happen then, Sergey!
What will be left in this world to believe in! But no, he couldn't be such a
scoundrel. I'm not worth the ground he treads on. Stop shaking your
head, my boy; it's true – I'm not!'

'Yegor Ilyich! Mamma is worried about you!' Miss Perepelitsyna's
unpleasant voice resounded from below; she had evidently been listening
at the open window and had overheard the whole of our conversation.
'Everybody's looking for you, where are you?'

'Good God, I'm late! More trouble!' Uncle exclaimed with a start.
'Sergey, in God's name, get changed and come down! I came to collect
you so that we could go down together . . . Coming, coming, Anna
Nilovna, I'm coming!'

Left alone, I remembered about my meeting with Nastenka and was
glad that I had kept quiet about it to Uncle – it would only have caused
him additional distress. I anticipated a terrible row and could not for the
life of me see how Uncle would be able to settle his affairs and steel
himself to propose to Nastenka. In spite of all my faith in his sense of

honour, I will repeat that I was nevertheless dubious of his chances of
success.

However, there was no time to waste. It was my duty to help him and
I immediately began to get changed. While I was smartening myself up,
which took me some time, Mizinchikov entered.

'I've come to fetch you,' he said. 'Yegor Ilyich wants you downstairs
immediately.'

'Let's go, then.'

I was now ready. We left the room.

'What's happening downstairs?' I asked on the way.

'Foma has assembled everybody,' Mizinchikov replied. 'He's not throwing tantrums, but he's gone all pensive and won't say much, just keeps
mumbling something through his teeth. He even gave Ilyusha a kiss – of
course, Yegor Ilyich was absolutely delighted. You see, he's instructed
Perepelitsyna to say he's not to be congratulated on the anniversary of his
name-day, and that he merely wanted to test our good faith ... The old
woman is still sniffing her smelling salts, but she's much less trouble now
that Foma has settled down. Nobody's breathing a word about what
happened this morning – it's as though it never happened. As long as
Foma keeps quiet, everyone else will too. He wouldn't let anybody near
him the whole morning even though the old woman begged him by all
the saints to come down for a discussion; she even stood at his door
trying to force her way in; but he locked himself in and answered that he
was praying for mankind or something of that sort. He's hatching
something: I can tell by his face. But Yegor Ilyich is incapable of reading
people's faces, he's in his seventh heaven at Foma's mildness now. What a
child he is! Ilyusha has brought along some poem and I've been sent to
fetch you.'

'And Tatyana Ivanovna?'

'What about Tatyana Ivanovna?'

'Is she there too? With the rest of them?'

'No; she's in her own room,' Mizinchikov replied curtly. 'She's resting
and crying. Maybe she's ashamed? I think that governess is there with her
now. What's this? Looks like a storm brewing. Look at the sky!'

'Yes, very likely a storm,' I replied, glancing at the darkening rainclouds
looming over the horizon.

We were mounting the steps of the terrace.

'But what about Obnoskin, eh?' I continued, unable to resist drawing
Mizinchikov on this point.

'Don't talk to me about him! Don't ever mention that scoundrel to me!' he exclaimed, stopping suddenly, stamping his foot and going very red in the face. 'The fool! the fool! To bungle such a brilliant idea! Listen: to be very frank, I'm an ass for not seeing through his tricks, and perhaps that's just the sort of admission you wanted from me? If he'd only managed to pull it all off, I swear I would have forgiven him – perhaps! The fool, the fool! Why does society keep and tolerate such people? Why aren't they sent to Siberia, into exile, hard labour! But they're all wrong! I'm not one to be outsmarted! At least I've learnt my lesson and we'll see who comes out best now. I'm working on another plan at the moment . . . Look, why should I be the loser just because some idiot from nowhere pinched my idea and then couldn't put it into practice? You must admit, it's unfair! And anyway, this Tatyana Ivanovna must get married – it's her vocation. If no one has locked her up in an asylum yet, it's only because she's still eligible. Let me tell you what my new plan is –'

'No, perhaps later,' I interrupted him. 'Look, here we are.'

'All right, all right, later!' Mizinchikov replied, his face contorted in a smile. 'And now . . . where are you off to? I told you, we're going straight to Foma! Follow me; you've not been there before. You're about to see another comedy . . . Since comedy is all the rage here . . .'

3

Ilyusha's Name-day

Foma Fomich occupied two large, magnificent rooms, which were decorated better than any of the others in the house. The great man resided in splendid comfort. Beautiful new wallpaper, bright silk curtains at the windows, carpets, a full-length mirror, an open logfire, comfortable, elegant furniture – everything spoke of the tender regard in which Foma Fomich was held by his hosts. Flower pots were arranged on window-sills and on little round marble tables by the windows. In the middle of the study stood a large writing-desk, its top covered in heavy red fabric, piled high with books and manuscripts. A splendid bronze inkstand and a bundle of pens, cared for and maintained by Vidoplyasov himself – all this seemed to testify to Foma Fomich's remarkable intellectual assiduity. I should perhaps add here that after spending eight years at this desk, Foma did not manage to produce anything of any consequence. In the end, after his departure to a better world, when we came to sort out his manuscripts, we discovered that they were a mass of utter rubbish. We found the beginning of a historical novel depicting life in seventh-century Novgorod;[35] then a dreadful poem, 'Anchoret at the Graveyard', written in blank verse;[36] then an absurd discourse on the significance and character of the Russian muzhik and how to handle him;[37] and finally, a tale of society life, 'Countess Vlonskaya',[38] also unfinished. That was all. And yet Foma Fomich had been compelling Uncle to take out expensive annual subscriptions to books and journals, many of which had not even had their pages cut. I do in fact remember numerous occasions when I would catch Foma Fomich engrossed in a Paul de Kock novel,[39] which he would hide when there were people around. A French window in the far wall of the study opened directly onto the courtyard.

Everybody was waiting for us. Foma Fomich was sitting in a comfortable armchair in an ankle-length frock-coat, but without a tie. He spoke little, and was indeed lost in thought. When we entered the room, he raised his brows slightly and looked at me curiously. I bowed; he responded with a faint nod which was actually rather courteous. My grandmamma, seeing that Foma Fomich had adopted a cordial attitude towards me, smiled and nodded to me. The poor soul could hardly have

believed that morning that her darling would receive the news of Tatyana
Ivanovna's escapade with such equanimity; consequently she was now in
very good spirits, although earlier in the morning she had indeed had
convulsions and swooning fits. Miss Perepelitsyna, having taken up her
usual position behind her mistress's chair, stood rubbing her bony hands
while a vicious, sour grin warped the thin line of her tightly drawn lips. A
pair of time-ravaged gentlewomen, hangers-on of the General's Lady, sat
close beside her without saying a single word. Also present was a nun,
who had wandered into the house that morning from goodness knows
where, and a neighbouring farmer's wife, advanced in years and also with
nothing to say for herself, who had called in after church to pay her
respects to the General's Lady. Aunt Praskovya Ilyinichna had made
herself inconspicuous somewhere in a distant corner of the room and was
darting furtive glances at Foma Fomich and Mamma. Uncle sat in an
armchair, beaming with joy. Ilyusha, in a red festive shirt and his hair
beautifully curled, stood in front of him like a little cherub. To please his
father, Sashenka and Nastenka had secretly taught him some lines for the
occasion, to show what excellent progress he was making in his studies.
Uncle was nearly in tears for joy: Foma's unexpected calmness, the
General's Lady's good spirits, Ilyusha's name-day, the poem – everything
had combined to put him in a state of euphoria, and he had triumphantly
sent for me to come and join him as soon as possible in order to share in
the universal happiness and listen to the poem. Sashenka and Nastenka,
who entered the room shortly after us, positioned themselves close to
Ilyusha. Sashenka was full of laughter and joy like a little child. Seeing
her, Nastenka also began to smile, although a minute earlier she had
entered the room pale and dejected. She was the only one who had
welcomed Tatyana Ivanovna on her return from her excursion and all this
time had been sitting with her upstairs in her room. Cheeky little Ilyusha
was also full of laughter as he watched his two instructresses. It seemed
the three of them had prepared a hilarious joke and were bursting with
impatience to play it on us ... Oh yes, and I quite forgot about
Bakhcheyev. He sat at a distance from everybody else, angry and red-
faced, with not a word to say for himself as he puffed and snorted and
blew his nose every few seconds, acting out a most miserable rôle in the
family celebrations. Yezhevikin was fussing close at hand; in fact he was
to be seen everywhere – kissing the hands of the General's Lady and her
lady-guests, whispering into Miss Perepelitsyna's ear, hovering about
Foma Fomich to attend to his needs. He too was evidently anxious to
hear Ilyusha's verses, and as soon as I appeared he rushed forward to

greet me, bowing and scraping as a mark of respect and devotion. It did not look at all as if he had come to defend his daughter and take her away from Stepanchikovo for good.

'Here he is!' Uncle exclaimed joyfully as soon as he saw me. 'Ilyusha has a poem ready, dear boy – who would have thought, what a surprise! You know, my boy, I'm quite astounded. I sent specially for you and asked for the recitation to be held up until you came ... Sit here beside me. We're all going to listen to it. Foma Fomich, admit it, my friend, it was your idea, wasn't it – to cheer me up in my old age? I swear it was!'

One would have thought that everything was going well, seeing that Uncle had adopted such a tone in Foma Fomich's room. But the trouble was that Uncle, as Mizinchikov had observed, was quite incapable of reading people's faces. After one glance at Foma, I had to admit that Mizinchikov was right, and that it looked as if something was about to happen.

'Don't worry about me, Colonel,' replied Foma Fomich feebly, in the voice of a man granting a reprieve to his enemy. 'Of course, I commend the idea: it speaks of a certain sensitivity and gentility in your children. Poetry has its merits, even if only to improve enunciation. But my mind was far from poetry this morning, Yegor Ilyich: I was at prayer ... as you know ... Anyway, I'm willing to listen to poetry.'

In the meantime I kissed and congratulated Ilyusha.

'That's right, Foma, I do beg your pardon! I quite forgot ... though I've every faith in your friendship, Foma! Go on, kiss him again, Sergey! Look what a brave little lad he is! Well, come on, Ilyusha, do begin! What's it about? Probably some kind of solemn ode, something from Lomonosov, I daresay!'

And Uncle swelled with pride. He could hardly keep still for impatience and joy.

'No, Papa, it's not Lomonosov,' Sashenka said, fighting back her laughter. 'But as you used to be a soldier and have fought the enemy, Ilyusha has learned a poem about war ... "The Siege of Pamba", Papa.'

'"The Siege of Pamba"? Ah! I don't remember ... What's Pamba, Seryozha, do you know? Something heroic, no doubt.'

And Uncle again assumed a dignified air.

'Begin, Ilyusha!' Sashenka commanded.

'Nine years now since Pedro Gomez ...'

Ilyusha began in a small, even-toned and distinct voice without pauses of any kind, in the manner of young children who have learnt their lines off by heart.

> 'Nine years now since Pedro Gomez
> Did besiege the town of Pamba,
> Milk has been the only diet
> Of the army of Don Pedro.
> All nine thousand brave Castilians
> Never broke their solemn vow,
> Never touched a crust of bread,
> Never drank a drop but milk.'

'What? What was that about milk?' Uncle exclaimed, looking at me in astonishment.

'Go on, Ilyusha!' cried Sashenka.

> 'Every day Don Pedro Gomez
> Weeps in fury at his weakness,
> Hides himself inside his cloak.
> Comes the tenth year of the siege;
> Now the wicked Moors in glee
> Celebrate their victory;
> And of all his mighty force
> Pedro has but nineteen left . . .'

'That's nonsense!' Uncle exclaimed in great agitation. 'It's just not possible! Nineteen men out of the whole force, when there was a sizeable corps to start with! What is all this, my boy?'

But at this moment Sashenka could restrain herself no longer, and burst into the most unbridled childish laughter; and although there was nothing much to laugh at, none of us could keep a straight face at the mere sight of her.

'It's meant to be a funny poem, Papa,' she exclaimed, overjoyed at the success of her prank. 'It's supposed to be like that, the author wrote it to make everybody laugh, Papa.'

'Ah! A funny one!' Uncle exclaimed, his face suddenly lighting up., 'Comic, that is! I was just going to say . . . Exactly, exactly, it's all a joke. It *is* funny, extremely funny! To keep a whole army starving on milk – and all for a vow! Can't see that he needed to do it really! Very witty though – don't you agree, Foma? You see, Mamma, it's one of those comic poems which poets sometimes write – isn't that right, Sergey, they do, don't they? Very funny indeed! Well, well, Ilyusha, so what next?'

> 'Nineteen men survived the slaughter.
> These Don Pedro now assembled:

> Thus addressed them: "My nineteen!
> All our standards we'll unfurl,
> Blow the trumpets, strike the drums;
> We'll retreat whence we have come.
> Pamba, true, still stands: however,
> We can swear by all that's holy
> We have all upheld our honour,
> Never have we broken once
> That most sacred vow we've taken:
> Nine long years we've nothing eaten,
> Not a morsel's passed our lips:
> All we've done is drink our milk!"'

'The blockhead! Why does he console himself with that?' Uncle interrupted again. 'Drinking milk for nine years! There's nothing virtuous in that! He would have done better to give everybody a roasted ram to eat instead of starving them! Wonderful, excellent! I see it, now I see it: it's a satire, or ... what do they call it, an allegory or something? ... And I daresay aimed at some foreign general,' Uncle added, raising his eyebrows and giving me a meaningful look. 'Eh? What d'you think? I trust it's an innocent, decent satire, which won't offend anyone! Splendid! Splendid! Above all it must be decent! Well, Ilyusha, do continue! Oh you pranksters, you pranksters!' he added with a loving look at Sashenka and a stealthy glance at Nastenka, who was blushing and smiling.

> 'Such a speech could not but bolster
> Warriors swaying in their saddles,
> And in voices weak and tired
> Nineteen warriors thus replied:
> 'Sancto Iago Compostello,
> Glory be to you, Don Pedro,
> Mighty Lion of Castille!"
> But his chaplain, named Don Diego,
> Muttered thus through clenchèd teeth:
> 'Had I led the army here,
> They'd have all had meat to eat,
> Washed down with strong Turin wine!"'

'There you are! What did I say?' Uncle exclaimed, utterly overjoyed. 'One man in the whole army with a bit of sense at last, and he would have to be some chaplain! Who exactly was he, Sergey, a captain of theirs, or what?'

'A monk, a holy man, Uncle.'

'Oh, yes, yes! Chapel, chaplain, I know, I remember! I read about them in Radcliffe's novels. They've got various orders, haven't they? ... Benedictines, I seem to remember ... It is Benedictine, isn't it?'

'Yes, Uncle.'

'Hm! ... I thought so. Well, Ilyusha, what next? Excellent, splendid!'

> 'This Don Pedro overheard;
> Laughing heartily, he spake:
> 'I admire him for his wit!
> Give the holy man a ram!"'

'Imagine laughing at a time like that! What a fool! He's seen the funny side of it at last! A ram, my word! So they had rams all along; why didn't he eat one himself? Well, Ilyusha, let's have the rest! Excellent, splendid! Devastatingly witty!'

'That's the end, Papa!'

'Ah! The end! But of course, what else was there to do indeed – am I right, Sergey? Well done, Ilyusha! Simply marvellous! Come and give me a kiss, my precious boy! My sweet little boy! And whose idea was it: was it yours, Sashenka?'

'No, it was Nastenka's! We came across the poem the other day. She read it out and thought: "How funny! Ilyusha's name-day is coming up: let's get him to learn it off by heart and recite it. It'll be such fun!"'

'So it was Nastenka? Well, I'm most grateful, most grateful,' Uncle mumbled and suddenly blushed like a child. 'Give me another kiss, Ilyusha! You too, Sashenka, my naughty little pet,' he said, giving Sashenka a hug and looking tenderly into her eyes.

'There now, Sashenka, it will be your name-day soon too,' he added, not knowing what to say for joy.

I turned to Nastenka and asked her who had written the poem.

'Ah yes! Who wrote it?' Uncle repeated with a start. 'Must be a very clever poet – don't you agree, Foma?'

'Hm!' grunted Foma Fomich.

All through the reading of the poem, a caustic, mocking smile had never left his lips.

'I've forgotten,' Nastenka replied, casting a meek glance at Foma Fomich.

'Mr Kuzma Prutkov wrote it, Papa.[40] It was printed in *The Contemporary*!' Sashenka burst out.

'Kuzma Prutkov! Don't know him,' Uncle said. 'Pushkin, that's another matter! ... Still, it seems he was a worthy poet – isn't that right, Sergey? And what's more, a thorough gentleman – that's plain as the sun at noonday! Might even have made an officer ... Well done! Anyway, it's a fine journal, *The Contemporary*! Must definitely take out a subscription if they have poets like that contributing ... I like poets! They're a good crowd! The way they put everything into verse! Sergey, do you remember the man of letters I met at your place in Petersburg? The one with the funny nose ... really! ... What did you say, Foma?'

Foma Fomich, who was getting more and more restless, suddenly began to giggle.

'No, I only ... it's nothing really ...' he said, as though barely able to contain his laughter. 'Carry on, Yegor Ilyich, carry on! I'll have my say later ... You see even Stepan Alekseyevich is enjoying your story of encounters with Petersburg men of letters ...'

Mr Bakhcheyev, who was sitting all by himself lost in thought, suddenly raised his head, went red in the face and turned aggressively in his chair.

'Don't you start getting at me, Foma Fomich! Just leave me alone!' he said, darting him a fierce look with his small, bloodshot eyes. 'I couldn't care less about your literature! Good health is all I pray for!' he mumbled under his breath. 'As for all your penpushers ... I confound them ... a bunch of Voltaireans, that's all they are!'

'Voltairean penpushers!' Yezhevikin spoke out, suddenly emerging on Mr Bakhcheyev's side. 'You're so very right, Stepan Alekseyevich, my good sir. That's just what Valentin Ignatych too was saying the other day. Even I've been accused of being a Voltairean – honest to God; though as everyone knows, I haven't written a great deal so far ... With some people, if the milk goes off in the jug, Mr Voltaire's done it! That's a fact!'

'Well, no!' Uncle remarked weightily. 'I think you're mistaken. Voltaire was a witty writer; he ridiculed prejudices; but he never was a Voltairean himself! His enemies are responsible for spreading that slander about him. Why should he get blamed for everything, poor man? ...'

Foma Fomich again sniggered maliciously. Uncle looked at him apprehensively, unable to conceal his discomfiture.

'I was only talking about journals, Foma,' Uncle said, visibly embarrassed and attempting to redeem himself somehow. 'You were perfectly right, Foma, to encourage us the other day to take out subscriptions. I feel we must too! ... Hm! ... really, it's a fact, they're spreading enlightenment and so on! How can you call yourself a son of your country when you haven't taken out a subscription? Isn't that right, Sergey? Hm! ... Yes! ... *The Contemporary* for example ... But you know, Sergey, the best journal of them all for science, if you ask me, is that thick one ... now what was it called again? With the yellow cover ...'

'*Country Notes*, Papa.'

'Ah yes, *Country Notes*, and a splendid title too, Sergey — isn't that right? Can't you picture the whole country sitting busily taking down notes? ... A brilliant idea! A most useful journal — and so thick! I'd like to see you publish an omnibus like that! The things you find in it would make your eyes pop out ... Came home the other day and there was a copy; I couldn't resist it, opened it and read three pages straight off. It made me simply gasp, it goes into everything. Take a broom, a shovel, a ladle, an oven-fork.[41] To the likes of me a broom is a broom, an oven-fork is an oven-fork. But, just hold on a moment, my boy! An oven-fork, looked at scientifically, is an emblem or a symbol of something or other; don't quite remember what of, but there you are, you see! They've got to the bottom of everything!'

I have no idea what Foma Fomich was planning to do after this latest flight of Uncle's, for at this moment Gavrila appeared on the doorstep and remained standing with his head bowed.

Foma Fomich cast him a meaningful glance.

'Ready, Gavrila?' he inquired in a low but firm voice.

'Yes,' Gavrila replied sadly, with a sigh.

'And have you put my bundle in the cart?'

'Yes.'

'Well then, I'm ready!' said Foma Fomich, rising slowly from his chair. Uncle was looking at him in astonishment. The General's Lady had leapt to her feet and was staring about her wild-eyed.

'By your leave, Colonel,' Foma Fomich began with dignity, 'I must now ask you to postpone your fascinating discussion on literary oven-forks; you may continue it in my absence. *I am now leaving you for good*, and I should like to say a few last words to you ...'

Astonishment bordering on terror seized the whole company.

'Foma! Foma! What's the matter? Where will you go?' Uncle exclaimed at last.

'I intend to leave your house, Colonel,' said Foma Fomich in a voice drained of all emotion. 'I've decided to go wherever fate and fortune take me, and I have engaged, at my own expense, a simple peasant cart for my journey. My luggage is loaded; it isn't much: a few of my favourite books, two changes of underwear – that's the lot! I'm poor, Yegor Ilyich, but never in my life would I consider taking your gold, the gold I turned down yesterday! . . .'

'For goodness sake, Foma! What is all this?' Uncle cried, white as a sheet.

The General's Lady uttered a shrill cry and extended her hands towards Foma with a look of utter desperation on her face. Miss Perepelitsyna rushed forward to support her. The lady companions sat petrified with terror. Mr Bakhcheyev slowly heaved himself off his chair.

'Well, there we go again!' Mizinchikov whispered at my side. At this moment there was the sound of distant thunder; a storm was approaching.

4

Expulsion

'I believe, Colonel, you asked: "What is all this?"' said Foma Fomich
solemnly, delighting in the general embarrassment. 'Your question astonishes me! Pray explain, how is it that you are still capable of looking me
straight in the eye! Do explain to me this final psychological mystery of
human shamelessness so that I can depart at least enriched by a new
insight into the depravity of humankind.'

But Uncle was in no state to make a reply: his eyes ready to pop out and
mouth hanging wide open, he stared at Foma Fomich, crushed and fearful.

'O Lord! Such passions!' Perepelitsyna uttered with a groan.

'Do you understand, Colonel,' continued Foma Fomich, 'that you
must now release me without any fuss or further questioning. In your
house even a man of my age and intellectual level cannot help being
concerned for the purity of his morals. Believe me that any further
probing on the subject will only lead to your total disgrace.'

'Foma! Foma! . . .' Uncle cried, and beads of cold sweat appeared on
his forehead.

'And therefore allow me without further ado to pronounce a few
farewell words of counsel, my very last in your house, Yegor Ilyich. The
mischief has been done and may not be undone! I trust you understand
what I am referring to. On my bended knees I beg you: restrain your
passions if you've still a spark of moral decency left in you! Dampen the
fire, lest the poisonous fumes of corruption engulf the whole edifice!'

'Foma! I assure you, you're mistaken!' Uncle exclaimed, gradually
beginning to regain his composure and fearful of the turn that the
conversation might take.

'Quell your passions,' continued Foma Fomich in the same solemn
tones, as if he had not even heard Uncle's exclamations, 'vanquish
yourself. If you wish to vanquish the world – first vanquish your own
self! That is my golden rule. You're a landowner; you should sparkle like
a diamond on your estates, but look what an example of gross licentious-
ness you set your subordinates! I spent nights in anguished prayer seeking
your ultimate happiness, but I found it not, for happiness resides in
virtue . . .'

'But this is impossible, Foma,' Uncle again interrupted him, 'you don't understand, you're off on the wrong track altogether . . .'

'And so remember that you are a landowner,' continued Foma Fomich, again ignoring Uncle's expostulations. 'Do not imagine that ease and lust are the privileges of the landed gentry. Perish the thought! It's not ease that's needed, but zeal towards God, Tsar and country! The landowner must toil, toil and toil again, like the meanest of his peasants!'[42]

'What! Must I go and plough the fields for the labourers, is that what you mean?' Bakhcheyev grumbled. 'I'm a landowner too, damn it . . .'

'And now you of the household staff,' Foma Fomich continued, addressing himself to Gavrila and Falaley, who had appeared in the doorway. 'Love your masters and be obedient to their will, be humble and meek. Your masters' love will be your ample reward. And you, Colonel, practise justice and compassion towards your servants. Behold, they are of humankind – moulded in the image of God, children so to speak, entrusted to your care by the Tsar and the land that he rules. Heavy lies the burden of duty upon you, but your reward will be great.'

'Foma Fomich, my darling! What are you thinking of?' the General's Lady cried out in despair, on the point of swooning in terror.

'Well, I think that will be all,' concluded Foma, paying no attention even to the General's Lady. 'And now to matters of detail; trivial, I grant you, but necessary. Yegor Ilyich! you still haven't cut the grass on that patch of wasteland in Khorinskaya. Don't leave it too late: have it cut and do it quickly. Such is my advice . . .'

'But Foma . . .'

'I know you wanted to clear that strip of woodland in Zyryanovsk; leave the trees alone – that is my second piece of advice. Forests must be preserved: for they retain moisture on the earth's surface . . . What a pity you sowed your spring crops so late; really, it is surprising how late you sowed your spring crops! . . .'

'But Foma . . .'

'Well, that will have to do! I could have said more, but this is not the time! I'll forward my instructions to you in writing, in a special notebook. Well, farewell, farewell all of you. God be with you and may the Lord's blessing be upon you all! Let me bless you too, my child,' he added, addressing himself to Ilyusha, 'and may God protect you from the noxious poison of your future passions! I bless you too, Falaley; have nothing to do with the kamarinsky! . . . And you, and all of you . . . remember Foma . . . Well, come along Gavrila! Help me into the cart, kind old man that you are.'

And Foma Fomich made for the door. The General's Lady let out a shriek and rushed after him.

'No, Foma! I shan't let you leave like that!' Uncle exclaimed, as he too caught up with him and grabbed him by the arm.

'So you want to resort to force, do you?'

'Yes, Foma ... force!' Uncle replied, trembling with agitation. 'You have said too much and you must explain yourself! You have misunderstood my letter, Foma! ...'

'Your letter!' shrieked Foma Fomich in sudden animation, as if he had been waiting precisely for this opportunity to vent his spleen. 'Your letter! Here is your letter! Here it is! I'm ripping this letter to pieces, I spit upon this letter! I trample your letter underfoot in performance of man's most sacred duty! That's what I'm doing if you mean to use force to extract an explanation from me! Here! Here! Here! ...'

And scraps of paper flew about the room.

'I repeat, Foma, you have misunderstood me!' Uncle shouted, growing whiter and whiter. 'I'm offering her my hand, Foma, I'm seeking my happiness ...'

'Your hand! First you seduce this girl, and now you think you can fool me with your offer of marriage! It so happens I saw you two last night in the garden, under the bushes!'

The General's Lady uttered a cry and collapsed swooning into a chair. A terrible commotion ensued. Poor Nastenka sat drained and utterly lifeless. Sashenka, terrified, had flung her arms around Ilyusha and was trembling as if in a fever.

'Foma!' Uncle yelled beside himself. 'If you give away this secret, you'll be guilty of the meanest trick on earth!'

'I shall give away this secret,' screeched Foma Fomich, 'and it will be the noblest deed that ever was! The Good Lord Himself has sent me to expose the world in its iniquity! I'm ready to proclaim your sordid misdeed from the thatched rooftop of a peasant's hut for the benefit of every landowner who lives here and everyone who passes through here! ... Yes, you should all know, all of you, that last night I caught him and this girl, who affects the most innocent airs, in the garden under a bush!'

'Oh, the disgrace of it!' Miss Perepelitsyna squealed.

'Foma! I'm warning you!' Uncle shouted, his fists clenched and eyes flashing.

'... And he,' Foma Fomich continued to screech, 'terrified that I saw him, has dared to approach me with a lying letter, expecting me, despite

my honesty and rectitude, to condone his crime – yes, crime! . . . because
you've turned a pure and innocent girl into a . . .'

'One more insulting word against her, and – I'll kill you, Foma, I
swear it . . .'

'I will say it, because you've managed to turn a pure and innocent girl
into a thoroughly depraved one!'

No sooner had Foma Fomich uttered these last words than Uncle
grabbed him by his shoulders, turned him round like a wisp of straw, and
hurled him violently through the French window into the courtyard. The
blow was so violent that the doors, standing slightly ajar, flew wide open
and Foma Fomich rolled head over heels down the seven stone steps and
ended up in the yard flat on his face. Bits of shattered glass cascaded
noisily down the steps.

'Gavrila, pick him up!' Uncle called out, white as a sheet, 'put him in
the cart and give him two minutes to clear out of Stepanchikovo!'

Such a turn of events was the last thing that Foma Fomich had
expected.

I can hardly attempt to describe what followed during the first few
minutes after this event. The General's Lady's ear-splitting scream as she
collapsed in her chair; Miss Perepelitsyna's stupor in the face of such an
unprecedented action on the part of the hitherto docile Uncle; the oohs
and ahs of the lady companions; Nastenka's near-fainting terror as her
father hovered around her; Sashenka's mortal alarm; Uncle's frantic pacing
to and fro as he waited for his mother to regain her senses; and, finally,
the lusty wailing of Falaley, lamenting his master's misfortune – all this
added up to a spectacle beyond my powers of description. I should add
that at this precise moment a violent storm broke; there were frequent
claps of thunder and soon the window-panes resounded to the patter of
heavy raindrops.

'What a party!' Mr Bakhcheyev mumbled, hanging his head and
flinging out his arms.

'It's a bad business!' I whispered to him, also in a state of shock. 'But at
least Foma has been got rid of for good.'

'Mamma! Are you all right? Are you better? Will you hear me out at
last?' Uncle asked, halting in his pacing in front of the old woman's chair.

She raised her head, folded her hands and regarded her son with
pleading eyes – never before had she seen him in such a rage.

'Mamma!' he continued: 'that was the last straw, you heard yourself. It
wasn't how I meant to broach the subject, but the hour had struck and
there was no delaying! You heard the slander, now you've got to listen to

my side of the story. Mamma, I love this girl – she's the noblest and most exalted creature in the world; I've loved her from the start and I shall always love her. She'll bring happiness to my children and will prove to be a faithful daughter to you, and now therefore, in your presence and witnessed by my friends and relatives, at her feet I solemnly plead to her to do me the untold honour of becoming my wife!'

Nastenka shook all over, and blushing crimson, jumped to her feet with a start. For a while the General's Lady regarded her son as though she had no idea what he was talking about, then she suddenly let out a piercing cry and flung herself down on her knees in front of him.

'Yegor, darling, bring back my Foma Fomich!' she cried. 'Bring him back at once! or I'll die before the day is out without him!'

Uncle was thunderstruck at the sight of his aged mother, always so domineering and capricious, kneeling at his feet. A pained expression flitted across his face; then, pulling himself together, he hastened to pick her up and seat her back in her chair.

'Bring back my Foma Fomich, Yegor my dear!' the old woman wailed on, 'please let me have my darling back! I can't live without him!'

'Mamma, please!' Uncle exclaimed in distress. 'You haven't listened to a word of what I've just been saying to you! I can't bring Foma back – try to understand! I cannot and I must not after his mean and slanderous attack on this angel of love and virtue. Can you not see, Mamma, that I am now duty bound, that it is a matter of my own honour to see that virtue is redeemed! You heard me: I seek this young lady's hand and beg you to bless our union.'

The General's Lady made another desperate turn and flung herself at Nastenka's feet.

'My dear, my precious girl!' she whined, 'don't marry him! Don't marry him, but do persuade him to return my Foma Fomich to me! Nastasya Yevgrafovna, my angel! All I have is yours for the taking, I'll sacrifice everything for you, if only you don't marry him. Old woman that I am, I haven't spent it all yet, I've still some little bits and pieces left since my poor husband passed away. It's all yours, my precious, I'll give it all to you, and Yegor will give you some too, only don't put me in my grave before my time is up, plead with him to let me have my Foma Fomich back! . . .'

The old woman would have gone on and on had not Perepelitsyna and all the lady companions rushed forward with howls and groans to pick her up, indignant that she should be kneeling in front of an employed governess. Nastenka was swaying on her feet with fright, while Perepelitsyna even burst into tears of anger.

'You'll be the death of poor Mamma,' Perepelitsyna shouted at Uncle. 'You'll be the death of her, sir! As for you, Nastasya Yevgrafovna, you ought to know better than to sow discord between mother and son; it is an ungodly thing to do . . .'

'Anna Nilovna, hold your tongue!' Uncle shouted. 'I've had enough! . . .'

'And I've had enough from you too! Just because I've been an orphan doesn't mean you have to reproach me with it! How long are you going to go on insulting an orphan? I'm not your slave yet, sir! I am a lieutenant-colonel's daughter myself, I'll have you know! I shan't stay a minute longer in this house, not a minute – this very day . . .!'

But Uncle was not listening; he approached Nastenka and graciously took her hand.

'Nastasya Yevgrafovna, you heard my proposal?' he said, looking at her with sadness bordering on despair.

'No, Yegor Ilyich, no! Let's forget about it,' Nastenka replied, also utterly dispirited. 'It's quite hopeless,' she continued, pressing his hands and unable to hold back a flood of tears. 'Yesterday was different . . . but nothing can come of it now, you can see that yourself. We were wrong, Yegor Ilyich . . . I'll always remember you as my benefactor and . . . I shall never, never stop praying for you!'

Tears prevented her from saying any more. Poor Uncle had apparently anticipated such a reply; he did not even attempt to plead or insist . . . He listened stooping slightly, still holding her hand, speechless and dejected. Tears welled in his eyes.

'I told you yesterday I couldn't be your wife,' Nastenka went on. 'You can see for yourself: I'm not wanted here . . . I knew it all along; your mamma will not give us her blessing . . . nor will *other people*. You might not have any regrets later yourself, being the noblest of men, but all the same you'd suffer on my account . . . with your kind heart . . .'

'*Kind heart*, the very word! You have a *kind heart*, sir! You're right there, Nastenka, you're right!' her aged father acquiesced, standing on the other side of her chair. 'You have used the very word.'

'I've no wish to be the cause of discord in your house,' Nastenka continued. 'And don't you worry about me, Yegor Ilyich: nobody is going to harm me, nobody is going to insult me . . . I'll go home with Father . . . today . . . Let's just say goodbye, Yegor Ilyich . . .'

And poor Nastasya again burst into tears.

'Nastasya Yevgrafovna! Is this really your last word?' Uncle pursued, looking at her in utter despair. 'Just one word, and I'll sacrifice everything for you . . .!'

'She's said her last word, her last word, Yegor Ilyich, sir,' Yezhevikin again chimed in. 'And she has explained herself so well to you – I'd never have expected it, I must say. You're the kindest person of all, Yegor Ilyich, truly the kindest, and you've been gracious enough to do us a great honour! A great honour, a great honour indeed! ... All the same, we're no match for you, Yegor Ilyich. You need a bride, Yegor Ilyich, who is wealthy, well connected and fabulously beautiful, with a fine voice, who adorns herself with diamonds and ostrich plumes as she moves about your house ... Maybe even Foma Fomich would be inspired to make a concession then ... and grant his blessing! You really ought to call him back! There was no need to hurt him so, no need at all! He was moved by the best intentions and carried away by zeal ... You'll be the first to admit it – mark my words! A worthier gentleman you never saw! And now getting soaked to the skin! You really ought to fetch him back now ... seeing as you'll be fetching him back sooner or later no matter what happens ...'

'Bring him back! Bring him back!' the General's Lady screeched, 'he's telling you the truth, my dearest! ...'

'Yes, indeed,' Yezhevikin continued, 'look how mortified your mamma is – and really no need for it ... Bring him back! And while you're about it, Nastenka and I will be on our way ...'

'Wait, Yevgraf Larionych!' Uncle cried, 'I beg you! One more word, Yevgraf, just one more word ...'

With this he withdrew into a corner, sat down on a chair and remained seated, his head hung low, shielding his eyes with his hands as if in deep thought.

At this moment a deafening clap of thunder resounded almost overhead and fairly rocked the whole house. First the General's Lady let out a cry, and then Perepelitsyna, while the lady companions, and with them Mr Bakhcheyev, all scared out of their wits, repeatedly made the sign of the cross.

'The prophet Ilya have mercy upon us!' five or six voices whispered together.

The thunder was immediately followed by such a downpour as though a whole lake had been tipped over the village of Stepanchikovo.

'Foma Fomich, what will become of him out in the open?' Perepelitsyna screeched.

'Yegor, my darling, bring him back!' the General's Lady wailed in despair and, like a woman demented, hurled herself towards the door. She was held back by her ever faithful companions, who clamoured around her, in turn snivelling, whimpering and attempting to comfort her. The pandemonium was terrible.

'All he had on was his dressing-jacket – not even a coat on him!' Perepelitsyna continued. 'And no umbrella either. He'll be struck dead by lightning, that's for sure!'

'He'll certainly be killed!' Bakhcheyev agreed, 'and soaked to the skin afterwards.'

'Don't you start!' I whispered to him.

'But he's human, isn't he?' Bakhcheyev retorted angrily. 'He's not a dog! You wouldn't go out in this! Go and try for yourself if you think it's such great fun!'

Foreseeing and dreading the outcome, I approached Uncle, who was still sitting in his chair as if paralysed.

'Uncle,' I said, bending down to his ear, 'you can't be thinking of having Foma Fomich back in the house? Can't you see it'd be the height of impropriety, at least while Nastasya Yevgrafovna is here?'

'My dear boy,' Uncle replied, raising his head and looking me straight in the eyes with a gaze of resolution, 'I've been considering my position, and I know what to do next! Don't worry, Nastenka shan't be offended – I'll see to it . . .'

He rose from his chair and went up to his mother.

'Mamma!' he said, 'calm yourself: I'll bring Foma Fomich back, I'll catch up with him: he can't have got far. But I swear, he'll come back on one condition only: that he confesses his guilt, publicly, in front of all the witnesses here present, and solemnly asks this most noble young lady's forgiveness. I'll have it my way this time! I'll make him! Or he will not cross the threshold of this house! I'll solemnly promise one more thing to you, Mamma: if he agrees to do this voluntarily, I'll be ready to fall at his feet and give him everything, everything that I can afford to give without depriving my children! As for me, I shall withdraw from everything from now on. My race is run, my star has set! I'm leaving Stepanchikovo. I wish you all peace and happiness here. I'm off to join my regiment – I shall live out my fated lot in clash of arms and storm of battle . . . Enough! I must away.'

At this moment the door opened and Gavrila appeared, dripping wet and covered in mud from head to toe, to add to the consternation of the company.

'What's the matter? Where have you been? Where's Foma?' Uncle cried, rushing up to Gavrila. The others surrounded Gavrila with avid curiosity, as literally rivulets of muddy water poured off his clothes. Oohs and ahs of disbelief followed every word he spoke.

'I left him by the beech grove about a verst and a half from here,' the old man began in a mournful voice. 'The horse bolted into the ditch from the lightning.'

'Well . . .' Uncle exclaimed.

'The cart overturned . . .'

'What about Foma?'

'He fell into the ditch.'

'Go on, finish the story!'

'He hurt his ribs and started to cry. I unharnessed the horse and rode back here to tell you.'

'Did Foma stay behind then?'

'He picked himself up and limped away on a stick,' Gavrila concluded, sighing deeply and hanging his head.

The weeping and sobbing of the womenfolk beggared all description.

'My horse!' Uncle cried and dashed out of the room. Uncle's horse was brought to the door; he mounted it bareback, and a moment later the sound of horse's hooves proclaimed the chase for Foma Fomich. Uncle had galloped off without even stopping to put on his hat.

The ladies crowded round the windows. Amongst the gasps and groans were some practical suggestions. There was talk of preparing a hot bath at once, of giving Foma Fomich a rub-down with surgical spirit followed by some herbal tea; it was remarked that he had not touched a crust of bread all day long and must now surely be starving. Miss Perepelitsyna suddenly produced his spectacles in their case, which he had left behind. This find had an extraordinary effect: the General's Lady seized the spectacle-case, weeping and wailing, pressed it to her bosom, and turned back to the window to keep a look-out on the road. By now the tension in the room was at breaking-point . . . In one corner Sashenka was comforting Nastenka; the two friends had their arms clasped round each other, and both were in tears. Nastenka held on to Ilyusha's hand and repeatedly kissed her pupil goodbye. Ilyusha too was sobbing, without knowing why. Yezhevikin and Mizinchikov were discussing something in a corner. I had the impression that Bakhcheyev too was about to start snivelling as he looked at the girls. I went up to him.

'No, my friend,' he said to me, 'Foma Fomich may leave this house one day, but the hour has not yet come: not until we provide him with gold-horned bulls for his chariot! Rest assured, my friend, he'll have his hosts out in the end and take the house over himself.'

The storm was over, and Mr Bakhcheyev had apparently undergone a change in his convictions.

Suddenly the cry went up: 'They're here! They're here!' and all the ladies rushed shrieking to the door. Barely ten minutes had elapsed since Uncle's departure, and it seemed impossible that Foma Fomich could have been brought back in so short a time. But the mystery was soon cleared up: after taking leave of Gavrila, Foma Fomich had indeed 'limped away on a stick'; but finding himself completely alone amid crashing thunder and pouring rain, had become simply terrified and turned back at once for Stepanchikovo, following Gavrila. Uncle had picked him up when he had reached the village. They had halted a passing farm cart, and Foma Fomich, by now much subdued, was helped into it by villagers who had arrived on the scene. Thus he was restored to the welcoming arms of the General's Lady, who all but went out of her mind when she beheld the state he was in. He was even muddier and more drenched than Gavrila. A terrible commotion ensued: some were for taking him upstairs immediately to change his underclothes; others advocated elderberry syrup and similar restorative remedies; everybody was talking at once and running around in panic without sense or purpose . . . But Foma Fomich seemed totally oblivious of what was going on around him. He was led into the room supported under both arms. As soon as he reached his chair, he slumped into it and closed his eyes. Somebody called out that he was dying: this was greeted by agonized screams; but it was Falaley who screamed the loudest of all as he desperately attempted to break through the female cordon to plant a kiss on Foma's hand . . .

5

Foma Fomich Creates Universal Happiness

'Where am I?' Foma Fomich uttered at last, in the voice of a man dying in the cause of truth.

'He makes me sick!' Mizinchikov whispered, standing next to me. 'As though he couldn't see for himself. There'll be no end to his play-acting now!'

'You're at home, Foma, with friends!' Uncle exclaimed. 'Calm yourself and cheer up! And you ought to change your clothes, Foma, or you'll catch a chill . . . I say, what about a drink, eh? A glass of something to warm you up . . .'

'I could drink some Malaga now,' groaned Foma Fomich, and closed his eyes again.

'Malaga! I don't suppose we've got any!' Uncle said, looking anxiously at Praskovya Ilyinichna.

'Yes we have!' Praskovya Ilyinichna hastened to reply. 'Four bottles — untouched,' and jingling her bundle of keys, she immediately scurried off to fetch the Malaga, accompanied by anxious exclamations on the part of all the women, who buzzed around Foma like bees about a honey-pot. But Mr Bakhcheyev was in a state of the utmost indignation.

'He wants Malaga, does he?' he growled, hardly bothering to lower his voice. 'A wine nobody ever drinks! Now who but a rogue like him would drink Malaga! Bah, confound you all! I don't know why I'm still here! What am I waiting for?'

'Foma!' Uncle began, stumbling over every word, 'now that . . . you've had a rest and are back with us . . . that is, I meant to say, Foma, I quite understand that just now, having so to speak accused the most innocent creature —'

'Where, O where is my innocence?' Foma rejoined, as though in feverish delirium. 'Where be the halcyon days of yore? Thou precious childhood, when I skipped about the fields, innocent and splendid, in pursuit of the spring butterfly? Where, where be those days of yore? Give me back my innocence, give it back to me!'

And spreading out his arms, Foma turned to each person in turn as though his innocence were hidden in somebody's pocket. Bakhcheyev was beside himself with rage.

'What will he ask for next!' he growled furiously. 'Bring him his innocence indeed! Does he want to kiss it or something? He must have been the rogue he is now even as a child! I swear he was!'

'Foma!' Uncle began again.

'Where, where be those days when I still believed in love and loved all humankind?' Foma shouted at the top of his voice, 'when I would embrace my fellow man and weep on his bosom? And now – where am I? Where am I?'

'Amongst friends, Foma, calm yourself!' Uncle called out. 'I wanted to tell you something, Foma . . .'

'I do wish you'd keep quiet,' Perepelitsyna hissed, flashing her reptilian eyes.

'Where am I?' continued Foma Fomich. 'Who are these people? Bulls and buffaloes pointing their horns at me! Life, what art thou? Does a man live on and on, in the end only to be disgraced, demeaned, humbled, beaten, and when he's dead and buried under the sod, will people only then come to their senses and crush his poor remains under a monument?'

'Holy smoke, he begins to speak of monuments!' Yezhevikin whispered, throwing up his arms.

'Erect no monument for me!' Foma shouted, 'erect none for me! I need no monuments of stone! Set me up a monument in your hearts,[43] and nothing more, nothing, nothing!'

'Foma!' Uncle interrupted. 'That's enough! Calm yourself! No need to talk of monuments. Just listen . . . You see, Foma, I appreciate, you may well have been fired by noble sentiments when you reproached me just now; but I must tell you, Foma, you got carried away – you overstepped the bounds of propriety – I assure you, you were in the wrong, Foma . . .'

'Will you never stop?' Perepelitsyna screeched again. 'Do you want to kill the poor man or something, just because he's in your power? . . .'

Following Perepelitsyna's example, the General's Lady herself was stirred to action, and her entourage with her; in no time at all they were all waving their hands at Uncle and bidding him to be silent.

'Anna Nilovna, be quiet yourself, I know exactly what I'm talking about!' Uncle replied firmly. 'This is a sacred matter! A matter of honour and justice! Foma, you're a man of sense, you offended a virtuous young lady and you must beg her pardon at once!'

'Whose pardon? What young lady have I offended?' said Foma Fomich, looking about him in bewilderment as though he had completely forgotten everything that had happened and had no idea what Uncle meant.

'Yes, Foma, if only you will agree of your own free will to make a noble admission of your guilt, upon my soul, Foma, I'll throw myself at your feet, and then ...'

'Whom have I offended?' Foma Fomich wailed. 'What young lady? Where is she? Where is this lady? Remind me of this young lady!'

At this moment Nastenka, frightened and embarrassed, approached Yegor Ilyich and tugged him by the sleeve.

'Yegor Ilyich, leave him alone!' she pleaded, 'there's no need for apologies! What's the point? Leave him!'

'Ah! Now I begin to remember!' exclaimed Foma Fomich. 'My God! I remember! Oh help me, help me to remember!' he pleaded in supreme agitation. 'Tell me: is it true I was driven out of here like the mangiest of dogs? Is it true I've been struck by lightning? Is it true someone threw me down a flight of steps? Is it all true, is it really all true?'

The weeping and lamentations of the ladies were eloquent response to Foma's question.

'Yes, yes!' he went on, 'I remember ... now I remember – after my fall I ran here pursued by thunder and lightning, to perform my duty and then vanish forever! Help me to my feet! No matter how weak I am, I have to perform my duty.'

Foma Fomich was immediately helped out of his chair. He assumed the posture of an orator and extended his arm.

'Colonel!' he cried, 'my mind is now clear; the thunder has not destroyed my mental faculties; true, I sense a deafness in my right ear, but that, I take it, is not so much the result of thunder as of my tumble down the stone steps ... Still, what of it! Who cares about Foma's right ear!'

Foma Fomich coloured these words with such a wealth of sorrowful irony and accompanied them by such a pathetic smile that the ladies were deeply moved, and lamentation broke out anew. They all looked at Uncle with sharp reproach, and some with unconcealed animosity, so that he began to show signs of capitulation in the face of such universal censure. Mizinchikov spat and walked over to the window in disgust. Bakhcheyev, barely able to contain himself, kept nudging me more and more violently with his elbow.

'Now listen, all, to my confession!' Foma Fomich cried out, looking about him with proud and resolute gaze, 'and while you're about it, pronounce your verdict upon the hapless Opiskin. Yegor Ilyich! I've had my eye on you for a long time now. I've been watching you with a sinking heart, and I could see everything, everything, when you did not even suspect that I was observing you. Colonel! I may be mistaken, but knowing your egoism, your boundless self-love, and your bestial appetite for carnal gratification, who would rebuke me for my involuntary concern for the honour of the most innocent of young persons?'

'Foma, Foma! . . . take care what you say, Foma!' Uncle exclaimed, looking anxiously at Nastenka's tortured face.

'What perturbed me most was not the innocence and gullibility of this person, but her inexperience,' Foma Fomich continued as though he had not even heard Uncle's words of caution. 'I beheld a tender sentiment opening in her heart like a rose blossom in spring, and my thoughts turned involuntarily to Petrarch, for was it not he who said that "there lies but a hair's breadth 'twixt innocence and peril"?[44] I sighed, groaned, and though I would readily have offered every drop of my blood in surety for this maid, who is as pure as gold, where was I to find a similar guarantor for you, Yegor Ilyich? Conscious of the recklessness of your unbridled passions, conscious of the fact that you would stake your all to achieve their momentary gratification, I was suddenly plunged into an abyss of fear and apprehension regarding the fate of this most virtuous of maidens . . .'

'Foma! did you really think that?' Uncle exclaimed.

'I watched you with a sinking heart. If you wish to know how I suffered, ask Shakespeare, he will tell you the state of my soul in *Hamlet*. I became suspicious and fearsome. In my deep distress and indignation I viewed everything in hues of darkness; but not the "darkness" of which we hear in the famous ballad[45] — rest assured! Hence my attempts to remove *her* from this house in order to save her; that's why you beheld me irritable of late, and out of sorts with the whole of mankind. Oh! Who will now reconcile me with mankind? I feel I may perhaps have been too demanding and unjust towards your guests, towards your nephew, towards Mr Bakhcheyev, whom I challenged on his astronomy; but who will blame me for the state of my soul at the time? Turning again to Shakespeare, I will confess that my vision of the future appeared to me like an unfathomable pool with a crocodile lurking at the bottom.[46] I felt that it was my duty to forestall disaster, that I had been appointed, created for that end — and what happened? You failed to appreciate the most noble aspirations of my soul, and paid me back with hatred, ingratitude, ridicule and humiliation . . .'

'Foma! If this is so . . . of course, I feel . . .' Uncle exclaimed in extreme agitation.

'If indeed you know what feeling is, Colonel, you will hear me out and stop interrupting me. To continue: my fault was merely that I was too concerned for the fate and happiness of this child; for truly she is but a child before you. My exalted love for mankind turned me at the time into a veritable fiend full of hatred and mistrust. I was ready to pounce upon people and tear them limb from limb. And do you know, Yegor Ilyich, that all your actions continually confirmed my mistrust and justified my suspicions? Do you know the thought that passed through my mind yesterday when you were showering me with your gold in order to reject me? "In me he's salving his own conscience so as to feel the more free to perpetrate his criminal act . . ."'

'Foma, Foma! did you really think that?' Uncle exclaimed in horror. 'Good God, and I didn't suspect a thing!'

'My suspicions were inspired from above,' Foma Fomich went on. 'Now judge for yourself, what was I to think when blind chance brought me last night to that fateful garden bench? What was I to be expected to feel at that moment – O God – when, finally, I perceived with my own eyes a glaring confirmation of all my suspicions? But a hope, albeit a slender one, still remained – and then what? This morning you yourself smashed it to smithereens! You sent me your letter; you set out your intention of entering into matrimony; you implored me not to reveal it . . . "Why should he," I reasoned, "why should he be writing to me now, after I have caught him out, rather than before? Why did he not come running to me earlier, joyful and radiant – for indeed, love does enhance the features – why did he not then fly into my arms, weep tears of infinite joy on my bosom, and reveal to me all, all?" Or am I a crocodile who would rather devour you than give you worthy counsel? Or am I some kind of vile insect which would sting you rather than be conducive to your happiness? "Am I his friend, or the most repulsive of insects?" was the question I put to myself this morning! "And finally," I thought, "why should he have summoned his nephew from the capital and betrothed him to this maiden if not to deceive us, along with the *frivolous boy himself,* while at the same time secretly pursuing his most criminal intent?" No, Colonel, if anyone did confirm my belief that your mutual love was criminal, it was you, and you alone! Moreover, your criminal guilt extends to this young lady too, for, innocent and virtuous though she be, you, by reason of your maladroit and selfish mistrust, have subjected her to the odium of slander and of grave suspicion!'

Uncle remained silent, his head hung low: Foma's eloquence seemed to have triumphed over all his objections, and he was already prepared to regard himself as an out and out criminal. The General's Lady and her company listened to Foma in mute reverence, while Perepelitsyna glared at poor Nastenka in hate-filled triumph.

'Defeated, agitated and undone,' continued Foma, 'I locked myself in my room and prayed for divine guidance! Finally, I decided to give you one last and public test. Perhaps I was unduly eager, perhaps I was too consumed with indignation; for all my noble aspirations, you hurled me through the window! As I fell through the window, I thought to myself: "Thus it is that virtue is always rewarded in this world!" Then I hit the ground and can barely remember what became of me!'

Yammering and groaning interrupted Foma Fomich's tragic recollections. The General's Lady was about to rush to him with the bottle of Malaga which she had just snatched out of Praskovya Ilyinichna's hands, when Foma, with a majestic sweep of his arm, waved aside both her and the bottle.

'Stop!' he cried, 'let me finish. What happened after my fall – I have no idea. The only thing I know is that standing as I do before you, drenched and liable to catch fever, I am intent upon being the author of your mutual happiness. Colonel! By virtue of numerous indications, upon which I shall not enlarge at present, I have finally come to the conviction that your love has been pure and even sublime, although at the same time criminally deficient in candour. Having suffered physical assault, moral degradation and being under suspicion of insulting a young lady, for whose honour I, in the manner of knights of old, would be ready to shed my last drop of blood – I have now decided to demonstrate to you the manner in which Foma Opiskin chooses to redress the wrongs done to him. Give me your hand, Colonel!'

'Gladly, Foma!' Uncle exclaimed, 'and now that you have so completely vindicated the honour of this excellent young lady ... of course ... here's my hand, Foma, and with it my sincere repentance ...'

And Uncle eagerly put out his hand without suspecting what would come of it.

'Let me have your hand too,' Foma continued in a subdued tone, addressing himself to Nastenka as he parted the crowd of women who were clustering around him.

Foma took it and put it into Uncle's hand.

'I join and bless you,' he said in the most solemn tone, 'and if there be any profit in the blessing of a sufferer mortified by grief, I urge you to be happy. Thus does Foma Opiskin take his revenge! Hurrah!'

The amazement expressed on all sides knew no bounds. This outcome was so unexpected that everybody was struck rigid with surprise. The General's Lady, her mouth wide open, came to a dead halt still clutching the bottle of Malaga in her hands. Perepelitsyna went pale and began to shake all over with rage. The rest of the female contingent threw up their hands and stood petrified, rooted to the spot. Uncle began to tremble and was about to say something, but could not bring it out. Nastenka turned white as a sheet and said meekly 'It isn't right ...' — but it was too late. Bakhcheyev — to give him his due — was the first to echo Foma's cry of hurrah, then I took it up, to be joined immediately by Sashenka's pealing voice as she rushed forward to embrace her father; then Ilyusha, then Yezhevikin; and last of all Mizinchikov.

'Hurrah!' Foma cried a second time. 'Hurrah! On your knees, children of my heart, on your knees before the tenderest of mothers! Beg her blessing and, if needs must, I too shall throw myself at her feet alongside you ...'

Uncle and Nastenka, scared, confused and not even having looked at each other, dropped on their knees before the General's Lady; everybody crowded around them; but the old woman stood stupefied, utterly at a loss what to do next. Foma Fomich was again quick to handle the situation: he himself knelt down before his benefactress. This had the effect of instantly dispelling her indecision. Through a flood of tears she finally pronounced her consent. Uncle jumped to his feet and embraced Foma in a bear hug.

'Foma, Foma! ...' he said, but his voice failed him and he was unable to continue.

'Champagne!' yelled Stepan Alekseyevich. 'Hurrah!'

'No, not champagne!' Perepelitsyna intervened, having had time to recover and weigh up the situation as well as to anticipate the consequences. 'We'll light a candle to the Good Lord to pray before the holy image and be blessed by it as befits all God-fearing folk ...'

There was a general rush to act upon this very judicious advice, which led to a fresh outburst of agitation. A candle had to be lit. Stepan Alekseyevich drew up a chair and clambered onto it to place the candle in front of the icon. However, the chair immediately collapsed under him and he fell down heavily on the floor, though he managed to stay on his feet. Not at all perturbed, he did not hesitate to give way respectfully to Perepelitsyna. The slim Perepelitsyna had the candle lit in a trice. The nun and the General's Lady and her companions began to make the sign of the cross and prostrate themselves. The image of Our Saviour was taken off the wall and brought to the General's Lady. Uncle and Nastenka again went down on their knees and the ceremony was performed under Perepelitsyna's devout instructions: 'Bow down to her feet; now pay your respects to the icon: now kiss Mamma's hand!' After the betrothed couple, Mr Bakhcheyev considered it his duty to venerate the icon, and he too did not omit to kiss the hand of the General's Lady. He was in a transport of joy.

'Hurrah!' he cried again. 'Now we'll have champagne!'

As a matter of fact, everyone was in a state of exultation. The General's Lady was weeping, but hers were now tears of joy: the union sanctified by Foma immediately became in her eyes both respectable and holy – but the most important thing of all to her was that Foma Fomich had excelled himself and was now to remain with her for ever and ever. All her companions, outwardly at least, shared in the general elation. Uncle, when he was not kneeling at his mother's feet and kissing her hands, was hugging me, Bakhcheyev, Mizinchikov or Yezhevikin in turn; as for Ilyusha, he nearly squeezed the life out of him in his arms. Sashenka had her arms round Nastenka and was showering her with kisses, Praskovya Ilyinichna was in a flood of tears. Mr Bakhcheyev, noticing this, went up to her and kissed her hand. Old Yezhevikin, profoundly affected, wept in a corner, wiping his eyes with the same check handkerchief that he had sported the previous day. Gavrila whispered in the corner opposite and regarded Foma Fomich with reverence, while Falaley went round the room howling at the top of his voice and planting kisses on everybody's hands. We were all overcome with emotion. No one had yet begun to speak or offer explanations; it seemed that everything had already been said and there was room only for exclamations of joy. Neither did anyone know how matters had come to such a swift conclusion. One thing only was accepted as an evident and incontrovertible fact: that the author of our happiness was Foma Fomich.

But not five minutes of the general rejoicing had elapsed when Tatyana Ivanovna suddenly appeared in our midst. By what means, by what powers of perception, closeted as she was upstairs in her room, she could have learned about the love match and the engagement that had just taken place, nobody will ever know. She flounced into the room with a radiant face and tears of joy in her eyes, exquisitely and seductively attired (while upstairs she had somehow managed to find time to change her dress), and with loud cries of joy flew to enclose Nastenka in an embrace.

'Nastenka, Nastenka! You loved him, and I had no idea,' she cried. 'God! they were in love, they suffered secretly, in silence! They were being persecuted! What a romance! Nastenka, my darling. I want to know the whole truth: do you really love this madman?'

In place of a reply Nastenka hugged and kissed her.

'God, what a lovely romance!' and Tatyana Ivanovna clapped her hands in excitement. 'Listen, Nastenka, listen, my angel: all these men are ungrateful, they're monsters, they're not worthy of our love. But perhaps he is the best of a bad bunch. Come here, you madman!' she exclaimed, turning to Uncle and grabbing hold of his hand. 'Are you really in love? Are you really capable of loving? Look at me – I want to look into your eyes, I want to see if these eyes are lying or not. No, they're not lying – they're shining with love. Oh, how happy I am! Nastenka, my friend, listen, you're not rich: I shall give you thirty thousand. Take it, for God's sake! I don't need the money, I don't need it; I'll still have a lot left over. No, no, no, no!' she cried, shaking her hands on seeing that Nastenka was about to object. 'You keep quiet too, Yegor Ilyich, it's none of your business. No, Nastenka, I've decided to give you a present; I've been meaning to give you a present for a long time now, and I've just been waiting for you to fall in love for the first time ... I shall rejoice in your happiness. You will insult me if you don't agree to accept; I shall cry, Nastenka ... No, no, no, no!'

Tatyana Ivanovna was so elated at that moment that it would have been cruel to argue with her. Nor did anybody venture to do so; it was decided to await a more opportune moment. She rushed forward to kiss the General's Lady, Perepelitsyna, and then all of us in turn. Bakhcheyev threaded his way towards her and with exquisite courtesy took her hand.

'Bless you, my dear sweet lady! Can you pardon an old fool for what he got up to yesterday: if only I'd known what a jewel of a heart you've got!'

'I've known you all along, you madman!' Tatyana Ivanovna replied, full of playful excitement, and dabbed him on the nose with her glove as she wafted past like a zephyr, catching him with the folds of her gorgeous dress. The fat man bowed respectfully to her.

'A most worthy lady!' he said with affection. 'I'll tell you, that German's nose has been glued back on!' he whispered confidentially, giving me a merry look.

'What nose? What German?' I asked in surprise.

'The one I ordered of course, with him kissing his lady's hand as she wipes away a tear with her handkerchief. My Yevdokim had it mended yesterday; I sent for it as soon as we got back from the chase ... It'll be here soon. A beautiful piece of work!'

'Foma!' cried Uncle, carried away with elation, 'you're the cause of our happiness! How can I ever repay you?'

'You can't, Colonel,' replied Foma Fomich, with a pinched expression. '*Continue to pay no attention to me*, and enjoy your happiness without Foma.'

Evidently he was piqued that amidst the general rejoicing he had somehow found himself neglected.

'It's because we're all so excited, Foma!' Uncle exclaimed. 'To tell you the truth, my friend, I hardly know where I am now. Listen, Foma, I've offended you. My life and my every drop of blood could not make good the damage done to you, and so I shan't say a word, not even by way of apology. But if ever you should require my head, my life, I'll willingly plunge into the deepest pit for you; command and you shall see ... I've no more to say, Foma.'

And Uncle, with a wave of the hand, conscious of the impossibility of lending any further conviction to his words, continued to gaze at Foma Fomich with eyes full of tears and gratitude.

'Now you see what an angel he is!' Perepelitsyna piped up, adding her contribution to the general praise of Foma Fomich.

'Yes, yes!' Sashenka put in, 'I had no idea that you're such a good man, Foma Fomich, and I've been disrespectful towards you. Do forgive me, Foma Fomich, you can be assured that I shall love you with my whole heart. If only you knew how much I now respect you!'

'Yes, Foma!' said Bakhcheyev in his turn, 'please forgive me too, fool that I am! How little I knew you! You're not only a scholar, Foma Fomich, you're a real hero! My whole house is at your disposal. I say, my friend, why don't you come over the day after tomorrow, and Mamma the General's Lady too, along with the betrothed pair, of course – look here, all of you come! I tell you, we'll have such a meal! I shan't brag in advance, but I'll lay on a feast fit for the Tsar. That's a solemn promise!'

In the midst of these effusions Nastenka also approached Foma Fomich, and without further ado hugged him warmly and gave him a big kiss.

'Foma Fomich!' she said, 'you are the benefactor; you've done so much for us that I simply don't know how to repay you, but I do know one thing, I'll always be the most gentle and loving of sisters to you ...'

She was unable to finish; tears choked her words. Foma Fomich kissed her on the head and himself let fall a tear.

'My children, children of my heart!' he said. 'Live, prosper and in moments of happiness spare an occasional thought for a wretched exile! As for myself, let it be said that misfortune may be the mother of virtue – Gogol's words,[47] if I'm not mistaken – that frivolous author's sometimes not devoid of a grain of sense. Exile is misfortune! I shall now go out into the world, a wanderer leaning on my staff, and who knows, through my misfortunes I may yet attain new pinnacles of virtue! This thought is the last comfort left to me!'

'But . . . where will you go, Foma?' Uncle exclaimed in terror.

Everybody shuddered and rushed up to Foma Fomich.

'Do you seriously expect me to stay in your house after what you did to me, Colonel?' asked Foma Fomich, with a most dignified air.

But he was not allowed to speak: his words were drowned in general outcry. He was persuaded to sit down; everybody kept pleading with him, weeping over him, and heaven knows what else. Needless to say, he had never had the slightest intention of leaving 'this house' either now, or earlier in the day, or the previous day when he had been digging in the garden. He knew very well that people would strenuously try to stop him, and would cling to him, especially after he had brought them happiness, after everybody's faith in him had been restored and everybody was ready to bear him aloft and considered it an honour and a privilege to do so. But it was probable that his cowardly return on taking fright in the thunderstorm niggled his pride and spurred him on to further display of heroics; and here indeed was another chance of acting the injured party, an irresistible temptation to hold forth and posture, to strut and make a show of his own virtues. It was a temptation he did not attempt to resist; he tried to break loose from those who would restrain him; he demanded his staff, he begged to have his freedom restored; to be allowed to go wherever he pleased, for 'in this house' he had been dishonoured and beaten; he insisted that the reason he had returned had been to secure the happiness of the household, and that, finally, he could never be expected to remain in 'a house of ingratitude and eat the soup that, however nourishing, was seasoned with beatings'. At last he ceased his remonstrations. He was again persuaded to sit down, but his eloquence was unimpaired.

'Tell me if I haven't been insulted here!' he yelled, 'tell me if you haven't been taunting me! Have you yourself, Colonel, not been pointing at me the finger of derision, like the unruly offspring of the vulgar classes on the streets of our towns? Yes, Colonel, I stand by this comparison, for though you may not have bean pointing at me with physical fingers of derision, you have done so in the moral sense; and moral fingers of derision are more offensive, on occasions, than physical ones. And I leave aside the beatings . . .'

'Foma, Foma!' cried Uncle, 'spare me the memory! Have I not been telling you that all my blood would not suffice to wash away the offence?

Show me your heart is in the right place! Forget and forgive and stay with us to witness our happiness! The fruits of your labours, Foma!'

'. . . I want to love mankind, to love mankind,' yelled Foma Fomich, 'but I'm not being allowed to see people, I am forbidden to love, they force people away from me! Give me, give me a man so that I may love him! Where is this man? Where has this man hidden himself? Like Diogenes with his lantern,[48] I've been yearning to find one true soul all my life long, but in vain, and I can't even begin to love anybody until I find that person. Woe to him who has turned me into a misanthropist! "Give me a man," I cry, "that I may love him!" – and I'm fobbed off with a Falaley! Should I love Falaley? Would I wish to love Falaley?[49] Could I love Falaley even if I wanted to? No! Why not? Because he is Falaley. Why do I hate mankind? Because mankind is made up of Falaleys, or beings like Falaley! I don't want Falaley, I detest Falaley, I spit upon Falaley, I'll make mincemeat of Falaley – and if you ask me to choose, I'd rather love the evil spirit Asmodeus[50] than Falaley! Come here, come here, my eternal tormentor, come here!' he screamed, suddenly turning on Falaley, who was standing on tiptoe and innocently peering from among the crowd that had gathered around Foma Fomich. 'Come here! I'll prove to you, Colonel,' screamed Foma, pulling the terrified Falaley by the hand, 'I'll prove to you the justice of what I said about those perpetual taunts and fingers of derision! Tell me, Falaley, tell me truthfully: what did you dream about last night? There, Colonel, you are about to witness your handiwork! Well, Falaley, speak up!'

The poor boy, trembling all over with fear, desperately searched the room with his eyes for deliverance; but all present could only quiver in terror as they anxiously awaited his reply.

'Well, Falaley, I'm waiting!'

In place of a reply, Falaley screwed up his face, opened his mouth wide and began to bellow like a calf.

'Colonel! Observe the pig-headedness of this creature! Do you suppose it's natural? I'm asking you for the last time, Falaley: what did you dream of last night?'

'I dreamed of . . .'

'Say you dreamt of me,' said Bakhcheyev, trying to be helpful.

'Of your virtues!' whispered Yezhevikin in his other ear.

Falaley rolled his eyes.

'I dreamed of . . . of your vir . . . of the white b-bull!' he finally brought out, bitter tears streaming down his face.

Everybody gasped. But Foma Fomich was in a rare state of magnanimity.

'At least I appreciate your honesty, Falaley,' he said, 'honesty which I fail to detect in others. God be with you. If you've been taught by others purposely to annoy me with this dream, God will reward you and the rest according to your deserts. If not, I respect you for your honesty, for even in the basest of creatures, such as you, I've taught myself to recognize the image and likeness of God ... I forgive you, Falaley! My children, embrace me, I'm staying! ...'

'He's staying!' everybody exclaimed in a transport of joy.

'I'm staying and all is forgiven. Colonel, give Falaley a lump of sugar: I can't bear to see him cry on such a day of universal joy.'

Naturally such magnanimity was greeted with amazement. To be *so* concerned, at a time like *this* – and on whose behalf? For Falaley! Uncle rushed to carry out the order for sugar. In a flash, God only knows how, the silver sugar bowl appeared in Praskovya Ilyinichna's hands. Uncle put out a trembling hand to extract two pieces, then three, then dropped them, realizing that he was too excited to do anything.

'Ah now!' he exclaimed, 'on a day like this! Wait, Falaley!' and he tipped the whole contents into Falaley's cupped hands.

'That's for being so honest,' he added by way of moral justification.

'Mr Korovkin,' Vidoplyasov announced, suddenly appearing in the doorway.

A comparatively slight commotion ensued. Korovkin's arrival was clearly ill-timed. Everybody looked to Uncle for explanation.

'Korovkin!' Uncle exclaimed in some embarrassment. 'I'm delighted, to be sure ...' he added, casting a meek glance at Foma Fomich. 'But, well, I don't know, should I invite him in now – at a time like this? What do you think, Foma?'

'Never mind, never mind!' replied Foma Fomich affably. 'Do invite Korovkin too; let him too participate in the general happiness.'

In short, Foma Fomich was in saintly mood.

'May I have permission to report,' Vidoplyasov remarked, 'that Korovkin is deemed not to be in a presentable state.'

'Not in a presentable state? What are you talking about?' Uncle exclaimed.

'Just so: he is not in a sober frame of mind, sir.'

But the mystery was solved even before Uncle had time to open his mouth again, blush, register his shock, and almost die of embarrassment. Korovkin appeared in the doorway, brushed Vidoplyasov aside and stood in front of the flabbergasted company. He was a short, thick-set man of about forty, with dark, greying, closely cropped hair and a round rubicund face with small bloodshot eyes; his dress comprised a close-fitting hair-cloth necktie fastened by a buckle at the back, the shabbiest of tail-coats covered in pieces of fluff and hay and with a huge tear under one armpit, a pair of *pantalons impossibles* and, held at arm's length, an unbelievably greasy cap. This gentleman was completely drunk. Having stumbled into the middle of the room, he stopped unsteadily, his head swaying back and forth with fuddled deliberation; then slowly his features melted into a wide grin.

'My apologies, ladies and gentlemen,' he said. 'I . . . er . . .' (with these words he gave his shirt collar a smart flip) 'have done it again!'

The General's Lady immediately assumed a pose of injured dignity. Foma Fomich, seated in his chair, looked the eccentric guest up and down ironically. Bakhcheyev regarded him with puzzlement not devoid of a certain degree of compassion. However, Uncle's embarrassment knew no bounds; he suffered heart and soul for Korovkin.

'Korovkin!' he began, 'listen!'

'*Attendez*,' Korovkin cut him short. 'At your service: a child of nature . . . But what's this? There are ladies present . . . Why didn't you tell me, you swine, that there were ladies here?' He looked at Uncle with a roguish grin. 'Never mind! Courage! . . . Let us introduce ourselves to the fair sex . . . My wonderful ladies!' he continued, moving his tongue with difficulty and stumbling over each word, 'behold one who is unfortunate enough . . . well, and so on and so forth . . . The rest is best unsaid . . . Musicians! A polka!'

'How about some sleep?' Mizinchikov asked, calmly walking up to Korovkin.

'Sleep? Do you intend to insult me?'

'Not at all. Just the thing after a journey . . .'

'Never!' Korovkin replied indignantly. 'Do you suppose I'm drunk? Not a bit . . . On second thoughts, where do they sleep here?'

'Come along, I'll lead the way.'

'Where to? The barn? No, my friend, you won't make a fool of me. I've spent one night there already . . . On second thoughts, lead on . . . Seeing as you're a good sort, why the hell not? No need for a pillow; a military man doesn't need a pillow. Fix me up a couch, a couch, my friend . . . And listen,' he added, coming to a halt, 'I can see you're a good fellow – fix me up with . . . you know what! a toddy, a toddy, just enough to drown a fly in . . . just to drown a fly in, just a thimbleful.'

'All right, all right!' Mizinchikov replied.

'Good . . . Don't rush me, I've got to say goodbye . . . *Adieu*, *mesdames et mesdemoiselles!* ... You have, as it were, pierced ... But enough! We'll talk later ... One other thing, wake me up when things get going ... or even five minutes before ... only see you don't start without me! Do you hear? Not without me!'

And the merry gentleman disappeared after Mizinchikov. No one spoke a word. Consternation continued. Finally Foma Fomich began to chuckle softly to himself; his mirth gradually gathered strength until it became full-blooded laughter. Seeing this, the General's Lady brightened up a little too, though she still preserved her aspect of outraged dignity. Involuntary laughter was gathering strength all round. Uncle alone remained dumbfounded, blushing and, for a time, quite inarticulate.

'Good Lord!' he muttered at last. 'Who could have known? But after all ... after all, it could happen to anyone. Foma, I assure you he's honest, gentlemanly, and in addition, exceptionally well read, Foma ... you'll see for yourself! ...'

'Quite, quite,' replied Foma Fomich, choking with laughter. 'Exceptionally well read, extraordinarily well read!'

'You ought to hear him talk about the railways!' Yezhevikin remarked *sotto voce.*

'Foma! ...' Uncle was about to launch forth, but his words were drowned in a general peal of laughter. Foma Fomich was splitting his sides. Watching him, Uncle too burst out laughing.

'Well, what of it!' he said with abandon. 'You're a noble soul, Foma, you have a great heart – I owe my happiness to you ... You'll bear no grudge against Korovkin.'

Nastenka alone did not join in the laughter. She regarded her intended with eyes suffused with love as if to say: 'Aren't you wonderful and kind and sweet, and how I love you!'

6

Conclusion

The triumph of Foma Fomich was complete and unassailable. Truly nothing would have come to pass without his intervention, and the accomplished fact stifled all doubts and objections. The gratitude of the blissfully happy couple knew no bounds. Uncle and Nastenka simply refused to listen to me when I tentatively hinted at the chain of events which had led Foma to agree to their marriage. Sashenka kept shouting: 'Good, kind Foma Fomich – I'll embroider a cushion for him in wool!' And she put me to shame for my scepticism. The newly converted Stepan Alekseyevich would probably have readily strangled me had I dared to utter a disrespectful word to Foma Fomich in his presence. He now followed Foma like a faithful dog, his eyes full of devotion, repeating as he went: 'You're the noblest of them all, Foma! You're a scholar, Foma!' As for Yezhevikin, he was beside himself with joy. The old man had been aware for a long time that Nastenka had turned Yegor Ilyich's head, and he had never ceased to hope and pray for the two to be wed. He had clung to his hope to the very last, only abandoning it when it had been impossible not to do so. Foma Fomich had changed matters. Of course, for all his elation, the old man could see right through Foma. It was clear that Foma Fomich would rule this household forever and that his tyranny would know no end. It is well known that even the most objectionable, the most capricious people relax, at least for a time, once their desires have been gratified. Not so Foma Fomich, who would become ever more fatuous and arrogant as his fortunes improved. Just before dinner, he appeared in a fresh change of clothes, sat down in his chair, summoned my uncle and in front of the whole family proceeded to read him a new sermon.

'Colonel!' he began, 'you are about to be legally married. Are you aware of the responsibilities? . . .'

And so on, and so forth; imagine a sermon stretching for ten pages, in the format of the *Journal des Débats*, in the smallest print and filled with the most arrant nonsense, which had nothing to do with responsibilities but simply paid unabashed homage to the intellect, humility, integrity, courage and generosity of Foma Fomich himself. Everybody was hungry and wanted to eat; however, no one dared to object and everyone felt obliged to listen deferentially until he reached the end of his ravings; even Bakhcheyev, with his prodigious appetite, sat stock-still through the whole sermon in an attitude of the most profound respect. Pleased with his own eloquence, Foma's spirits rose and he got a little the worse for drink at dinner, which caused him to propose some very extraordinary toasts. These he followed by quips and jokes, mostly at the expense of the newly betrothed. Everybody laughed and applauded, but some of the jokes were so obscene and unambiguous that even Bakhcheyev was embarrassed. At last Nastenka jumped up from the table and ran away. At this Foma Fomich went wild with delight; but he immediately pulled himself together, in a few brief but well-chosen words depicted Nastenka's virtues, and proposed her health in her absence. Uncle, who a moment before had felt distressed and embarrassed, was now ready to embrace Foma Fomich. On the whole, both the betrothed behaved as though they were slightly uneasy in each other's presence and overwhelmed by their good fortune. I noticed too that not a single word had passed between them since they had received their blessing, and they were even avoiding each other's eyes. As everyone was rising from the table, Uncle suddenly left the room. I went out to look for him and wandered onto the terrace. There, sitting in a chair over a cup of coffee, Foma Fomich was holding forth, very much the worse for drink. Standing near him were Yezhevikin, Bakhcheyev and Mizinchikov. I stopped to listen.

'Why,' shouted Foma Fomich, 'would I be ready to go to the stake this minute for my convictions? And why would none of you be prepared to go to the stake? Why, why?'

'Wouldn't it be overdoing it somewhat, Foma Fomich, I mean to go to the stake!' Yezhevikin was pulling his leg. 'What's the point? First, it would be painful, and secondly, you'd go up in flames — what would remain of you?'

'What would remain of me? A handful of sacred ashes would remain of me. But how can I expect you to understand, to appreciate me! You, for whom great men don't exist apart from Caesar or Alexander the Great! And what have your Caesars ever done? Whom have they made happy? What has your famous Alexander the Great ever accomplished? He conquered the whole world, did he? Well, you give me an army like his and I'll conquer it too, and so will you, and so will he . . . But he killed· the worthy Clitus and I never killed the worthy Clitus . . . The brat! The rogue! I'd give him a good birching instead of celebrating him in the history of the world . . . and the same goes for Caesar!'

'Spare Caesar, Foma Fomich!'

'He was a fool!' cried Foma.

'Well spoken!' Stepan Alekseyevich chimed in, also under the influence, 'don't spare them; they're all a bunch of whippersnappers pirouetting on one leg! Sausagemongers all of them! Who was it the other day that tried . to set up a scholarship? And what's a scholarship! The devil knows what it is! Bound to be some new trick or other! And that one who came strutting into polite society swaying on his feet and asking for rum! Nothing wrong with having a drink, I say! Have all the drink you want, but stick to your own side of the fence, then have another one if you like . . . No need to spare any of them. They're all scoundrels! You're the only learned man about, Foma!'

Once Bakhcheyev had sided with somebody, he did it heart and soul.

I found Uncle in the garden in the most secluded spot, by the pond. Nastenka was with him. As soon as she saw me, she dashed out of sight into the bushes as though overcome by guilt. Uncle came forward to meet me, his face beaming and tears of exultation in his eyes. He took both my hands and clasped them warmly.

'My boy!' he said, 'I still can't believe my good fortune . . . nor can Nastenka. We can only marvel, and praise the Almighty. She was crying just now. And believe me, I'm still not myself: I believe it and yet I don't believe it! Why should it be me? Why? What have I done? What have I done to deserve it?'

'If anyone deserves it, it must be you, dear Uncle,' I said with warmth. 'I've never met such an honest, such a wonderful, good-natured person as you . . .'

'No, Seryozha, no, you're exaggerating,' he replied in a note of chagrin. 'That's just the trouble – we're good (I'm speaking only of myself, you understand), just so long as all is well with us; but the minute things go wrong, nobody must come near us! I was discussing it with Nastenka just now. No matter how much Foma Fomich used to shine, you know, I didn't quite believe in him until today, even though I had been trying to convince you of his perfection; and even yesterday, when he refused my gift, I still wasn't absolutely convinced of his true merit. Shame on me! My heart shudders when I think back to this morning! But I lost control of myself . . . When he talked about Nastenka it was like a stab in the heart. I went out of my mind and turned on him like a tiger . . .'

'It can't be helped, Uncle, it was only natural.'

Uncle waved his hands in protest.

'No, no, my boy, don't say that! It's simply my corrupt nature which is to blame for everything; I'm such a base, selfish, lascivious brute – I will let my passions run away with me. Foma said so too.' (What could I say to that?) 'You've no idea, Seryozha,' he continued with deep feeling, 'the number of times I've been short-tempered, cruel, unjust, arrogant – and not only towards Foma! You see, now it all comes back to me, and I'm ashamed that so far I've done nothing to deserve my good fortune. Nastenka feels the same about herself, though I really don't know what sins she could have committed – she's an angel, without a human fault! She said to me, we're deeply beholden to God and must try to improve ourselves and be forever charitable ... If only you had heard how passionately, how beautifully she put it all! My God, what a girl!'

He paused, overcome with emotion. A moment later he continued: 'We've decided, my boy, to be especially considerate towards Foma, Mamma and Tatyana Ivanovna. Dear Tatyana Ivanovna! Isn't she the noblest creature that ever was! Oh, I've been so bad to everybody! To you ... But just let anyone hurt Tatyana Ivanovna ... Still, never mind! ... Must do something for Mizinchikov too.'

'Yes, Uncle, I've changed my opinion of Tatyana Ivanovna! One can't help respecting and feeling sorry for her.'

'Exactly so, exactly so!' Uncle snapped up my words eagerly, 'one can't help respecting her! Take Korovkin, for example; I'm sure you're laughing at him,' he added, looking timidly into my eyes, 'and weren't we all laughing at him? That's unforgivable of us, you know ... perhaps he's altogether the nicest, kindest person you could imagine – it's just his fate ... the misfortune he has endured ... You don't believe me, but it could very well be so, I assure you.'

'No, Uncle, why shouldn't I believe you?'

And I began to explain with fervour that even the most degraded people still manage to retain the loftiest human feelings, that the depths of man's soul are unfathomable, that we should not despise the fallen, but on the contrary should seek them out and raise them up, that the commonly held standards of goodness and morality are false, and so on and so forth – in short, I got carried away and even touched upon the Natural School;[51] in conclusion I quoted the poem: 'When from the darkness of depravity ...'[52] Uncle was delighted.

'My dear boy, my dear boy!' he said, profoundly moved, 'you understand me perfectly, you've put it better than I could ever have done. Precisely, precisely! God! Why should man be wicked? Why is it that I'm so often wicked if it's such a pleasure, such a joy to be kind? Nastenka said the same thing just now ... But look – what a glorious spot this is,' he added, looking around. 'What a countryside! What a picture! Look at that tree! You couldn't get your arms round it! All the sap! The foliage! The sunshine! How joyful and washed everything looks after the storm! . . . I'm sure trees have understanding and feelings and know what joy it is to be alive . . . They do, don't they – eh? What do you think?'

'It's very possible, Uncle. In their own way of course . . .'

'Quite right, in their own way . . . Marvellous, marvellous Creator! . . . Surely, you remember this garden, Seryozha: the way you played and romped when you were small! You know, I can still remember you as a child,' he said, looking at me with eyes full of inexpressible love and happiness. 'One thing you weren't allowed to do on your own was to go near the pond. Remember one evening when Katya – bless her soul – called to you and began to cuddle you . . . you were all hot and flushed from running in the garden; you had such fair, curly locks of hair . . . She stroked them and played with them and then said: "I'm glad you brought the little orphan here." Do you remember?'

'Just about, Uncle.'

'It was evening, I remember, but there was still plenty of sunshine, and it shone on you both, and I was sitting in a corner puffing my pipe, watching you . . . I go to town to visit her grave every month, Sergey,' he added, lowering his voice, which betrayed great emotional stress. 'I was telling Nastenka about this just now – she said in future we'll both go together . . .'

Uncle stopped in an effort to suppress his agitation.

Vidoplyasov came up to us at this moment.

'Vidoplyasov!' Uncle exclaimed with a start. 'Have you come from Foma Fomich?'

'No, sir, it's more on my own account.'

'Ah, splendid! Do tell us about Korovkin. I meant to ask you a while ago . . . I told him to keep an eye on Korovkin, you see, Sergey. Well, Vidoplyasov, what's wrong?'

'If I may be so bold as to remind you, sir, of your promise yesterday to consider my request to intercede on my behalf, sir, with regard to the insults to which I'm subjected daily.'

'It's not about your surname again, is it?' Uncle exclaimed, horrified.

'What's to be done, sir? There's no end to the insults.'

'Oh, Vidoplyasov, Vidoplyasov! What am I to do with you?' said Uncle, disheartened. 'What insults are you talking about? You'll drive yourself out of your mind and end up in a lunatic asylum!'

'I'm sure, as regards my sanity –' Vidoplyasov began to retort.

'All right, all right,' Uncle interrupted, 'I didn't mean any harm – I was thinking of your own good. There now, who on earth would want to insult you? It's just some nonsense again!'

'They're the poison of my life!'

'Who?'

'Everybody, but Matryona's the worst. She's made my life a misery, sir. You see, sir, discriminating people, people who have known me from childhood, they agree I have a foreign look about me, largely due to my features. Well sir, because of this I have no peace at all now. Everywhere I go, I get called all sorts of awful names – even the little children, they ought to be chastised . . . They jeered at me again as I was coming here . . . I just can't take any more, sir. Help and protect me, sir!'

'Oh, Vidoplyasov! . . . What exactly do they say? Probably something so stupid it's not worth bothering about.'

'It wouldn't be decent to repeat.'

'Come on, what is it?'

'It's really too awful!'

'Go on, say it!'

'Grishka the monk, he sat on my trunk.'

'There you are! And I thought it really was heaven knows what! Why don't you just ignore it?'

'I tried, it was even worse.'

'Listen, Uncle,' I said, 'he's saying that it's not much of a life for him in this house, so why don't you send him to Moscow, for a time at any rate, to stay with that calligrapher friend of his? You did say he had been staying with a calligrapher.'

'Well, my boy, that one came to a tragic end.'

'Really?'

'The gentleman in question, sir,' replied Vidoplyasov, 'had the misfortune to appropriate property not belonging to him for which, his talent notwithstanding, he was confined to gaol, sir, where he perished most irrevocably . . .'

'All right, all right, Vidoplyasov, you calm down and I'll sort it all out,' Uncle said, 'it's a promise! Now what about Korovkin? Still asleep, is he?'

'No, sir. The gentleman's just departed. This is what I came to report.'

'What do you mean, departed? What are you talking about? How could you have let him go?' Uncle exclaimed.

'I didn't have the heart not to let him go, sir; it was a most pitiful sight. When he woke up and recalled the whole episode, he beat his brow and bawled his head off, sir . . .'

'Bawled his head off . . .?'

'To put it more graciously: he uttered a variety of lamentations, sir. He cried: "How can I face the fair sex now?" And then he said: "I'm not worthy of belonging to the family of man!" And carried on most pitifully, in the most delicate vein, sir.'

'There's a sensitive soul for you! What did I tell you, Sergey . . . But how could you let him go, Vidoplyasov, after being specially told to look after him? My God, oh my God!'

'It was more than my heart could bear. He begged me to keep it secret. His coachman fed and harnessed the horses himself. As for the sum he was lent three days ago, he instructed me, sir, to convey his profoundest thanks together with his assurance that the loan would be returned by the earliest post.'

'What sum is he talking about, Uncle?'

'He mentioned twenty-five rubles in silver,' said Vidoplyasov.

'I lent it to him at the station, my boy. He found himself a little short. Of course, he'll send it back by the first post . . . Oh my God, what a pity! What about going after him, Sergey?'

'No, Uncle, I think it would be better not to.'

'So do I. You see, Seryozha, I'm no philosopher, of course, but it seems to me there's far more good in every person than appears on the surface. Same with Korovkin: he just couldn't face the disgrace . . . Anyway, let's go and see Foma! It's time we did; he might take offence at our ingratitude and neglect. Let's go to him. Oh, Korovkin, Korovkin!'

My story is finished. The lovers were united and the genius of goodness, in the shape of Foma Fomich, was installed in the house. A number of convenient reasons could be given for this, but in the light of present circumstances all such reasons would be wholly superfluous. Such is my opinion at any rate. Instead, I merely propose to say a few words about the subsequent fate of my heroes, without which, as is well known, no tale can be considered complete; anyway, it is required of me by prescribed procedure.

The nuptials of the 'happy pair' took place six weeks after the events described above. It was a quiet family affair without undue pomp or too many guests. Mizinchikov was Uncle's best man, while I was charged with looking after Nastenka. Of course there were guests. But the principal and most important personage was, naturally, Foma Fomich. Everybody danced attendance on him. However, it so happened that at the height of the festivities he was missed out in a champagne round.

There was immediately a scene – reproaches, wailing and shouting. Foma Fomich dashed upstairs to his room and bolted the door, shouting that he was being despised, that 'new people' had been installed in the family circle and he had therefore been reduced to nought, to mere flotsam. Uncle wrung his hands in despair; Nastenka was in tears; the General's Lady went into convulsions as usual. The wedding festivities began to assume a funereal air. Seven more years of such life with their benefactor Foma Fomich fell to the lot of my hapless Uncle and poor Nastenka. Right up to the moment of his death (he passed away last year) Foma Fomich dissembled, sulked, shammed, raged, swore, but the veneration in which he was held by the 'happy pair' not only did not diminish but grew in direct proportion to his caprices. Yegor Ilyich and Nastenka were so wrapped up in their own happiness that they were even apprehensive of their good fortune, considering that the Good Lord had been altogether too generous to them, and that before long they would have to bear the cross of suffering to atone for the happiness which they did not deserve. Of course, Foma Fomich was able to do whatever he liked in this docile household. And he certainly indulged himself to the full during those seven years. The mind boggles at the resourcefulness of his corrupt, idle, degenerate mind in inventing the most refined, morally Lucullan[53] caprices. Three years after Uncle's wedding the General's Lady died. The orphaned Foma was beside himself with grief. To this day people in the house still speak with awe of his condition at this time. When it came to the burial, he struggled and begged to be interred with her. For a month or more he was given neither knife nor fork; and on one memorable occasion his mouth had to be forced open for the extraction of a pin which he was trying to swallow. One observer maintained that in the course of the struggle Foma Fomich had a thousand opportunities of swallowing this pin and yet he missed every one of them. However, this suggestion was greeted with frank indignation and its author was soundly condemned for callousness and indecency. Nastenka alone kept her peace, and even could not hold back a little smile, which caused Uncle to look at her with some anxiety. Generally speaking it must be owned that, although Foma Fomich continued to be as full of himself and as capricious as ever in my uncle's house, he no longer indulged in quite the same despotic extravagances towards Uncle as previously. He moaned, wept, reproached, complained, ridiculed, but he no longer showed his former cruelty – there were no more 'Your Excellency' scenes, and this, it would appear, was thanks to Nastenka. Almost imperceptibly she managed to compel Foma to make a concession here, to submit to the will of others there. She refused to see her husband humiliated, and succeeded in getting her way. Foma Fomich realized very well that he held almost no secrets for her. I say *almost*, because Nastenka too venerated him, and supported her husband wholeheartedly whenever he chose to praise his mentor. She wished to see her spouse respected by everyone in all regards, and for this reason openly supported his attachment to Foma Fomich. I am equally convinced that in the sweetness of her heart Nastenka had long since forgotten all former wrongs and bore no further malice against Foma Fomich in gratitude for uniting her with Uncle; and furthermore, she probably fully embraced Uncle's belief, in all seriousness, that too much ought not to be expected of a former 'martyr' and jester, that on the contrary, one ought to give succour to his heart. Poor Nastenka, herself from the ranks of the *insulted*, had endured suffering, and memories of it were still fresh in her mind. Within a month or so of the wedding, Foma became quieter, meek and even amiable; but then he began to have entirely new and unexpected fits, and to fall into trances, which terrified every member of the household. One moment he would be talking happily, or even laughing, and the next he would stop dead, paralysed, in precisely the same posture in which he had been a split second before the fit; if, for example, he had been laughing, then the expression would remain, a smile fixed on his lips; if he happened to be holding something in his hand, say a fork, it would remain in his extended hand, suspended in mid-air. Of course, eventually the grin would relax and his hand would be lowered, but Foma Fomich would have no feeling or recollection of anything, including dropping his hand. He would sit staring in front of him, occasionally blinking his eyes, saying not a word, hearing and understanding nothing. An hour would then sometimes pass, the whole household tiptoeing about with bated breath, in fear and trembling and in tears. At last Foma Fomich would come to, utterly exhausted, and quite refusing to admit that he had been aware of anything untoward during all this time. To what unimaginable lengths of posturing did the man go in subjecting himself to hour-long, self-imposed torture merely in order to say later: 'Look at me, my feelings are more exalted than yours!' Eventually the day came when Foma Fomich condemned Uncle outright for his 'continued insolence and disrespect' and moved out to live with Mr Bakhcheyev. Stepan Alekseyevich, who after Uncle's marriage quarrelled with Foma Fomich on numerous occasions, though he always begged his pardon in the end, now took his side with enormous fervour, greeted him with open arms, entertained him to a splendid meal, and offered on the spot formally to sever all ties with Uncle, promising for good measure to take out a writ against him. There was somewhere a small plot of land disputed between them, which, to be sure, they never quarrelled about because Uncle was always quite ready to assign it to Mr Bakhcheyev. Without further ado Stepan Alekseyevich requested his calash to be made ready and galloped off to the town, where he made out a claim for the land to be formally made over to him together with full compensation for costs and damages in just punishment for his peremptory behaviour and rapacity. Meanwhile Foma Fomich, having the very next day become thoroughly bored at Mr Bakhcheyev's, decided to let bygones be bygones, granted Uncle his pardon when the latter came to see him to offer his apologies, and returned with him to Stepanchikovo. Mr Bakhcheyev's rage, on his return from the town, to find Foma Fomich gone, beggars description; but three days later he suddenly turned up at Stepanchikovo offering his sincere apologies and, tears streaming down his face, begged Uncle for his forgiveness with assurances that he had withdrawn his claim. The same day, Uncle persuaded Mr Bakhcheyev and Foma Fomich to make it up between them, and Stepan Alekseyevich once again began to follow Foma about like a dog, repeating after his every word: 'You're a wise man, Foma! You're a learned man, Foma!'

Foma Fomich is now resting in his grave next to the General's Lady; it is marked by a magnificent tombstone of white marble engraved with lachrymose inscriptions and laudatory epitaphs. Every now and then, whilst out walking, Uncle and Nastenka will turn into the churchyard to pay homage to Foma Fomich. To this day they cannot speak of him except in tones of deep feeling, lovingly recalling his every word, his favourite meals, his likes and dislikes. His personal belongings are preserved and treasured. In their bereavement, my uncle and Nastenka have grown all the closer to each other. God has not blessed them with children; although this grieves them in the extreme, they never think of complaining. Sashenka was married a good while ago to a splendid young man. Ilyusha is studying in Moscow. Thus Uncle and Nastenka have ended up living on their own, and they are blissfully happy in each other's company. Their anxiety for each other is almost morbid. Nastenka spends all her time in prayer. I think that if one of them were to die first, the other would hardly survive a week. But may God grant them a long life! All who come to see them are welcomed with open arms, and they are ready to share all they possess with anyone suffering misfortune. Nastenka is fond of reading the lives of the saints, and maintains with remorse that good deeds alone are not enough, that really they ought to distribute everything to the destitute and seek happiness in poverty. Had it not been for the need to provide for Sashenka and Ilyusha, Uncle would have done just that, since he readily agrees with his wife in all things. Praskovya Ilyinichna continues to live with them and delights in indulging them to the full; she is also responsible for managing the household. Mr Bakhcheyev proposed to her not long after Uncle's marriage, but she turned him down flat. It was consequently assumed that she would enter a nunnery, but this did not happen either. One peculiar trait in Praskovya Ilyinichna's character is that she is utterly self-effacing as regards those she has chosen to love: she will be totally unobtrusive in their presence, look into their eyes, submit to all their caprices, follow in their footsteps, and wait upon them in all things. Now that her mother is dead, she feels duty bound to stay close to her brother and to pamper Nastenka to the full. Old Yezhevikin is still alive, and has lately been coming to see his daughter more and more regularly. At first he thoroughly exasperated Uncle by totally dissociating himself and his small fry (as he calls his children) from Stepanchikovo. None of Uncle's invitations seemed to have any effect upon him; he was not so much proud as touchy and sensitive to a degree. This sensitivity, indeed, sometimes verged on the pathological. The very thought that he, a pauper, might be tolerated in a well-to-do household out of charity and thus be considered obtrusive and tiresome thoroughly mortified him; sometimes he would not even accept assistance from Nastenka unless it was in the bare necessities. As for being helped by Uncle, he would not even hear of it. Nastenka had been quite mistaken in telling me that time in the garden that her father acted the fool for *her* benefit. True, he was most anxious to marry her off, but his clowning was to a much greater extent the result of an inner compulsion to find an outlet for his own pent-up spleen. Mockery and ridicule were in his blood. He would portray himself, for example, as the most obsequious and despicable of flatterers; but he always made it clear that he was play-acting; in fact, the lower he stooped in his obsequiousness, the more pointed and extreme became his mockery. Such was his nature and he could not help it. All his children were placed in the best educational establishments in Moscow and Petersburg, but only after Nastenka had made it clear to him that this would be entirely at her own expense, that is, paid for out of the thirty thousand given to her by Tatyana Ivanovna. As a matter of fact, they had never actually taken this thirty thousand from Tatyana Ivanovna but so as not to hurt or offend her they had assured her that if ever there was an urgent family need her help would be sought first. And that was exactly what was done; to placate her, two fairly substantial loans were negotiated from her on two separate occasions.

But Tatyana Ivanovna died three years ago, and so Nastenka received her thirty thousand in any case. Poor Tatyana Ivanovna died very suddenly. The whole family was preparing to go to a ball given by one of the neighbouring landowners and she had just put on her evening-gown and adorned her hair with a charming garland of white roses, when she suddenly felt nauseous, sat down in her chair and died. She was buried still wearing the garland. Nastenka was desperate. Tatyana Ivanovna had been cherished and cared for in the house as though she were a child. To everybody's surprise she left a remarkably sensible will: Nastenka's thirty thousand apart, all the rest, nearly three hundred thousand rubles in cash, went towards the upbringing of orphaned girls and cash gratuities on completion of their education. The same year that Tatyana Ivanovna died saw the marriage of Miss Perepelitsyna, who had stayed on in the house after the death of the General's Lady in the hope of inveigling herself into the wealthy spinster's favour. The erstwhile clerk and present landowner in Mishino, the little village which had seen the episode with Tatyana Ivanovna, Obnoskin and his Mamma, had in the meantime become a widower. This man, an incorrigible litigant, had a family of six by his first wife. Suspecting Perepelitsyna of having money, he began to ply her with offers of marriage, and she immediately accepted. But Perepelitsyna was as poor as a church mouse: three hundred rubles in silver was all she could claim to possess, and even this was out of Nastenka's pocket, given her to help with the wedding expenses. Husband and wife are now at each other's throat all day long. She pulls his children by the hair and boxes their ears; she scratches his face (or so people claim) and constantly reminds him that her father was a lieutenant-colonel. Mizinchikov too has now settled down. After prudently abandoning all his designs on Tatyana Ivanovna, he began to show an interest in agriculture. Uncle recommended him to a wealthy count, a landowner, who would occasionally come to review his estate, which had three thousand serfs and which was situated about eighty versts from Stepanchikovo. Having recognized Mizinchikov's abilities and considered my uncle's recommendation, the Count offered him the management of his estate, dismissing on the spot his German predecessor, who, in spite of the much-vaunted German honesty, had been swindling his master at every step and turn. Five years later the estate was unrecognizable: the peasants had prospered; new ventures had been initiated which had not previously been considered viable; profits had nearly doubled – in short, the new manager had excelled himself and word of his unique business acumen spread throughout the province. The Count's bewilderment and mortification may be imagined when at the end of five years Mizinchikov, despite all pleas and inducements, firmly resolved to leave his post and announced his retirement! The Count believed that his employee had been enticed away by the other landowners of the neighbourhood, or even to another province. But what was everybody's surprise when two months after his retirement Mizinchikov suddenly turned out to be the proud possessor of an excellent estate of his own of a hundred serfs, situated at a distance of precisely forty versts from the Count's property, and purchased from a former friend of his, a hussar, who had frittered away his money and found himself totally destitute! He at once mortgaged the hundred serfs, and a year later acquired sixty more from the district. Now he is an established landowner and his estate is unrivalled. People cannot stop wondering how he came into possession of the necessary capital in the first place, others merely shake their heads in total disbelief. But Ivan Ivanovich is quite unperturbed and feels perfectly within his rights. He has brought his sister over from Moscow, the one who parted with her last three rubles to enable him to purchase his boots when he was setting out for Stepanchikovo – as sweet a soul as ever one could wish to meet, no longer in her prime, but very meek, loving and well educated, though extremely subdued. She previously eked out a living in Moscow as a paid companion to a rich patroness; now she worships her brother, runs the house for him, complies with his every whim, and is perfectly contented with life. Her brother does not indulge her overmuch. In fact he is rather repressive towards her, but she does not seem to mind. They have taken a great liking to her in Stepanchikovo, and rumour has it that Bakhcheyev is quite partial to her. He would surely have proposed by now but for his fear of being turned down. As for Mr Bakhcheyev, it is our intention to say a good deal more of him in another story.

That, then, should be all ... No! I nearly forgot: Gavrila has grown very old and completely forgotten all his French. Falaley has turned into a very capable coachman, but poor Vidoplyasov was put in a madhouse a long time ago, and there I understand he met his end ... I shall be going to Stepanchikovo shortly and must remember to ask Uncle about him.

NOTES

1. (page 6) *Ivan Yakovlevich Koreysha*: a 'holy man' in Moscow who was particularly famous 1820–30. Semyon Yakovlevich in *Devils* is based on this figure.

2. (page 11) *The Liberation of Moscow, Ataman Storm, Filial Love – or Russians in 1104*: popular pseudo-historical adventure novels of 1830–40. Of *Ataman Storm* Belinsky wrote in a review published in 1835 that it 'belongs to that particular category of works, the initial idea for which is born in the market-place'.

3. (page 11) *Baron Brambeus*: pen-name of O. I. Senkovsky (1800–51), a clever, witty but superficial critic who delighted in reviewing and ridiculing insignificant works.

4. (page 11) *Thirty thousand people will throng every month to attend my lectures*: a reference to Gogol's appointment in 1834 as assistant professor of history at St Petersburg University. The appointment lasted one year only and proved a disastrous failure. His lectures were often dull and consisted of nothing more than a catalogue of bare facts.

5. (page 11) *he, Foma, was destined one day to perform a great feat*: cf. Gogol's letter to the writer S. T. Aksakov of 13 June 1841 (first published in 1857): 'My work is great, my endeavour salutary. I am dead now to everything that is trivial . . .'

6. (page 11) *he was to compose a profoundly searching magnum opus of a spiritually edifying nature that would shake the world and stun all Russia*: in Gogol's 'Testament' in *Selected Passages from Correspondence with Friends* we read of a 'Farewell Novel', '. . . the best to come from my pen and that I have been carrying in my heart a long time as my greatest treasure'.

7. (page 12) *Foma, scorning glory, would withdraw to a monastery . . . for the salvation of his motherland*: cf. Gogol's statement in *Selected Passages*: 'I shall be praying at the tomb of Our Saviour for all my compatriots excluding no one.'

8. (page 14) *You've got to be doubly considerate to someone in your debt*: a similar sentiment is expressed in Dostoyevsky's letter of 14 August 1855 to A. E. Vrangel: '. . . I know very well that you appreciate better than anyone perhaps how one must treat a person beholden to you. I know you will be twice, three times more considerate with him; a person indebted to you must be treated with care; he is apprehensive; *he is forever imagining that in treating him carelessly and. familiarly people are trying to make him repay his debts.*' (Dostoyevsky's italics.)

9. (page 14) *on Foma's express orders my uncle was compelled to shave off his splendid reddish-brown side whiskers*: Nicholas I in a special ukase of 2 April 1837 forbade civil servants to wear beards or moustaches.

10. (page 15) *Foma Fomich invariably adopted this tone when conversing with the*

'*shrewd Russian peasant*': in the letter 'Russian Landowner' in *Selected Passages*, Gogol gives the following advice on how to address a negligent peasant: 'You unwashed mug! Look at you covered in soot to your eyeballs and still refusing to pay homage!' Belinsky quotes these words with indignation in his letter to Gogol of 15 July 1847.

11. (page 39) *Frol Silin, a charitable man*: see note to page 77.

12. (page 50) '*The Misfit*': a popular novel by A. F. Pisemsky first published in 1850. The narrator here identifies himself with Pisemsky's hero, Pavel Vasilyevich Beshmetev, a young nobleman of good education, but clumsy, ungainly and with no experience of life, which eventually leads to his downfall.

13. (page 57) *the Kholmsky family*: the title of a long novel running into six parts by D. N. Begichev published in 1832, relating the life-story of four sisters belonging to a large family of the Russian nobility.

14. (page 58) *My dear sir and benefactor! The simple man is the one I'm afraid of most of all!*: in a letter of 22 February 1854 to his brother Mikhail, Dostoyevsky writes: 'It's the simple man I'm afraid of more than the complex one.'

15. (page 61) (*the young man is a notary in Malinov now, a brilliant fellow with an all-round education!*): the town of Malinov is the setting for the second part of A. I. Herzen's amusing sketch 'Notes of a Young Man' published in 1841. Malinov is referred to as 'the worst city in the world, because one cannot imagine anything worse for a city than its total non-existence . . . Malinov lies not within the pale of the world, but somewhere outside it.' Rostanev's reference to the legendary city of Malinov, 'which you will not discover on any map of either the ancient or the new world', indicates his confused and abstracted state of mind.

16. (page 68) *I've stuffed myself with pie like Martin full of soap!*: one of the numerous expressions used by Dostoyevsky in *The Village of Stepanchikovo* which are recorded in his *Siberian Notebook*.

17. (page 70) *The band consisted of two balalaikas, a guitar, a fiddle, and a tambourine*: cf. the band described in *Notes from the House of the Dead* part I, chapter 11. The repertoire is similar too: dance tunes ending invariably with the kamarinsky.

18. (page 73) *Only a stupid society dimwit could conceive of such senseless niceties*: an almost verbatim quote from the third of the 'Four Letters to Various People apropos "Dead Souls"' in Gogol's *Selected Passages*: 'Only a stupid society dimwit could think of anything so stupid.'

19. (page 74) *Was he a manorial peasant, a crown peasant, a free peasant, an obligated or economical peasant?*: 'manorial peasants' belonged to the landowner; 'crown' or 'state peasants' to the Tsar and the state. 'Economical peasants' belonged to monasteries. 'Obligated peasants' were a category of peasants still not fully entitled to the land allotted to them by their landowners.

20. (page 75) *What have all these Pushkins, Lermontovs, Borozdnas been doing up to now?*: in 1852 a collection of poems came out in St Petersburg entitled 'Forget-me-not. A Lady's Album Containing the Best Examples of Russian Poetry . . .' The poets featured ranged from Pushkin and Lermontov to such obscurities as I. P. Kreshnev, I. P. Borozdna and K. I. Korenev. Opiskin and the compilers of 'Forget-me-not' were happy to lump all poets into the same category.

21. (page 75) *People are dancing the kamarinsky, this apotheosis of drunkenness*: the music critic F. Tolstoy (pen-name Rostislav) complained bitterly about the contemporary trends in art which sacrificed aesthetic taste to the demands of naturalism. In an article on A. Rubinstein's opera *Fomka the Fool* published in 1854 he wrote: 'What pleasure is there in the contortions of a dishevelled, stupid muzhik? The drinking-house and all that it entails is, of course, a matter of considerable significance, but is it worth depicting it in an aesthetic work?' Dostoyevsky was rather impatient with such arch-conservatism.

22. (page 75) *I know Russia and Mother Russia knows me*: quotation from N. A. Polevoy's foreword to his historical novel *Solemn Vow at the Tomb of our Lord* (1832), for which he was frequently held up to ridicule, notably by Belinsky.

23. (page 76) *Let them portray this peasant ... glorifying his poverty and indifferent to the gold of the wealthy*: cf. Gogol's advice in 'Topics for a Contemporary Lyric Poet' in his *Selected Passages*: 'Depict their glorious poverty so that it shine forth in everybody's eyes like an object of sanctity and induce each one of us to wish he were poor.'

24. (page 77) *the immortal Karamzin ... 'Frol Silin'*: N. M. Karamzin's *History of the Russian State* was published in eleven volumes in 1816–24, an unfinished twelfth volume appearing posthumously in 1829. The tale *Frol Silin, a Charitable Man* first appeared in 1791 and was reissued in 1848. Frol Silin is an industrious settler in the Simbirsk Province who in times of hardship distributes bread and alms to the poor and needy. Dostoyevsky was impatient with Karamzin's cloying sentimentality and in his article 'Bookishness and Literacy' exhorted his readers 'not to judge' the spirit of the nation 'by Karamzin's novels and their bone china landscapes'.

25. (page 77) *'The Mysteries of Brussels'*: a very inferior imitation by an anonymous author of Marie-Joseph (Eugène) Sue's *Les Mystères de Paris*. It appeared in translation in St Petersburg in 1847.

26. (page 77) *'The Scribe'*: a reference to the pen-name of the writer and critic A. V. Druzhinin, who in 1849–52 wrote articles in the journal *The Contemporary* (*Sovremennik*) under the heading 'Letters of a country subscriber', representing the views of an enlightened landowner who kept abreast of all the current literary events.

27. (page 82) *Monsieur Chematon*: from the French *chômer* – to be unemployed or idle, hence 'Mr Ne'er-do-well'.

28. (page 99) *Why is it I am always happy, always content, in spite of all my anguish; ... any pity at all*: cf. Gogol's 'Testament' in *Selected Passages*: 'weak though I be and insignificant, I have always heartened my friends, and no one who has associated with me lately, no one in his moment of gloom and despondency has observed on me a dejected aspect, although I too have had my moments of difficulty and suffered no less than others ...'

29. (page 100) *For all he knew, it might have been Machiavelli or Mercadante sitting before him*: Foma mentions at random two similar-sounding names which have nothing in common. Mercadante's operas and vocal pieces were frequently performed in the 1830s and 1840s in St Petersburg theatres and his name was therefore well known. It is more likely that Foma meant Mirandola, the fifteenth-century Italian philosopher whose claim to erudition was far greater. It was said of Pico della Mirandola that he knew everything there is to know and much else besides.

30. (page 102) *Miẓinchikov*: from *miẓinets*, Russian for the little finger or toe. The name conjures up the image of a diminutive but perky individual.

31. (page 107) *I set the fashion, like Burtsov*: Aleksey Petrovich Burtsov (died in 1813) was an officer in the hussars, famous in his revelry and merry-making. The poet Denis Davydov immortalized him.

32. (page 117) *first you wanted to be called simply 'The Faithful' — 'Grigory the Faithful'; then . . . some damned fool turned it into 'Disgraceful'*; a possible reference to the infamous informer against the Decembrist Movement, Ivan Vasilyevich Sherwood. Sherwood, the son of an English engineer, was brought to Russia at the age of two. In adulthood he served in the army and was able to obtain for the authorities evidence of a major conspiracy. In recognition of his 'service' Nicholas I awarded him the title of 'Faithful' and he came to be called Sherwood the Faithful. In society, however, where his rôle was well known, his new title was soon changed to Sherwood the Disgraceful.

33. (page 117) *Now tell me, my friend, what could be more ridiculous than Uhlanov?*: U(h)lanov is a common Russian surname derived from *uhlan*, a light cavalryman. For Rostanev, himself a former hussar, the idea of the effeminate Vidoplyasov being called 'Uhlanov' is quite ridiculous.

34. (page 117) *Bolvanov*: derived from *bolvan*, Russian for a hatter's dummy, hence numskull.

35. (page 150) *the beginning of a historical novel depicting life in seventh-century Novgorod*: a reflection on Foma the 'scholar' — Novgorod was founded in the ninth century.

36. (page 150) *a dreadful poem, 'Anchoret at the Graveyard', written in blank verse*: the title parodies early nineteenth-century mystico-philosophical poems written predominantly in blank verse.

37. (page 150) *an absurd discourse on the significance and character of the Russian muẓhik and how to handle him*: a parody on Gogol's 'Russian landowner' in *Selected Passages*, on N. M. Karamzin's 'Letter from a Villager' (1803), as well as on 'Testament to my Peasants or a Moral Homily to them' by A. S. Shishkov (1843).

38. (page 150) *a tale of society life, 'Countess Vlonskaya'*: the society novel was a popular genre in the 1830s to '50s. Cf. A. P. Glinka's tale *Countess Polina*.

39. (page 150) *Paul de Kock*: contemporary French novelist. Russian conservative critics of the 1840s regarded him as 'obscene'.

40. (page 155) *Mr Kuẓma Prutkov wrote it*: Kuzma Prutkov was the collective pen-name of the writers A. K. Tolstoy and brothers A. M. and V. M. Zhemchuzhnikov during the period 1850–60. Kuzma Prutkov is a fictitious, grotesquely humorous poet-bureaucrat with the mock-official title of Director of the Assay-House. He is self-opinionated, dull, but not ill-intentioned. 'The Siege of Pamba', an actual product of his pen, was published in the satirical supplement to *The Contemporary* in 1854. In *Winter Notes on Summer Impressions* (1863) Dostoyevsky describes Kuzma Prutkov as 'a wonderful writer, the pride and joy of our time . . .'

41. (page 157) *Take a broom, a shovel, a ladle, an oven-fork*: a reference to A. N. Afanasyev's article 'The Pagano-religious Significance of the Slav's Hut', in which the author endowed the peasant's hut and its contents with far-fetched mystical symbolism. Afanasyev's article was frequently held up to ridicule in the press. Dostoyevsky himself wrote of it disparagingly in his article 'Mr − bov and the Question of Art'. Just before the publication of *The Village of Stepanchikovo* in Krayevsky's journal, Dostoyevsky wrote to his brother on 20 October 1859: 'You remember Col. Rostanev's pronouncements on literature, on journals, on the erudition of *Otechestvennyye zapiski* and so on. Here is an indispensable condition: not one line is to be omitted by Krayevsky from this conversation . . . Please insist on it. Make a special point.'

42. (page 160) *You're a landowner; you should sparkle like a diamond on your estates . . . Do not imagine . . . like the meanest of his peasants!*: cf. Gogol's homiletic instructions to the Russian landowner in *Selected Passages*: 'Get on with the work of the landowner as one ought in the true and righteous sense . . . God will call you to account should you abandon this calling in preference to another, for each and every one must serve God according to his own station . . . See to it that at the beginning of every task . . . you . . . join [the peasants] in their work and be their leader, exhorting them to do their best, praising the keen one and rebuking the lazy one . . . Take into your own hands the axe and the scythe . . .'

43. (page 170) *I need no monuments of stone! Set me up a monument in your hearts*: ironic reference to Gogol's statement in his 'Testament' in *Selected Passages*: 'It is my will that there should be no monument standing over me, nobody should even think of such a folly, which is unworthy of a Christian. Those of my nearest to whom I have been truly dear, they will erect for me a different kind of monument . . .'

44. (page 172) *'there lies but a hair's breadth 'twixt innocence and peril'*: Foma's own vulgarized rendering of what would seem to be a line from the third sonnet of Petrarch's *Canzoniere*.

45. (page 172) *but not the 'darkness' of which we hear in the famous ballad*: a popular sentimental ballad of the time, 'Hues of darkness, hues of gloom'. Its author is unknown.

46. (page 172) *Turning again to Shakespeare . . . with a crocodile lurking at the bottom*: this poetic image does not go back to Shakespeare but to Châteaubriand. In his novel *Atala* (1801), Chactas the Indian says: 'The purest of hearts resembles a pool in the savannahs of Alachua; its surface is clear and calm, but when you gaze into its depths you see a crocodile.'

47. (page 178) *let it be said that misfortune may be the mother of virtue − Gogol's words*: cf. Gogol's letter 'Concerning Help for the Poor' in *Selected Passages*: 'misfortune mollifies a man; his nature then becomes more receptive to matters that are beyond the comprehension of one who remains in the usual, day-to-day state'.

48. (page 180) *Like Diogenes with his lantern*: the ancient Greek philosopher cynic was once observed walking in the street at noon with a lighted lantern in his hands and in reply to questions said: 'I'm looking for a human being.'

49. (page 180) *Should I love Falaley? Would I wish to love Falaley?*: cf. Gogol's lament in *Selected Passages*: 'But how can one love one's own brothers, how can

one love people? The soul yearns for beauty, but people are so imperfect, and there is so little beauty in them!'

50. (page 180) *the evil spirit Asmodeus*: see Tobit, iii, 8.

51. (page 187) *and even touched upon the Natural School*: a literary movement initiated by the critic Vissarion Belinsky (1811–48) during the 1840s, which insisted that literature should be relevant to social questions, and show compassion for the least privileged in Russian society, the peasantry and the urban poor.

52. (page 187) '*When from the darkness of depravity*': a poem by N. A. Nekrasov published in 1846 in *Otechestvennyye zapiski*. Its theme of the spiritual rehabilitation of a fallen creature was very close to Dostoyevsky's heart, and he used an extended extract from the poem as an epigraph to the second section of *Notes from Underground*.

53. (page 191) *Lucullan*: pertaining to Lucius Licinius Lucullus (c. 144–57 BC), a Roman statesman celebrated for his fondness for luxury; hence a term characterizing excessive indulgence.